# THE QUEST
# FOR THE KEY

Cover and illustrations
**Agnieszka Czyżykowska, Agnieszka Sowała-Kozłowska**

Editor
**Anna Basara**

Publisher
**Dom Wydawniczy Klucz**

Translator
**Alexander Hayes**

DTP
**Anna Krych**

ISBN  978-83-944491-7-9

Margaret Borkowska

# THE QUEST FOR THE KEY

Warsaw 2016

# Chapter one
## A BORING HOLIDAY

He was walking down the road, bored. The holidays had only just begun and he already knew that nothing good was going to happen. He had no plans and he was utterly fed up with sitting at home and continually arguing with his Mum about playing on the computer too long. As for Dad – well, he wasn't going to be there anyway.

He walked past a bookshop and stopped. Maybe he would go in and see if there were any new games? But what was the point? He didn't have enough money anyway. But still, he turned back. He could at least have a look and see what was new.

But he was kidding himself. His friend Peter always had his parents buy him everything the day it came out so he wasn't going to see anything that Peter didn't already have. Peter...Thinking about his friend sent a nasty shiver down his spine. He didn't want to think about what had recently happened. Tough! Maybe he would see if there were any interesting books. He liked fantasy.

He made his way over to that section. It didn't look like there was anything new. But... His eye was caught by the cover of a book with a dragon and some kind of gryphon battling it out in a blizzard. "The Quest for the Key," he read. He took a look at the description on the back: something about a journey through an unknown world and discovering the truth about oneself. This last bit irritated him. He didn't like such preachy books. But it looked as if there was nothing more interesting in the bookshop. And anyway the drawing of a sailing ship on the back cover looked quite intriguing.

He liked building model ships and, even though he didn't like admitting this to himself, he dreamt of going on a voyage on such a vessel. His grandmother lived in Gdansk and she had a captain for a neighbour who had travelled around the world. He had told him all sorts of stories about his sailing adventures and had even once taken him on a short cruise.

Tough! He'd take the book. At least he would have something to do when Mum told him again that he couldn't play on the computer. He just had to check that he had enough money. He did. He paid and walked out.

He began to make his way slowly home. The sun was shining but still everything, the people, the trees, the houses all seemed to emanate greyness. Yes, Warsaw remained bleary even in the sunshine. His dark eyes peeped out from underneath a shock of blonde hair. How he longed for something at last to happen. Anything. Again he thought about how he was going to spend the holiday alone at home before he began his final year in his lower secondary school. Again he thought about Peter; after all he could occasionally play with him. He preferred not to think about their last argument.

To say it was an argument was putting it lightly. Peter was the only one in his class with whom he could share his dreams. He would tell him about his longing to travel, to experience an adventure of a lifetime… And above all about his need to find sense in the world. Perhaps deep down his friend shared his longing, but his admission of this was only a shrug of the shoulders and to grunt "you philosopher". Paul nonetheless knew that this snide comment was cover for a deep liking. His other classmates didn't hold back with their numerous unpleasantries, which they dealt him out because of his passion and dreams. They thought that life was no fairy tale and that it was simply better to act crazily in the here and now. Just before the end of the school year he had gone into the class just before the bell when he'd heard those cruel words.

'What are you hanging around with him for anyway? He keeps on telling you so much rubbish about all of his plans and dreams. Doesn't it make you laugh?'

'Yeah... well it is kind of funny. That's why I listen to him. It's a good laugh,' Peter replied quietly.

The blood rushed to Paul's head. Somewhere in his heart a voice was telling him that he knew Peter better than that, that he hadn't wanted to say such a thing and that he was afraid of standing up to the others... But his ears were still burning and for every doubt he found just one answer: "coward".

He marched into class. Peter saw him straight away and went pale. The other boys burst into sneering laughter. Since that day he hadn't spoken with his friend and the day before the end of the school year he'd pushed Peter so hard on the stairs that he'd fallen. It was strange that he hadn't tried to hit back.

Paul's fury was mixed with the realisation that the holidays without Peter were going to be really terribly boring and uninteresting.

Slowly he made his way up the stairs to his flat. Maybe, he thought, he would spend a while reading. He lay back and made himself comfortable on his bed and then opened up his new book. It didn't have a very interesting start. He quickly flicked through the first few pages. The hero was some boy whose grandmother had been taken ill and he was to travel and look after her. He yawned out of boredom. He decided that he was going to play on the computer after all. He was just getting up to turn it on when his mother returned. She was exceptionally early.

'Paul, are you there?' she called out from the door.

'Yes I am Mum. I'm in my room,' he replied.

She stood in the doorway and it was clear that she was upset.

'What's wrong Mum?'

'Oh Paul, you can't imagine; I got a call at work. Granny's feeling really very poorly. It seems to be something serious. We talked on the telephone and she needs help. She asked us to come over because she's got nobody to look after her. But I can't take the time off work so I was wondering if maybe you couldn't live for the time being with Granny and help her while she's ill.' She stopped and then added, 'I know that this is a big responsibility and it's probably nothing very interesting for a boy of your age, but I'm really worried about Granny and I've got no one else I can ask in such a situation.'

Paul listened to his mother in silence. This really wasn't a very attractive prospect, looking after the ill... But it so happened that his grandmother wasn't an everyday person. The boy had always thought that there was something exceptional about her. They didn't see each other very often because she lived far away and even worked at weekends, so there weren't many opportunities to spend time together. However Paul always felt extremely good whenever he was with her. It also sometimes happened that Granny would take him to her work. She cooked and sometimes even cleaned in a children's home. The home was called the Little Sun, which Paul thought didn't really suit a place where so many sad children lived. He himself liked to go there. No one there would ask him where his parents worked, whether he had any brothers and sisters, what kind of pet he had or if he'd been given the latest games console as a present. He could simply just be there and play with the children who weren't particularly interested in the details of his life. Of course now that Granny was ill, she wasn't going to be taking him to the Little Sun. Suddenly, Paul realised that even staying at home with an ill grandmother, who at least always told him various interesting stories, was still going to be better than sitting alone in Warsaw continually building the same model ships.

And so with quite some certainty in his voice he said, 'Of course Mum, I'll be happy to go to Granny's and help her out.'

'O, Paul!' exclaimed Mum with undisguised joy. 'I'm so happy! You really must already be a mature boy since you're taking on such a task,' she added.

Paul wasn't so sure that he really deserved such praise, but he said nothing. The next day they were already sitting on the train to Gdansk on their way to his grandmother's. It was a Saturday so his Mum could come with him and have enough time later to return to Warsaw before yet another week of work. The bus took them most of the way from the train station to Granny's house. Just after getting off, they passed by a smallish house where Granny's neighbour Captain John Wronski lived with his brother. The boy had only seen Mr Ralph Wronski a few times and only in passing, which he didn't regret since the man always had such a sour expression as if nothing nice had ever happened to him throughout his life. He had just begun to think about the other brother and his countless sea adventures when they reached Granny's house. The door wasn't locked. When they entered, it turned out that Granny had deliberately left it open because she was already so weak that she was unable to get out of bed. Before their arrival, John (who was Mr Wronski to Paul) had been helping out, but now it was the boy who was to take over caring for her.

'I'm glad you agreed yourself to come and help me, Paul,' said Granny greeting her grandson with a large smile on her face. 'It was really nice of you. John's been helping me a lot, but he works and all the time he's been preparing for his next voyage, while I can't even now get up by myself. Thank you Mary for finding the time to bring him here,' Granny said turning to Mum, who at that moment was fixing her pillow.

The next evening Mum went back to her flat and her work in Warsaw and Paul spent the following days helping Granny. It was quite a tedious and sometimes even unpleasant job. Worse still was that the whole house was covered in cobwebs so the boy spent much of his free time trying to clean out all the corners. However he was under the impression that the more fervently he fought with the cobwebs the quicker new ones would appear. To his disappointment Granny was so weak that she didn't have the strength to tell any of her stories... Paul consoled himself with the fact that for company, he still had Granny's cat, called Tiger, who was a very peculiar creature. Above all his fur was most unusual with black and ginger stripes, just like a real tiger. Moreover the tomcat also had long strands of hair at the tips of his ears, as if he were a lynx. Unlike typical members of his species he loved to accompany people and would either demand that Paul should play with him or would lie on his lap to rest awhile. He also had a passion for hunting the larger spiders, which often hid in spaces in the furniture and other equipment.

## Chapter two
# FRIEND

One day at the very end of July Granny said, 'Paul, tomorrow I'm going to have a very important guest and I would like you not to go away but to keep us company while we talk. I think you'll like my friend.' Paul was a bit surprised by such a request but overall he had nothing against it. The next day just before the visit, he made the tea and when the guest arrived, he opened the door and led him to his grandmother's room where together they sat by her bed. The boy was surprised that the stranger didn't introduce himself, but the boy didn't ask anything and just observed him carefully. He was a young man who was nonetheless still quite mature with curly dark hair that reached down below his ears and surprisingly bright blue eyes. He was wearing a simple pair of jeans and a white collared shirt.

'Welcome my friend,' said Granny reaching out her hand to the guest. 'I'm glad that you're here. As you can see my dear grandson is also here with me. I think he'll be perfect for the task that you've given me.' Paul froze with surprise. Up until that moment Granny had said nothing about any task.

'For sure, he's just right for it. Have you already told him something about it?' asked the stranger.

'No. I thought it would be better to explain everything with you being here.'

They both turned at the same time to look at Paul.

'Paul, up until this moment I haven't said anything... but... I didn't ask you and your mother to come just to help me here. I need you for something far more important. Unfortunately your mother couldn't stay so the entire burden of this task will now rest on your shoulders. But since my friend says that you'll be able to cope, I'm sure you'll be all right.

Suddenly Tiger jumped onto the bed and turning towards the guest he clearly meowed, 'Hi.'

'Hi Tiger,' replied the man.

Everything happened so quickly and in such a natural way that Paul didn't have the time to feel surprised. He didn't even know what was more unusual: this particular task that Granny and the stranger wished to entrust to him or the fact that an animal was speaking with a human voice and that nobody apart from him appeared to be surprised by this.

Meanwhile the cat planted himself comfortably on Granny's lap and looked at Paul. Now there were three pairs of eyes following the boy.

'Well, what are you staring at?' said Tiger, speaking again. 'You look like you've just swallowed a dead mouse.'

'You... can speak!' exclaimed a rather disorientated Paul.

'Of course I can speak. I could always do so. It's just that you couldn't always understand.'

'And how come I seem to understand now?' Paul asked feeling confused.

'That's because you now know Friend,' the cat replied calmly.

'Well actually I don't think we've been introduced,' interrupted Friend. 'Can I be your friend?' he asked stretching out his hand to the boy.

Paul looked at the man suspiciously. Not only had he not introduced himself but he was also going to give him some task which he still knew nothing about and he'd caused Tiger to start speaking. But most of all what stopped Paul from taking the hand of this so-called friend was the memory of Peter's betrayal. He felt so injured by his former friend that his heart would not allow him to trust some stranger too quickly. How was this man supposed to be his new friend, he kept thinking. Meanwhile the eyes looking at him became ever more intriguing and strangely blue. There was something in them that made the boy want to like this man.

'I don't know...' Paul said quietly, 'Someone we call a friend sometimes turns out not to be one...' he hesitantly added.

However, Friend did not take back his hand but said in a calm voice, 'I know that Peter hurt you, but when you get to know me, you'll understand that he really didn't want to.'

Friend knew about Peter. What a horror! And maybe he even knew about the week before the argument with his friend when he'd laughed at the jokes those boys made about Peter? Paul began to feel really awkward and uncomfortable.

'I would like to be your friend. I promise I will never let you down,' the stranger said.

His hand was still outstretched and his eyes shone with such joy that almost in spite of himself Paul put out his hand. When he grasped Friend's hand, all of his doubts instantly disappeared and he realised that he himself was smiling.

Suddenly something started buzzing near his ear. The boy waved his hand to chase away the bee that had most probably come from a neighbouring hive. The insect evaded and flew away from Paul. But he noticed that although the insect was yellow in colour, it was far bigger than a bee, more like the size of a small bird. He looked at it very carefully as it settled on a dusty bookshelf and in amazement he realised that what he had taken for a bee was in fact a strange little creature with quickly beating clear sparkling wings that looked as if they were made of crystal. The creature was indeed of a yellowish colour but it was difficult to say if this was the colour of its body or rather of the clothes that covered it. The boy remembered that he had read before in fairy tales of the existence of similar small creatures that were known as elves. He now no longer knew what surprised him more: whether it was the appearance of this strange creature or the fact that suddenly it seemed to him completely natural that remarkable things happened in the presence of Friend.

'Is that an elf?' he asked.

'You can call him that if you want. He belongs to you,' replied Friend.

Tiger stared at Elf – since that is how Paul still thought of the creature – with ravenous eyes. However you could see that he was using all his willpower to stop himself hunting down this little creature.

'I don't understand anything' said the boy with resignation in his voice. Up until this moment everything was so normal and just like usual and now Tiger suddenly starts speaking with a human voice and Elf appears. What else could happen?'

'Aah, this is only the beginning of everything. And what might happen next? Hmm, well I suppose anything. Anything that you want and decide to be worth happening,' explained Friend in a rather mysterious manner.

'And what about this task?' Paul went on.

'Well Paul,' said Granny with life returning to her voice, 'That's a difficult matter. You see, my dear, that I really am very ill. For me to get better, I need the key to the Crooked World. It's there that I will recover. I want you to help me find this key,' she explained.

'The Crooked World? And where is this?' asked the boy, his interest piqued, 'I've never heard of it before.'

'The Crooked World is where Friend and all of these strange creatures you see come from. And where is it? Hmm... It's a difficult question.'

Matters were becoming even more complicated. Paul had the impression that he understood less and less while at the same time everything seemed to fit together. Friend sat without moving smiling at the boy. Suddenly, he winced as if something had suddenly started itching and scratched his back. When he brought back his hand it turned out that there was a small bee sitting on it – although whether it was actually a bee or yet another smaller elf, Paul wasn't quite sure.

'Oh. You're here!' exclaimed the man with undisguised joy. 'Fly off to Traveller and tell him that we will be coming over to him shortly, ' he told the bee and turning again to Paul he said, 'I forgot about your new name. You are Knight of the Rabbit.'

'What?' said Paul lost for words.

He had no idea what this thing about his name was and what was worse, he wasn't very happy with it either. As much as being a knight by itself sounded like something to be proud of, being the knight of some rabbit seemed not that honorific.

'I give a name to everyone I meet,' began Friend, 'For instance your grandmother is Good Fairy, although that's hardly original. As far as I know the children from the Little Sun call her the same thing.'

'But why Knight of the Rabbit?' asked Paul feeling unconvinced.

'Because only a knight can perform the task that will save Good Fairy. And why of the rabbit? Well...' Friend seemed to be considering something. 'Maybe the Fairy could say something about that?'

'That's simple. You're going to have your own rabbit, Paul,' Granny stated and then she put out her hand in which she held a short stick, waved it quickly and suddenly there was a rabbit sitting on his lap. It wasn't any ordinary rabbit; one ear was crooked and the other was the colour red. Next its eyes were different colours: one was purple and the other was orange.

'Hi!' said Rabbit. 'it's nice to meet you. I've always wanted to have my own knight.'

Paul was feeling less and less happy with the turn of events. Even though a speaking Tiger and little Elf seemed very likeable, he was not impressed by this strange rabbit. And the prospect of being its knight seemed to Paul completely abhorrent.

'I don't want to be the Knight of the Rabbit,' the boy protested.

'Well, you've got to be somebody's knight. And anyway it's already happened. Fairy has conjured up a rabbit for you so you don't have a great deal of choice.' replied Friend, seemingly unmoved.

'What do you mean? Since Granny's only just conjured him up, how could he have always wanted to have his own knight?' Paul asked in amazement.

'Aah but since he exists that means he is someone doesn't it? And that means he may want different things and have very strange characteristics.' On saying this Friend looked at Rabbit as if he wasn't convinced himself of his theory being right. 'After all, you are someone even though you yourself once didn't exist. Somebody wanted you just as you are.'

'But I was born this way. Nobody designed me.' The boy defended his opinion with desperation in his voice.

Paul realised that he was getting dangerously deep into a contrived discussion that could lead to nothing sensible and certainly wouldn't free him from Rabbit. At the same time he felt that this strange creature was making itself comfortable on his lap and was beginning to look at him in a very friendly manner.

'Paul, it's not how you think. I wanted you to be exactly as you are,' argued Friend.

'But we've only just met,' Paul said in amazement although Friend's enigmatic smile alone seemed enough to convince the boy of everything he was hearing.

'You've only just met me, my boy, but I know you and I wanted you to be born for a long time,' said Friend.

The words sounded like a secret declaration of love and Paul felt somehow strangely moved by it. He thought that maybe the time would come for a more precise explanation. In the meantime he just wanted to know what this task was all about.

'Let's say that I believe you,' he uncertainly ended the previous topic and then quickly added, 'Could you at least explain to me exactly what it is with this key? Where am I meant to go looking for it?'

'How am I supposed to know?' bridled Granny, 'If I knew where to look for it, it wouldn't be necessary to find it and I wouldn't need your help,' she said more calmly.

Paul thought that this wasn't a very helpful comment but he decided not to say anything. Instead he asked a few further questions:

'What in that case am I meant to do?'

'You're to go on a journey,' said Granny as if there was no need to add any more.

Paul felt irritated with such a large number of unknowns. He wanted to find out at last what it was all about. However before the anger had begun to well up in him, Friend explained more precisely, 'Your grandmother, as you heard, needs the key to the Crooked World. It's not known where it is exactly. In order to find it, you'll simply have to set off on a journey. However, you won't be alone. Traveller, who lives not far from here, is going to be your guide. You'll be accompanied by Rabbit and Elf.' How did Friend know that that was what in his heart he was continually calling the quiet creature sitting on the shelf? '… as well as Little Lula.'

Suddenly there was a loud and indignant, 'Meeeow I think you've forgotten about someone.' Of course it was Tiger who all the time had been following both Elf and Rabbit. However now he looked unhappily at Friend.

'Of course, Tiger, if you want you can also go with Knight,' Friend reassured the cat.

'And who is Little Lula?' asked Paul. He no longer felt irritated with the number of secrets. At last his mission was beginning to take on a concrete form and looked rather interesting.

'Lula is a little girl who lives in the Little Sun,' explained Granny, 'She very much likes Friend and he promised her that she could go with him on a long journey.'

'And so you're also coming with us?' asked Paul turning to the man. It seemed to him that if Friend was coming with them, the journey would certainly not turn out to be difficult.

'I'll be by your side when you need me, but you won't always know about it. Just remember that in times of danger you can always call the lion Arie.'

Paul felt both disappointed and intrigued by this answer. Disappointed because in the depth of his heart he very much wanted Friend to come with them and intrigued because the vision of this Arie appearing seemed fascinating.

'And who is Arie?' Paul asked.

'You will find out when you meet him. It is impossible to describe who Arie is,' answered Friend.

'But the world is full of lions and people who could be called lions because of their courage. How will I know this is the real Arie?'

'In the Crooked World everyone has their own name and no one else can be called the same. When you meet Arie you will know that it is him,' explained Friend mysteriously.

'But we're not in the Crooked World, this is the normal world. We're only now meant to be looking for the key to the Crooked World,' Paul consciously protested.

'Do you really believe this is the normal world?' said Rabbit.

'I think it's about time we left,' said Friend cutting the conversation short and he added, 'Traveller is waiting. I'll take you to his home.'

'Wait a moment,' Paul interrupted again while quickly bidding farewell to his grandmother. 'Since we're going to be setting off somewhere, surely I have to first pack...'

'Just do it quickly.'

Without thinking for long, the boy ran to his room and threw everything into his bag that he had brought from Warsaw. He spent a moment considering whether to leave the book that he'd bought recently but in the end he decided he might however have some time for reading on the journey.

## Chapter three
# IN TRAVELLER'S HOME

On the way to Traveller's home, Paul looked carefully at those taking part in this strange expedition. Friend and Tiger looked rather normal but next to them there was Rabbit tirelessly jumping and Elf was sometimes flying in front of them and sometimes behind them as if continually looking to find his place.

The boy didn't stop wondering what he himself was doing among them... Why had he trusted this strange man so easily, who after all had said nothing about himself? What after all does the statement "I will never let you down" mean? What kind of reassurance was that? Why was he supposed to believe him? All these strange things that happened around Friend, the revelation that Granny was Good Fairy... It all showed that this mysterious acquaintance was no ordinary person but in that case who was he? Was it wise to set off into the unknown with a band of strange creatures to find the key to a world about which he knew nothing? Yet Granny had asked him to do it. But it wasn't only her request that had strengthened his resolve that it was worth undertaking such a quest. The truth was that Paul had always wanted to experience something remarkable. He had always dreamed of something happening to him that went beyond normal grey of reality. He had always wanted a wonderful fascinating world full of fairy tale creatures to be hiding somewhere under everything that is called normality. And indeed there was. It seemed as if he really had found himself in the middle of an extraordinary adventure but the old woman who passed them in the street didn't even bat an eyelid in surprise, when Elf flew directly in front of her face and when she almost tripped over Rabbit she only muttered, 'Oh, these pavements.' Similarly when they passed a group of children playing in a garden, they too didn't notice anything unusual. Why not?

'It's not always enough to look in order to see. You need to want to see,' Friend stated unexpectedly and again Paul had the impression that he was reading his mind.

'But I always wanted to see such things; why couldn't I?' the boy asked with regret.

'You wanted to and that is why you met me and now you can see,' replied Friend with a melancholy voice. 'Not everything happens straight away. Most often people discover the Crooked World little by little and only then is the desire to meet me awakened. You had the luck to meet me in Good Fairy's home and straight away you can see many of the effects of the Crooked World.'

'I still don't understand how it's possible that Granny needs the key to the Crooked World since this world is already here,' said Paul.

'It seems to you that this other world is here already but that certainly doesn't mean that it is here in its entirety...' Friend stopped and added, 'Look, we're coming up to Traveller's house. I don't think I need to introduce him to you.'

At that moment Paul, who had been distracted with the conversation, noticed that they had arrived at the house of Mr Wronski. He could have guessed, after all John Wronski loved to travel.

Friend knocked on the door. They waited a moment until at last it was opened by Mr Wronski's brother Ralph. He wasn't a very tall man but he was very thin with dark blond hair. His thin lips were normally pursed and his eyes always squinted slightly. Most often he dressed in a slovenly manner in creased trousers and a stained shirt and as a result his appearance seemed a little repellent.

'Welcome Grouch,' blurted out Friend.

The boy froze in amazement. Although the term "Grouch" undoubtedly did suit Ralph Wronski, who the boy most associated with complaining about everything, these words spoken in such an undisguised direct and impudent manner still sounded strange in the mouth of Friend, who from the beginning had seemed to Paul to embody gentleness itself.

Friend turned to the boy and told him quietly, 'I see that you underestimate me, Knight. I always call things by their name.'

'Oh, it's you again...' stated Ralph Wronski with resignation in his voice. 'And what's this group you've brought along this time?' he asked with clearly bitter expression.

'These are my friends.' Turning to them, Friend appeared to pay no attention to the tone of Grouch. 'Can we come in? Is Traveller in?'

'But you know he is,' blurted out their host. 'He's waiting for you.'

Ralph Wronski, or Grouch (since this nickname instantly stuck to the owner of the embittered face) let them in through the door. Everyone clearly new the way since they went straight to the drawing room where John Wronski was indeed standing and leaning over various documents. His tall thin shape emanated confidence. On his head he had quite a lot of hair that had faded in the sun and from his permanently suntanned face shone out a pair of clear grey eyes that expressed calm and self-control. He quickly welcomed them and then the boy noticed that he was dressed in simple dark trousers as well as a sailor's shirt with epaulettes[1]. After a while Traveller sat down on the sofa by a table with maps spread out over the top. Paul, who very much liked Geography, noticed straight away that these were not ordinary maps of the world. Although it seemed that he recognised the outlines of some of the continents, in his opinion on the map, there was... more. There were both more bits of various lands as well as more seas and strange patches attached to those continents that Paul did recognise. He decided not to ask but to wait and let events take their course.

'I see that you've been doing your preparation,' observed Friend.

'What! If I didn't prepare, your Crooked World would already be totally twisted up,' replied Traveller while leaning over a map. 'Luckily I am the one normal and simple person in your band of twisted mad men.'

As John Wronski was talking Paul realised that he shared one characteristic with his brother. Both of them could be malicious. But in as far as Ralph Wronski's malice resulted from his bitterness, the acerbity of his brother seemed rather pleasant.

'I thought that you would come with Little Lula,' said John Wronski looking up from his maps. Traveller clearly knew of the plan of taking Little Lula with them and also didn't seem at all surprised by the presence of even the weird Rabbit. He must have been so well acquainted with the Crooked World

---

1 Epaulette – (or shoulder board) A piece of material sewn on between the top of the sleeve and the collar of a uniform shirt. Normally fastened with a button.

that such things no longer made any impression on him. Then Paul noticed Grouch, who a moment before had slipped into the room. Now he stood behind everybody and with a disdainful expression he looked at Elf who was sitting on a lamp. Then having felt the gaze of the boy on him he turned around and retreated to the corner of the room where there stood an armchair. Even from far away it seemed dirty and covered in cobwebs. Paul was surprised that in such a tidy house there was such a neglected piece of furniture. Grouch sat down and picked up a newspaper. The boy felt however that he hadn't at all taken his eye off the guests.

'Don't pay any attention to Grouch, Knight,' said Friend quietly.

Paul almost jumped. He had been certain that Friend was looking at the maps.

'He simply doesn't like me and detests everything associated with me.' Friend smiled at the boy and continued: 'We met a long time ago and Grouch was very happy to know me. He was at school and wanted to become a carpenter. But then when I met his brother and helped him to become Traveller, Grouch became envious. It seemed to him that since I was spending more time with John, he was more important to me.' Friend stopped speaking for a moment as if he were considering how much he would say. 'But that wasn't true. Nevertheless from that time on he stopped liking me, and now around fifteen years have passed. But I still haven't lost hope that he will come back to me.'

'Do you want to listen to my plans or do you prefer to depend on each other on the journey,' interjected Traveller.

'No, no dear Traveller. We're listening to you now,' Friend returned his attention to their host, sitting on the sofa.

'I've already prepared a ship. We can set sail at any moment. We need to collect Little Lula quickly, because my people are not going to want to sit idle waiting in port. I've already collected together all the necessary maps and weapons,' Traveller quickly concluded.

'I'm sorry? Did you say weapons!' Paul was speechless.

So far there had only been talk of finding a key. Nobody had mentioned anything about danger. However if he thought about it, he would have to say that in all the novels and computer games, there was always an evil villain, a monster or a wizard that would appear and who wanted to harm the heroes. Why should it be any different now?

'Of course, and how are we supposed to fight Enemy?' Traveller seemed quite surprised at the ignorance of the boy.

'There's no hurry,' Friend reassured everyone. 'Paul has only just met me. There was no need to tell him of all the details and dangers. In the end he's safe with me,' he added.

'Yes, but you yourself have reminded me many times not to forget about the weapons,' said Traveller with a little acerbity and added, 'You are supposedly always at our side, but when you're needed that's exactly when you're nowhere around. It seems to me that you're not quite the hero you claim to be!' Again a malicious spark appeared in the eye of Traveller but at the same time it could be seen that the corner of his mouth quivered in an attempt to hold back a joyful smile. Friend also smiled, clearly understanding this hidden stab.

'So listen Paul,' explained Traveller, 'There is Enemy. Now Enemy is not going to want us to find the key and will do everything to stop us.'

'And what does he look like?' the boy asked a little bit frightened.

'That's... a difficult question. He looks the way the circumstances allow him to look. You could also say that he looks the way he wants. It's just...' Traveller paused to think a little, 'it's difficult to say that he has a defined look. Just before he comes, it grows a little darker and you'll feel an inner unease or even fear.'

'Aah so then it's quite easy... Since you say...' despite it all Paul was not feeling too confident.

'Actually no. Because, it'll always seem to you that there's some reason or other for it to get dark. Also something will always happen that really will give you true cause to be scared and you will not be expecting Enemy to use your fear in order to appear. There's no point worrying about it in advance. We've got weapons. Arie can always turn up and besides the devil is not so black as he is painted. Enemy, it is true, is dangerous but fear only makes it easier for him to appear,' Traveller ended his talk.

'OK, and where are we sailing to? When I asked earlier no one knew where the key was so how do we know which direction to take?' asked Paul. He was getting used to the fact that there were certain questions that it was better not to raise because with time they would be cleared up anyway. But the matter of the destination of their voyage seemed rather important to him.

'The most important thing is to know what we seek, and the road will find itself. Anyway even if we were to get lost, Friend would certainly give us a hint. You just have to listen very carefully,' replied Traveller cryptically.

And it was just at this moment that Paul realised that Friend, who had for a long time been sitting quietly, had simply disappeared. Meaning not so much that he had disappeared, but that he was no longer in the room.

'Well and again he's hung you out to dry, or rather just left you,' Grouch maliciously commented, 'He just gives you your orders and as soon as it comes to anything, he's already gone.'

'Oh, don't complain Ralph,' snorted Traveller, 'Friend always appears when he's really needed.'

Paul thought that just a moment ago Traveller had stated the exact opposite, although half-jokingly. Further discussion had to be put off till later since Grouch with a terrible cry jumped out of his armchair.

'What kind of little monsters are these!' he shouted.

And indeed, from beneath his chair a group of little rabbits appeared identical in every way to the one that Granny had conjured up.

'Oh, come on! Rabbits always reproduce, and as you can see, these magic ones can do it by themselves,' Traveller shrugged. 'Come on, it's time to go.'

'Just take those jumping fur bags with you. I don't intend to set up a breeding centre for those monstrosities!' Grouch shouted still angry.

'You've got to be mad if you think I'm going to take them on the ship. They'd reproduce so often that we'd sink for sure! – Traveller shouted out in reply. 'Rabbit, I absolutely forbid you to reproduce while we're voyaging on the ship,' he told the animal sitting on the piano.

'Oh Traveller, you lot were being so boring that I had to do something. On the ship I'm sure there'll be many more interesting things to do,' replied Rabbit, hopping off towards the door in the company of the equally bored Tiger and the carefree flying Elf.

This was the exact manner in which the companions left Mr Wronski's house. With maps under their arms and dragging behind them a gigantic trunk, they left behind them Grouch dumbstruck with anger and a herd of little rabbits running around the garden. It was high time to go and fetch Little Lula.

**Chapter four**

# A TOAD IN
# THE GARDEN

On the way to the Little Sun children's home they had an unexpected adventure. Tiger, who had already managed to become completely bored in Traveller's home, ran far ahead of the others and looked with interest at the houses they passed along the street. Suddenly, as quick as lightning, he jumped to the side and ran underneath a nearby fence. Paul immediately chased after the cat but ran into an obstacle in the form of a gate blocking his access to the courtyard. Unfortunately he couldn't see the cat through the gaps between the slats. Traveller suggested that under such circumstances, they should either leave Tiger to find his own way home where he would stay with Granny or jump over the fence and start looking for him. The first proposal was abandoned at the moment when Rabbit too ran under the fence and disappeared into the bushes. Even though they could have left Tiger behind, they couldn't go anywhere without Rabbit; after all Paul was his knight. This argument sounded somewhat absurd, however the adventurers had been left with no other choice but to look for Tiger and Rabbit. The boy thought that jumping over someone else's fence in broad daylight and moreover in the middle of the town would not be very sensible. He decided to buzz the intercom in the hope that someone would open the gate for them.

'And what are you going to say?' asked Traveller. 'That you've lost a talking cat and a magic rabbit?'

Traveller's objection seemed to Paul to be quite reasonable, but he didn't have any better ideas and anyway he'd already rung the buzzer. Suddenly a woman stepped out of the building and waved her hand inviting them in. The gate wasn't shut properly so they went in. As they went up to the woman,

Paul noticed that she was young; she wasn't too pretty but she certainly had a pleasant face. She had short curly black hair and deep green eyes. She was wearing a purple woollen dress, which looked simple and attractive on her. When she saw them she smiled, and her smile was so wide that it took up almost all of the bottom half of her face.

'Welcome. What are you looking for?' she asked.

And it was at this moment that Paul realised how difficult the task was just as Traveller had warned him. Even though they could say they were searching for a cat, they couldn't give away the fact they were also searching for Rabbit, who since he didn't belong to this world, the woman wouldn't be able to see at all.

'Errr, our cat ermm...' Paul was plucking up his courage while Traveller stood to one side aloof and silent. '... ran in somewhere under the fence and he's almost certainly hiding in the bushes. We'd like to go and look for him.'

'Of course. It's no problem,' replied the stranger. 'It seems to me I also saw your rabbit in my garden.'

At that moment both Paul and Traveller stared wide-eyed at the woman.

'And so you too know Friend?' Paul asked.

'Whose friend?' replied the still smiling woman.

'Well... Friend.'

At that moment Paul realised that it couldn't be explained. Firstly, how do you explain to someone what it meant to know Friend. Anyone who knew Friend, would know which friend was being talked about. And secondly, how could he be described in a few words? This was simply impossible. Suddenly it seemed to Paul that although he had met Friend only a couple of hours ago, he already knew him quite well.

'Hmm, I'm not really sure what you're talking about,' and this time the stranger smiled less confidently but after a while her smile broadened again. 'But I see your rabbit's turned up.'

And indeed, suddenly Rabbit had appeared by Paul's legs. The boy looked again at the Beautiful Lady – How had it happened that suddenly he had started calling her that in his head? Especially when she wasn't really that beautiful? – He remembered that Friend had mentioned that some people first see the effects of the Crooked World before they meet him.

Suddenly, surprising even himself he blurted out, 'Do you want to come with us on an expedition?'

He could palpably feel how Traveller, who was standing behind him, froze and had fixed his eyes upon him with a disapproving gaze.

'An expedition? Yeah sure! And where are we going?' The Beautiful Lady was very much taken by the proposal. He wanted to reply to her but then Traveller coughed and interrupted, 'I am in charge of this expedition, madam. The boy was being quite incautious to propose it to you. It is likely to be a rather exhausting and dangerous undertaking,' he said sharply.

Paul wondered why when faced with such a beautiful smile from a woman, Traveller hadn't become enraptured. He thought that Mr Wronski must have been spending too much time with his maps, which was why he wasn't able to appreciate the company of nice people.

'But that's not a problem! The more dangerous and exhausting, the better!' At that moment the woman's smile stopped shining for a while and it seemed to Paul as if the sun had suddenly gone down. For a split second he was under the impression that in her eyes he could make out a boundless sadness, which however immediately passed and again the woman beamed a broad smile.

Strangely that single moment changed Traveller's attitude: 'Well since that's so, you're sincerely welcome. We need resourceful people.'

'Brilliant, in that case let's go. But, but it seems that we've still got to find the cat.' With all her extraordinary etherealness, she was nonetheless quite practical. 'You lot go and look for him and I will pack something to eat for us all.'

For a moment Paul felt really surprised. Everything today was incredible and magical, but here was suddenly something so prosaic. Taking care of food seemed to him something so unlike a fairy tale that in no way did it fit the events of the day, nor did it fit this unusual lady. Well as clearly could be seen, even the heroes of marvellous adventures must sometimes eat something.

'Oh, I haven't introduced myself,' The Beautiful Lady stepped back from the door, 'I'm Stacey Gherkin. And what are you called?' she asked.

And once again Paul froze. Firstly because never in his life had he heard of someone with such an ill-suiting surname and secondly because Traveller stated without hesitation, 'I am Traveller, this is Knight of the Rabbit, and Elf is sitting there on the window sill.'

'Wonderful, in that case we already know each other,' Lady replied without the least surprise and she waved at Elf. Then she turned round and went into the building.

'How can it be that she doesn't know Friend and yet she can see everything and it doesn't surprise her?' Paul asked turning to Traveller.

'I don't know, but you don't need to know everything, Knight. Anyway, since she can see everything, sooner or later she will meet Friend so there's no reason to worry. Come on,' Traveller added encouragingly, 'we've got to find Tiger. Rabbit, have you seen him?'

'No, but if I know Tiger, he's sure to have gone hunting something and now he's enjoying his meal,' replied Rabbit.

So they started their search. First, they beat the bushes that grew in front of the house but they found nothing. Then they decided to go into the back garden. They were amazed by its size, it was indeed large as well as wild and overgrown. Interestingly it also seemed to them strangely enticing.

It's just like Lady, Paul felt deep down. Meanwhile Elf had flown into a thicket.

'Err, maybe I'll wait for you here,' Rabbit said straight away and seated himself on the side of the porch.

'What, are you afraid?' teased Paul.

'No, I'm just a little bit tired,' explained Rabbit, 'It's time for my nap.'

Traveller had already disappeared into the undergrowth but there was no telling why Paul felt a little uncertain as he walked among the trees. He slowly made his way deeper into the bushes until he suddenly realised that he had no idea where Elf and Mr Wronski were. It was true he could hear the beating of Elf's tiny wings as well as the heavy breathing of Traveller as he made his way through the undergrowth, but he was unable to say from which direction these sounds were coming. He wondered how it was possible for such a strange thickly growing garden to find itself in the middle of the suburbs. Before he could come to any conclusions, suddenly something jumped on him and cursed in anger. It seemed to Paul that it had cursed because the "meee-ow" that he had just heard had sounded particularly spirited.

'Oh Tiger, you're here. We lost you. We've been looking for you for ages,' Paul said worriedly.

'I got lost? But I've been here all the time. It's that dreadful toad that's been hiding somewhere here all the time,' replied Tiger as if nothing were amiss.

'It would be better for you, you disgusting cat, if you looked after your owners,' suddenly interrupted the toad, peeking out from under a pile of leaves lying on the ground.

'How dare you! I'm a free cat. I don't have any owners! I'm as fierce and terrible as a tiger and you're better off never coming out of hiding,' shouted the cat ready to spring, when suddenly Beautiful Lady was standing next to them.

'Oh there you are Toad. I've been looking for you everywhere. Did you know we're about to go on a long journey with the Knight and his cat?' she explained with a smile.

It was hard to know who was more surprised by this statement: Paul, Tiger, or Toad. Immediately from behind Lady Rabbit also appeared, who clearly felt no fear of entering the undergrowth in her presence. At the same time Traveller and Elf also appeared.

'Excuse me! You want to take that Toad with us?' Traveller was clearly unhappy with the turn of events.

'Of course, I couldn't leave her here all alone! After all she wouldn't be able to look after herself. I'm sure she won't be a problem. She's really very nice.'

Everyone looked doubtfully at Toad. Probably the last thing they could say about her was that she was nice. She looked just horrid and moreover her vivid yellow eyes seemed to look at them sneeringly.

'Oh, how wonderful, I've always wanted to go on a distant journey and I'm sure with you there will be lots of great adventures,' Toad gave them a loathsome smile. Paul and Traveller swapped glances. Neither of them much fancied the idea of taking that vile amphibian with them but it appeared that leaving her behind would also mean giving up the company of Beautiful Lady. At that moment an unspoken understanding was formed between them as both of them really wanted to take the owner of that angelic smile with them although each of them clearly had different reasons. Tiger however objected:

'What's this! No! Toad's not sailing anywhere with us for sure. Either you give up the company of Toad or you yourself are not coming on this journey.'

Tears welled up in the eyes of the woman. She didn't want to pass up this unusual adventure, but she also could not leave Toad.

'Ahh tough. In that case we'll take Toad. But you've got to make sure that she doesn't cause us any trouble,' decided Traveller. Tiger looked at Mr Wronski in a fury, but he didn't have too much to say so he turned around and stuck his tail up in the air aggressively and walked briskly off towards the house and then further along the fence to the exit. The others followed on after him together with Toad and Lady, who carried a bag filled with food on her arm.

## Chapter five
# THE SEARCH
# FOR LITTLE LULA

They walked down the road towards the Little Sun. Paul tried to explain to his new companion that they wanted to collect Little Lula after which they were to go to a ship and later that evening set sail. The fact that the boy himself knew very little about the entire expedition was no hindrance to him in his explanation and moreover he didn't know Little Lula at all and he could see no particular reason for taking her on a sailing ship. However it was important to Friend that the girl should sail with them and because of this Knight wasn't going to object.

When they got to the Little Sun, they introduced themselves to the door-man and he directed them to the director's office. While they were waiting for her Paul asked Traveller on what basis they were going to ask her to entrust Little Lula into their care. As far as he knew, you couldn't just take some-one from a children's home. Traveller looked at the boy surprised. Clearly he hadn't thought of this himself.

'Good afternoon. How can I help you?' The director had suddenly appeared.

'Err...' Traveller was clearly hesitating.

'We've come to ask Little Lula out for a walk,' interrupted Lady. 'We haven't seen her for a long time and we wanted to surprise her.' The charming smile of their companion was evidently winning over the director, who smiled back.

Nevertheless, to their horror she replied, 'That's most kind of you but I don't know of anyone with such a name. Who exactly is Little Lula?'

Everyone froze. None of them knew what the little girl was actually called. It wasn't enough that they wanted to steal some child from an orphanage, they did not even know her name.

Beautiful Lady started wading in further, 'When we were here last time, she introduced herself as Lula so we call her more familiarly Little Lula. We thought that was actually her name.'

'Ahh, well you see I'm new in this position and I don't yet know all the children well. I'll just go and ask one of the carers about this girl.'

What an indescribable relief. Everyone breathed out. Thanks to the guile of Lady they'd managed to pull themselves out of a difficult situation so they waited patiently feeling elated with their success.

However when the director returned she was alone and wore a frown.

She spoke to them being evidently wary, 'The carers state categorically that there is no Lula living in the Little Sun and they're also certain that no girl would introduce herself in such a manner.'

'Aha… ' concluded Traveller, 'And couldn't we just walk round the building and have a look around? Maybe we'll meet her.'

At first Paul thought that this was senseless; how were they supposed to recognise her when they had never met her. But then it came into his head that if Little Lula was somehow connected to the Crooked World, there was in fact a high chance that they would recognise her. This time however the director wasn't so amicably inclined.

'I would prefer that you go. I am not certain of your intentions and I wouldn't want to let strange people wander freely around this institution.' This time the voice of the director sounded almost threatening.

Next the director led the entire party with a quite deliberate step all the way to the gate. When the lock sounded in the gate, everyone froze. They'd let down Friend. They were going to have to set off without Little Lula. They looked at one another glumly and once again they realised that Rabbit was not with them. The last time they had seen him was in the director's office where he had clearly been sniffing something out. Going back inside was no longer possible seeing as they had been treated with a great measure of suspicion. Searching for Rabbit, who was invisible to everyone, would be all the more poorly taken. However it was Tiger who came to their aid.

'Maybe I'll go look for him,' and having said this he tensed his entire colourfully striped body and with a single bound he was on top of the fence. 'You lot go to the ship. We'll catch up with you there,' after which he disappeared over the other side.

'Good,' answered Toad. 'Now we don't need their company. Meanwhile we can settle in on the ship and maybe we can eat something?'

'That's a good idea. Don't worry boys. Tiger is sure to find Rabbit and we will soon be able to set sail,' added Lady. 'Although we're probably not going to make it before nightfall anyway since the light is beginning to fade.'

Paul thought that Traveller's face when he had been called a boy had looked extremely funny but he held back from saying anything. He was worried that they were splitting up at such an early stage of their journey, even before they had managed to set sail. They went on, but now at an evidently slower pace. The tension could be felt in the air. The further they left the Little Sun behind them, the more Paul felt uneasy. Just as much as Paul didn't doubt that Tiger and Rabbit would be found, the idea of leaving without Little Lula was hard to accept. After all, Friend had promised her that she would go sailing. And they were supposed to leave her? And in such an out of hand manner they would cause Friend to break his promise?

'This is not right,' Lady suddenly called out. Her smile had disappeared somewhere and now she looked angry. She was completely changed. 'We can't just simply leave the little girl.'

Her words cut straight into Paul. They couldn't. In one moment he knew that he had to return to the Little Sun. He looked at Traveller, who had a determined look on his face and was gazing at the horizon, clearly thinking about the opportunity they had already missed to sail that evening.

'I'm going back. I'll look for her. You lot go on,' Paul said feeling really determined.

'I'm going with you. It'll be better,' added Lady, 'Traveller, you can go to the ship and prepare everything to set sail.'

Now Mr Wronski's face expressed sheer rage.

'I'm the leader of this expedition. It's I who decides what we do. If you want to sail with me on my ship, you have to obey me,' he shouted.

The air around them clearly thickened. Silence fell. Everyone was considering what to do in such a situation.

Suddenly Toad spoke up: 'Well that was to be expected. You are a terribly mismatched crew, but I think, my lady, that you are right. We can't leave the little girl.'

Her words resonated for a long time in the silence that ruled between them. Paul thought about how it was Toad who had encouraged them to leave Tiger and Little Lula and make their way to the ship and now she was saying the exact opposite. He had an uneasy feeling that this vile creature was manipulating them, but he couldn't think about this for any longer because Traveller, with a clearly determined expression spoke up.

'Do what you like. I'm going to the ship and preparing to sail. You'd better be back on time. Goodbye.' And with these words he turned around and left.

Lady looked torn. She clearly understood that she should not have spoken like that to this man whom she had barely just met but at the same time she felt similarly to Paul that it wasn't right to set off without Little Lula.

Paul said, 'Please go with Traveller. It will be easier for me to get into the Little Sun alone. They'll take me for one of the children who live there. And you for sure will be able to stop Traveller.'

This proposal seemed quite sensible. Lady looked at the boy with evident relief.

'I'm glad that you've come up with such a clever idea. If you need my help, I'm sure you know your way to the port. You'll find me there,' she replied.

'I can accompany him. I'm happy to help,' added Toad.

Paul wanted to object strongly but before he could Lady said, 'Oh yes, that would be best. You see, Knight, Toad will tell me if anything happens.'

Every fibre of the boy's body told him that this was a very bad idea but he was unable to refuse this strange woman. With clenched teeth he just nodded his head and waved Lady goodbye. He turned around hoping a little that Toad herself would not want to accompany him. But after a few steps he noticed that she was following him.

It was only when he reached the gate to the Little Sun that he began to consider his plan of action. It looked as if it was already getting late and there was nobody outside, which gave him a chance to get inside by climbing over the fence. But what then? He would have to go with the flow.

When he found himself in the courtyard, he realised that it was quite a large property on which there was a playground, woods and a large field which was probably used by the children as a football pitch. At first glance there was nobody to be seen, so he marched off quickly in the direction of the building. Walking around along the wall, he was looking for a back door, which – as far as he remembered – used to be there. Suddenly he came to a wooden door that was in the bend of a wall. Just as he should have expected, it was locked. All of a sudden he noticed a thick piece of wire lying on the ground. Paul remembered how with just such wire he used to try to make picks for various locks with his father, who once had more time for him. So the boy grabbed it and with dexterous fingers he tried to make it fit the keyhole in the door. Out of the corner of his eye he saw Toad, who had been following him the entire time, watching him intently. Suddenly he felt the lock resist and with one swift motion he turned the makeshift key and the doorway stood open before them. However what a disappointment it was. The door led down to a cellar. Paul froze. He wondered whether it was worthwhile at all to go down the stairs, since there was no knowing if there would be another way up. Moreover the descent into the dark opening didn't look particularly inviting. He already wanted to turn back and look for another entrance when he heard a terrible noise behind him which made him jump forward and slam the door.

'Wait, wait! Open up!' Toad shouted from outside. 'I knocked over a bucket.'

It was only then that Paul felt relief. Not only had no one seen him jump down into the cellar, he had also managed to get rid of Toad. He wasn't going to turn back any more. Besides there should be some way up out of here. One problem however was the lack of light. The boy was unable to find a light switch anywhere and the little moonlight that shone through the skylight in the ceiling was not enough to allow him to get his bearings in this space.

Unexpectedly something moved in the twilight...

# Chapter six
# THE STRUGGLE

Paul froze.

He felt absolutely certain that something was hiding nearby among the different pieces of furniture and equipment stored in the cellar. Suddenly with terrifying clarity he remembered the words of Traveller about the signs of Enemy. Yes for a long time he had been feeling uneasy and for quite some time it had been getting darker. Just like parts of a puzzle everything fitted together. It did not matter that Paul did not know who in general Enemy was or what he looked like. He was hiding somewhere there in the darkness. The boy was certain of this and felt an increasing panic.

He began involuntarily walking back to the stairs that could just be made out in the darkness. Suddenly he realised that before he would be able to open the door again with his lock pick quite some time would pass during which Enemy would be able to attack him freely from behind. There was no sense to this. The only option was to face the danger. Besides Friend did not doubt him and had repeatedly told him that he could do it...

And like a distant light in a tunnel, like a cool breeze blowing on a sunburnt face, the thought of Friend gave him strength. Paul went forward with a quick step and passed by the furniture placed along the wall. It already seemed that he was rushing down a narrow path through the mess when suddenly...

He fell. He had tripped over a bag full of junk. He grabbed it so that he would have something in his hands to defend himself and in one moment he felt that there was a long fat torch inside of it. Pulling it out he knew that there was someone standing in front of him. He found the switch...

In the light of the torch the figure of a short wrinkled old man made a disturbing impression. The old man had a long beard and his eyes seemed so dark that it was difficult to differentiate the irises from the pupils. Paul's heart pounded like mad but his mind wandered off to Friend as his last hope of being saved. The boy stood up and for a short time the two of them looked at each other in silence.

'And so you've broken in here. I know what you're looking for,' he said.

'You don't know anything. I got lost. I'm looking for the way out,' retorted Paul.

'Ha ha, that's a good one. My dear, I'm not going to be taken in by such fairy tales. I already know boys like you: small inconspicuous blonds with dark brown eyes who pretend innocence,' the man laughed disturbingly.

It was only now that the boy felt that fear was suffocating him and pressing down on his chest. The old man blinded by the torch couldn't see him so clearly. He knew what Paul looked like. No matter what this meant, this was Enemy. Suddenly it seemed to him that an ice cold hand lay on his heart. Friend hadn't prepared him for this meeting...

'Yes, Friend...' The old man laughed sneeringly and Paul understood at this moment that Enemy could read his mind. 'You don't mean anything to him. He only needs you to fulfil his goals.'

Paul felt a warmth, which seemed to melt his already icy heart.

He noticed that throughout all this time they hadn't been alone. In the deafening silence that reigned in the cellar, he suddenly heard the beating of little wings. Elf had flown near his ear and with a melodious voice reminiscent of the ringing of bells in the wind which the boy now heard for the first time he said, 'Whoever Enemy is, at the moment he's just an old man. Remember this.'

The very presence of Elf had a soothing effect on Paul. Suddenly he understood the full meaning of his companion's words. He still didn't know the real identity of Enemy but if he was only an old man right now, then he could be beaten like an old man. The boy suddenly realised that he was holding a big heavy torch in his hand. He swung his arm with all his strength and hit the man standing in front of him in the chest. He fell with a terrible howl on the floor and in one bound Paul jumped over him and ran forward straight to the door, which could now be seen in the narrow beam of light. Before he could try the handle, he heard a squealing cry from the man lying on the floor.

'I'll remember you.'

The door was unlocked and in the next moment Paul ran out into an empty corridor with many doors leading to children's bedrooms. The boy leaned against the wall and tried to catch his breath and out of the corner of his eye he looked at Elf, who had sat down on a window sill as if nothing had happened. For the first time it crossed his mind that up until that moment he had never tried even to talk to him. But nonetheless he was still there when he was needed. His simple words had allowed Paul to escape from that horrible place and leave Enemy behind. He really wanted to ask something more, to find out who Enemy was and why he had allowed himself to be so easily beaten and why he wasn't chasing him. However the silence of Elf, who was looking in total calm at the clear rising moon left the boy abashed and wordless. It seemed out of place to ask him about anything.

Suddenly Paul realised that he could hear a cacophony of children's voices coming from the rooms. It brought him back from the reverie that he had momentarily fallen into. He walked slowly along the corridor and without a thought opened the door to the room from where the loudest din was coming from.

'Hey, who are you?' a tall blonde girl, who seemed to be about nine, asked him straight away.

'Errm, I'm new here. I just wanted to look around and see what was going on...' he replied uncertainly.

There were six children in the room, all of about the same age as the girl. Clearly they had been playing some board game and he had interrupted them. Everyone looked at him intently.

'And your carer hasn't shown you the entire building?' the girl asked him dubiously.

'No of course, I mean she showed it to me but now I want to see it for myself...' stammered Paul.

'Errr, you're up to something. New kids don't simply go walking around by themselves looking into different rooms. And anyway you're older so you probably live on the second floor?' Despite her clear suspicions, the girl seemed willing to help.

Suddenly it dawned on Paul that he would be best off owning up about everything.

'You know actually, I'm not from here,' he began to explain. 'I'm the grandson of Barbara Hengel, who was until recently the cook here. Now she's very ill and I'm helping her during the holidays. Granny very much wanted me to bring her Little Lula. I was here earlier and I talked with the director, but she didn't know who I was talking about. She seems to be new. So I thought that I would go from room to room and ask to see if I could find her myself...'

'Oh dear,' exclaimed the girl. She looked enchanted, 'Good Fairy is your grandmother. We're all so sad that she's ill; she always was so good to us... I'm Amelia. You're looking for Little Lula? Her room's not far, but...' the girl seemed to hesitate.

'What, can you lead me to her?' he asked worried.

'Well actually, you see today something strange happened. While we were in the garden Little Lula found some rabbit. She said that he had come especially to find her, that she had to go. I don't know how this is possible but she went up to the gate that is always locked, opened it and went out. We wanted to chase after her but the gate had already slammed shut. We didn't tell the carers about this because well,' Amelia clearly didn't know how to explain it, 'if you knew Little Lula, then you'd know why.' She finished speaking.

'And the rabbit, what about the rabbit?' Paul asked anxiously.

'The rabbit?' the girl seemed surprised that such a detail would catch the attention of the boy. 'Well, I don't know. It seemed to me that she'd hidden it under her coat and was holding it, but I'm not sure. Really, I didn't even see this animal. She just said that she had found it. Interestingly enough, there was also a big cat that looked a little like a miniature tiger running after her.'

When Amelia had finished her tale, Paul felt an indescribable relief. It seemed that everyone including Little Lula had been found and was heading for the ship. Maybe they had even got there. He was happy and didn't really feel any regret on having returned unnecessarily to the Little Sun and having met Enemy. He was under the impression that somehow the entire adventure had worked out for him. He was also glad that he could see how much the children appreciated his beloved grandmother. She really must have been Good Fairy for them.

'Thanks, in that case I think that she must have gone to our house. I'm going to go too. Really, thank you very much for all your help,' he said with undisguised gratitude.

'It's no problem,' Amelia smiled at him and returned to her game with the other children.

Paul decided to leave the Little Sun quickly. However he didn't want to go back out through the dark cellar. He tried to quietly find the main entrance to the building. Luckily one of the carers who passed him by didn't pay him any attention. The doors were locked, but he dealt with it. Light from street lamps also fell on the forecourt of the institution and as a result he had no problem finding his way. Climbing over the fence turned out to be a real challenge. On the inside there were no rails on which he could get a foothold. He remembered however that by the door to the cellar Toad had knocked over a bucket. Maybe he could use that to climb up onto the fence.

Paul hesitated. And what if that vile amphibian was still waiting for him? Wouldn't it be better just to leave it here? Toad would certainly be able to look after herself. Something was telling him however that he shouldn't just leave her like that. After all how would he explain her disappearance to Lady? For a moment he regretted that he had even remembered about the bucket, he turned around with a silent curse on his lips. He returned to the orphanage wall and walked along to the bend in the wall, where the entrance to the cellar had been and suddenly he froze. For a moment he was out of breath. He stared dumbfounded at the place where the door used to be and there was now only... a blank wall. The bucket was still standing there with Toad waiting beside it but the door had disappeared.

'Oh you're here,' she croaked unpleasantly, 'Well I really waited a long time for you.'

'But, but...' Paul still couldn't get a grip on himself, 'Where is the door?'

'What door?' asked Toad, clearly surprised.

'The door to the cellar. I slammed it shut when you knocked over the bucket and that's why you stayed here.' The boy was no longer sure of what he was saying.

'What on earth are you talking about? The back entrance to the building is over there behind the corner. You ordered me to stay here because you were scared how people would react to the sight of a boy with a toad,' she said as if it were nothing.

Paul walked further along. He passed the bend and there indeed was the back door to the Little Sun. Bewildered he turned around and suddenly noticed Elf, who had been after all following him throughout all this time. And so there was a witness to his adventure in the cellar. The gentle smile of this illuminated creature seemed to answer Paul's doubts. Whatever had happened, it wasn't just his imagination.

After the children's home had disappeared from view, the boy realised that he should start hurrying. Traveller had threatened to set sail without waiting for him. He paced quickly down the streets of the port, which were now illuminated only by the glare of street lamps. When he got to the quay where Mr Wronski normally moored his ship, he saw a girl who looked about five years old standing in the middle of it. She was wearing a long black coat and a cat was standing at her legs as well as some other kind of animal that had to be Rabbit.

Paul shouted out with joy and started to run straight ahead at full pelt while Toad hopped after him. However before he managed to reach the person he thought was Little Lula, He was surprised by the sight of a great big ship at the end of the quay. Paul didn't know himself from where the thought came to him that this was the sailing ship that they were to sail on. So he looked around thinking that maybe he would see Traveller's yacht, but it was nowhere to be seen. Suddenly he realised that Little Lula had disappeared from sight. So clearly she must have boarded. When he ran up to the ship a whole host of questions ran through his mind... How could such a small crew like theirs manage to steer such a large sailing ship? And where had it come from? Most of all he was struck by the realisation that right now the adventure of his life was just beginning and he was completely unprepared. And why was he meant to be taking part? Because he wanted to. And because Friend wanted him to.

# Chapter seven
# ON BOARD

As soon as Paul ran onto the deck he saw Traveller dressed in a dark captain's jacket. He greeted him with evident joy, gave him a manly hug and with a wide swing of his arm he showed him the ship.

'Look what a beautiful sailing ship we have. This is The Whaler. You've also got to meet the crew.'

'But where did you get a ship like this? And where did the crew come from? I thought it was only us who would be sailing on your yacht,' exclaimed Paul.

'Oh yes, I didn't tell you this earlier. Friend knows someone who offered to lend us The Whaler. And as for the crew, well what did you expect? That I was going to sail with you, Rabbit and Little Lula? No my lad,' Traveller's voice sounded mysterious. 'Friend assured us that we would have a good, well trained crew. Now come with me. I have to show you the maps. We don't know yet where to find the key but we're going to sail to the nearest island archipelago in the Crooked World. Maybe we'll find out something there.' Suddenly Traveller turned to a well-built middle-aged man: 'Mr Fratel, we set sail tomorrow morning. Please prepare everything so that we can cast off at dawn.'

'Traveller, is everyone already here? Did Lady get here after you? I saw Little Lula on the quay but did she get on board the ship?' Paul was fretting.

'Ah yes; everything in turn. Lady arrived just after me, but I haven't seen Little Lula. I thought that since she didn't come with you, that you hadn't been able to find her...' Traveller hesitated.

No, I... It's a long story...' Paul explained in an agitated manner. 'Anyway, when I managed to get to the Little Sun, the children there told me that Little

Lula had found Tiger and Rabbit and she had simply left through the gate. I followed her and I tell you I saw her here on the quay.'

'Hmm, that's a surprise. And tell me, did anything else that was worrying happen to you while you were searching for her?' asked Mr Wronski.

'Well, yes. It's a rather strange matter, but I met Enemy.'

'What, you met Enemy? Where?' Traveller appeared very concerned about this event.

'In the cellar of the Little Sun... Elf helped me out. It's just that it was something very strange, because the cellar door, where I went in, later disappeared... I really don't know what to make of this,' explained Paul.

'Oh, that's nothing much. When you get to know the Crooked World a little bit better, you'll get used to such things happening. But the fact that you ran into Enemy sounds really ominous. This probably means we have to sail straight away, since Enemy knows of our plans and has already tried to waylay you.' Traveller walked quickly up to Mr Fratel, who was clearly the first officer.

This train of events worried Paul. He looked around the deck and suddenly he saw Tiger, who was sitting unconcerned on the barrier and licking his paw. Rabbit was sitting beside a barrel that stood below. The boy was so happy that he ran up to them straight away.

'Tiger, Rabbit, oh I'm so happy to see you. I was already beginning to think that you had got lost again,' he called out with relief.

'But we've been sitting here for ages. While you've been chatting away happily with Traveller, I've already had enough time for a nap,' replied Tiger yawning.

'Me too,' added Rabbit.

'But tell me, what about Little Lula?' the boy asked further.

'Well what do you want to know? We all boarded this ship together and she must have wandered off when we decided to have a rest.'

Paul clearly now felt frustrated with continually looking for Little Lula. He didn't understand why this little girl was always disappearing somewhere on him. One thing seemed certain however – she had made it to the ship. He stood looking around the deck and thinking about the strange train of events when he noticed the crew were working more busily. They really were preparing to cast off. Suddenly from below deck Beautiful Lady appeared with a bright smile upon her face and she started walking over in their direction.

'I'm happy to see you at last, Knight. Oh, and you've found Tiger and Rabbit. How wonderful!' Tiger gave an offended snort. 'I see that we're already setting off. Luckily, Traveller was quite easy to placate and agreed to wait for you. And what about Little Lula and Toad?'

Paul no longer had the strength to answer the question about Little Lula, but the question about Toad reminded him once again about this horrid creature.

'Err, well really I don't know. She should be here somewhere, she was jumping after me on the quay...'

'Aah, she's sure to turn up.' Strangely enough, Lady did not look worried.

Meanwhile Traveller called out for them not to get in the way while the ship was being cast off so they obediently moved out of the way of the crew and watched as the ship moved away from the shore. When all the moorings had been untied, Paul walked over to the bow to look at the sea opening up before him. It was indeed an incredible sight: the black night illuminated only by the stars and a few lights on the ship reflected in the breaking waves. Far out in the distance, there was the empty dark horizon that hid the surprises that they were going to meet on their voyage. However, the monotonous blackness into which they made their way seemed in no way terrifying, but rather invited them to embrace it and to surrender themselves to the unknown.

While Paul was standing so lost in thought, a quiet voice interrupted his reflections.

'How fascinating this all is! I'd like to now be somewhere far away. I miss Friend. He's always so jolly.' And suddenly this little voice burst out into a cascade of laughter as if the memory of Friend's antics was in itself one big joke.

The sound of this laughter made Paul giggle happily as well without any reason at all. Only after a while could he make out a small dark figure sitting on the bowsprit. Now he was sure that Little Lula had really made it on board. She turned towards him and in the harsh light of the lamps on the bow he could make out the face of a little girl with blonde hair and dark eyes. She had a thin nose and a small but prominent mouth. In Paul's opinion she was the embodiment of a little angel with the only difference being that her eyes were not sky but a remarkable navy blue.

'You made it here! I spent so long searching for you that in the end I didn't know if you'd set sail with us,' he said.

'Oh, Friend wouldn't have forgotten about me. Besides that's why he sent Rabbit to the Little Sun. He keeps his promises,' she replied.

The boy thought that the girl must indeed know Friend very well, since she was so certain of her words. However, he himself felt that Friend would never let him down, despite having only spoken with him for such a short time.

'I ran into Enemy in the cellar of The Little Sun...' Paul himself had no idea why he had told her that.

'That old man? I see him sometimes. He always looks to me as if he's going to be sick. His stomach must always be hurting him,' she added lost in thought.

'Who is he?' asked Paul, not knowing why he expected her to answer.

Little Lula frowned for a moment as if she were thinking but after a moment her little face was lit up by a happy smile and she exclaimed, 'Come on, it must be time for supper! There's a terrible rumble in my tummy.' With one bound she leapt from the bowsprit and ran towards the main deck. Paul felt a little disappointed that she hadn't answered his question, however after a moment he himself began to feel hungry and he went after her towards the mess.

As they were going down the stairs leading below deck they heard clearly angry voices coming from somewhere around the cabins.

Traveller was shouting, 'But explain to me what the hell you're doing? Why did you come here? To poke around? Did you want to steal something?'

'You're a fool. I wanted to bring you the bag with your things before you set sail,' said a voice that must have belonged to Grouch.

'I've been on board the whole time. You could have come up to me. I know you and I'm certain that you haven't just turned up here without some twisted reason,' shouted Traveller still angry.

Quite a crowd had already gathered in the corridor out of curiosity. Paul squeezed his way past the tall sailors certain that Little Lula was following. When he got to the cabin from where the voices were coming he saw a furious captain as well as a grim-looking Grouch.

'What's happening?' asked the boy.

'What's happening?' exclaimed Traveller, 'My dear brother has sneaked aboard for some unknown purpose and now that we have cast off he is going to have to sail with us.'

Little Lula pushed her way in front of Paul and went up to Grouch.

'Oh no,' she said clearly worried. 'You've no way of getting back home. But don't worry. You're sure to have fun here with us,' she added with a laugh.

The faces of the two brothers seemed truly funny. One of them felt clearly embarrassed by the little girl's courtesy, which contrasted with his own anger, while the other tried to put on a contemptuous face, which utterly failed to come out right. So he shrugged, not quite knowing how to react to such sincerity.

'Oh well it's just tough. What's happened has happened.' Traveller responded with resignation in his voice. 'Since you're here now, we'll have to find you somewhere to sleep. This was to be Paul's and Little Lula's cabin. Here are some things for you two.' He pointed with his hand to a small wardrobe. 'Come on Ralph, I think I've got another free berth. Maybe we can find you some spare clothes.' With these words Traveller started walking out and Grouch silently followed him. After a moment Paul and Little Lula found themselves alone. The little girl took out some stones from her pocket and began playing with them on the bed.

'We were supposed to be going to supper,' said the boy.

'Oh yes, I'm terribly hungry,' the girl declared emphatically.

After supper when they were getting ready for bed, Paul was getting changed when he discovered that in his pocket was the piece of wire shaped like a key that he had used to open the door of the cellar. The door that wasn't there.

## Chapter eight
# THE VOYAGE

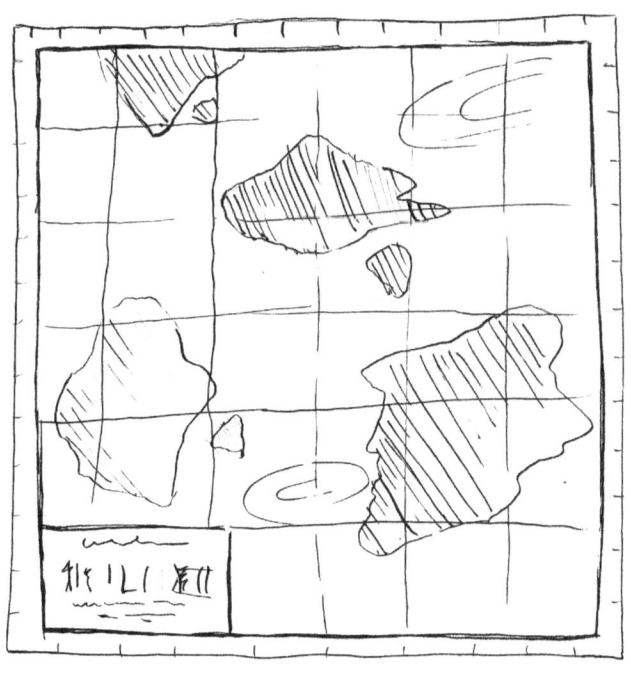

It took the first week of sailing to get used to the ship and learn to sail it. Paul had read a little bit on the subject but the reality turned out to be far more complex than the examples in the book... He had to take in the daily system of watches, help with the reefing of the sail, to climb the mast and sit in the crow's nest as a lookout. Nobody treated Paul as a child of whom less could be demanded. Even Lady and Grouch had to do all kinds of different jobs on board the ship. Only Little Lula had allowances made for her by everyone and it sufficed for her to sit on the bridge and make the work more pleasant for everyone by playing happily with Tiger and Rabbit.

Throughout this time not much was spoken about the quest that was just beginning. However Paul liked to sit on the deck beside Beautiful Lady and tell her about himself: about his parents, who were never there for him; about his grandmother, who would tell him the most fantastic stories, which now the boy suspected were actually true stories from the Crooked World; about the dog that had once come to him and had later been hit by a car; about the gang of boys at school who terrorised everyone and had turned him against Peter... Lady would always listen to Paul with interest as she stroked Tiger who would sit on her lap. She would never, however, say anything about herself. Whenever he tried to ask her anything, her enchanting smile would go out and in her eyes that same boundless sadness would return that had appeared on her face on the day that he had met her.

Every time they sat and talked, it would seem to Paul that Traveller had something extremely important to do on deck. However he never approached them nor did he join in the conversation. Sometimes Grouch, who for no known reason would like to listen in, would throw in some snide remark of his own. During these times Little Lula would run all over the entire ship squealing with delight after Rabbit who would be hopping around. At these blissful and joyful moments even Toad would occasionally take part in these chases. Elf, however, had found himself a place high up on the yardarm and rarely appeared on deck. When night fell, his crystal wings would begin to shine brightly and he sometimes could be seen as he left the ship and flew up to the stars. There were moments when it seemed to Paul that the other golden points in the night sky weren't stars at all, but other elves, who were watching over their voyage. And so the days passed. It seemed to the boy that the voyage was taking an eternity.

One day after around two weeks of sailing, the captain called everyone together including First Officer Fratel to the captain's quarters for a meeting. There he showed them drawings in which the Baltic Sea was far larger than what is shown on any ordinary map. Paul spent a long time looking at the faded papers, wondering if they didn't have secret bulges that were not visible to the naked eye. It looked as if in certain places known on standard maps there would be strange bulges that indicated a part of the Crooked World. And also the islands that they were heading to found themselves on one of the biggest bulges. There were seven of them with the largest of them, which was called Shemesh, being an almost perfect circle. Just next to it there was a small islet called Karev. The other islands had equally unusual-sounding names.

We're approaching that archipelago that I mentioned to you. It's high time to make concrete decisions in regard to the search. I must therefore explain to you all what these islands are. You won't find them on any ordinary map. They're quite wild and steep. On Shemesh, the first of these, there are lots of waterfalls with entrances to caves underneath. I think that this is a good place to start our search. The tunnels stretch out under the seabed and come out on the island of Karev. Mr Fratel, you will take command of the ship during my absence and anchor it next to the shore of this island so please listen carefully. We, which means Knight, Little Lula, Lady, Grouch and I will set off...' Traveller was interrupted by a loud grunt.

'And what about us? Supposedly animals don't have a vote any more. I'm not going to stand for that,' interjected an outraged Rabbit. His orangey-purple eyes took on an intense shade as if a storm were gathering.

'OK, OK, the animals are also coming with us,' the captain placated. 'So we're going to make our way into the middle of the island of Shemesh and if we can we'll make our way via the caves to the island of Karev where we will reunite with the crew, which will temporarily be under the command of Mr Fratel. In short that's probably everything.'

They sat awhile in silence considering what Traveller had told them. Once again Paul couldn't stop himself and began asking questions.

'There's something I don't understand. How do we know we'll find anything at all in the caves? Why are we taking this way and not some other seeing as we have no clues as to where the key may be hidden?'

Traveller gave him a searching look, and considered how much he could reveal.

Suddenly Little Lula squealed with laughter, 'But it's obvious! Everyone knows that the most difficult road is the one with the highest chance of finding the key. If it were easy to find, why should we bother trying?'

The captain glanced at the girl in a fright as if she had just revealed some dangerous secret. Paul didn't understand what it was all about. Although Little Lula's argument wasn't just nonsense, it was still unclear to Paul why the hardest road should be the basis of any kind of search.

'This isn't any kind of search, Knight.' On hearing those words, Paul froze. After all, he had not stated aloud exactly what he was thinking. He looked around at all those there assembled, all of whom looked just as surprised. He looked into the corner of the cabin where he had heard the voice come from. He already knew in his heart that, underneath the large mirror in the ornamental frame, he would see Friend. However before Paul could say anything, Little Lula had let out a loud squeal of joy and now threw herself into the arms of the man who rose from his chair, caught her under the arms and span her round in a circle, while laughing loudly all the time.

'Hello my dear. I'm glad that we're together,' and with these words he stuck out his tongue at her.

The little girl burst out in laughter and for a moment they both played at sticking out their tongues. To Paul it seemed that an uncomfortable silence reigned among the others, as if it seemed to them that it wasn't fitting to join in with such a childish game. Friend however paid this no heed and it was only after a moment that he addressed them.

'Welcome. I was listening to your plans and I was glad to see you were so keen to act. It's wonderful that we've finally got to meet each other, Daisy,' he said turning at the end to the only woman in their company.

Beautiful Lady sat as if carved from stone. Her figure did not even twitch, even when everyone was looking at her in silence. Then Paul remembered that Lady, or maybe Daisy, had never met Friend before, but could see many of the effects of the Crooked World. There was tension in the air. The boy was surprised that his older friend, Lady, hadn't jumped in the air with joy to grasp the hand of Friend. Her eyes were always lively, but now they expressed nothing in particular, as if there were some internal conflict that she wished to conceal from everyone there present. Suddenly tears flowed from her eyes.

'I was waiting for you,' whispered Lady.

'Yes, it took a long time but I'm here now.' And with these words Friend walked up and kissed her on the cheek. 'After all, you're no longer alone,' he said reaching out to everyone with his arms.

Daisy smiled, but it was not the wide and lively smile that Paul had become accustomed to, only a discreet and peaceful one that banished the hint of desperation that hid deep in her eyes.

'But you two supposedly don't know each other,' blurted out Traveller.

Friend burst out laughing, but Daisy became grave.

'No, we met once, but it's hard to say that we know each other,' she explained.

'We still only barely know each other, but that will change,' added Friend. I'm going to accompany you a little on the voyage. I think someone here needs a few words of explanation,' he said turning to Paul. 'This isn't any kind of search, Knight,' he repeated. The boy looked at him uncertainly. What was that supposed to mean?'

'What this means is that the search for the key is a matter of the utmost importance. You don't have to choose the most difficult way when you're searching for a lost sock; that would be ridiculous.'

Little Lula giggled and a hidden laugh shone in Friend's eyes:

'The road to the key to the Crooked World is one of the most difficult, but also one of the most fascinating. What is more exciting: a walk down a paved road to a shop, even when you can buy millions of sweets, or a dangerous expedition across seas, through forests, through underground caves, and over high mountains where at the end you find something no more extraordinary than a key? Answer that question for yourself. Anyway you're not going to get this key in a shop. If you go looking for it, you must take the most difficult path,' he said finishing his explanation.

Paul looked at Friend in silence. It crossed his mind that no one had explained this to him when they had set out on this expedition. Friend smiled. However the boy felt that at the beginning of the journey, this had not been the most important information. After all, he had wanted to set off for at least two reasons: to find the key for Granny and to experience something. How could he now complain that something extraordinary now awaited him?

'That's clear... I mean maybe I don't understand completely why we're going to go such a way, but let's just say that it's ... OK,' agreed Paul.

'Well good. Does anything else need explaining, Traveller?' asked Friend.

'I don't think so. We'll land on Shemesh tomorrow. Please can you all pack any necessities and get ready to set off,' said Traveller, finishing the meeting.

The preparations took up all of the day. They were each allowed to take only one small bag so they had to think very carefully about what they would need. Paul was surprised when Traveller brought him a long dagger asking him, as far as it was possible, to keep it on him at all times. Next the man stood in front of Little Lula with a small knife in his hand clearly debating whether such a small girl could be given such a thing to hand. However in the end he put it into his pocket and quickly went out. He returned carrying a quaint pocket watch on a chain shut in a gold case. When Paul looked at it closer with Lula, it turned out that it didn't have any hands. The captain did not however explain what the object could possibly be used for. It crossed Paul's mind that it could only be used to give someone's head a good bashing but he didn't share this thought with the girl. Traveller left quickly to hand out weapons to the remaining members of the expeditionary party. Mainly these were long swords. The boy was surprised that this old-fashioned weaponry, which could have come from a mediaeval legend, gave the entire expedition the charm of a secret knightly quest.

After the preparations were completed Paul went out on deck hoping to meet Friend, but he could not find him anywhere. Then he saw Lady standing at the bow illuminated by the reddish light of the setting sun, or should it be Daisy, even though of all the names that had so far been given by Friend this one seemed least suited to its owner, well apart from maybe his own. This mysterious woman despite her broad smile and accessible character in no way reminded him of a cheerful wild flower so in his thoughts he still called her Lady.

'Why are you standing here alone? Come on, let's go and find Friend,' proposed Paul.

However she didn't seem very interested by this idea. On the contrary, she was for her surprisingly sad. Paul noticed that Toad had sat next to her. He had the vague impression that in the presence of this amphibian, it was much harder to talk with Lady.

Meanwhile Friend himself had appeared beside them.

'Are you ready to go? Then come with me. I've asked Traveller if we can dance on deck. Did you know that Grouch can play the guitar? He can play the music for us,' he said merrily.

Then Paul noticed Traveller who with guitar in hand was talking passionately with his brother, who stood however with crossed arms and clearly wasn't being persuaded to help with the dance.

Suddenly Little Lula appeared, who laughing loudly had of course come out from below deck chasing after Rabbit, and ran straight into Grouch.

'Watch out where you're going, little one!' he shouted in anger.

'But why are you standing in the middle like a post? Tag, you're it!' The girl gave him a slap on the hip and ran away laughing.

Grouch's expression looked just indescribably funny. But to everyone's surprise he began to run after the child. The little girl ran between Paul and Friend and with one bound jumped onto the bowsprit, where Grouch could not reach her so easily.

'Next time you won't escape me so easily,' he said.

Little Lula gave a snort of laughter and Grouch looked at her with slightly narrowed eyes. Although his expression was as grim as ever a joyful spark could be seen in his eyes.

'You've lost. Now you've got to play for us,' Lula triumphantly exclaimed

Mr Wronski clearly wanted to rage about this ultimatum, but somehow he was unable to. With a somewhat sour face he took the guitar from his brother and began to play some lively tune. Paul felt a little bit awkward because he didn't really know how to dance, but in the meantime Friend had led Daisy out onto the main part of the deck and there they began to have fun. Clearly they were not doing any particular dance, just joyfully jumping up and down and twirling to the music. The boy looked at Daisy. At first she seemed almost abashed by Friend's invitation, as if she hadn't entirely wanted to accept it but after some time her smile shone again. Suddenly, Knight saw Toad, who had been sitting next to Daisy, with a quiet croak jump below deck.

There was no cause for delay. Little Lula grabbed Paul by the hand and they went out to dance together. Soon part of the crew, those not on watch duty, had also joined them. And everyone leapt about to the lively tunes played by Grouch.

They partied late into the night. Friend was clearly keen to take part in their fun and at the same time it seemed that his own joy burst out from deep inside and he didn't need the dancing at all to be full of delight. Paul despite being physically exhausted, had probably never felt before such an internal relief of tension while everyone else clearly felt the same. Only Tiger seemed to become quickly bored and left for his cat nap.

**Chapter nine**

# IN THE RAINBOW
# WORLD

In the morning they were all woken up by Traveller himself asking them to ready themselves since one of the crew was soon going to take them by boat to the island, where they would search for the key. Coming out on deck Paul noticed that during the night they really had approached close to Shemesh. It was a mountainous island with thick vegetation. Even from far away one could hear a powerful roar. Traveller explained that there were over one hundred waterfalls and the thundering of falling water was indeed immense. When the entire expeditionary party was assembled on deck, First Officer Fratel lowered a boat into the water in which they towed Traveller, Grouch, Lady, Paul, Little Lula and all the animals together with seaman Darek to land. Friend also accompanied them.

They landed on a golden beach. It seemed to Paul that he had an Eden before him, but when he placed his bare foot on land, it turned out that the scorching sand burnt the skin on his sole and walking up the shore in shoes was also absolutely impossible as the feet were sucked into the loose ground as if wading through blancmange. Everyone cried out in pain. Only Friend maintained his calm unperturbed. After some time they managed to make their way to the edge of the forest and they slowly waded their way into the woods. It was a strange place. The thick vegetation similar to that of the Mediterranean, which made the Knight really doubt for a moment that they were even on the Baltic, made it truly beautiful. There was nothing there that could in any way threaten them – in no way did it resemble the overgrown garden at the back of Lady's house. Paul was under the impression that the place was dead. He didn't see any animals, not even the smallest of insects. The land slowly rose. All around grew tall trees, which reminded Paul of Polish pines although they branched out decidedly more. Their canopy was so dense that it completely blocked out the sky. The low and equally dense forest undergrowth made their journey laborious. They pushed on in the strange green half-light. It seemed to the boy that no light could break through the top between the trees. He thought that maybe it was the vegetation itself which emitted this weird aura that gave the light its colour. Certainly they did not feel here totally at ease. There was something disturbing in the prevailing silence.

Suddenly the boy heard a quiet weep behind him. He looked back and saw that Daisy was clearly lagging behind. She was the one crying as she looked around the forest. Paul thought that in her deep misfortune he could hear an unassuaged grief as if in mourning. He sensed that Lady wanted to be alone which was why she had cut herself off from them. Everyone, including Grouch was walking somewhat scattered anyway in silence as if everyone was looking for some sign of animals or insects along the way... Only Friend walked on without looking around himself anywhere whereas Rabbit and Tiger pattered on immediately behind him, clearly disconcerted. Suddenly the boy heard the drumming of hooves and in the blink of an eye a roe deer jumped out from behind the bushes after which it stood before them. They all froze. This was the only living creature they had come across since they had landed on the island. It lasted only a moment but it seemed to Paul that they stood for a long time looking into the eyes of this wild animal that was clearly not afraid of them. Suddenly the deer looked at Friend and gave a snort before suddenly bounding off and disappearing into the undergrowth.

During the march, the thunder of the waterfalls grew ever louder. The ever brighter light, which was penetrating the forest canopy, showed that they were approaching the edge of the forest. And so they all moved closer to one another as if in fear of what awaited them. However, when they finally crossed the tree line, their eyes were greeted by a stunning sight. Water thundered over dozens of falls and fell between the lush vegetation covering the rocks into a huge lake... Water droplets were thrown into the air and in the bright sunlight seven rainbows reigned over a stunning landscape. They decorated the entire horizon like the most beautifully inlaid crown.

They stood a long time in silence. Friend was the first to speak.

'I see that you're all delighted. Believe me this is only the beginning. We must go deeper in; only then will you see truly heavenly views. Let's go.'

No one replied. They probably lacked the words to express what they felt. As they approached the lake, Paul saw that the water was crystal clear but not dark like the sea but sandy-blue. It was so bright that it dazzled the eyes. After a while the boy noticed a large number of fish swimming in it, but he wasn't able to say what kind they were. He had the impression that they were making their way through that magical land with unusual caution, since it seemed to them that the slightest movement could destroy its spotless beauty. The ground around the lake was fertile and abundant in wild flowers, while the green of the plants had an emerald hue. They walked along the edge of the lake towards the waterfalls. It was only as they came closer that Paul noticed that among the rocks ran a path leading up the slope. They slowly climbed up among the cascades. On every level they found numerous lakes and the boy saw how this mass of water reflected countless rainbows threw up by water droplets splashing everywhere. Their colours were so intense that he could not focus his eyes on them.

The path led along a rocky ledge behind the widest of the falls to the other side of the lake. When Paul looked through the curtain of water at the lake's surface, he began to feel dizzy. Everything turned into an amazing blur and flickered in the continually falling water. Suddenly he felt something rub up against his leg. When he looked down, he saw Tiger.

This time the ever-jovial cat looked at him sadly and with a quiet meow said, 'We can't stop here. Come on. The others are already way ahead of us.'

Indeed, it was only now that Paul realised that he must have been staring at the landscape for quite some time. But why did they have to go? Was there anywhere on Earth more beautiful than this?

'Tiger, I want to stay here. Why should I go on any further? Will I ever find a more beautiful place in the world than this?' asked the boy.

'But Knight, can't you see? There's no life here. How could you stay?' Tiger asked him sadly.

'What do you mean, there's no life here? And what about the deer we saw? And the fish in the lake?' Paul most of all was trying to convince himself with these questions as deep down he knew that Tiger was right.

If it weren't for the thunder of the water, the place would have been terrifyingly silent. But where, if there was no life here, had the deer and the fish come from? The boy felt as if he was about to break down in tears out of despair. He so wanted to stay; he so longed for this wonderful island to be filled with life. He looked down at his fingers. They twitched. They twitched as if bursting with a life-giving force. But how was it possible when everything here seemed dead? He felt how the warmth circulated through his body – this was that delightful life force that poured through his veins like honey. And he had to leave this place. Suddenly tears flowed by themselves down his cheeks. No, he wasn't going to move. He was staying. Somewhere at the back of his mind questions were forming about how he was going to live and what he was going to eat but he stubbornly pushed them out of his consciousness. He closed his eyes and felt as if his chest was being constricted by a terrible longing and a moan was forming in his throat that transformed itself into a cry. As well as his own voice he could hear Tiger calling his name and suddenly he felt the rough touch of a cat's tongue on his face and he realised that he must have fallen down. He was well aware that had it not been for the care of the cat he would have gone mad but still it had been too little to save him from this madness that was taking him over. Lying on the ground he could feel convulsions running through his entire body. He desperately wanted Friend to appear before him and free him. He screamed and screamed and screamed and screamed until suddenly somebody's cold hand moved the hair from his forehead and the last scream came from his chest. There was silence. The boy could hear only the thunder of the water and the beating of his own heart. He was completely overcome by a feeling of peace, but he could feel the tears still running down his cheeks. Slowly he opened his eyes and as he expected, he saw Friend squatting beside him and looking at him with a sad expression on his face. He could see that the others were standing around a little farther off, gathered together into a group. Only Rabbit was sitting at his feet. Paul could see in the eyes of the animal this same desperate madness that had possessed him just a moment ago. The colourful eyes of his companion now shone with all the colours of the rainbow. The thought came to the boy that maybe Rabbit had been here before and this was where his eyes had taken on such crazy colours as if they had kept the reflection of this strange world.

'I want to stay here,' he told Friend with a gravelly voice. It seemed that he only needed his agreement and he would find his place here.

The man kept looking at him sadly and then said, 'This is not yet the place for you. Anyway as you can see it still remains empty. Now it's just waiting for the right moment to fill with life.' Friend fell silent as if he was wondering how much he could reveal to the boy. 'You couldn't survive here. There is too little strength in you to bear this shocking beauty.'

Paul silently considered these words. What did he mean by saying that this was not yet the place for him? Did that mean that one day it would be? And just like usual Friend replied to his thoughts.

'Yes one day you will come back here and you will be able to stay. And then everything will start to live.'

'But why? After all I saw creatures here. I don't understand what is happening here. Why is there no life?' Paul doggedly continued.

Friend looked at him in silence. Was he hiding something? The boy wondered for a moment if he had seen the deer or the fish at all, since everything here was dead.

'You're right,' Friend admitted as if he were reluctant to do so, 'there is life here. It could even be that it is full of life here. It's just that there isn't enough life in you to see it.' These words cut into him like a sword. The longing that a moment ago had led him to the edge of madness, again began to press down on his chest. In his ears drummed only his own desire: I want to, I want to, I want to, I want to stay here. I don't want to return to the sad grey world. I want the blood in my veins to thunder like a waterfall. Here is life and I want to live. I don't want only to vegetate from day to day.

Friend took him firmly by the arm and whispered, 'You will come back here. I promise. Do you think that I'm leading you this way, my Knight, only for you to die of despair? This is just the beginning of the journey. You've got to gather up enough strength to go on. The power of this place will intensify in you until one day it will flow full stream in your veins. And you will return here. I promise.' He repeated with more emphasis.

Paul looked at Rabbit. The madness in his colourful eyes only now began to speak to him. Was anyone able to look at this place and remain normal?

Friend gave him his hand and they both stood up. Rabbit followed on after them. Paul noticed that Tiger stood up very slowly as if he were very tired. His eyes, which usually blazed with joy, looked matt and sad. Daisy and Traveller were standing not far off and looking into the curtain of water full of diffracted rainbows. They too were sad, but at the same time calm. In the eyes of Lady, you could still see the inconsolable regret, which had emanated from her eyes in the forest. The captain just appeared to be somewhere else. It was difficult to say if he was feeling anything. Paul wondered if everyone could see the same thing as himself. Only Grouch sat among the broken rocks and quietly snored. Clearly nothing here made any impression on him. The boy couldn't understand how they could all be so indifferent when confronted by this secret place.

Everyone slowly began to move on again waking up Grouch as they left. They came out from underneath the waterfall and between the hills they passed by more lakes and cascades pouring out from everywhere. For a long time they walked in silence, admiring the wonders of nature. Then suddenly a peal of laughter interrupted their reveries. It was Little Lula who had run on quite far ahead. She had stopped for a while and was playing by the banks of the lake with a fish that was jumping out of it. Paul thought that he would like to be as joyful as she was. Suddenly the girl stumbled. The boy was terrified that she would fall into the water. But she just danced on that spot and with as much agility as a roe deer, she jumped back. Then she looked behind herself and started running in their direction.

'Why are you lot being so slow? Come on. It's so wonderful here. Let's dance for joy and run on,' she called out and threw herself into the arms of Friend who caught her and started spinning in a circle.

How come there was so much joy in them? Paul felt a little too exhausted by all of these emotions to join in with the fun. He also thought that the others didn't feel like dancing but he was surprised to see Traveller take Daisy by the hand and start dancing with her, just like their last night onboard the ship. Paul sat down on a rock and looked at them in silence while Grouch and the animals slowly went on. Tiger could barely drag his legs and looked almost ill.

Looking at the dancing couple the boy had the impression that the waterfalls were playing secret music that was enchanted in their thunder. When, after a while they stopped, they smiled happily at one another. Lady's face was particularly full of peace and joy. It was only now that Paul realised that her lively smile up until now had not had much true joy in it.

Traveller stood for a while staring at her, after which with uncharacteristic gentleness he said, 'I've heard a lot about this island but nobody ever mentioned that it was so beautiful. Among the sailors of the Crooked World stories are told of the burning sands, the hideous mountains and lakes where monsters live, but none of this is true apart from maybe the baking sands on the beach. Really I do not know where these stories come from. In the end nobody I know has ever dared to sail here.'

'So why did you decide to sail here?' asked Paul with astonishment. Even though he remembered about the necessity of choosing the hardest way, this seemed to him to be exceptionally foolhardy.

'There would have been no point going any farther if we hadn't been able to cope with the most terrible dangers here,' Traveller mused. 'Only here it isn't dangerous.'

'Isn't it?' Friend suddenly asked. 'Knight, what do you think?'

Paul was surprised by the question. After all Mr Wronski was right that nothing threatening had happened here. But nonetheless the boy hesitated. Just behind the waterfall he had been overcome by a terrible longing, a kind of despair... Maybe that was where the danger lay? What would have happened if Friend hadn't woken him from that state? Would he have stayed on that rocky ledge crying for eternity? He looked at the nearby lake. What might it mean to say that monsters lived in it? Even though he felt safe here, he sensed that the secret of this place was far greater than his understanding and in it there could lurk something dangerous. Suddenly he looked around himself because the thought came to his mind that he hadn't seen Elf for some time. In fear he realised that his brightly shining companion was nowhere around. They couldn't continue their deliberations because at that moment they were interrupted by the terrifying scream of Grouch coming from behind the rocks up to which the path led. As they had just been talking about danger, Paul's throat tensed with fear. And so there was still something waiting for them? Maybe the morbidity of this place really did mean that something dangerous lived here?

When they ran up to the place where the scream had come from they saw the older Mr Wronski lying on the ground and rubbing his hands clearly in pain. Rabbit was trying to calm him, but Mr Wronski was desperately scream-ing. Tiger was nowhere to be seen.

'What's happening Ralph?' asked Traveller sharply.

'Ow.. it hurts, it hurts. My hands are burning up,' exclaimed Grouch.

'But what happened? What did you do?' said the captain continuing with his interrogation.

'And again everyone's turning on me. I didn't do anything. I wanted to go further along the path but suddenly – I don't know why – I hit this rock.' Grouch pointed to a huge boulder blocking the path. 'I tried to climb up to see what was beyond and if we would have to turn back, but when I tried to do it the rock burnt me,' he finished with a cry.

And so there really was a secret to this place. Everyone but Little Lula and Friend took a step back as if they were afraid of the boulder.

The girl ran forward right up to the huge rock and said, 'But there's nothing here.'

And at that very moment she took just one more step and disappeared into the rock that was blocking their way. Paul could feel his whole body stiffen in fear. Lady let out a quiet gasp and Traveller ran forward hitting the rock with his fists, after which he retreated with a cry looking at his scalded hands. Only Friend stood calmly still.

'No, No! This isn't possible. We can't just leave her. I won't let her just vanish on us!' cried the captain clearly in a state of tremendous shock.

'Are you sure? It seems that at first you wanted to set off without her and leave her in the Little Sun and now you despair?' Friend seemed just cruel in his coolness. 'But don't worry. She'll turn up. Nothing on this island can disappear.' And saying this he turned to Paul as if in answer to his earlier musings about whether it hadn't been monsters that had made this island so dead.

'I told you about this before. It's you who cannot see life on this island but that doesn't mean it's not here. Your eyes are too weak to see the whole wonderful secret of this place. You have too little strength to survive it,' he calmly continued. 'But now we have to forget about such considerations and find another path. Everyone forget about Little Lula for the time being. She's safe.'

He turned on his heel and went back down the path. The others slowly picked themselves up and followed on behind. Just for a moment Paul thought that somewhere deep among the rocks he could make out the figure of a cat but he felt so lethargic that he didn't tell the others. When they returned to the lake by which they had so recently been dancing, it turned out that within the undergrowth they had missed a path that led to the side. This time it took them a long time to wade through the thickets, which seemed almost like a jungle. A number of times they happened to fall into rather deep miniature lakes that were more the size of puddles. Next to their road at every step there ran narrow streams, which fell from a height into the lake that they had left behind below. Now no rainbows were thrown in the shade of the bushes and trees, although whenever the sunlight did manage to penetrate through the foliage the water droplets that were everywhere in the air changed into the most wonderful colours. The path became ever steeper and ever more often frightening rocks would appear here and there. Soon the vegetation grew sparser and there were waterfalls that thundered down from lakes in the hollows of the rocks disappearing into the lower waters. It crossed Paul's mind that maybe they'd soon be able to find the entrance to the cave that Traveller had been talking about.

Suddenly some large figure rushed by between the rocks. The boy tensed fearing some monstrous creature, but he obediently followed behind the others. A little later the path once again led them behind a curtain of water. Paul hesitated out of fear, remembering what had happened the last time they had walked behind a waterfall. This time, however, when they passed by the first bend in the rock leading in, the darkness became ever deeper. Then he understood that they had entered a hidden grotto that was the mouth of a cold and dark cave.

**Chapter ten**

# THE DWELLER
# OF THE CAVE

They made their way into the depths of the grotto. The light from the sun held out for quite some time, but it slowly became ever darker and colder. Traveller ordered a rest to which Friend, who had up to now been doggedly leading them on, also agreed. From their bags, they took out clothes and torches that they had taken with them just in case. Unfortunately it turned out that none of the torches worked. But how was this possible when they had all been checked on the ship?

'Don't worry. This cave is inhabited. We should soon find an old oil lamp. And we've also got matches,' said Friend.

'Inhabited? And who would live in such a hostile place as this?' asked Daisy.

Friend was clearly lost in thought, since he said nothing. They decided to eat. It was only now that they began to feel truly hungry – after all they hadn't eaten anything for many hours, the last time having been when they'd been on the ship. They silently ate the sandwiches that the ship's steward[2] had prepared for them. They also had rusks and a variety of spreads. Paul secretly hoped that the journey through the tunnel to Karev would be short since there didn't seem to be enough food for a longer excursion. While they were eating Grouch mumbled a complaint about the culinary experimentation of the chef. Rabbit spent the time napping by the boy's legs.

Shortly they gathered together and dressed in warm jumpers they set off again on their journey. Just as Friend had predicted, they soon saw an oil lamp

---

2    Steward – a cook on a ship, a person who prepares meals for the crew and is certified by the maritime authorities

hanging on the rock wall, which had clearly been prepared for visitors. Paul wondered for a moment who in this place their host could be, who had so kindly facilitated his guests' entrance into the depths of the grotto. When the light shone out it seemed to the boy that he could make out for just a moment some huge figure at the edge of the area illuminated, after which it suddenly dived into the shadows.

'Friend!' exclaimed Paul. 'I think someone or something is watching us.'

'I thought so too' added Grouch, who up until now had been silent.

'Are you afraid?' asked Friend.

The boy considered his answer. He did not feel particularly safe at this moment but at the same time it seemed to him that he had nothing to fear in the company of Friend. So he took a deep breath and followed the others. After him Grouch followed mumbling, 'To hell with it.'

They spent a long time walking along the dark empty tunnel which gradually led them downwards. Paul began to notice that on the walls he could see ever more varied rock formations. In the dull light of the oil lamp the roof of the cave could be seen to be getting ever higher. Now it was at least ten metres above them full of stalactites pointing down. The light falling on them threw fantastical and somewhat frightening shadows on the walls.

Friend was walking at the front and behind him followed Daisy. Already for some time Paul had been under the impression that Lady did not feel the slightest disquiet at the difficult conditions and the disturbing atmosphere. Since the time they had danced, only once had she seemed scared – the time when Little Lula had disappeared. She was dressed in a tight sporty dress that went down to her knees and strapped around her waist was a belt from which hung a long dagger. Paul remembered how when they'd first met, Lady had stated with bravado that no danger worried her. Here in this dark cave her bearing confirmed those words. As if she could feel someone's eyes upon her, Daisy turned her head and looked behind her. On meeting the gaze of the boy, she smiled happily and stopped to wait for him. Soon they were walking together.

'You look exhausted,' she said eventually.

'No...' Paul hesitated, 'I mean I've got enough strength but it's been a difficult day. I just wish we were all together. I'm worried that Little Lula and Tiger aren't here. Nobody seems concerned about their absence. Other than that there's something following us; I'm sure of it. Friend has always been understanding and pleasant but now I don't seem able to talk to him...'

'Oh Knight, this all really must be difficult for you. You see... It seems to me that everyone has their own road on this island. Little Lula simply took another path but since Friend says she's safe he's sure to be right. And as for Tiger... he was so tired, maybe he stayed behind to rest. The same for Toad. I haven't seen her for a long time but I'm sure she'll turn up,' said Daisy.

'How can you be so calm? How do you know that everything's going to be OK?' Lady's explanations probably only annoyed Paul. Grouch, who was walking just behind them, snorted being clearly irritated. Clearly he too was not very optimistic.

'I don't know... You see I've found my inner peace on this island. I was missing it for a long time. But for you it's probably just a beginning. You were really upset at the waterfall?' Daisy looked at him questioningly.

'Yes. It was terrible. I so wanted to stay on this island and I couldn't. I don't know why. So much so that something hurts me in the chest when I think about it.' Paul could feel his chest tighten terribly.

'Hmmm...' said Lady in thought, 'I don't think it was for nothing that Friend called you Knight. You are still going to have to fight to return to Shemesh.'

'And you? Don't you want to return? Since you found peace there on the island, surely you would prefer to stay on it?' objected Paul.

'No, I've brought the peace with me. You've brought longing. That's why I told you that everyone has their own road on this island. Anyway, it seems to me that you've taken something of that place with you,' she said finishing with a smile.

'What?' Now the boy couldn't understand anything. 'What do you mean that I've supposedly taken something with me?'

Lady let out a peal of laughter.

'When you look in the mirror, you will understand,' she exclaimed and she ran forward to where she had been walking before, just behind Friend.

Paul froze. Looking at his hand he almost walked into a huge limestone column but he didn't see anything. He thought that there must have been some change in his face. He turned round to Grouch and asked if maybe he could see something strange in him, but he just grimaced and said, 'Err it's nothing. It's just woman talk. But, but... actually you do look different,' he chuckled.

With these words Paul felt no better at all. He'd had enough of everything; he felt that his chalice had overflowed and he was going to sit down among the spiky stalagmites that rose from the floor and stay there. Something nudged him on from behind. It was Rabbit who was doggedly following him. He clearly sensed that the boy was in a rebellious mood and needed support. The thought occurred to Paul, however, that he'd had enough of such support. Neither Friend nor Lady and certainly not Grouch had helped him.

'You're sad, aren't you?' asked Rabbit. At least he seemed to understand the boy. His colourful eyes shone in the darkness.

'Yes, I am. Are you too?' Paul asked almost hopefully.

'Yes, I wanted to stay there too,' explained his little companion.

'So why didn't you? As for you, nobody would have stopped you.'

'But I couldn't leave you. Besides, I think I was a little afraid. That huge eagle that was flying above us looked as if he could swallow me whole,' explained Rabbit.

Paul froze. Not for a moment on this entire excursion had he seen any eagle. Like lightning, the words of Friend came to his mind about how it was that life was too lacking in them to be able to see it on the island. Maybe Rabbit simply saw more. Suddenly Grouch walked into him.

'Why are you dawdling like this? We've got to get moving on and shouldn't be standing in the middle here like sheep,' he exclaimed. 'I've had enough of this journey. Does anybody know anything about where we're going? My imbecile brother is so pleased with himself at having chosen the hardest route and so he's happy.'

Grouch's remarks could be heard by those walking at the front and made them stop.

Traveller with uncharacteristic gentleness said, 'I think we should have a short break. I see, Ralph, you're already tired. It's a difficult route. Let's rest.'

Grouch only snorted but he stopped and let his bag fall to the ground. Friend turned round and it could clearly be seen that there was no longer within him that harshness which could be seen earlier.

With a warm smile he turned to them and said, 'That's right. We've got to gather up our strength before we enter into the heart of Enemy's cave.'

**Chapter eleven**

# THE BATTLE
# IN THE AIR

This time Paul was certain that it wasn't only him who had stopped in surprise. After all, when Friend had mentioned that the cave was inhabited and that their host left a lamp for guests, he hadn't even mumbled that it was Enemy himself.

Traveller, even though he seemed to know Enemy's tricks well, protested, 'Wait a moment. You never mentioned anything about us making our way straight into Enemy's den. We were meant to go looking for the key and I somewhat suspect that we're not going to find it here. Isn't this a little bit too risky anyway? We're inviting some misfortune on ourselves by doing this.'

'You're right, Traveller. This really is risky. But are you sure that safety should be our main concern? You yourself having travelled for many years have put yourself in danger on numerous occasions. But still you haven't stopped continually setting off on new voyages. Besides I'm coming with you so that we can face down Eyma together.'

'Eyma?' interrupted Lady.

'Yes, at the very bottom of this cave, Eyma has his lair. As Paul has already found out, Enemy takes on many different forms, but Eyma is one of his most ancient. Once he lived in the sea surrounding the island but later some mysterious event took place which meant that he had to hide here in the depths. The cave that he most often visits is the deepest of all underneath the seabed,' Friend explained.

'What was this mysterious event?' asked Paul.

'If it weren't mysterious, then it would be possible to talk about it,' Grouch interjected acerbically.

'Don't worry. It's possible you'll soon find everything out. The secret of the island has been enchanted in a Book hidden somewhere here. Our task is to find it,' explained Friend coolly. His words sounded really mysterious and fascinating; however Paul didn't understand what this had to do with finding the key for Granny. And just as usual Friend answered his thoughts:

'The key can't be found without the Book. When you got worried earlier that we didn't know where to look for it, you were partially right. It's unbelievably difficult to find something that is hidden without any kind of clues. The Book will help us. But you have to remember that opening it might be really dangerous.'

'Why?' asked Grouch with interest.

'Because reading it is absorbing,' replied Friend with a wink.

They sat for a while longer in silence. Lady handed out some nuts she had in her bag, but soon Friend ordered that they set off again. Now they were going to go steeply down. He warned them that soon the tunnel would go below sea level so it might sometimes become stuffy. If someone started feeling unwell, they were to call out to the others for help.

At first the way seemed just as monotonous as it had been before, only it was sometimes more difficult to avoid the stalagmites that were ever more densely sticking out of the ground. Soon, however, the way down became very steep and it really was becoming stuffy. When Paul stopped and closed his eyes, which were already tired, he could see in his head the strangest of images. He saw a green sun with upside-down trees growing out of the sky, their canopies pointing downwards so that their fruit fell like hail onto the ground; he saw fantastical many-eyed creatures… As soon as he tried to examine these oddities more closely, the picture changed. Dreadful bugs crawled out from the earth, the sun became black and in the ears of the boy sounded someone's monstrous laugh, which instantly awoke him from his torpor. Then he soon noticed that Lady was walking next to him and looking at him with concern in her eyes. Grouch on the other hand was cursing more and more with every step. Only Friend and Traveller were marching forward blithely. Rabbit had long ago hidden himself away in Paul's bag, which unfortunately made it even heavier. And so they walked on for a long time without a word.

Suddenly Lady put her foot on a rock that was sticking out and shouted out aloud. The ground beneath her feet began to move and she hurtled down as if on a slide and smashed into Traveller. The light of their lamp went out and both of them rolled downwards. Paul could feel the ground tremble beneath his feet and a moment later he too slid down in an avalanche of gravel and stone. Behind him he only heard the cries and curses of Grouch.

Unexpectedly, while screaming horrifically, he felt himself land on a rock ledge. Above him the gravel rain still fell. After a moment everything went quiet and Paul found himself lying in the darkness trying to catch his breath. At least the disturbing visions had not returned. When the rockfall went quiet, a dead silence fell.

He did not know how long he had been lying there. Maybe he wouldn't have even found the strength to get up at all had it not been for the whimpering that came from his bag. It was a relief to realise that he wasn't completely alone. Even the company of Rabbit was a consolation at that moment. He blindly opened the bag and let out the shaken creature from it.

'Aaah, aah, what a nightmare! You could have been a little more careful, couldn't you?' blurted out Rabbit in pain.

'It wasn't my fault!' protested the boy vehemently. 'It was Lady who caused the rockfall.'

'OK, it's OK now. You can't imagine what a nightmare it is to fall like that in that bag,' said Rabbit soothingly.

'I can't imagine!' The boy was still angry. 'So you think it would be more pleasant to fall without a bag? I've been completely bashed up by the rocks,' he added massaging his injured forearms.

'And where are the others?' asked Rabbit.

'The others? I don't have the foggiest idea,' replied Paul.

'Not the foggiest? Well I don't have any clear ideas either,' snorted Rabbit in the darkness. 'Hey Elf, could you help us out a little. I'm sure it won't be any loss to your honour to shine here awhile for us.'

And at that moment, as if it were nothing, a little light shone out. In a daze, Paul saw Elf, whose existence he had long ago forgotten about, sparkle with a pleasant warm light behind him. The light emanated from his entire figure with his wings shining particularly brightly. A powerful urge came over the boy to ask Elf where he'd come from, after all he hadn't seen him on the island. But once again, just as it had been in the Little Sun he felt that it wasn't right to ask this strange being about its secrets.

'Well now we're stuck,' commented Rabbit.

Indeed, they were sitting on quite a wide rock ledge. But the unusually steep sides made a descent impossible. The space below them was no longer a narrow passageway but a vast cave. In Elf's light they could see no one.

'I don't understand,' blurted out Paul; 'Didn't Friend know that the descent was like this? Why didn't he warn us? Couldn't he have predicted that something like this was going to happen?'

'It wouldn't have done any good,' Elf unexpectedly answered. 'It was Daisy who tripped over. Friend is sure to be at the bottom and we must get to him.'

'That's easily said,' interjected Rabbit. 'Maybe you could enlighten us as to how we are to do it?'

'You've got to call Arie,' answered Elf without the slightest irritation.

Paul began to wonder. Friend had indeed once said that he could always call on Arie. Traveller too had mentioned him. The mystery, however, was how he was supposed to do it. It crossed his mind that in this strange twisted world he could try to do it very simply in this way:

'Hello, Arie!' he shouted. 'We need your help.'

His voice echoed throughout the cave. The answer seemed to be complete silence. But after a while Paul noticed movement up by the high ceiling of the cave.

'Oh no! Not that monster. Help!' squealed Rabbit, after which he began running desperately round in circles.

The boy didn't really know what was going on but after a while he saw that something resembling a giant eagle was approaching them, circling ever lower.

'What have you done? What have you done?' shouted Rabbit terrified. 'You've revealed our hiding place.'

Paul wanted to say that Elf's light had long ago given it away but he decided that this wasn't the right time to quibble with an hysterical Rabbit.

He looked at Elf out of the corner of his eye trying to assess if he had any chance in a fight with an enormous eagle. Unfortunately the bird could swallow him whole. Paul took out the dagger he had strapped to his belt. The eagle was already circling just a few metres above them. After a moment, however, instead of seizing them as prey, it landed majestically on the rock ledge. Just in case the boy held the blade out in front of himself. They stood awhile in silence looking at each other, while Rabbit hid behind the leg of his knight. The eagle took a step forward and it was only then Paul noticed that instead of an eagle's talons, it had two lion's feet. It was such a surprise that he lowered the dagger while carefully examining the animal.

Now he realised what an astounding figure he had before him. He understood that this wasn't any normal animal, but rather an unearthly creature that was both majestic and dangerous and yet it posed no threat to them. The predatory paws of the beast grew out of the gigantic body of an eagle which was at least twice the size of Paul. Suddenly the boy saw that the folded wings of the creature looked more like those of a dove – they were densely feathered and white completely unlike the compact wings of a bird of prey.

Paul had no doubt any more that this creature had answered his call. There was no other way to look at it other than that Arie in all his fantastic glory was standing there before them.

'You know who I am,' said the creature in a low voice that sent a shiver down Paul's spine.

'Yes, I think so,' he answered with hesitation. 'We need help and … I don't know really… Apparently you can help us.'

It seemed to the boy that it wasn't right to ask for help of such a majestic being, however this was the very creature they were meant to turn to when in all kinds of jeopardy. Arie didn't answer. He lowered his eagle head and with piercing eyes that suddenly changed colour from black to green he turned to Rabbit:

'You think I'm going to eat you?' he asked.

'Eeeee' squeaked the creature in answer. 'And won't you?'

'No, although I assure you that if I were to it would be the best thing that would meet you,' answered Arie mysteriously.

'I, however, will say no thank you. I feel perfectly happy at the moment in my rabbit skin. When I feel like I want to be eaten, I will be most happy to inform you,' and having said this Rabbit came out with his ears raised from behind Paul's legs. Clearly he also had the impression that one assurance from Arie was enough to believe him completely.

'I will help you. That's surely why you called me,' he said as if it were nothing.

'Yes… yes,' replied Paul. 'What do we have to do to get away from here?'

'You must sit on my back and we'll fly down together.'

Paul felt a lump in his throat. Even though he felt certain that Arie would in no way harm them, he still cut an imposing figure. The boy, although he didn't know why, had the impression that if he were to touch this creature's feathers, it might hurt. Arie was, however, clearly waiting for them so Paul slowly approached him. The eagle sat back on his lion paws allowing the boy to climb up onto his back. When he fearfully touched the bird a shiver went from his fingertips all the way through his body. It wasn't painful at all, it was just the opposite: pleasant, full of strange delights such as eating the most delicious ice cream. Then with one bound he jumped onto Arie's back and breathed out a deep sigh of relief. He hadn't felt so good for a long time.

Behind him Rabbit slowly climbed up wheezing and muttering under his breath, 'It's OK, it's OK. Not too bad.'

When Arie spread his wings and took off into the air Elf's light suddenly went out. Only then did Paul realise that they were surrounded by a strange ephemeral light. It didn't pour out from within Arie, as it did with Elf, but it would be better to say that they were surrounded by a bright pale glow. Suddenly the boy felt that eagle was descending. They slowly flew down into the cave and further down a passage into the depths all the way to the lowest chamber. The first sign of impending danger was when Rabbit sitting at the back began nervously sniffing. Paul heard the hiss of air moving quickly through the nostrils of the creature. Suddenly he noticed something rush by beside them. When he was staring into the darkness something flapped loudly on the other side. Rabbit squeaked.

Paul felt beside him the warm presence of Elf, who with a gentle voice whispered, 'Hold on tight. Remember this is not your fight. Just look after yourself and Rabbit.'

Not understanding anything he picked up Rabbit and placed him in front of him after which he grabbed on tight to the base of Arie's wings. He already knew that they were surrounded.

Suddenly the whole cavern shone with a blinding light, which seemed to emanate from the entire figure of the eagle. The giant monstrous birds that surrounded them tried with a terrifying squawk to jump out of the brightness that dazzled them. Paul noticed that they had long sharp beaks and their entire silhouette was that of a skeletal bird covered in tight skin. The boy thought that they looked a little like the pterodactyls that he had once seen in a film about dinosaurs. There was no true life in them. Really, thought Paul, that's how one could imagine death. Every now and then their white eyes shone out from a distance and the monstrous shrieks went right through the ears.

And then the dance began. The terrible dance of death between Arie and this flock of ghoulish creatures. The eagle every now and then would swerve out of the way in flight, either of a limestone column or of one of the hideous monsters. He would bank so sharply that his passengers almost fell off. Paul had already lost count of how many birds they had fought against. Arie would occasionally dazzle them with his brightness and when suddenly an exceptionally large swarm appeared, he opened his beak wide and from it instead of an eagle's shriek there came a deafening lion-like roar, which resounded with a dreadful echo throughout the entire cave. The birds scattered around the walls and Paul felt his throat tighten when he saw them walk upside down on the ceiling and stare at them with empty white eyes. The entire gigantic underground cavern was now illuminated with a bright light and everywhere as far as the eye could see there were birds sitting on the walls. Momentarily stunned by the glare and Arie's terrifying roar, they lurked gathering up their strength ready for another attack. When they came Paul felt a shiver beneath his fingers. The eagle's wings tensed and his whole body shook. The boy nevertheless understood that Arie wasn't quivering in fear but in anger. In such a terrible fury powerful enough to destroy everything in its way. Arie prepared for battle and it was a battle the outcome of which was already predetermined. It was only then that Paul understood that they weren't being attacked. The birds were desperately trying to defend themselves against the power of Arie, which was illuminating their cave with a destructive glare that suffocated and killed with its power. That was why their eyes shone with the pale light of burning innards. The last chance for these monsters to survive was to throw themselves at the intruder. For one short moment the eagle slowed his flight. At that moment they were completely surrounded to such an extent that they could see nothing other than the compacted bodies of the birds. And then Arie jumped. With a terrifying roar he threw himself at the monsters and tore them to pieces in his jaws. Paul no longer knew if he saw the beak of a bird or the jaws of a predatory cat. Everything happened so fast that he heard only the death cries of these monstrous creatures, which lifelessly fell into the abyss below them. This was more than could be borne. He shut his eyes with all his strength.

He was sitting in a meadow full of blood-red poppies. Far off on the horizon he saw the outline of mountains and heard from there the powerful roar of waterfalls. He was surprised because when they were walking across the island they never saw such a beautiful clearing. He walked slowly forward. He realised that his feet were bare and the earth over which he walked was softer than the finest powder. He had the impression that he was falling into it as if into an eiderdown. Suddenly he heard a laugh and turning around he saw Friend who was dressed in poppy red and was sitting in the meadow.

'Look out in case you fall. Hold onto the flowers.' For a moment it crossed Paul's mind that this was absurd, but when he grabbed a handful of poppies he felt that they were as hard as rock. He came to and realised that he had caught hold of Arie's wings more firmly. Now he really did open his eyes. Silence reigned in the tunnel and the faint glow of the eagle illuminated empty space all around.

He didn't know how much further they flew, but he felt a surprising calm. He wasn't even that concerned about the fate of his companions. The cave no longer seemed so terrifying. For a moment it seemed to him that he heard someone whisper into his ear, 'this is only the beginning,' but when he looked around he saw that Elf was far behind him and he thought that he must have imagined it. On Arie's back it was quite comfortable so he leaned over so that he would have some support underneath him and again closed his eyes. This time, however, he fell asleep, which was dominated by normal darkness and all that could be heard was the distant roar of the waterfalls.

## Chapter twelve
# TOGETHER

He was awoken by the light landing of the eagle. Rabbit quickly jumped out of his grasp and hopped off towards their companions whom they had lost earlier and who were sitting nearby. They were spread out over the flat bottom of the cave and they were eating by a bonfire chatting away calmly. Paul jumped down from the back of Arie and ran towards them happily. However Rabbit let out a desperate squeal and jumped to the side making Paul turn his attention to the big carnivorous creature that came out from behind Friend. At first glance one could see that a tiger stood before them, a real tiger.

'What mate, don't you recognise your old buddy?' the tiger asked with a rasping growl.

At first Paul didn't know who the animal was addressing until he heard the squeaky answer of Rabbit hiding behind his legs.

'I, I... don't know what you're talking about.'

'Hmm, what a coward you are, just like all rabbits. I thought that if no one else, you'd recognise Tiger. After all for that you don't need too much of the intelligence that you're lacking anyway,' sneered Tiger.

'Tiger is that really you? I thought we'd left you on the island,' interrupted Paul, 'and... you look somewhat different now. Somewhat more... impressive.'

Meanwhile Rabbit jumped out from behind the leg of the boy and ran straight at Tiger falling between his paws while he turned over onto his back. After a while the predator got up and walked over to Paul. He wanted to rub up against him, like before, but it didn't work out quite so well since he pushed the boy over with the huge weight of his body. Little Lula burst out laughing. 'So everyone is together,' thought Paul with relief. Tiger helped him to stand, but was already looking in a different direction. He took a serious look at Arie who was standing at the back. Suddenly he bowed his head low. The boy thought it looked like a cat making a bow. Arie growled quietly and moved forward. Having passed by them all, he stood in front of the darkness that awaited them. He seemed to be protecting them. Meanwhile Friend stood up with the others rising after him and together they walked over to Paul in order to greet him.

They sat for a long time by the fire that Traveller had lit with scraps of wood that they had found in the cave. There was no end to the stories. And so it turned out that it had been Tiger who had been following them in the darkness of the cave. As they had been walking across the island, the cat had felt ever worse. He had been staggering almost blindly forward, and so he had not even noticed that he was alone. Clearly he must have, just like Little Lula, walked through the magic rock before Grouch or Rabbit had reached it. Soon afterwards he had felt that he hadn't had the strength to go on. He had lain down by a bush and it seemed to him that he had fallen into a very deep sleep, but not one that was pleasant in the slightest. He could only breathe with difficulty and everything around him had become foggy. He wasn't able to say how long he had slept. When he had awoken, he noticed that he was much larger than he had previously been. On reaching the nearby lake, he had looked in the water and realised that he had turned into a real tiger. He had returned to the path and begun to follow them. He had been scared to reveal himself as he thought he might frighten them. It was only when there had been the rockfall in the cave that he had fallen with the others to some cavern from where they had made their way to this place. Nothing in particular had happened to them on the way. Only Daisy had been badly bruised, but Traveller had tended to her injuries. It crossed Paul's mind that he hadn't paid so much attention to the injuries of Grouch, who was continually moaning. At that time Toad had turned up again. All the time since leaving the ship she had been hiding deep in Lady's bag.

In short, that was the entire story. But what most interested Paul was what Tiger had seen beyond the rock blocking the path. When he asked the question, Tiger looked at him with a blank expression as if he didn't understand the question.

'I don't know. I don't really remember. I think it must have been beautiful there, colourful... It's difficult to say...'

Paul sighed. The secret of the island remained undiscovered. He looked at Little Lula for a moment, who was now having a lot of fun playing and trying to catch a hopping Rabbit. Suddenly she jumped heavily on Tiger who fell on his stomach and tousled her delicately. It was a beautiful idyllic sight. Suddenly he realised that no one had explained how Little Lula had turned up. He looked questioningly at Friend, who was looking at the fire.

However after a moment he said, 'She flew here on Arie's back before you called him. But don't ask her what she found beyond the stone. She won't remember. There are places that are better left unexamined.'

And again Paul let out a sigh.

Suddenly he jumped. He felt something moving down by his feet. He looked down and saw many white little creatures. At first he wanted to jump away in fear, but then he realised that they were only little rabbits.

'Oh forgive me, I couldn't help myself,' said Rabbit jovially.

'Rabbit,' exclaimed Traveller, 'I forbade you from multiplying like that.'

'Oh yes, yes!' replied Rabbit. 'You forbade me to do so on the ship but now we're in a cave.'

The undeniable logic of such an answer forced the captain to keeping silent about the entire situation. For some time little rabbits bounded between their legs before scattering out in the darkness.

'What's going to happen to them?' asked Paul. 'Are the monsters going to eat them?'

Friend smiled warmly.

'Don't worry Knight. They'll be all right. Rabbits reproduce so quickly that I would rather worry about Enemy,' he finished with a curious smile.

They spent a long time just resting. The boy wondered how it was possible for scraps of wood to burn so slowly. They were tired so they all agreed to go to sleep. It was difficult to say exactly how quickly time passed in this place but since the time they had left the ship at least a whole day had passed. It could be no surprise that everybody felt exhausted. Before Paul fell asleep, he wondered for a moment what had happened to Granny and whether Mum was worried about him and whether he would get back in time to go back to school in September… With the remainder of his strength keeping his eyelids from closing he looked at Friend who sat in front of their little camp next to Arie. Both of them looked silently into the darkness in front of them. Paul was no longer able to stop himself from falling asleep. At the last moment it seemed to him that Arie stood up and walked off into the darkness with his pale glow gradually fading. In a moment the boy was already asleep.

It was difficult to say how long they rested. After Paul woke up he saw Friend standing nearby and carrying a large flaming torch. It was only now in this light that Paul noticed that not far from their camp there was a huge heap of wood. This was most probably where the scraps of wood had come from for the fire.

'Why does Enemy leave a lamp and wood in the cave to allow the way down to be lit? It's illogical. It would be easier for him to hide if people were to wander around in the darkness,' said the boy.

'But he wants people to make their way as deep as possible. How would he be able to eat them if they lost their way?' Friend answered with a question.

'What, eat them?' The squeal of Rabbit perfectly reflected Knight's feelings. 'No one has said anything about being eaten before.'

'Well, dragons have a habit of eating their victims,' replied Friend coolly.

'A dragon? How fantastic. I've always dreamed of seeing a dragon,' exclaimed Lady enthusiastically.

Everyone looked at her out of the corners of their eyes. Grouch simply mumbled, 'women'. But in Friend's eyes a terrible sadness could be seen.

'Is something wrong?' Daisy asked uncertainly. 'Don't you think it will be great to fight against a dragon?'

'Do you really believe that a person would have any hope in a fight with a dragon?' asked Friend challengingly. 'Besides this dragon wasn't created in order to live in misery and eat its victims. It was the most beautiful creature on the entire island. Its scales shone reflecting all the colours of the rainbow and the flapping of its huge wings created a beautiful draught that cooled the inhabitants of this land. And what is it here? A monster. Its scales now only absorb the impenetrable darkness of this place and its wings allow it to fly up only as high as the top of the cave. It has become a prisoner of its own monstrousness.' Friend screamed out these last words in anger. Lady shrank and was afraid to say anything.

The silence was only broken by Toad croaking, 'I, however, have a fondness for reptiles.'

Friend gave her a hard stare. 'You're a miserable thing yourself. Your poisonous skin won't save you when the time comes. Watch out for Arie, because his sharp beak will tear out your guts!'

Paul was terrified. He had not expected that Friend was able to be so angry when he wanted and the threat he had made to Toad sounded particularly unpleasant.

'Why are you threatening Toad? What has she done to you?' Lady asked with tears in her eyes.

'What's she done to me? This creature cannot do anything to me. It's your heart she's been injecting with venom ever since it was torn by the death of Violet,' replied Friend.

Paul was beginning to get lost in what was happening but suddenly he remembered how Lady looked when they were walking through the forest on the island; her eyes had been full of sadness as if in mourning and her words about how she had at last found peace.

'I wanted to console you then but you wouldn't allow it. Will you now allow me to kiss you?' this time Friend's words sounded gentle and soothing as if all the anger in him had evaporated. Lady cried. Toad croaked something so quickly that Paul didn't understand at all what it was about. She was clearly angry with such a turn of events.

Suddenly Grouch, who was standing behind the boy, interrupted, 'Well I can see some tearful melodrama's been taking place here. What about we get moving? Since we're to be eaten by some dragon, let's not keep him waiting for his supper.'

Apart from Traveller, who hissed with rage at his brother on hearing these words, no one reacted. During this time Friend had walked slowly up to Lady, clearly wishing to embrace her. Daisy took a step back. 'How could I allow you to comfort me? It was you who took Violet when she died,' she wept. 'And then you didn't return. I thought that at least you would explain to me what had happened.'

Her crying echoed throughout the cave. Toad jumped angrily at Friend, but before she could even reach him, Arie emerged as quick as lightning from the darkness and caught her in his beak devouring her hideous body. Lady gave a short cry. When she stood like that looking at the place where Toad had been taken, Friend went up to her, embraced her, and kissed her on the forehead.

'It's OK. Now you're safe,' he said to her quietly.

Paul stood dumbstruck. His feeling of disgust at seeing Toad being torn apart mixed with relief that she was no longer around and that Lady would be happier. Suddenly he heard a quiet laugh behind him.

'Much too good for the likes of you, little brother.'

Traveller looked angrily at his brother. And then Paul noticed that the captain indeed did not look happy at the turn of events. But he said nothing. He just bent over and packed everything straight into his bag.

The boy thought that nothing further could surprise him that day, even the appearance of Dragon, but a moment later he realised that he was wrong. Little Lula, who up to this point had been looking at everybody surprisingly calmly, laughed and ran up to Lady and Friend. 'Don't worry, Daisy. Violet is safe.'

And at this moment, from her pocket she pulled out a little violet that looked as if it had only just been picked. Lady smiled radiantly without any surprise. She leaned over and kissed Little Lula. She took the flower from her and put it in her hair. The intensely violet petals stood out in the black background of her locks. Paul remembered that when he had first met her she hadn't seemed at all beautiful to him, but her smile had seemed irresistible and that is why he had named her then Beautiful Lady. Now he had to admit that she fully deserved her title.

He heard a silent sigh and looked at Traveller, who suddenly turned his head around and in a sharp voice demanded, 'Can we finally get ready? Since we have to fight Dragon it would be better to do it while we are rested.' 'Why didn't you tell us that Eyma is a dragon?' asked Paul when they had set off.

'Because Eyma isn't a dragon. Eyma lives in this cave and guards it. And Dragon... well he's the master of all the creatures that are Enemy,' Friend explained mysteriously.

**Chapter thirteen**

# THE BOOK CHAMBER

They quickly packed the remainder of the things; they lit one more torch, put out the fire and moved off. Paul noticed that Elf had begun to delicately glow and most strangely other flying creatures had appeared next to him. The boy couldn't say for sure that they were elves since despite many similarities, they were nonetheless very different. His elf was golden, like a large bee with crystal wings, while a green figure floated closest to him with wings that looked as if they were carved out of ruby; a little bit behind that one on the other hand flew a beautiful blue being with sapphire wings. There were at least a dozen of these many-coloured creatures. Furthermore many of them had beautiful golden hair. And from the round heads of others seemed to grow red manes.

The presence of such creatures poured reassurance into Paul's heart. He already knew, it was true, that he could depend on Friend and Arie but he felt that the care of the elves was a particular gift for him and his other companions.

They walked a long time in the middle of the empty cave with Arie flying lazily above them. The journey took so long that they had to make a number of stops for meals. Then in the light of the torches they were surprised to make out that the way was blocked. Before them there was only a smooth wall. When Traveller and Grouch began to feel it looking for a bend, which would have shown of a passageway leading onwards, Friend stood unmoved.

'Do you know which way to go?' Paul asked him.

He answered him with a silent look of his blue eyes. The boy could feel that Friend was waiting for something. Or maybe he was just giving them a chance to prove themselves.

'I think you're the one who knows how to open locks without using a key,' he said after a while.

Surprised Paul realised that he was right. In his pocket he even had the lock pick with which he had opened the door to the cellar of the Little Sun. A non-existent door he suddenly thought. Something was telling him that he would be able to use this pseudo key. But here there wasn't any door or lock…

When he was thinking about this he noticed a small recess in the rock. It was strange that no one had noticed it before. Involuntarily he moved to the front, taking the lock pick out of his pocket. He was no longer surprised when this provisional key fitted perfectly into the opening. Paul turned it to the side and it cranked. The others stepped back and with their weapons pulled out, they stood by Friend. Slowly, even majestically the rock began to open up. At first it seemed that there stretched out beyond it just like behind them an empty passageway but Paul noticed that it widened more to the sides creating a great stone cavern in the middle of which far out in front of them flickered a shining point. The boy looked back to Friend who smiled and said, 'So we're here.'

The others did not look equally happy. Although no huge monster had attacked them yet, there could be no doubt that within the near vicinity lurked something terrifying. It was difficult to see this as cause for joy.

'Let's go,' ordered Friend. 'We have to get to the Book.' It was only now that Paul noticed that in the distance in the feeble light of this shining point lay a huge Book. The space between them and the Book, which was illuminated only by the flames of their torches as well as the colourful light coming from the elves, appeared empty. For a single moment like lightning Arie's powerful light flashed. Paul felt sick. In the dazzling brightness that lasted only a second he saw a terrible monstrosity of creatures hiding in the cave. He saw thousands of inhuman faces, or rather what looked like masks twisted in anger looking at them from the walls. He saw tens of tentacles twisting towards him along the ground. He saw in different places things in the shape of abdomens of huge vile insects. Involuntarily he grabbed the arm of Traveller, but he didn't give him any support. His arm was as soft as clay and he was clearly swaying on his legs. Grouch gave a furious hiss. Little Lula began crying. Only Lady shouted out threateningly and lifted her sword in the air while Tiger gave a hostile growl.

Darkness fell again, illuminated only by the torches. The knowledge, how-ever, of what was waiting for them in hiding meant that for a long time no one moved.

And suddenly Paul noticed that Rabbit, whom he had paid no attention to earlier, was hopping towards the Book as if it were nothing. For a moment he froze in fear, after which he threw himself like a madman into chasing after the animal. Behind him he heard a shout, but he no longer cared about anything. He ran through the darkness being fully aware that he did not have a chance of catching up with Rabbit. The hisses of monstrous creatures came to him from the sides. Suddenly some tentacle blocked his path but in one swipe of the dagger, he cut it from its abdomen. After a moment he was cutting blindly with the blade all around him, feeling that the enraged monsters were reaching for him with their long limbs at every moment. For a second he thought that it was surprisingly easy to wade his way through this forest of stinking tentacles, however he saw a majestic figure, which flying above them tore up everything in its path. It was Arie. He was fighting with Eyma.

In the powerful glow given off by the eagle, Paul noticed that what he took for a thousand monsters was actually one monstrous slimy octopus with thousands of hideous carapaces from which came millions of limbs.

His companions were now beside him. They slowly waded forward fight-ing with Enemy. Only Friend walked forward calmly holding Little Lula by the hand and Eyma didn't even try to attack him. It was an astounding sight. A tall man with a slow gait led a little girl through a field of battle as if he were wandering through a meadow. Paul did not know how long this had all lasted; he was slowly running out of strength. He saw colourful flashes of light where the elves were fighting. Suddenly something grabbed him by the ankle and pulled him across the ground away from the Book. Then he heard a roar. A large striped predator jumped over Paul and threw himself on the tentacle that was dragging the boy. At that moment Knight was glad that Ti-ger had turned into a real tiger. Lady rushed to their aid cutting everything around her with her sword in a fervour befitting the best of warriors. But with every moment the advantage of Enemy grew. Paul noticed out of the corner of his eye that Friend and Little Lula stood by the pedestal on which the Book lay. When the man went forward to climb on the step from which he could reach the bound tome, the terrible monster screamed in rage. Eyma, however, was clearly unable to do anything to stop Friend. At the moment when he placed his hand on the Book, everything happened at once. Arie roared and shone with light, the whole cave shook as if in a terrible rage and Eyma retreated into the impenetrable darkness and disappeared.

Friend turned to the others and waved them over with his hand so that they would come and join him. They gradually collected themselves together wounded and very tired. Paul noticed in dismay that he couldn't see Rabbit anywhere. Arie circled above them keeping guard.

When they all stood before the pedestal, Friend pointed to the Book with his hand and explained, 'This is the Book, which Eyma was guarding the access to. In it we'll find all the clues we need, including how to find the key for Granny as well as above all how to defeat Dragon, with which we still await to do battle. Yes my dears, Eyma, who guards the Book, and Dragon are two separate incarnations of Enemy and we still have to confront this second form, which is the most fitting for him. You've also got to remember that reading the Book is very dangerous.

'Why's it dangerous?' asked Lady.

Paul very much wanted to know the answer to this question, but he was more worried by the disappearance of Rabbit. He didn't know if Friend had answered it at all. He was only awoken from his torpor by the man's comment.

'Knight, it seems that you are worried about your little companion.'

'Yes, Friend. I haven't seen him anywhere since I started chasing after him and the monster got to me,' replied Paul.

'My dear, I'm afraid that Rabbit has gone.'

Paul tottered. Although he had expected that something terrible might have happened to Rabbit, this direct answer from Friend was devastating.

'No… how's it possible? Why?' Some part of Paul still didn't want to accept the truth.

'I'm very sorry… But if you want to save Rabbit… well, know this, it's not too late yet,' replied Friend mysteriously.

His words slowly sank into Paul. How could it be that it wasn't too late? If the monster had eaten him, there was nothing left of him. But since Friend was saying this…

'What does that mean, Friend?' interrupted Lady.

'Rabbit can certainly still be saved. But for this we need the Book. If we find him in it then we save him.'

'What do you mean? How can we find Rabbit in the Book?' asked Traveller.

'A bunch of nutters,' Grouch snidely remarked, after which he turned on his heel and walked away from them. He sat down at a distance from them, took his provisions out of his bag and began to eat.

Paul felt at that moment that he too was really hungry but he also felt too impatient about wanting to know what had happened to Rabbit to lose time on eating. Little Lula ran after Grouch clearly trying to encourage him to come back.

'Knight, it's your Rabbit. Do you want to find him in the Book?' asked Friend.

'Yes, whatever that might mean,' replied Paul not feeling very sure.

Friend turned around and placed his hand on the lock that bound the Book. He stood there a moment until at last a click could be heard. When Friend removed his hand, the Book opened by itself somewhere in the middle. Paul moved forward. Even though only a couple of steps separated him from the Book, it seemed to him that it took an eternity before he found himself next to it. When he at last looked at the ancient pages, it seemed to him at the first moment that he couldn't read anything. But soon he noticed that the strange signs began to sort themselves out into words that were understandable to him.

He began to read:

*The journey was very tedious. The dry sand of the desert stripped the skin off his naked feet and a powerful wind dried his burnt cracked lips yet more. Only the ever lighter baggage was a kind of relief which was overshadowed by the knowledge that he was losing the weight of water, which was so valuable to him,*

When he read it went through his mind that also his lips were completely dry and that he was thinking with ever greater longing for even a drop of water. Worse still, the light that illuminated the Book was so dazzling that the boy had to squint to be able to read further:

*The sun must have been at its zenith. The whole horizon quivered because of hot rising air. It was difficult for him to look at the road that stretched out without continually screwing up his eyes. The heat and stuffiness made every step an almost superhuman effort.*

Paul wondered how long he could hold out in this blinding light. He half-closed his eyes for a moment…

When he opened them he saw the unchanging horizon filled with golden sand. He thought that maybe it would nonetheless be worth stopping and at least wetting his lips. Then he heard a low purring behind him. He turned around.

'How could you think that you could leave me behind!' barked Tiger in an offended manner. 'After all, Rabbit was my companion too.'

'Oh Tiger, I'm sorry. I didn't want to leave you. I'm glad that you managed to catch up with me,' replied tired Paul.

'I can assure you it wasn't easy in the slightest in this infernal heat. Do you still have a little water?' asked the predator.

They drank a little after which they set off in silence. It was swelteringly hot. Even the loose fitting white clothes that Paul wore didn't give him any protection. They walked on slowly falling into the soft sand. Suddenly Knight felt a cold drop of rain on his nose. He looked up but there was not a cloud in the sky. Surprised he thought that maybe he was hallucinating although he had never heard of visions being one of the first signs of heatstroke. He was more expecting to see mirages. However a second droplet of rain, which hit him on the cheek, made him stop and look up again.

Tiger mumbled, 'You felt it too?'

'What, the rain? Yes. A second drop has fallen on me but there are no clouds here,' replied Knight.

Suddenly he saw that directly above them in the sky was a white point. It was true that it was difficult to call it a cloud but theoretically… And when he was thinking this he noted that the point was growing in front of his eyes. It looked like above them was developing a small white cloud. It was drizzling ever harder. They looked at each other surprised and moved on. The cloud followed them. They walked in the rain for a while and were astonished to see that beyond the boundary of the cloud following them the desert remained dry. Paul wondered what strange joke of nature would decide for no known reasons to give them rain. He came to the conclusion, however, that he shouldn't be complaining. If it were a joke it certainly wasn't malicious as the coolness that this little downpour brought was exactly what he had dreamt about. When they were soaked to the skin, the rain began to weaken until it stopped completely. Again they felt the heat of the sun but now it wasn't so distressing.

## Chapter fourteen
# THE SECRET MEETING

They walked on in silence not feeling any particular need to talk to one another. After some time they could make out a dark point growing bigger on the horizon. Soon it turned out that they were approaching a large tree. Although Paul had earlier decided not to be surprised by anything, nonetheless he found this astonishing. Such a large lone tree growing in the middle of the desert? He soon recognised it as a gigantic and majestic oak and with its branching canopy it resembled the largest of such trees in Europe. Its roots spread out through the desert going many metres out and it seemed to Knight that they twisted and turned between the numerous offshoots that here and there stuck out of the sand. When they approached close enough they could see three men sitting by a table under the spreading branches, enjoying some drink. They looked at the travellers with amiable curiosity, showing no fear at the presence of Tiger. They must be used to the various peculiarities of the Crooked World, thought Paul.

'Come join us,' one of them called out.

'Thank you. It'll be a pleasure,' replied the boy courteously. 'I'm the Knight of the Rabbit and this is Tiger.' For a moment the boy wondered which thing was stranger: his name or calling a tiger simply Tiger. The men smiled amicably and pointed to an empty chair at the table. But they didn't introduce themselves.

'You both must be tired,' said the next men. 'I see that you needed the downpour.'

'Yes. Thank you for the invitation,' said Paul, not quite knowing why. 'We're looking for Rabbit,' he added after a while.

'Ahh, yes,' replied the man who had first spoken to them. 'He went by this way some time ago, but he was in a big hurry. He said that he was heading to the tower.'

'Are we definitely talking about the same Rabbit?' interjected Tiger. 'Our rabbit is small with one red ear and colourful eyes.'

'Yes, of course. We're talking about Mad Rabbit,' answered the stranger.

Paul had to secretly admit that such a name suited his companion and he also had the impression that the men knew Rabbit better than he did himself.

'Which way did he go?' he asked. The man looked at him and gave a somewhat avuncular smile.

'It doesn't matter,' he said.

Paul frowned. He didn't like this answer. 'But it does matter. We really do need to catch up with him. Would you gentlemen please be so gracious as to tell us which way we should go to look for him?' he asked in a superior tone.

His interlocutor laughed wholeheartedly and explained, 'I see that my words have annoyed you. I didn't want to say that I didn't care which way you went or that I didn't care about your search. I only meant that it's unimportant which way you go because in the end you will catch up with him anyway. Though the truth is not all the roads will be equally easy and pleasant for you.'

Paul was fed up with puzzles. He just wanted to know where Rabbit had gone.

Tiger once again joined in the conversation: 'You're telling us that all roads lead to our companion, that all roads lead to the same place?'

The second man tilted his head a little and replied, 'You can put it that way. But it would probably be simpler to say that although many different things might happen, depending on what you decide to do, if it is written that your fate is to find Rabbit, then you should succeed. After all, you are in the Book.'

Paul had a foggy memory that indeed they had found themselves here when they had started to read the Book. He suddenly looked at the second man with a clear head and thought that there was something about him that reminded him of Friend. He was tall with dark hair and blue eyes, but his looks were more oriental. He looked at the others. The man they had mainly been talking with was also similar to Friend, but a bit older and his eyes were a shade of light grey. The third man, who so far hadn't spoken even a word, had a thick mass of ginger hair, green eyes and a long hooked nose.

'OK, but your mate told us not every road's equally easy and pleasant,' said Tiger. 'In that case could you show us which one's the easiest?'

'That's a good question,' answered the oldest man completely unfazed by Tiger's lack of formality. 'I think the easiest thing would be for you to go around the tree because it won't be so hot in the shade.'

This time both Paul and Tiger narrowed their eyes. Even though they could accept that every road would simply sooner or later lead them to their goal, walking around the tree sounded senseless.

'You might think it's a rather strange way to go travelling, but surely it won't hurt to give it a try?' said the second stranger. 'Anyway, do what you will. If you change your minds you can always come back to us.'

On saying that he pulled out a chessboard from under the table, on which they must have already been playing earlier, since the pieces were set out in various positions on the board. He placed it on the table top and he and his older companion leaned over it to continue the game.

'And so – what's your decision?' asked the grey-eyed man unexpectedly. 'Are you going to go around the tree?'

'Let's say… the answer's yes…'

Then their silent companion took the knight in hand, circled the white king a number of times with it and made a classic knight move by placing it on a a square next to the rook[3]. The other two turned their attention to the game.

Knight feeling completely stupefied by the conversation moved away obliviously when Tiger nudged him on the hip with his wet nose in the right direction. They began walking around the tree.

The oak was a real giant and its huge roots stuck out of the earth forcing the travellers to go out of their way to avoid them. After a while the three men disappeared from sight obscured from view by the great tree trunk. Knight tripped over a number of times but Tiger deftly jumped over all obstacles. After some time Paul noticed that there was no point on the horizon with which he could assess from where they had started. They had been circling the tree already for some time when he began to get an uneasy feeling that they weren't going back to the table where the three men were sitting. It occurred to him that the advice of the strangers wasn't quite so absurd and by going

---

3   In Polish the rook chess piece is called a tower

around the tree they could get to a completely different place than the one from where they had set off.

After a while they saw that they were approaching a large dark opening in the trunk of the tree. It was clearly the entrance to a huge hollow. They stopped to have a look inside. At first they saw nothing but soon after crossing the unconventional threshold, their eyes were greeted by a strange sight.

They were standing on the porch to a house in some – at least to Paul's mind – oriental city. From here they could see the busy streets of the city full of market stalls among buildings of sandstone and marble. Everywhere shone the intense colour of clothes and tunics and the air almost vibrated from the calls of traders. Knight thought that he would very much like to go down and walk through those narrow streets to ask the people how such a large city could fit in a tree. But he knew such a question would be a bit absurd, since standing in the middle it could not be seen at all that they were inside a giant oak.

Suddenly a dark-skinned man shouting at a young beautiful woman in a nearby alley caught his attention.

'Give me a break! Are you going to carry on telling me such rubbish? I know what it's like. I've lived my whole life in this lousy city and I've never met anyone who believed that anything else existed in the world. I know how it is. There is no sense wasting time looking for some fairy tale land. You'd better forget about Dominique's babbling and at last get down to some work. This dirty linen needs washing, otherwise we're going to drown in filth!'

Paul stepped back. He was sure he didn't want to stay here a minute longer. Maybe he was afraid that if he stayed too long in this place, he would be prepared to believe the words of the man and wouldn't have enough strength to find the exit. Tiger, however, gave him a stern look.

'And you? You're already going to go?' he asked.

'I don't want to stay here,' replied Knight. 'I prefer the Crooked World.'

'Obviously, but how can you simply run away leaving that poor girl here?' said a clearly outraged Tiger. 'You didn't think that you should help her get away from here?'

Paul wasn't sure if he wanted to risk his own skin for some woman who certainly didn't know anything about their world anyway. Besides in this place there could be many more people who dreamed of another reality. Surely they weren't going to save everybody? None of his objections made the least bit of difference to Tiger. With one bound he jumped over the balustrade and ran quickly after the girl, who had almost managed to disappear from them in the crowd of street hawkers. Paul had no other choice than to follow after him.

As he passed by grimy stalls, among the curses he heard people haggling for various items. Here and there stood groups of bitter old women evidently gossiping about the others on the street. Luckily no one paid any attention to the boy and the tiger. The narrow streets, along which stone houses stuck out, led downwards. It gave the impression that the city was built on a hill. Behind the buildings below them sparkled sky blue water. So they were on the coast.

When they walked through the city square surrounded by huge marble buildings supported by majestic columns, some tall, well-built man stood on a dais and shouted, 'Don't believe in nonsense. Rather than listen to rubbish about other lands, it is better to concentrate on the development of our own settlement. There is no other world beyond our City. Anyone who claims otherwise really hates our City and wishes to destroy it. But we have the right to have our City!' While the man was making his speech, Paul realised that this was City with a capital 'C'. 'We are free. We can do with our land what we want. No one is going to tell us that we have to adjust to the ways of people from other lands. Every citizen of our wonderful City is free and will never bow down before oppressors who try to convince us of something else! We must not lay down our freedom!'

Knight felt truly disgusted. He did not know if he should laugh or cry on hearing such words. It came to his mind that he should shout out at the speaker about what a miserable freedom it was when you were not allowed to believe anything other than what others permitted. But he wanted to catch up with the girl and get away from there as fast as possible. The fiery speaker shouted on but Paul had turned round and was running after Tiger when all of a sudden he froze in fear...

Standing in the middle of the square he saw an enormous black dragon sitting on a circular building with a roof that was supported by an impressive colonnade. Knight stood like a statue. For a moment he stared at the monster. Its entire body shone. One had the strange impression that the skin and scales that covered it had such depths that they were like mirrors. But the only thing that was reflected in them was darkness, infinite darkness. When in fascination and at the same time in revulsion he examined Dragon more carefully, he noticed that in the blackness of the scales could be seen a shape, like the reflection of City, but it was so caricatured, twisted and deformed that it made him feel unwell. He looked at the creature's maw and realised in fear that the beast was looking straight at him with its yellow eyes. Their eyes met. The monster's head was so hideous that Paul felt another wave of nausea. He ran off chasing after Tiger aware that they had to escape this awful City as quickly as possible. Only now did he see how filthy the streets were, how wretchedly clothed people lying here and there contrasted with the opulence of some of the buildings. While he was running it occurred to him that these poor inhabitants had no idea what was happening, since they did not see this terrible beast nor were they aware of the chase which was taking place on the streets of their very own town.

Suddenly he noticed that he had already run up to the outskirts of City. His heart was pounding ever harder, when all of a sudden a shadow blocked out the sun yet he preferred not to look up for fear of what he might see. At last he saw Tiger, who at full pelt was closing in on the woman carrying the basket of underwear in her arms. The predator leapt. With one bound he caught the girl in flight and they both fell into the entrance of some derelict home. Knight ran after them almost tripping over the washing that was lying about. When he jumped through the door of the building, he heard behind him a terrible roar and felt the soles of his shoes beginning to burn. He hadn't even noticed that Dragon was pursuing him with his monstrous fiery breath. The doors closed behind them and it was only then that Paul noticed that they were standing in the desert and behind them grew the enormous oak in which there was the huge dark opening that led to the hidden city.

## Chapter fifteen
# VOICE

'My goodness, what a monster...' wheezed Tiger with the remainder of his strength. 'We were all lucky to escape from there.'

Paul wanted to ask how the predator had known that it was exactly that door that would lead them out of City for good, but at that moment he looked at the woman they had snatched. The stranger put aside the laundry basket and began to calmly look around the place where they had wound up. She had short black curly hair and a pleasant face. When she looked at the boy, she parted her lips in a broad smile that took up the entire lower half of her face. Knight had the inescapable feeling that he knew this woman from somewhere and then suddenly he spotted a beautiful little violet in her hair.

'Lady,' he blurted out involuntarily.

'Thank you so much, my dears, for taking me away from there. My name is Margarita[4].'

'How do you do? I am Knight of the Rabbit and this is Tiger,' he replied almost mechanically.

'Oh, so you're Knight of the Rabbit!' exclaimed Lady. 'Well, I really didn't expect to meet you quite so quickly.'

There was clearly no end to the surprises.

'Errr... Of course. You mean... you know Rabbit?' he asked uncertainly.

'Yes, I met him just this morning. He looked so incredible... Anyway I had the strange impression that I had seen him somewhere before. So I asked him straight away where he had come from and he began to tell me about his amazing adventures in other lands. I so very much wanted then to

4   Margarita – (Spanish) Daisy

get away from that accursed City!' said Lady. 'I'd always felt that there was something more. I couldn't believe that Violet had simply gone. She's got to be somewhere.'

Her smile faded and in her eyes could be seen an indescribable sadness. Paul felt he could no longer hold back the question that had been bugging him for some time.

'Who is Violet? What happened to her?' he asked. Margarita gave him a melancholic look. She seemed lost in her thoughts.

'Violet was my dearest child. In fact she wasn't mine because I didn't give birth to her. But I was the one who loved her like a mother. She was everything to me; she was my entire life. What else could bring me joy in this abhorrent place? But one day Violet disappeared, simply disappeared. I spent a long time looking for her in City but I didn't find her. One day I met someone who claimed he had seen Violet. But he didn't want to tell me where. He said that Violet had left me because she wasn't mine. And that it would be better if I let her.' Margarita spoke these last words with clear anger in her voice. 'How could he? And still he had the gall to call himself Friend!'

The individual pieces started to fit together to form a whole in the mind of Knight, like in some strange puzzle. He still didn't understand, though, what was the sense to it all. It crossed his mind that he didn't even know who he himself was nor where he had come from.

'You're only just beginning to find that out,' a voice replied to him. 'You have to read on.'

'Read on?' Knight did not know if he had said those words aloud or if they were just thoughts.

'Yes. Only in the Book can you find the answer to every question. If you get to the end you'll learn your name,' said Voice.

'But I know my name,' Knight defended himself.

'You know it because I gave it to you. But do you really know what it means?' his interlocutor questioned further.

'Who are you?' asked a stunned Knight.

'I am the Author of this Book. For you I am simply Voice. It is I who is writing this story,' explained Voice.

Knight considered these words for a moment. Did that mean he was only a puppet? A character from the Book with no free will?

'Of course not!' denied Voice. 'Besides I told you that you were free to choose any road and you will still arrive where you want to. In other words I chose you as the hero of my tale but while I'm still writing you may still affect its form. But I have already chosen the ending.'

Knight was overcome by the vague feeling that he had recently heard something similar. For a moment it even seemed that he had heard the sound of that voice before. But he was feeling very tired. It occurred to him that he hadn't eaten for a long time and he was surprised to realise that he wasn't hungry at all.

'No, you don't need to eat here. But if you want, rest and have a meal. Here, this is for you.'

At that moment, as if it were nothing, a table appeared before them laid with a lot of food. There were all sorts of different types of fruit upon it as well as a lot of white cheese and honey. Knight was happy that they would be able to have such a light meal. When he sat down he realised that Lady and Tiger were looking dumbstruck at what was happening.

'But, but...' stammered Tiger. 'Where did this all come from?'

So the entire conversation had taken place in Knight's head and it was going to be difficult to explain everything, so he brushed his companion's question aside.

'Oh, don't think about that, just eat. Enough has happened to us already today; are you really so surprised by the ordinary appearance of a table?'

Clearly Tiger wasn't able to think up any counter arguments. He only moaned, expressing his dissatisfaction with the menu and at that moment a huge meat roast appeared on the table.

'That's a bit better,' he added this time without the least astonishment.

'Your country is really surprising,' said Lady, who was also sitting down to eat. 'Overall, I'm not surprised that the inhabitants of City prefer to know nothing about it.'

Knight wondered awhile how he might explain to her that this wasn't in any way their country and that at present they were in a Book. He decided that it was pointless to become embroiled in the twists and turns of a story that clearly was not his.

The sun slowly went down. Margarita didn't know where Rabbit had gone after he had met her, but there wasn't any point anyway in looking for him after dark. They decided to lay out their tunics and to sleep on the soft sand between the roots of the tree. They were however afraid to sleep near the opening so they walked a little further around the oak and only then did they lie down to rest.

After some time Knight awoke thinking that he felt well rested. But when he opened his eyes, he discovered that it was still night. He lay for some time in the darkness trying to sleep but he couldn't. He thought about everything that had happened to him so far. Today he could remember a lot more clearly the events before he had entered the Book. What was bothering him was the question about what it all meant. How could it be possible that all the clues that were needed in their own lives would be right here, if this was only a story being spun by some Author. He came to the conclusion that he would probably have to believe Voice just as he had without any explanation believed Friend and allow himself to be led through this adventure of a lifetime, no matter how strange such words would sound in the mouth of the hero of some story… He was bothered by these doubts…

He got up and moved away from the tree, far enough for its spreading branches not to block out his view of the sky. He looked up at the dark blue firmament. It was speckled with many of the same stars as in his world. Paul didn't know much about astronomy but he was able to recognise various constellations and knew that those he saw here were exactly the same as those seen in the sky outside the Book. Was it that this heavenly vault was really a dark flat canvas full of yellow points painted by the hand of the Book's Author? Or was it like the real world where behind the view of the heavens hid an endless universe sown with huge fiery heavenly bodies? The thought came to him somewhere deep down that it was here where real life was: fascinating life full of adventures of which he had always dreamed. But he wasn't sure if it was he who had thought this or whether it had been whispered to him by Voice.

When a streak of light slowly began to appear on the horizon, Knight went back beneath the oak to wake up his companions. They reluctantly began to collect themselves together. Suddenly they were startled by sounds coming from the somewhat distant dark hollow. Whatever it was, it sounded none too pleasant, besides they had no real desire to meet anything that might come out from there, and especially not with Dragon. So they quickly threw the few things they had into Knight's bag and while they were clearing the last of the fruit from the table, a terrible cry came out from the hollow in the tree. It was however no scream of fear, but more a war cry. They ran off at the same time as a great band of armed men jumped out from the hollow, led by the person whom Knight recognised as the speaker of the previous day.

In a split second the thought crossed Paul's mind that in the desert there wasn't the slightest chance of shelter anywhere. But when he turned round running he noticed that the desert was disappearing. In front of them huge trees sprang out from the sand… Everything happened so quickly that in a moment they were running through growing shoots into a great forest that was so dense it seemed like a jungle. All of a sudden they heard a terrible roar. Knight looked over his shoulder and saw the muzzle of the gigantic Dragon emerge from the small opening of the hollow. Its yellow eyes burned with rage and black venom oozed from its whole body and burnt everything onto which it poured. Even the sand was in flames, which when they went out left glass behind. Dragon spread his wings over the inhabitants of City, who as if oblivious, chased the travellers still shouting with forks and staves raised high. The sight was truly terrifying, but at the same moment they managed to hide in the forest thickets.

'We've got to run further away,' said Tiger, catching his breath. 'They're still going to chase us for sure and besides that monster could burn down the forest with its breath or with its stinking venom.'

At that moment, Knight tripped over a root that stuck out and fell spectacularly flat on his face onto the forest floor. He cried out in pain. The grass was as hard and sharp as a sword. The distant memory of the meadow filled with poppies where he had seen Friend flashed like lightning into his mind. There too it had turned out that the flowers had been like rock. Despite the numerous injuries over his body, he felt inner relief.

'No, these plants are like steel; Dragon won't be able to burn them. However the thugs for sure are not going to stop chasing us. At least we have some shelter,' he gasped out to his companions.

They ran on, hearing the shouting of their foes behind them, but now they sounded less combative. From time to time a faint light would penetrate through the dense forest canopy. But it was almost immediately blocked by Dragon spreading its wings out. So it was following them, flying above the forest. At a certain moment the monster clearly accelerated and its shadow passed between the trees in front of them. Knight felt a growing sense of unease.

They ran out into a forest clearing covered in rockfoil and moss. Far out in front of them they saw the missing Rabbit, who – unaware of the powerful Dragon descending from above – was hopping around the meadow without a care. Some unknown force that had once made Paul throw himself after his companion almost into Eyma's jaws, now pushed him forward. Although it seemed to him that he had been running as fast as he was able, he now ran even faster. Behind him he heard the roar of Tiger and the cry of Margarita. He took out the sword from his belt… Sword? Not long ago he had had a dagger; he collected together his distracted thoughts. As if it had come out from under the ground, a powerful white horse appeared between his legs, which bore him towards Rabbit and the approaching Dragon. He heard a scream of rage come from the reptile's throat. The beast on seeing Paul began to turn its huge body slowly around.

They rushed towards each other. A rider on a horse with a drawn sword and a powerful black Dragon. The monster opened its jaws. As if in slow motion Knight saw a stream of fire from within. He did not know when he had learnt to fight but in a single moment he was standing in the saddle and was preparing to jump. When the waves of fire almost reached the horse's head he leapt with all the strength of his legs from the back of his mount and jumped with one bound onto Dragon's head that was approaching at breakneck speed and was just about to devour them. For a moment he felt sorry for his steed, but he didn't have the time for such sentiments. Dragon scales burnt his feet, but with all his strength he lashed out and began to cut the monster's neck. He knew that he couldn't allow himself to look at his terribly deformed reflection, which for a moment he caught a glance of in the mirrored shell of the beast. Out of the corner of his eye he saw his companions who were fiercely fighting the band of thugs. The monster began to wave its head. Knight stumbled but just in time managed to catch Dragon's crest. He cried out in pain. His reflection twisted into a ghastly smile. Without a moment's hesitation, holding on with one hand to Dragon's thrashing neck, he stuck the blade straight into the part of the reptile where he saw the twisted sneering face. He heard only the protracted scream of the beast, while he himself felt a terrible pain cut through him.

Everything went dark and in the gloom of his own mind he called out in despair, 'Friend! Friend! Help!'

A cool hand brushed the hair from his forehead. He felt relief.

'I'm here. You no longer have to be afraid,' answered a familiar voice.

Paul slowly opened his eyes. He was lying on the ground in the Book chamber and Friend was kneeling by him. At a certain distance sat Grouch, who was eating and talking with Little Lula. Traveller was standing – as if torn – between his brother and the Book, while Tiger and Lady were by the pedestal still absorbed by the Book. Did it mean that it had all been a dream?

'I think you know the answer to that,' said Friend. The boy looked at his injured hands and touched the wound on his face. He remembered being cut by the grass.

Daisy pulled herself away from the Book and said, 'You were very brave. I didn't know you could fight like that.'

For a moment Paul wanted to ask her how the fight with Dragon and the inhabitants of City had ended, but he was interrupted by Grouch.

'Well what? Did you find that hare? Was he there somewhere between the pages?'

'Oh, stop sneering,' Traveller rebuked him. 'What happened?' he asked this time turning to Paul.

'I... No... I mean I saw him but...' The boy just could not find the words to describe what had happened so all he did was sigh in resignation.

'He ran through the forest but disappeared somewhere when Knight was fighting Dragon,' Daisy explained on his behalf.

'I saw him run between the trees. I don't think he noticed anything,' added Tiger.

'He ran into the forest,' mused Traveller, 'and you don't know anything about where he went?'

'Wait a moment, but I do,' exclaimed Tiger triumphantly. 'That man under the oak said that Rabbit wanted to get to the tower.'

Paul was slowly coming round. The memories of all these events were coming back to life in his head.

'Yes, to the tower,' he at last gasped out. 'And there's something else. That third man, the red head with the aquiline nose... He circled the king with the pawn...' At that moment Paul hesitated as it seemed to him that he had muddled everything, 'and he placed it near the rook. So it seems Rabbit's heading there. Only I don't understand why in that case he circled the king… It makes no sense…' he finished with resignation.

'No, it's not completely senseless,' objected Traveller. 'On the island of Migdal there is a tower which stands in the middle of a huge forest. So maybe it is there that we should be heading?' Traveller's enthusiasm was contagious for Lady, Tiger and Little Lula.

Only Grouch added disparagingly, 'The amount of rubbish you're spouting has reached its zenith.'

Paradoxically, Paul also felt unimpressed. He did not know on what basis he should take what had happened in the Book seriously and be led by it. He hazily remembered that they were supposed to find all the necessary clues in the Book. But now he felt too tired to set off on a further search. Friend looked at him closely. The boy turned his eyes away. For a moment a shiver went right through him and before his eyes stood the memory of his twisted reflection in the scales of Dragon. No longer did he want to see it and he felt that he did not want Friend to ever find out about it. So he was unable to let on too much about what had happened in the Book.

'If you think so,' he said indifferently. 'I just want to rest a bit before we set off.'

'That's not very sensible,' Traveller answered him. 'Even though Eyma has hidden away in the darkness, I still have no desire to set up camp here. Let's move on at least a little further.'

Everybody picked themselves up and moved on but Paul dallied. Was he simply supposed to leave the Book?

Friend turned around to him and said gently, 'Don't worry. You will return there. The Book is in every place where the darkness deepens because only it will light up the darkness.' With these mysterious words he moved off.

The boy took a few steps continually dragging his feet. For a moment he wanted to turn back but when he looked behind he saw Arie protecting them. Their eyes met. The green eyes of the bird chased away the bad thoughts from Paul for a moment and filled him with hope. The time had come to make their way to the castle.

**Chapter sixteen**

THE MIRROR

The way up out of the cave passed by calmly. The only unfortunate incident during the journey was when Little Lula twisted her ankle. But fortunately Arie took her on his back and as a result nothing further disrupted their journey, apart from of course the constant complaining of Grouch. At one moment they felt sleepy so they set up camp and had a rest. After a couple of hours sleep, they set off again on their journey.

Paul was still bothered by his memories of the events in the Book, in particular his reflection in the scales of Dragon. The more he thought about it, the more he was afraid that this had been a true picture of his face and not just a deformation. It frightened him to remember that Lady had earlier mentioned some change in his appearance. He grasped at the hope however that if he did look so nightmarish, she wouldn't have reacted so calmly. Sometimes he glanced at Friend. He was afraid that he would penetrate his thoughts so he tried to walk as far back towards the end as he could.

Slowly the light of the sun flooded into the cave. After the darkness that had surrounded them for those past few days, it was a real relief. They put out their torches and enjoyed the sunlight, which ever more brightly illuminated the cave. In the end they ran out into a large clearing covered in many colourful flowers on the island of Karev. Arie shot out from inside the cave like a bullet and began to do the most varied rolls in the air to the rhythm of the joyful hoots of Little Lula. Everyone was overcome with joy so unexpectedly quickly that even Grouch was as happy as a child.

When after some time they all collected together again, Traveller noted with some regret, 'So he's left us again. Oh well, at least we know which way we should go on.'

It was only now that Paul noticed that Friend was no longer with them. Indeed the last he had seen of him was his silhouette in the bright sunlight of the cave mouth. He felt regret, but at the same time a certain relief. He glanced at Arie, who was still gliding in the sky, fearing he might see the unease he was repressing within himself, but he immediately understood intuitively that the eagle was no longer going to keep them company. So he didn't have to worry about inconvenient questions from him. And indeed when in the evening they reached the shore, where a boat with two crew members was waiting for them, Arie place Little Lula on the ground and took off quickly into the air. He flew off in the direction of Shemesh, which was barely visible.

At first the next part of the voyage went smoothly. Traveller spent much of his time with his maps and it was only after some time that Paul realised that he looked worried. In the end the captain explained to them that the way to the huge pear-shaped island of Migdal was strewn with rocks that stuck out from the water, the avoidance of which would present a number of difficulties. They could, it was true, try to go around them and approach the island from the other side, but such a manoeuvre would take them many days. This was not advisable since Good Fairy was ill and needed the key in the not too distant future.

The mention of his grandmother awoke a lot of emotions in the boy. On the one hand he missed her and he thought that he would very much like to find the key for her, but on the other the unease that he had been feeling for some time, forced him to think that maybe Granny was not at all depending on him and had actually sent him on this quest without any care for his fate or safety… Somewhere deep down the boy felt that this was impossible. Granny knew after all that Friend would be accompanying him. But he wasn't accompanying him all the time at all… And such was the internal dialogue that was taking place in Paul's heart, which meant that ever more rarely did he want to join in with the conversation of the crew. He chose rather to be alone, in particular he liked to climb up onto the yardarm and stare out at the horizon. He was very irritated by the continual companionship of Elf, although he was silent and discreet. Little Lula tried on many occasions to engage the boy in play but he stubbornly refused and after some time he was surprised to see that Grouch had become her main companion. Well, she was the only one who could stand his company, Paul thought with some disdain.

The strangest thing was that the boy no longer wanted to look in the mirror. Such a state of affairs had lasted since the time when they had boarded the ship from Karev. Paul had made his way directly to the captain's cabin, where an enormous mirror hung, to see how his physiognomy had changed. At first he was very surprised because he saw absolutely no changes. It seemed to him that he looked exactly as he had before. When he leaned in a little closer something pushed him away from the glass. His hazel eyes had completely changed colour. Now they were a shade of sandy blue. Paul didn't have to think long before he realised where he had seen such a colour before. He remembered the beautiful sky blue of the lake located on the island they had left. Why? How was it possible? Paul looked in amazement at his reflection, which physically seemed to show the heart-rendering longing he had then felt. In terror he realised that nothing of those experiences remained in him. He looked at himself as if it were the face of some unknown person. The though came to his mind like lightning that although the reflection in the scales of Dragon had not shown his physical likeness, it could have been a reflection of his inner self. Yes, that had to be the truth. The reflection of City had also been terribly deformed but it hadn't shown what could be seen at first glance, but rather the ugliness in the hearts of its citizens. In that case who was he himself? Was he that terrible creature that he had seen then? Or rather a sensitive boy with eyes the colour of clear water? Or was he – as some inner voice suggested – Knight, who had rushed on horseback with drawn sword to do battle with Dragon?

Immediately he felt the bitterness that was poisoning his heart. Friend had promised him that he would find a clue in the Book that would help him defeat the beast. Now it seemed that he was as far as possible from finding it. Dragon's venom had entered the guts of the boy... Friend.... had lied.

After a week of sailing, they reached the area where according to the map there were many rocks. An uneasy Traveller spent all his time tracking their course from the captain's bridge. They reefed the sails and slowly made their way along a narrow course between the rocky islets. It took them all of three days. At every turn the loud shouts of the crew could be heard warning of another obstacle appearing in their path. To make matters worse, the weather very much deteriorated. Traveller would curse with rage looking into the dark sky, which every now and then would help them to a heavy downpour. Paul heard the captain talking to Mr Fratel considering whether they should turn back from this area. But the First Officer pointed out correctly that they had already sailed along quite a large part of the course so turning back would in no way be any safer. Everyone avoided being in sight of Traveller when he marched quickly down the deck. In principle it was harder to state what filled the crew with more fear, whether it was the danger that threatened them or rather the anger of the captain. Only Lady seemed to make nothing of his moods and it was she who most often would accompany him. Next to her he would become somewhat milder.

On the third day of this slow sailing the misty outline of Migdal island could be seen. Paul had the impression that everyone breathed out with relief. Only Traveller shouted furiously exhorting everyone to take care. With every moment he became ever more irritable. In the end Grouch accosted him.

'Little brother, relax. Most of the rocks are behind us now; the ones here might be bigger, but there are a lot less of them. I don't know, it's true, what insanity has made you sail to this island but the danger has already passed.'

This was too much for Traveller, 'You fool, what do you know about the sea! The water breaking on the rocks in a high wind will often form whirlpools in this region. Do you have any idea what it is to sail in such a vortex?'

This was for sure unexpected news. Having been sobered by this information, Grouch ordered Little Lula to lock herself in her cabin. Everyone else assembled on deck to carefully observe the sea. The tall ship occasionally floundered. It was like a paper boat on the great ocean of the world and they were like little ants subject to a greater power over which they held no sway. Paul thought that here in this world they were mere puppets at the mercy of the elements, whereas in the Book, Voice had made them into characters that were able to contribute to their own story. This thought gave him comfort. If he could be a hero there, then why not here as well?

He ran out onto the bridge to stand next to Traveller. It was difficult to say whether in front of them lay real danger because the water breaking on the huge rocks turned into a spray of a million droplets and became a thick fog. Was there a vortex before him? For a moment in the blue sky between the clouds, Knight saw a powerful flying figure. At first he thought that maybe

Arie was watching them, but when again he saw the outline of this figure, as well as its long twisting tail, he realised that it was more likely to be Dragon that was following their progress. Everything was blocked out by rage. The fear and doubts that had been gnawing at him for the past week disappeared. He was not going to surrender to that beast. He wouldn't give it the satisfaction of seeing their destruction. For a moment he wanted to take the wheel as if he had the conviction that he himself could sail the ship through dangerous waters. Common sense told him, however, that he had better leave that to Traveller. He felt that some inner force was pushing him and he couldn't sit still doing nothing. Elf appeared as if he had been called.

'What should I do?' Knight called out to Elf.

'Take the key and go to your cabin.'

This advice didn't seem very sensible to Knight, but he had grown accustomed to strange orders. He closed his hand around the lock pick that he had kept in his pocket all this time and went down to his cabin. Little Lula sat in the middle of the room playing with the watch that Traveller had once given her. Paul walked up and took a closer look at it. Then he noticed that on the side there was an opening for a little key, which most likely was to open up the mechanism inside and wind up the watch. For a moment Paul hesitated wondering if this really was what Elf had meant, but he took the watch from Little Lula and started to bend the wire to fit into the tiny keyhole. He heard a click, and he had succeeded. He looked at the numerous cogs inside. Suddenly it occurred to him that it was stupid anyway: this watch had no hands so how could he set the time? The girl watched curiously over his shoulder. The ship still rocked violently.

'What's this?' and saying this she pointed to a cog that did not seem to suit the rest of the mechanism. It was attached with a little screw but it made no contact with any other cogs. The ship floundered. Paul turned the wheel a number of times. For a moment he expected some sort of fireworks since he had already grown used to the Crooked World being full of surprises, but nothing happened. He closed the case looking around the cabin wondering if maybe Elf had meant something else; however, he didn't find anything that could be opened with his lock pick. He gave back the watch resignedly to Little Lula, preferring not to answer her question. He left the cabin to go back up on deck and the girl followed.

He was surprised to see that the fog had disappeared and they were now sailing on a calm sea with the dangerous rocks already far behind them. Lady ran to him and joyfully caught him in her arms.

'We're safe now! What joy! Hasn't Traveller steered us brilliantly through all these dangers?' she called out enthusiastically.

Out of the corner of his eye Paul saw the captain standing proudly with swollen breast. He was smiling deep down. Only Grouch clearly grimaced as if he were not happy with the turn of events. Paul looked around the deck again in search of Elf. He wanted to ask him what it was about the key and what in principle he was supposed to have done. However, he noticed that his silent companion was already sitting high up in the rigging so he sighed in resignation as well as in the hope that sooner or later he would be able to have the matter explained.

Meanwhile they were approaching the island. When they had gathered in the Captain's quarters, Traveller admitted to them that it really was a vast island and they didn't have a chance to cross it. The tower was situated closer to the side of the atoll from which they were approaching. It would be better if they anchored the ship somewhere leaving the crew on board and made their way themselves to the turret.

'And what is this building? Do we know anything about it?' asked Tiger.

'Well, yes and no,' began Traveller ambiguously. 'Once on the island there was a large city, but that was a few centuries ago. For unknown reasons, the island was deserted, and an enormous forest grew over the ruins of the town. Even the castle slowly fell to ruin and became overgrown. The only building intact is the tower, but I don't know what it was used for in those times.'

'What do you mean: "The castle fell to ruin",' Paul asked. 'But buildings don't just simply fall to ruin.'

'Yes... Well at least that's normally the case. What happened on the island isn't known. There's no evidence of any battle nor the signs of any natural disaster. There are only ruins. On the mainland there are stories of the wealth of the people that once lived here. Nothing more is known. I once came here before myself, but I admit I didn't make my way to the tower. I don't know what is inside.'

This story sounded quite interesting although there was something threatening in it. Paul felt uneasy. What if something lived in the tower? What if some danger was awaiting them? Suddenly the large mirror flashed before his eyes in which for a split second he caught his reflection. He turned his head. He was not certain that he wanted to go there.

**Chapter seventeen**

# THE RUINS

They climbed slowly upwards. They had been making their way through the thick forest that covered the island for a long time, when suddenly Grouch tripped over a large stone cube and landed on the ground with a thud. The sound was surprisingly hollow. Picking himself up, Mr Wronski put his leg into a large pile of leaves and suddenly the ground gave way under him and with a terrible scream he fell into the depths that opened up beneath him. Traveller ran forward and leaned over the opening calling his brother. At the bottom of the cavity a bruised Grouch lay moaning. The others breathed a sigh of relief, because obviously the same thought had crossed everyone's minds: what if their companion had just disappeared in the same way the former inhabitants of this city had done? Mr Wronski, however, was clearly not comforted by this, since he shouted at them angrily, demanding immediate assistance.

When they had succeeded together in pulling him out, it turned out that the poor fellow had twisted his ankle and he had to be supported by Traveller in order to go on. Neither of the brothers seemed too pleased with such an arrangement. What was worse, it made their climb even slower. In the thick forest they began to ever more often see stone ruins here and there. They were so completely destroyed and overgrown that it was difficult to make out from them what kind of buildings might have once stood there. They also had to watch out because here and there they came across deep holes like the one into which Grouch had fallen. They guessed that they might have been the cellars of the buildings that were once located there. After some time they stopped in order to rest. Lady suggested they make camp, since it was the afternoon and they had no chance of reaching the tower before nightfall.

Tiger objected, 'I don't very much fancy sleeping in this place. I don't know whether it's because of Traveller's tales or whether these stone ruins really do have something threatening about them, but I don't think we'll be spending a peaceful night here.'

'But where else should we stop in your opinion?' Daisy was not giving up. 'These ruins are sure to stretch out to the tower itself. It's highly unlikely we'll find a place where there are none. We're not going to get to the tower before nightfall. And also I don't know if sleeping there would be any safer.'

'And what do you think Traveller?' Little Lula said unexpectedly, although she seldom commented on their decisions.

Meanwhile Traveller was leaning over some map, which he had taken out from his bag earlier. He looked at them deep in thought. After a moment he spoke.

'I have here an old sketch of the city. It survived due to the few who had left the island for the mainland before those mysterious events took place here. It's difficult for me to say exactly where we are, but it looks as if we are somewhere near the city gardens. If we're scared of the ruins we could try to find that place and make camp there.'

Traveller's suggestion sounded sensible enough. Paul leaned over the map and the accompanying drawings in order to help establish where they were. They were studying the maps together. Suddenly the captain pulled out from under the map a sketch that showed a large building. A shiver went down Paul's spine. He took the drawing to look at it closer. He had already seen the building somewhere before. He had been standing in a large square looking at a city hall on which there had sat a monstrous Dragon. He dropped the drawing as if it had burnt him. He didn't want to be here. He simply didn't. He looked around him at the forest. Everywhere there were the ruins of sandstone buildings. Something tightened in his throat. This was some dreadful dream. None of this could really be true. Maybe it only seemed to him that way.

Submissively, he followed the others. They were looking for the place Traveller had spoken about. As if in a daze, he barely registered their conversation. When they decided to set up camp he didn't even know if they had made up their minds to sleep in the ruins or if they had found the former park. He ate the meal prepared by Lady almost unconsciously, but he felt nauseous so he announced that he had to sleep. He lay without moving while his companions talked of their plans for the next day. Together with the darkness, silence fell, but for him there was no sleep. Possessed by a strange urge, he stood up. He lit a torch from the fire that was burning down and set off again on the journey alone.

At night everything really did look terrifying. Illuminated only in the torch-light, the trees had a ghoulish appearance. Knight walked on without thinking with only the vaguest recollection of Traveller's map in his head. Strangely he no longer feared the mysterious power that had made all the people disappear from this island. City must have been destroyed. Now he felt that this should have been obvious to him when he had been listening to the ranting of that speaker. He was more disturbed by what he himself was doing. Why did he feel it was so necessary for him to reach the tower first? Here, in City he had seen Dragon for the first time. He must be frightened that here he was also going to have to face the fear that had come to him after the battle with the monster. He did not want the others to see this. He wanted to be alone. The thought came to him that the tower could be the lair of the beast. Was he going to have to do battle with it again? Maybe. But somehow that did not frighten him. Maybe he was frightened of his reflection… Or maybe it was more that he wanted to see it. Maybe he had to find out the truth about himself.

The sight of the dark lone tower standing on a bare hill with the starry sky for a background made an unusual impression on Paul, who slowly climbed the steep side. Nothing had waylaid him on his journey. He even considered if this wasn't some trap. When he had almost reached the very top, he looked back. He had indeed climbed up high. High enough that behind the trees he saw the sea illuminated by the light of the moon. It was a beautiful view. The waves refracted the light and with a silent rumble broke on the shore. He thought how strange it was that it was so empty here and yet the depths of the sea hid a world that teemed with life. That was not the world for him. At that moment he had to face whatever it was that waited for him in the tower. He turned to the tower and took it in for one last time with his eyes before entering. Out of the corner of his eye he could make out a brightly glowing golden star, which had appeared surprisingly close to him. It was somewhat heartening to know that he was not totally alone after all. Elf had remembered about him.

Inside the turret seemed completely ruined. In the poor light of the torch he could barely make out bits of furniture, fragments of broken statues, and various unidentified equipment. All of these things were tightly packed together but in a certain disorder. Obviously, this large room had been used as a storeroom for unnecessary furniture and things. Knight looked around. Everything was covered in cobwebs. There was a sudden movement from behind that startled him. When he turned around he saw a spider as big as a hand sitting on the banisters to the stairs. Revolting, he thought. Nonetheless, he decided to ascend the tower. Down there at the bottom he couldn't find anything of interest.

He spent a long time climbing up. Each individual floor he passed was empty and even the cobwebs did not have many places to stick to. The higher he climbed, the narrower the winding stairs became. Eventually, he reached a large empty room. He was already tired from the climb, so he decided to rest awhile and have a walk around.

He went up to a narrow window. The night was black with a few golden points in the sky. When he looked again at the sea, he was reminded of their dangerous passage between the rocks. He looked around to find Elf. He wanted to ask him what it was he was meant to open with the key in the cabin. But his faithful companion stayed motionless as if hanging in the air, beyond the light of the torch. His glow went out and in the darkness he looked more like a large fly.

Knight shivered. For the first time he felt truly terrified. He looked again at the cobweb hanging in the corner. The thought of poor pallid Elf caught in a web nauseated him. Only now did it occur to Paul that the presence of the spiders might not be a complete coincidence. And so there was something lurking here. He retreated towards the stairs. Suddenly he noticed that from this level a pair of spiral staircases, which perfectly overlapped each other, led upwards. It seemed strange. For a moment Knight wondered which of them he was to choose and whether they led to two different places. In the end he chose the stairway that began closest to him. Each time he passed by the other stairway, he looked around nervously as if he was afraid that someone was coming. He even had goose pimples. This time there were no further floors to the tower, so he spent a long time walking up the stairwell, every now and then looking around him. He couldn't see Elf anywhere. He didn't know how many stairs he had already climbed, but he felt truly exhausted when he realised that he was already approaching the top. The stairs came out at the very top into some room. He tried the handle and briskly walked in and the door slammed behind him.

He was dazzled by the incredible light of fire. It was as if everything around him was burning. His eyes, which had become accustomed to the dark, hurt him taking in so much light. Screwing up his eyes, Knight could only make out that everywhere around him there were many figures – in front of him, behind him, on the ceiling and under his feet – it seemed a whole army of figures that almost stretched out to infinity was looking at him. When he had managed to open his eyes wider, he understood that what awaited him was exactly what he feared the most. Everywhere he looked he saw the reflection of himself a countless number of times. Mirrors, mirrors everywhere, mirror walls, mirrors at every angle. The whole shining room limitlessly filled with the fire from his torch and his reflections. He had to look at himself. With a mix of dread and fascination, he realised that each of these reflections looked completely different. In some he looked beautiful and in others deformed, sometimes he saw himself as he seemed to be in reality but here and there that sneering facial expression he had seen in the scales of Dragon flashed before him. Some of the reflections were so distorted that it was difficult to find any similarity to the boy at all.

Paul felt the blood pulsate ever quicker in his temples. He looked frantically around himself, with everywhere his eyes falling on a plate of glass and confronting his own self. He staggered around like a madman. Where was the exit? He was shocked by the realisation that he did not know under which mirror the door was and that from this accursed room that was reflecting him ad infinitum, he might never be able to find his way back. He was in a cage – a cage with himself, having been endlessly replicated. And there was no one there to help him. He heard a scream come out of his throat and recognised a terrible note of panic in it. But he had the impression himself that he could no longer feel anything.

When his voice died in his larynx, with the rest of his strength he gasped out the one word that might give him hope of liberation, 'Friend.'

He fell. His torch hit the floor and unexpectedly went out. All the reflections vanished and darkness reigned all around him. He stuck to the floor. It seemed to him as if he was in his own coffin, without the slightest ray of light. The only thing he felt was the cold touch of the mirrored floor and only this brought him relief. He did not know how long he had slept. When he awoke he did not want to open his eyes. It didn't make the slightest bit of difference as he was surrounded by the impenetrable darkness of the mirrored room. Suddenly he felt some pleasant cold touch on his face. A gentle breeze of air breathed out from a wet nose helped him come to. He opened his eyes. As he had expected there was no way he could make out anything in the darkness, but after a while he heard a timid little voice.

'Is that you, Knight?'

There could be no doubt that in this nightmare something good had oc-curred; he had found Rabbit. The presence of someone close brought Paul a certain relief.

'Yes, Rabbit. Where did you come from?'

'I saw you go up the other staircase in front of me but you must have en-tered through a different door because I couldn't find you anywhere in... Well, at first I thought it was a garden, but that garden looked terribly similar to the island on which there were the waterfalls... Then I heard your terrible scream and I went back to the door to get to you via the other staircase.'

Even in spite of the great tiredness he still felt, Knight realised that there was something suspiciously strange about Rabbit's tale.

'What door? After all you said you were on an island,' he asked with a per-plexed voice.

'Well, yes,' answered his companion as if it were nothing. 'But I got onto that island through a door. It was carved into a big stone that stood in the middle of a path, if that's what you're asking about.'

Knight felt inexpressible relief. So somewhere near here there was an en-trance that led onto the island. His island. The memory of it was so sweet and refreshing for Paul. He still had no idea how to get out of the mirror room but the tale told by Rabbit reminded him that somewhere beyond this nightmar-ish place lay another world. A beautiful world that was worth seeking out. Actually it was a good thing it was dark here. At least he didn't have to look at an endless number of reflections of himself. But how was he to get out of here?

'I've also been thinking about that,' wheezed Rabbit.

His companion's reply made Knight realise that he had spoken his ques-tion aloud. But actually... did it really mean that? Maybe Rabbit could read his mind just like Friend? The thought of Friend made Paul calmly think about what he had advised them to do when in danger. They could certainly try to call Arie. Suddenly he remembered something else Friend had said: that the Book was always in the place where darkness deepens. Well for sure, the darkness in that place was absolute. Knight stood blindly.

'Come on, we've got to look for the Book,' he said turning to Rabbit.

'That certainly is an idea,' replied his companion without surprise, 'but there is a slight catch.'

'What?' asked Paul surprised.

'Well have you ever read without light?'

Rabbit's reasoning wasn't without logic, although Knight also thought that he could equally well have wondered how they were supposed to find the Book in the darkness. But there wasn't any sense in arguing about these difficulties; it was time to begin searching.

They used their sense of touch to find their way around. After a while they came to the wall. Moving their way along they came across a shape that was obviously a handle. Paradoxically, the place seemed less threatening in the dark than in the light. Since not a single ray of light was being reflected in the mirrors, they could at least slowly and calmly become acquainted with the layout of the area. In this way they were able to make their way through another chamber. And yet another. They had a vague feeling that the rooms surrounded the stairwell, which was located in the centre. Suddenly the wall turned left and at that same moment they were engulfed by a weird brightness. There in the next room a surprise awaited them.

In the middle of the room stood a pedestal on which lay the open Book lit by a light from an unknown source. What was strangest of all, however, was a bright glow surrounding the pedestal in the mirrors as well as their illuminated figures but the Book was not reflected. Knight no longer wanted to look in the mirrors so at a quick pace he approached the thick tome hearing Rabbit panting quietly behind him. He leant over and began to read.

*The stairway is ten steps to the left.*

Paul stared wide-eyed. He knew that the Book gave hints but he hadn't expected it to be so direct. After all he had expected to be pulled into the story. He read on.

*If you want to read on, you should be aware that the battle with Dragon, which I'm writing about, is still ongoing. The beast is free and is distorting the truth about this world, the truth that I want to show in my Book. This is no story for the gullible. This is life itself. This is a war that has been fought since the dawn of time and which will last until the end of this story.*

Knight read while holding his breath. At last. At last Voice spoke again.

*Do you see how devastated City is? They turned away from the truth. The truth that I myself wrote for them in my tale. They preferred their impoverished world built with their own hands. But in my story there is no place for anything that isn't mine. When I write the final chapter I will immortalise only faithful heroes.*

The words of Voice sounded very threatening but at the same time they poured hope into Knight's heart. Even though he had never seen the owner of Voice with his own eyes, he had no doubt that he was a good Author who would never let Dragon win so the ending of the story had to be good. And he, Knight, was the hero anyway and he felt that he wanted to remain faithful to Voice.

*If that is the case, go ten even steps left and there you will find the door. However, first you will have to open the windows of the lighthouse and then sail away from this island. Everything here has been destroyed. It's time that you made your way to Alta. You must go overland.*

This was the bottom of the page. Knight was a little tempted to turn over and read on but he felt that he ought to do what Voice had asked. Only what did 'open the windows of the lighthouse' mean?

'Rabbit, what do you think this thing about the lighthouse is all about?'

'But it couldn't be simpler. After all you heard. All you have to do is open the windows.'

From the left the voice of Traveller could be heard. Paul turned his head and saw Traveller standing in the doorway, which indeed was just ten steps away. He was with the other companions and in his hand he held an electric torch.

'You gave us a fright, you little rascal, running away like that,' he said scathingly.

'I still don't understand what us having to open the windows means,' said Paul ignoring Traveller's remark.

'Well, if you had been good enough to wait for us, you would have heard that this isn't any kind of castle tower, as legend would have it, but an ordinary lighthouse. But I see that today's youth doesn't have much by way of brains. We have to open the windows so that the light that emanates from the Book has the chance to get outside,' said Traveller.

'I still don't understand anything,' said Paul stubbornly.

Grouch gave a sneering laugh.

'Next time, brother, you're going to have to look after the children better,' he said putting clear emphasis on the second last word while looking at Paul.

Meanwhile Traveller slid a large mirror opposite the door out of the way and the warm morning light flooded in. All the mirrors shone with a bright shine, reflecting a thousandfold wonderful views of the billowing sea.

Only then did Knight look carefully around himself. Everywhere his own reflections that had been replicated an infinite number of times looked back at him. But now he looked at them without fear. Maybe it was because of the shock that he had just had or it was because when he had called out to Friend... help had come. And so Friend hadn't pushed him away after all. And maybe it was because in the mirrors Paul didn't see his own horrifying ugliness that had appeared in the reflection in the scales of Dragon?

The boy slowly went up to one of the mirrors and looked closely into the flat pane, from which his own face looked out. Fair hair, blue eyes, or rather sandy sky-blue eyes, a nice straight nose... Nothing horrible. Rather the opposite. But maybe he had let himself be deceived? Maybe the monstrous mask that had stared back at him from the shiny scales of the beast wasn't his true visage? Maybe it had all been a big lie? But if that was the case he had let himself be deceived. And that had been his biggest downfall. He remembered how he had avoided Friend after he had returned from his journey into the Book. Now he was overcome by real shame. How could he have doubted him? How could he have been taken in by that vile Dragon and believed that Friend had cheated him? How strange it was. Deep down two different feelings were fighting with each other: relief that that monstrous mask had only been a lie and shame that he had been so faithless. His reflection mirrored this internal battle. In his blue eyes he saw depths that he had never seen before, as if his own soul was opening up before him and showing him the precipice upon which he stood. That's how he saw it now. The picture of him in the scales of Dragon was a lie, but it was also a possibility that could have become reality had he just believed in it. And there in the depths of his being, which faintly shimmered in the distance of the infinite reflections, yawned the gap. The gap from which the fumes of disbelief could rise to infuse his soul and poison it with Dragon venom. And so the evil was in him. He saw it as plain as day, although it was hidden. Was there any escape? Was there any way to prevent this monstrous reflection from becoming true?

His mind wandered for a while aimlessly. He looked at his blue eyes. They reminded him of something or rather someone. Bright water in the land of happiness. The blue of an unsullied lake. Eyes. Irises that looked at him with sadness to promise him that one day he would return. A gaze that changed him and allowed him to take the shining eye colour with him forever. Friend. Yes, he was the only rescue. It couldn't be doubted. The blue water of this faith would clear the fumes of the destructive venom that was poisoning him from within.

'Are you lot ready?' said a female voice breaking the silence. 'Can we go now?'

While Paul had been looking into the mirror, Traveller together with Lady had gone around all the chambers and opened up the enormous shutters. Tiger, however, at every turn had bumped into some mirror and tried to sniff out his own reflection. Slowly what the captain had been talking about began to sink in for Paul. Indeed he was standing in the middle of a gigantic lighthouse. Its rooms were covered in mirrors to magnify the light that came from the Book that was placed on the pedestal. He swore deep down. He had almost convinced himself that this fairy tale place had been built specifically in order to entrap innocent victims.

'You've got to admit that it's an incredibly large lighthouse. Normally buildings such as these only have one round room at the top, which will not have mirrors arranged so carefully around it as they are here. Well, it's time to open up this lighthouse and make our way back to the ship. Then we'll sail on to the port in Luleå at the very northern edge of the Baltic and then on to Alta,' announced Traveller, who had walked around and reached them from the other side. He had clearly heard the last words Paul had read from the Book.

They began to go down together. Little Lula held onto Grouch's hand. Paul looked around everywhere in case Elf had become imprisoned somewhere. His absence was worrying him. Was it possible for him to fall into some spider's web?

When they reached the very bottom, he felt that he couldn't simply leave. After all his companion had to be somewhere. He stood indecisively.

'What is it, Knight?' asked Daisy.

'Elf's not here... The last time I saw him was in the tower but that was before I got to the top... Do you think he could have been caught and devoured by some spider?'

Lady looked at him uncertainly.

'Not really... Elf has great power. He wouldn't simply let himself be eaten.'

'But I don't think those were ordinary spiders. They were... really bad spiders,' Paul felt that he didn't even sound convincing to himself.

'Knight, listen. Why do you think that the only building to have survived on this island is a lighthouse?' Daisy asked out of the blue.

'What do you mean? What has that got to do with Elf?'

'You read it yourself. City was destroyed but as you can see the lighthouse has survived. Why?'

'I don't know. I don't think I know what you're on about.'

'But I do. You see, I lived here. The lighthouse was one of the oldest buildings and it was meant to help sailors navigate on the sea. Both those from here who sailed out in search of distant lands and foreigners. It was also meant to encourage people to stay. But then the inhabitants no longer wanted to have anything to do with foreigners. They preferred their very own City. The lighthouse remained but nobody lit it. For some reason, however, it was not knocked down and for those who still believed in the existence of other countries it was a sign that their faith made sense,' explained Margarita, while the others walked down the slope. 'That's why it was never destroyed. Now that it has been lit again the island can come back to life.'

These last words she said as if to herself. Paul listened in fascination. He didn't know why she was telling him this. After leaving the Book they hadn't talked even once about what had happened to them. Only now did he understand that everyone had had their own story in the Book.

'You lived there. You have many memories of living in City. When I began to read, I simply found myself in the desert. I don't remember much about my past in the Book.'

'I remember. Yes, even quite a lot. Sometimes it even seems to me that my life in Gdansk was very similar to my life in City, if not the same. I wanted to believe that there was something more than just the normal grey daily routine. Sometimes it would happen that I would see some strange creature. I could talk with certain animals. But it was as if I were tethered. Just like in City. It was only after meeting Friend that everything changed; only here with you lot I am truly alive. This here is the real world. It may be called the Crooked World, but its only here that everything is truly OK.

They walked slowly down the slope. Rabbit also listened to the story. Thinking about Lady's words, Knight suddenly felt that he couldn't go on any further. He had to return for Elf. Even if the lighthouse was the only good place on the whole island and you could deduce from this that the spiders couldn't completely overrun it, he still couldn't leave Elf there.

'Forgive me. I've got to go back. I hope that you will tell me more about yourself, but I feel that I cannot leave Elf. Don't tell anyone that I've gone back. I'll catch you up.'

## Chapter eighteen
# AUTHOR

Paul went back towards the tower. He didn't even have to turn round to know that Rabbit had followed him. Again he entered the room on the ground floor. In the light of day the dusty cobweb-covered furniture no longer looked so sinister. It rather presented a sorry sight. He went up, looking around everywhere. He reached the very top and ran through all the rooms. He couldn't find Elf anywhere. So there was only one thing that could be done. He went up to the Book, which still lay open on the pedestal.

He looked at its surprisingly empty pages and asked aloud, 'Where is Elf?'

He didn't know what in principle he was expecting. Was the answer meant to appear on the pages as if on command? He touched the Book with his hand and then he saw that letters were emerging from the depths of the pages becoming ever darker:

*Elf is always with you even when you cannot see him. It's not you who is supposed to be looking after him.*

Although such words should have cheered up Paul, he felt disappointed. Deep down he wanted to know more so he read on:

*What do you want to know?*

'Anything,' Paul thought to himself deep down. 'Whatever helps me to understand. I'm wandering around as if I were blind, not knowing what I'm really looking for. Apparently it's a key for Granny. However I'm under the impression that it's all a pretext. That you're pulling me into your story, that you're making me into its hero, although I've not been given even a moment to decide if that's what I want. Who are you?'

For a moment Knight felt that the Book couldn't be read further. His silent question resounded in the silence of disordered letters. Had he assumed too much for himself? And maybe the Book would close in front of him not wishing to give an answer? Why should Author betray his secrets?

Suddenly the words again became legible. Knight with bated breath followed them with his sight.

*Am I to reveal to you the secrets of my story? Who are you to demand answers from me? A reader? No, you come into my story. You become a part of it. I made you up. You arose from the letters written by my hand. And you dare to ask who I am?*

Knight felt his stomach tense. And so Author wasn't going to answer his question. More words however were forcing themselves into what he was reading:

*Who am I? You'll understand that when you finish reading. Only then will you know if I am a benevolent author and why I am writing this story.*

'But what is the point of this all? What am I here for? Where am I heading? I need some kind of sense that would let me understand how this story fits together. Something strange happens at every moment and I don't know when to expect something magical to occur or when nothing special will happen.'

*Sense? But don't you see how I'm looking after you? I gave you Elf for protection, I showed you the island that you long for, I let you face your fears so that you could free yourself from them and when you wanted to fight with Dragon, I gave you a horse to help you. Can't you see how much I do for you?*

'Yes, that's true. But still I have no feeling of purpose. I want to know why,' he asked both himself and the Book.

You want to know why? Well, let it be. Into my beautiful fairy tale world, which one evening I dreamt up for my beloved little son, Dragon crept in. Well, not so much crept in as betrayed my story. The story of Shemesh where I wanted to create the most beautiful of worlds. Since that chapter my tale has been that of the battle with Dragon.

'Why can't you just cross Dragon out?'

Because I like giving freedom to my heroes. Would freedom make any sense if I were now to say, 'And so it's the end. I don't like my heroes', and if I were to burn the Book in the fire?

'But didn't you destroy City?'

They condemned themselves to destruction through their own choices. Can one exist in my tale without accepting the truth of the world I'm writing about? Can a hero deny his own existence in the Book? No. Then he would erase himself from the pages of the story. Even Dragon does not deny the existence of the Book. He only tried to hide it, since he was unable to destroy it. And they didn't want to see it even though I placed it in the very centre of City at the top of a lighthouse. I made it the light of their country and they abandoned it considering it to be a collection of imaginative fairy tales. So in that case why should I have continued to write about them? They forgot about the story so the story forgot about them.

'Since that is the case, how are we meant to fight Dragon? How can we win when you have given him freedom and made him such a powerful being?'

I sent you my son, whom I started writing this fairy tale for. The story is for him so he'll finish it. You're safest with him. He loves you, the heroes of the tale, so much that he always talks of you as friends and he absolutely had to take part in your story. Could I have done more for you as Author?

Knight stopped reading. The words he'd seen seemed too wonderful and inconceivable to be true. But still he believed in them. The darkness that had dominated his heart, now gave way. He still had many, many questions in his head. Suddenly he felt his companion impatiently nudging his leg. Clearly Knight had been absorbed in the Book for too long. He could feel that involuntarily a question was forming in his head: 'Why Rabbit? Who is Rabbit?'

*You still haven't worked it out? Rabbit is you. Or more precisely a part of you. You were an insanely reluctant hero. You concentrated only on your model ships and computer games, dreaming of distant worlds but without doing anything to really see them. To make you move off, I had to force you to chase your own self. But I think you've found your goal so you don't need such a companion.*

Knight felt he didn't need to look down. He knew he wouldn't find Rabbit any more. That did not worry him at all. He already knew which way he was heading.

'And Granny? What about the key for Granny? Am I to still look for it?'

*But of course! Everyone needs a key to their part of the story. The fact that you have found your key and have become a part of the Crooked World is not enough for the whole story to come to a happy end. Good Fairy has spent her whole life working hard in the Little Sun, so now it is time that others helped her. It might turn out not to be so difficult at all.*

'And one more thing. You still haven't explained to me why everything is so magical. Until recently, until I met Friend, I had a peaceful life and nothing strange happened around me. Why as Author are you making this story ever more like a fairy tale?'

*It isn't I who is making this story ever more like a fairy tale. It has always been so. When you were still unaware that you were a participant in my tale, you considered the whole world ordinary and boring. Only now when you allow me to write your story and you take part in it of your own free will, do you see how wonderful my imagination is and what strange things I am able to think up. It's you who is only now allowing yourself to see the truth about the world I created. The deeper you go into my story, into my Crooked World, the more mysterious and fascinating it will be for you. Being Author, I simply like to spring surprises.*

Reading these words, Knight reached the end of the page. He knew that he had no time to read on. His companions must have already gone a good part of the way back. So he ran quickly down the stairs and down the side of the slope. He ran as if he had wings. He felt truly happy. Going down the hill went a great deal easier than going up. He didn't even notice that when he caught up with his companions, they were already halfway to the ship.

Hearing his panting, Traveller, who was leading the expedition, looked back.

'Well how was it?' he said as if it were nothing. 'Did you at least resolve your doubts?'

'What are you talking about?' asked Knight suspiciously.

'Oh, never mind. I thought that you just wanted to know where we were heading, but since you're in no way interested...' he said with an amused look in his eyes.

'You knew it, didn't you? You knew that we were in the middle of a story. You knew we were fighting with Dragon?'

'Well, it's not the first time that I've had the opportunity to meet him during my travels. But you know, I don't think about it in that way.' Traveller thought awhile. 'In the end, it's not me who's meant to fight Dragon so at the moment I'm making use of the opportunity to delight in this world. It is truly beautiful and like a fairy tale. I love getting to know it. And since I can also lead others on expeditions and help them find their keys I am more than willing.'

Knight wondered for a moment about these words. Traveller in his calm approach to all of the wonders of this world really was a strong support.

'And Grouch, what about him?' asked Paul suddenly.

'Oh, but he just wanted to be a carpenter. And then he realised that others had a much more interesting role in this tale and since that time he has become terribly embittered. I don't know. I'm still counting on Friend finding some place for him.'

**Chapter nineteen**

# VOYAGE
# IN THE SUNSHINE

They reached the ship that same day in the evening as the way down went a lot easier. They cast off and the sea bathed in the bright light of the lighthouse looked exceptionally inviting that night. Looking at the island disappearing into the distance, Knight thought what an extraordinarily beautiful place this was and maybe, just as Lady had said, there would come a day when people would come to live on it again, enticed by the brightness of the Book, which lit up the sea for many miles around. Somewhere high up in the rigging, he could make out a small shining point and with a smile he thought about how pleased he was that for a moment earlier Elf had disappeared. In the end it was thanks to him that he had returned to the Book.

This time they were able to circle the island in such a way that they didn't have to manoeuvre between the rocks. Traveller explained that Alta was a city on the mainland and lay at the very north of Norway. First they had to reach the northern Baltic port of Luleå from where they would still have around twenty days of travel, unless they could find some means of transport. The captain wasn't ruling out such a possibility, but he was assuming that a journey on foot awaited them.

They sailed for around five weeks. Looking at the maps, Paul was surprised to discover that the Baltic was very much bigger in the Crooked World. Even in his dreams, it couldn't contain so many islands and isles. Traveller showed him, however, that the way from Luleå to Alta was not that different from the passage that they would have marked out on an ordinary map.

It led precisely to the north of the Scandinavian Peninsula beyond the Arctic Circle. The boy felt a shiver of excitement. He'd always very much wanted to visit the far north and experience the Midnight Sun when night never fell.

The Captain warned him that in August the polar day in Alta was already over and that by the time they arrived there the day would certainly be almost of ordinary length. Besides after some time the lack of darkness would be tiring and the regions they were to traverse were very difficult to cross due to the numerous lakes and mountainous terrain. Moreover they had to be prepared for low temperatures.

The voyage was calm and did not present them with too many difficulties, but they were troubled by short periods of dead calm[5], which resulted in their voyage taking a little longer. One day Paul was a little anxious to realise that the school year must have already started, but this didn't matter much because even if he had wanted to he was already unable to stop the quest.

Memories of his parents came to him with surprising poignancy. For some time, he tried to push them out of his mind, because they made him feel a sadness he'd never known before. But where could one escape from one's memories? One day he finally gave in and looking at the setting sun, he let his thoughts run to a smallish flat in grey Warsaw. Mum was never there. She worked until late and it was better not to think of Dad. He worked in a freight company and was always travelling abroad. When he was small he used to dream that his father would take him travelling with him. They had even planned up together where they could go. Mum had looked at them then with a smile. These had been moments full of joy and happiness for the boy. He had liked to imagine the whole family crossing the desert on camels or wading through the jungle. He had also dreamed that he had younger siblings who he could teach to fight with machetes.

Paul had slowly grown up, however, and these dreams had not been fulfilled. Dad had been promoted and ever more often went abroad. He would bring back model ships for him from his trips. Mum, sadder with every year, spent more of her time working in the office. They didn't have time. Paul was torn by the longing for the world of his childhood, which having passed had taken with it its family warmth.

Yes, once it had been different... From the gloom of memory an image appeared of childhood games with his parents, filled with laughter and joy. What had happened to make it all go?

---

5 Dead calm – no wind at sea

He did not know... Well tough... Such was life. Over time Paul had become accustomed to the thought that that was the way it was. What is good passes and what remains is everyday life without hope. Sometimes the boy felt a deep-down objection; something screamed out in his heart, 'NO! I do not agree to this. I want to live differently. I want to take in the world. To love people. To be happy.' But this internal whisper broke through to the surface too weakly. And in the end nothing changed. An empty home, boring homework to be done, old models of ships to be put together. And another day the same.

There was a time he had rebelled against the ever increasing absence of his parents. He had demanded that they spend more time with him and sometimes they had met his demands. He very much liked the time they spent together. But with the course of time he had stopped wanting this and even, despite himself, showed them ever more indifference. In the end what? Was he supposed to play with them? He wasn't a child any more. Everything they did had begun to irritate him. And they had sensed it and spent ever less time at home. His friends envied his freedom but somehow he was not entirely happy with it.

Was there anything that really made him happy? He had always wanted to experience something. Some great adventure in life. Some voyage over distant seas. To visit foreign countries and meet interesting people. He dreamed of becoming a great traveller.

Suddenly he thought about his model ships and in particular the one that Dad had brought him from South America. Although he had difficulty admitting it, he still was happy to remember the times he had spent with his father. He had felt then so... grown up. Dad was the only one who treated him like a man. He wasn't even able to say how. Maybe during the times he was at home he preferred to spend time with his son rather than forcibly try to bring him up. Maybe that is why Paul so loved those models. They reminded him of the presence of a man, who simply normally saw in him another man.

Suddenly he heard a low male voice calling his name. For a moment it seemed as if his father had in some strange manner found himself aboard the ship, but when he turned round he saw Traveller, who was calling him into his cabin. With difficulty he tore himself away from his memories and was surprised to note that a strange warmth spread through his body as if some joy and longing for his parents had once again made a home in his heart.

More days passed. He spent them mainly in conversation, playing social games, or simply playing with Little Lula, who made the time for them more enjoyable with her constant mischief. Only Tiger became irritated at the length of the voyage and almost destroyed the deck with his excess energy. Knight wondered why no one had asked about Rabbit, as if everyone knew why he had gone. He also noticed that Tiger, who had been Rabbit's closest companion, now chose him, Paul, for company, most probably feeling that he had found his lost companion in him. They enjoyed rolling around together on deck. Knight really did need a lot of strength for such games since on more than one occasion the powerful paws of the predator pinned him to the ground. The huge cat, however, remained gentle in these wrestles and never used his claws. Paul was grateful for these fighting lessons, guessing that in the future they might come in useful.

One day Traveller noticed that Paul had grown a lot, during so short a time as their voyage. The boy now was of a comparable height to the rest of the crew. The captain decided that under such circumstances it was not sensible for Paul to continue to wear such a small dagger. Having a sword, however, would require a certain amount of skill and that meant intensive practice. Mr Fratel was happy to take on the task and so in this way Knight's days slowly began to fill with duels with the first officer and other crew members.

This was a very enjoyable time for Paul. He felt himself become physically fit at lightning speed and with it came the feeling that he was truly capable of many things. Deep down he realised that the name that Friend had given him was an augury of a number of battles, which were not necessarily going to be in defence of an already non-existent Rabbit. Now while he was fighting the battle for his very self and had taken on his role written in the Book, he knew that a much more important challenge awaited him. It no longer filled him with fear. He tried not to waste a single opportunity to practise.

At one time when once again he was practising some basic sword strokes in his cabin, the captain interrupted him.

'My boy, I think we should talk.'

'Yes, Traveller? Has something happened?'

'Yes and no. What I mean is that I can see you're using almost every opportunity for physical training, which certainly is important, but it's beginning to worry me a little bit,' he explained.

This was quite unexpected information for Paul.

'What do you mean?' he said surprised.

'Well, you know… As I was saying it's very good that you're practising a lot. In the end I myself encouraged you to do this. But physical training isn't the only thing that you need.'

'Oh no…' yelped the boy. 'Now, you're going to give me a lecture about how sometimes it's necessary to remember about rest. But I've had enough of rest. Now it's time for work.'

As soon as he had said these words, Paul had already had the time to regret them. In truth he didn't imagine that such platitudes that are the typical blandishments adults use with children could ever fall from the lips of Traveller. The man raised one eyebrow in an amused manner.

'Well, since rest is so unpleasant for you… What can I say? But despite what seems apparent, this is not at all what I was on about. I only wanted to say that true battle doesn't only depend on vigorously waving a sword about, no matter how accurate it might be. It doesn't even depend on physical stamina, which you're now working on so avidly. In battle you always need a strategy, an idea, a concept of how to win without working too hard.'

It sounded perfectly sensible, although Traveller's argument was no longer convincing Paul so much. In the end, wasn't it worth working hard for the sake of winning?

'I know that you're very enthusiastic,' continued the captain, 'but I would like you to concentrate on other activities, even things that seem completely unrelated to our quest. You could play chess sometimes. Did you know that Grouch was once a master of chess at school? That was a long time ago, I know, but I think that he would be happy to play with you. As well as your muscles, it's also worth developing your mind.'

Knight was far from convinced by this proposal. His last memory of chess was from the Book, where the three strangers had been playing with the fates of the heroes under the oak tree.

'I can see you grimace. If you don't like chess you could also read. I've got many interesting books in my cabin. But it's important to me that you spend some time on other activities and not only physical exercise.'

Even though reluctant at first, Paul allowed himself to be convinced. Traveller's words reminded him that he had after all brought a book with him. He reached for his bag which he hadn't finished unpacking, but nowhere could he find the story. He'd hardly had the time to begin it at home. Where could it be? It had a terrible dragon on the front cover and a ship on the back. A strange shiver went down Paul's spine. 'The Quest for the Key': that was the title and how did it begin? A boy went to look after his ill grandmother... But surely that was impossible...

All of a sudden, with a squeal of joy Little Lula ran into the cabin, chased by Tiger. The girl ran into Knight and began to call out with a laugh, 'Save me, save me!' Paul reached for his sword and pointing it at the predator he pretended that he was fighting him. Shortly afterwards the dinner bell rang and all three left the cabin. On going out the boy once again looked into his open bag, but soon he decided that he must have left the book at Granny's. And besides, such a title and such a cover... It all had to be a coincidence.

In the end Paul allowed himself to be talked into a game of chess. Grouch really did turn out to be a chess master and with uncharacteristic patience, he explained to Knight the secrets of the most various openings and moves. It was true that he also didn't spare him his regular malicious comments such as, 'with a brain such as yours, my friend, you're not going to go far.' But on the whole he was bearable. The boy discovered that there was a lot of playing through a sly sequence of moves, and moreover he was a very quick student. When Traveller asked Grouch how well they were doing, Paul was surprised to hear himself being praised.

After five weeks at the very beginning of October, the outline of land could at last be made out on the horizon. This pleased everyone, because although the time spent on the ship had passed by most pleasantly, everyone longed for dry land beneath their feet. After mooring in the port of Luleå, they decided first to go into town and have a little bit of a look around. Paul looked carefully at the low brick tenement buildings, among which here and there also sprang up newer buildings. There was nothing special to be seen that indicated the proximity of the Crooked World. After a pleasant evening spent along the streets of the port they returned to the ship. They spent the next day packing. Because a long overland journey awaited them they had to prepare for it with the utmost care. Their bags could not be too big, but at the same time they needed all sorts of varied equipment to help them make camp or cook food. Knight wondered for a moment if they wouldn't look strange with swords strapped to their belts, but this time he hadn't taken into account the wiliness of Traveller. Swords being the most reliable weapon in fighting Enemy, were essential for the expedition but captain tried to ensure that they were not too conspicuous. He chose modern weapons with blades that had a spring loaded mechanism, which meant the swords could be folded up relatively small and hidden in layers of clothing. Because they expected it to be cold, they packed lots of warm clothes and thick sleeping bags.

Being thus prepared they went to bed in order to be able to set off fully rested on their journey the next morning. Traveller had arranged for Mr Fratel to take command of the ship and to head north along the Scandinavian Peninsula and further on along the Skagerrak strait into the North Sea and the Norwegian Sea until they reach the port in Alta. Such a voyage, taking into account that they were sailing in accordance with maps of the Crooked World, was going to take the ship around two months. The captain's decision surprised Paul a little.

'We still don't know what kind of task awaits us there, but it could still take us a little time. Anyway, I hope that when the Whaler reaches Alta, we'll be ready for the return home. For sure, we're not going to be capable of walking back to Luleå,' explained Traveller. 'Anyway for the next three weeks we've got a seven-hour hike every day ahead of us. It really is going to be exhausting. I do hope that we find some form of transport, although we have to avoid normal travel on the roads.'

'And why's that?' Paul asked, his interest piqued.

'And how do you expect to pack Tiger onto a bus? We've got to keep well away from people, although honestly I've got to admit that I've been wondering if others will be able to see him at all, since he belongs to the Crooked World. Besides the region through which we'll be walking is sparsely inhabited so I don't think that public transport operates there.'

Knight had to accept this explanation. Besides he was looking forward to the expedition; the harsh conditions appealed to him. Traveller took two large tents for them. Luckily in Scandinavia, one could camp in any place as long as it was at least one hundred and fifty meters away from a household and these were very seldom seen in this region. Thick roll mats took up a sizeable portion of their baggage as the terrain was quite rocky and – as the captain claimed – after a day of physical effort, there is nothing more important than a good comfortable sleep. They also had gas cylinders with which they planned to cook their meals. This time they also packed some tinned food and some dry bread, not too much so that they were not overburdened but enough in order to be able to last out the trek on which they couldn't expect to find any shops. Traveller also took care to pack two shotguns as well as a fishing rod in case they would have to go hunting animals themselves. A number of moose and even more reindeer lived there. But the reindeer mainly migrated in herds that were tended by Sámi, the native people of the far north.

**Chapter twenty**

# ON THE ROAD

They began their trek in the early morning of the next day. They had to leave the port for the edge of the city in order to then walk through the local fields. Paul thought that even though the landscape looked undoubtedly harsher than in Poland, it was not, nonetheless, utterly different from what he knew.

'Wait a moment,' said Lady when he shared this observation with her. It turned out that she had once already visited the northern regions of Scandinavia. After college, she had set off on a survivalist expedition with her friends. They had camped in tents and travelled mainly by hitch-hiking. Once again Daisy had surprised the boy. He wondered if maybe that was why she seemed completely unconcerned by the difficult conditions that they were going to have to travel in.

The first thing to surprise Knight was how extremely rocky the entire vicinity was, so much so that it was indeed difficult to find a good place to put up a tent. The thick roll mats that Traveller had ordered them to take, turned out to be a blessing. They spent the first night on the edge of someone's field, which luckily had been cleared and was as a result a relatively flat floor. But Mr Wronski stated that the next day they would most probably be sleeping in a forest so they would have to spend more time on looking for a place to camp. He explained that a series of glaciers had littered the land with rocks and boulders.

The next day brought a new discovery. The landscape there undulated with numerous but not high hills that were interspersed with many lakes filling the hollows created between them. Only now did Paul see that their way truly did weave in between large bodies of water. During one of the breaks in the trek, he sat down next to the water and looked into it. He saw numerous stones at the bottom of the lake. They formed a background for the flickering reflection of clear skies as well as of the hills that surrounded the lake like a crown. He was struck by the raw harshness of the landscape and thought that it well reflected how he was feeling, which after the initial euphoria that had been caused by the revelations made to him by Author of the Book had now become more resolute. He knew he had to save his strength for the long trek as well as for the battle with Dragon that awaited him. It was true that he had no idea how this was going to happen and what he was going to do then, but he felt that Friend would not leave him by himself. Somewhere within him a feeling of pride was germinating that it was he who was Knight and that Voice had chosen him as hero for his Book. He didn't feel any particular fear of what awaited him. He knew he could depend on Author. His reverie was interrupted by a sudden splash and the circles expanding over the surface of the water that broke up the crystal reflection of the landscape.

'Hey what're you doing staring at the water?' asked Tiger irritatingly. 'It would be better to eat something before we set off again. Or at least sleep.' And on saying this the predator lay down on a large boulder sticking out from the lake just next to the bank. In these cold green and grey surroundings, the intensity of his garish colours jarred and seemed a reminder that reality hid many secrets only visible to someone who knows the Crooked World. This thought terrified Knight, who stood up from the stone he was sitting on and looked into the black depths in the middle of the lake. Who knew how much danger cold be hidden there? A shiver of unease ran through him. He looked behind at his companions who were resting. They were so calm. It hadn't even entered their minds that Enemy might lurk here. Suddenly he heard a noise and out of the corner of his eye he saw small waves appear on the water. His hand grabbed the hilt of his sword that was hidden beneath his clothing. He waited. The wind died down and the lapping of the water slowly became quieter. Nothing happened. Paul wondered if he really had sensed some danger here or whether his imagination had put the idea into his head. He waited some more time ready to fight, but nothing happened. He thought that nonetheless it was worthwhile to have some rest so he laid out his roll mat and tried to lie down in a comfortable position. However, sleep did not come. The constant fear of not knowing what it was that hid beneath the surface of reality did not give him rest. Under the skin he still felt that they were not alone.

Only in the evening did he feel that two days of constant walking were having an effect on him. He was tired, and blisters had appeared on his feet. He was already counting on having a longer rest. Traveller was really enforcing discipline so everyone would have to rise without a murmur at dawn and spend a long time walking before they stopped for their first rest, which would last barely an hour. Grouch complained all the time but his brother paid him not the least bit of notice. Little Lula was enchanted by the journey, which she spent mainly on Tiger's back, who at every turn would ensure extra fun for her, jumping from stone to stone. Lady however resolutely bore every discomfort without complaint. Furthermore, it was she who rested the least of all of them since the short moments that they stopped she would often use for cooking the meals. It was hard to count Elf as a member of the company, since only occasionally would he appear in front of them like some bird flying by and when night fell he would shine on them somewhere from high up in a tree like a tiny torch. This however gave Paul a feeling of safety. The boy now had the impression that all of these fantastic adventures in which he had lately taken part, were only a distant dream. The presence of Elf was for him a guarantee of the truth of what Voice had revealed to him.

The trek was indeed hard. Even though it seemed they had a lot of time to chat, they walked largely in silence, except for, of course, Grouch's snide comments. Only Lady, like all women, would often engage some of them in conversation. There was one time when Paul noticed her try to encourage Grouch to say something about himself. Her attempts did not land on fertile ground. It was after all Ralph Wronski who normally interfered in the affairs of others, while keeping his own secret. So all the more, he must have felt threatened by Daisy's interrogation regarding his life. Discouraged by his demeanour, she quickly gave up and went to chat with his brother. Traveller was decidedly more willing to talk with Beautiful Lady. However it could be seen that similarly to his brother, he felt constrained when talking about his life. Clearly he didn't wish to offend so he tried to steer the conversation onto other topics, to talk about travelling and also to ask Daisy herself about her story.

How strange it is, thought Paul. Now he still had no resistance to tell others about his life, school matters or even the painful relationship he had with his parents. He looked at his feet, trying not to trip over more and more new stones that appeared along the way and he wondered whether there would come a time when he would find it equally difficult to talk about himself like the older companions on his journey. Why did they keep quiet? What was so difficult about telling one's own story? For the first time Paul was truly glad that he was still young and felt no awkwardness. He enjoyed the moments he could tell Daisy about his experiences and at last feel that someone was really listening to him. Suddenly the though crossed his mind that the brothers were ashamed of their past. He was able to understand the silence of Grouch, but of Traveller? His expeditions were fascinating after all. But no. After all, Lady wasn't asking the captain about his voyages, but about himself, his experiences and longings... Could John Wronski have some unfulfilled dream? He had visited the entire world, he had had count-less adventures. But... he was alone. Yes, Paul could not imagine a life alone. He knew that many people live in just such a way but for him it was a com-pletely alien thought. The pain of his parents being absent was still too fresh in him to be pleased with the thought of a life spent alone. Could anyone really want such a thing?

He looked around over the empty wilderness. Up to the horizon all that could be seen were empty spaces filled with rocks and lakes shining in the distance. How miserable the picture of loneliness was. Maybe when people go through life alone a long time, they clam up like oysters so as to hide their dream of being loved in the hard shell of their own insides?

But Traveller knew Friend. He knew that he was loved. He was suddenly hit by the memory of their meeting in his house in Gdansk, when the captain felt so responsible for organising the expedition and Friend had sat in silence before in the end disappearing. Maybe Traveller knew Friend but did not want to allow him to lead.

The trek had really gone on for a long time. They had been hiking for al-most ten days, covering almost twenty miles a day. Even Grouch had long ago fallen silent and with a determined face brought up the rear. Lady already seemed tired with the journey and now Traveller often took on the chore of cooking, while she lay on a roll mat with Little Lula and quietly told her var-ious tales.

It turned out that there were almost no settlements so after a few days they decided to throw their fishing rod into a lake. This meant their stop had to become longer, since catching enough fish for meal took up a great amount of time. The captain then stated that they would have to change to hunting, since it was not worth losing so many hours on fishing. This idea didn't please either Daisy or Little Lula, who were clearly opposed to killing animals. Traveller only shrugged at their complaints and the next day he went off for some time to later bring back a hare. The delicious fresh meat smelt so tempting that despite their initial reluctance the girls could not refuse to try it. From that time on Traveller and Tiger, who up to then had gone off himself at meal times, hunted regularly. Little Lula demanded that they swore to never hunt any of the moose that they sometimes happened to see afar in the most deserted places. The little girl was so delighted with these creatures that she could not agree to any such barbarity.

The tenth day, however, brought with it a real crisis. In the evening, they made camp on the edge of a small empty plain, which stretched between hills. They were very tired so it did not take long to convince Traveller that maybe it wasn't so important to set off at dawn the next day. Besides the early mornings in the parts of Sweden through which they were travelling were already rather cold so it was even harder for them to leave their warm sleeping bags.

So the next day they clearly overslept since they were awoken by foreign voices outside their tents. Knight froze, listening to the unknown sounds. While he was on the coast he had heard a little of the Swedish language so he was certain that the people standing in front of the tent where he slept with Traveller and Grouch were not Swedes. The captain jumped up and looked outside. Paul leaned out behind him and was dumbstruck. A number of men with wide smiling faces and dressed in blue costumes with large red belts stood around. An entire herd of reindeer grazed on the grass next to them. Knight hazily remembered Traveller's stories about the Sámi, the native people of Scandinavia and Caucasia. Indeed the faces of the newcomers did not have typical European facial features. But they were so sincere and open that Paul was glad to meet such welcoming people. They scrambled out of the tents and bowed to the strangers, but straight away a fundamental problem became clear: no one knew any language which they could use to communicate. That is apart from gestures, which their captain used quite effectively. So straight away he began to talk with the men, who invited them to share a meal. As could have been expected, it turned out that they had quite a lot of delicious reindeer meat. Paul was quite surprised to see that it was almost black and it had an exquisite aromatic flavour. As Traveller explained, and as could be seen by looking at the herd with the naked eye, reindeer lived mainly off mosses and lichens, which had a wonderful fresh smell and gave the meat an exceptional after-taste.

The Sámi encouraged them to stay with them longer, but Traveller showed them on the map where they were heading. Then the Sámi spent a long time discussing things among themselves, after which they were able to show the captain with gestures that they could help with the journey. It turned out that not far away in their encampment hey had left carts, in which they sometimes travelled. It was only necessary to harness them up to reindeer. Traveller happily agreed to such an offer, so one of the men left for the encampment. It was time for them to have a longer break. Over the day Paul and Little Lula looked at the reindeer. In the early autumn before being shed for the winter, the reindeer's antlers now looked truly impressive. Some individuals had such gigantic antlers that they held their heads close to the ground being unable to hold up such a heavy burden. Paul thought they looked very similar to those from pictures of Father Christmas that were so popular at Christmas time, and at the same time there was so much unperturbed calm about them that it was hard for him to imagine them running in harness. Interestingly, the reindeer, unlike their herders, clearly sensed the presence of Tiger, however they seemed to have absolutely no fear of him, and rather looked at him with a certain amount of interest. The tomcat was also not interested in hunting, and only studied them carefully.

They spent the day resting with the Sámi by a fire. For dinner they had the opportunity to eat the delicious reindeer meat, this time roasted in honey. For the travellers tired out by the long journey this was a particularly nourishing meal. Paul was also glad about the company of other people, even though he didn't know their language. The men turned out to be particularly friendly, all the time laughing about something. They didn't seem to mind that their new friends hardly understood anything at all and they continually told them things. Only Little Lula repaid them in the same coin and she happily sat on their laps trying to engage them in conversation. Strangely it seemed as if she was able to communicate with them quite well. Then it occurred to Paul that it was more important to communicate with the heart than with the head, especially with these tribal men who overflowed with childlike joy. Strangest of all was Grouch's behaviour. Paul had expected their mean companion to become even more dour as a result of such company. But it turned out the Grouch accepted the presence of the Sámi in silence and afterwards even tried to communicate through gestures with one of them.

In the evening a cart arrived pulled by four reindeer with two additional animals at the sides. To Paul's surprise, the driver was not the man who had gone off to the village earlier, but a Sámi woman of a similar age to Lady with a broadly smiling face and dark eyes. She didn't speak to them, only waved her hand energetically, after which she busied herself with looking after her animals. Later, when they were all sitting next to the fire, listening to the traditional music of the Sámi, she joined them, but she didn't speak even once, not even to her own people.

The next morning they quickly packed up for the journey. The reindeer were already harnessed to the cart and the girl was waiting for them. They bade farewell to the herders and they also received some dried meat for the road from them. Traveller showed the Sámi woman where on the map they wanted to go, at which she nodded her head in understanding and set off quickly. In a moment Tiger also jumped into the cart.

They rode a long time in silence. In the end Grouch couldn't hold out any longer.

'At last, I thought that I couldn't take any more of that continual walking. It's a pity only that this cart is so rubbish. It looks like it's just about to fall apart. And that woman's probably not seen soap in a month.' Traveller gave him a murderous glance, but said nothing.

Little Lula, who sat wrapped in a blanket under the arms of Daisy, spoke for him.

'But, she's so nice, when I got up this morning she put me for a moment on the back of one of the reindeer. I'm really glad that she's the one who is driving us.'

Grouch fell silent as if offended. After a while he spoke up in a softer voice: 'Well, maybe she is nice but I was only saying that she looks none too clean.'

'Better to be dirty than mean.'

Such a direct comment from Little Lula completely threw him. Lady spoke up quickly to put an end to the unpleasant topic.

'The girl really is very nice. But I'm glad above all that we don't have to go on foot, because I really was tired. But do you know, Traveller, where she is taking us? I don't believe she will go with us all the way to Alta.'

'No, for sure not. Yesterday when I showed the map to her companions they showed me some point more or less halfway to Alta. That's the region where the tundra starts anyway.'

'Well, that is quite a long way anyway.'

'And what is tundra?' interrupted Little Lula.

'There are hardly any plants there,' said Traveller after some thought. 'There's not going to be many places to hide.'

'To hide?' said Paul worriedly.

Traveller gave him a cross look.

'Did you think that there was no threat to us? Enemy is somewhere near all the time. The fact that he hasn't attacked us yet means nothing.'

'What? You really think he's following us?' Lady seemed just as surprised as Paul.

'Yes, besides,' and now the captain turned directly to Paul, 'I think you felt his presence at the lake. You looked really scared.' This observation surprised the boy. He'd been convinced that nobody had seen anything.

'How do you know? I thought you were asleep.'

'I was lying down trying to sleep but that wind had an ominous murmur to it.'

'Then why didn't you do anything? After all, he could have attacked us.' Paul was indignant. Since Traveller had known about the presence of Enemy, why hadn't he done anything?

'He didn't do anything to us. He only wanted to give us a scare.'

'But how were you supposed to know that? You should have been alert.'

The captain's eyes flashed angrily. 'Alert? What do you think? I was the only one of us that knew about his presence and you're talking to me about not being alert? If I'd just grabbed the hilt of my sword like you, I'd have only provoked him to fight. It was better just to pretend that I hadn't noticed him,' Traveller snorted in rage. Paul felt like a fool. It did indeed look as if Traveller had acted cautiously. 'I told you that you shouldn't only be learning how to fight but strategy as well,' continued the captain. 'Enemy is a master of trickery and most often will not attack head on. If we want to measure up to him, we have to be clever. That's why I'm thinking about what we can do in the tundra. We're not going to have anywhere to hide but on the other hand Enemy's not going to have too many opportunities to ambush us.'

This conversation seemed to Paul unusual. Since leaving the island, there had not been so many strange things to remind them of the Crooked World, not mentioning, of course, Tiger and Elf whom they had already grown accustomed to. Talk of Enemy and fighting seemed now so unrealistic and Knight wondered if it was all true, or whether he was just an ordinary tourist visiting the world with friends... And where was Friend anyway? He'd left them such a long time ago that Paul had slowly stopped thinking about him. Now he felt a longing for his warm voice and gentle smile. It crossed his mind that he wanted to be very much like him. So calm and sure of himself. Fearless. And what am I like? he wondered. Suddenly before his eyes he saw the image he had seen in the scales of Dragon. He closed his eyes. No, that wasn't true. After all, Voice wouldn't have made him Knight if he was someone so awful. This evil only smouldered somewhere deep down inside his being. Besides Friend...

The delicate touch of someone's hand on his cheek awoke him from his musings. He opened his eyes. Lady was looking at him with a look of concern. Little Lula was sleeping in her lap.

'Is everything OK? You look really troubled.'

'No, no, there's nothing wrong. I just suddenly remembered something, but it's nothing important.'

Paul looked away. He could feel that Daisy didn't completely believe him, but in any case he could not tell her the truth. After a while he looked at her again. She was still looking at him searchingly.

'Do you sometimes think of Friend?' he asked.

She raised her eyebrows as if she were surprised by the question.

'Of course, every day. After all, it's thanks to him that I feel alive. He's the one who gave me back my sense of existence!' she exclaimed emphatically.

The others looked at her with surprise. Only Tiger stared at the horizon, unperturbed.

'What do you mean?' asked Traveller attentively.

'Oh! What was life without him? It seemed to me that the future held nothing for me, that I would always dwell in my loneliness with Toad… And now… It's not even that I'm having the adventure of a lifetime. What gladdens me most is simply that I'm here with you… and that maybe… I will meet Violet again.' After these words she lightly shook her hair where the fresh violet still was and she looked out into the distance in front of her.

Paul smiled to see her happiness, but suddenly he saw that Traveller had a strangely unclear expression. He looked as if he wanted to stand up and leave the speeding cart, which was being driven by the silent Sámi woman.

All of a sudden, Lady turned to him, caught his hand and said, 'Thank you for letting me come with you on this journey. It's been very important for me that I can count on your support. You've been a real pillar of strength for me.'

Under normal circumstances the captain would have burst with pride on hearing such words, but this time he only frowned. Only now did Paul understand how eaten up with jealousy he was of Friend. It was true that Knight did not think of himself as an expert in matters of relations between men and women, but the feelings of Traveller towards Daisy were becoming for him ever more self-evident. The rivalry between the captain and Friend seemed to him completely abstract: he was unable to imagine the latter as a romantic hero. Friend cared about everybody and although it was clear that he very much loved Daisy, he certainly did not single her out as a lover. Traveller as a result had no reason to regard him as a rival.

'You look very much in love…' Grouch's comment was a clear attempt to taunt his brother.

'In love? What do you mean?' Lady blushed and withdrew her hand. She glanced at Traveller, 'I… don't know what you're talking about.'

'Well,' Ralph Wronski clearly felt that his malice had been way off the mark. Traveller immediately gave Daisy a studied look, 'I was talking about in love with Friend.'

'Aaah…' the girl breathed a sigh of relief. 'Well… you know. We all love him, don't we? I was wondering how one couldn't love him. He's such a good man.'

'Love? Him?' Grouch snorted in anger. Paul nonetheless noticed that his jaw tensed and when he turned away, his eyes took on a surprisingly sad look.

Any further discussion had to wait, because at that moment the Sámi woman had slowed and was now bringing the reindeer to a stop. It was clearly time for a break. Traveller looked very pleased.

**Chapter twenty one**

# THE SECRET OF
# THE CART DRIVER

They ate a meal nearby a lake from which the animals drank water. Despite what one might think, rusks with dried meat were truly exquisite. Furthermore in the nearby vicinity there grew many berries, which they ate for dessert. Paul felt as if he had eaten the most wonderful feast. He lay down on the moss to take a nap. He did not know how long he must have slept, but when he awoke he heard that the others were already preparing themselves to set off.

'But where's that girl got to?' he heard an unhappy Grouch ask.

Indeed the girl was nowhere nearby.

Paul proposed to go and look for her. The entire area was filled with huge boulders and small hills, behind which she might have been hiding. Knight had been searching for quite some time when he came to the conclusion that it would be better to return to the place they had stopped and wait: after all, she wouldn't have abandoned the cart and reindeer. Suddenly he heard a strange monotone sound, similar to singing. He went up a little further and took a look around a huge rock. The sight that was laid out before him filled him with wonder. On a small meadow covered in Arctic flowers lay Tiger, and beside him humming a bizarre tune knelt the Sámi woman. With this she stroked his soft fur.

Paul did not know what surprised him more: whether it was the fact that the girl was not mute, as he had expected or rather that she could see Tiger who other members of her tribe could not make out. Earlier, after all she had not paid him any attention. Was it that she knew Friend? Or maybe the Crooked World had suddenly appeared to her as it had done to Daisy?

He stood there a long time listening. Tiger lay quietly, like he seldom ever did, almost thoughtfully. Suddenly the Sámi woman looked straight at Knight and smiled, as if she had known all along that he was standing there. She fell silent, after which she stood up and slowly began to walk in his direction. They returned to the others in silence. Tiger followed on behind them. Paul promised himself to ask him about this unusual girl.

'At last, I thought that you had got lost,' said Grouch commenting on their return.

Traveller helped the girl harness up the reindeer. Only now did Paul take a close look at their cart. As well as wheels it also had runners, which were placed just above the ground. Clearly once the wheels were taken off, it was used by the Sámi as a sleigh. It was not very large – hardly did they all fit in – but it was pulled from the front by four reindeer. Paul was surprised to see that the two reindeer at the sides had also been harnessed up. At first he had thought that they were running along so that they could replace those at the front pulling the cart. However on closer inspection of the animals, he realised that they were much more slender than horses so they had much less strength, which was why six were needed to pull the cart.

'We're off,' announced Traveller, interrupting Paul's thoughts.

When they had all squeezed into the cart, Paul whispered to Lady, 'Did you know she has a voice? I heard her humming some melody to Tiger.'

'Tiger?'

'Yes. She saw him.'

This time he had no opportunity to ask the predator about the Sámi woman, since the cat had not sat in the cart with them having wanted to run around awhile.

'Maybe she knows Friend?' Lady wondered aloud.

This thought surprised Paul. Somehow he hadn't imagined that someone from this half-primitive tribe might know Friend.

'You look surprised,' noted Lady. 'But he certainly also appears here. Why should he be treating us in any special way?'

'Maybe. I hadn't thought about it earlier. I just assumed that maybe she could see certain effects of the Crooked World in spite of not knowing Friend. Wasn't it that way with you?'

'It was a little like that. But now I know that I had met Friend before I got to know him. But wait a moment… Before that I had also met a talking animal. Maybe in fact… I still however believe that we shouldn't rule out her knowing Friend.'

The journey continued in silence. They had to make a long stop every two hours as the reindeer quickly grew tired pulling such a heavy load. As soon as they had eaten, Paul went over to Tiger to ask him about the Sámi woman.

'Mmmm, I don't really know,' the tomcat replied thoughtfully. 'I mean she's seen me from the start and then she simply came up to me. She wanted to stroke me and then she started to hum that tune. But I haven't heard her say anything.'

Paul was very disappointed. He had hoped that he would find out something. So he turned to Traveller, who knew the most about the Crooked World.

'I agree with Daisy. We cannot rule out that she knows Friend and even if she doesn't know him, it could be that she is close to the Crooked World with her heart and so she sees it.'

'But why doesn't she talk? I heard her hum a tune, so she must have a voice.'

Traveller looked at him seemingly unconvinced. 'I don't know if I would make such a big thing out of it. Maybe she simply knows that she won't communicate with her language so she stays quiet, but that doesn't stop her occasionally singing.'

Knight waved his hand and turned around. He decided to have a look around where they were. There were a few trees growing around but there was no possibility of calling the place a forest. Along their way ever more often there would appear patches of ground covered with low vegetation, which meant that they were already indeed in the far North. Moreover it was getting ever cooler, which was also beginning to make itself felt.

Paul wondered why he was so determined to find something unusual in this girl. She looked perfectly ordinary and the explanations of Traveller and Lady were completely acceptable. But something seemed odd to Paul. If she did know Traveller, shouldn't there be some glimmer of understanding between them? Since in this foreign world they shared a common secret, shouldn't they be able to understand each other without words?

The journey continued monotonously. The Sámi woman continued to stay silent. The lack of change in the landscape affected Paul's mind and it seemed to him that he was beginning to stop thinking about anything. The hoof clops on stone and the squeaking of the cart put him into a kind of apathetic state, from which even his companions didn't wake him.

Two days later when during a stop he decided to have a walk around, he again heard the strange tune. Being unable to walk away, he moved in the direction from where the sound came. Among a nearby clump of trees, which grew up at the foot of a small rock, he saw the Sámi woman stroking the head of a small bird that rested in her hand. Again it was a beautiful idyllic sight. Paul stood looking at this ethereal scene.

Fire.

There was fire everywhere.

Flames.

Flames that reached up almost to his heart, but still he couldn't tear his sight away from this secret girl with the bird in her hand standing motionlessly in the heat. Underneath the tune he heard the crackle of fire. But why didn't the flames touch either her or the trees in which she stood? After all, they were so close. He wanted to run, to get away from this place, but his legs seemed planted in the ground. He couldn't move. He wanted to at least shout out to warn her of the danger but he was unable to make a sound.

He would have probably allowed himself to be consumed by the flames, if it hadn't been for the sudden realisation that he was cold. Very cold. Instead of burning him, the fire was chilling him to such an extent that he was beginning to shiver. And then everything stopped. He stood once again near some trees on normal grass that had in no way been scorched.

The Sámi woman noticed his presence and fell silent.

She smiled, 'Dát Ipmil.'

Of course, Knight did not understand what she wanted to tell him.

The girl pointed at the bird, which she still held in her hand, 'Duvvá dát Ipmil.'

Paul's expression must have still showed a lack of understanding since the Sámi girl began to wave her hand as if pointing all around herself.

'Dolla. Ipmil dá,' she said slowly and clearly as if trying to get through to him with these individual words. Knight, however, was unable to understand anything. The girl grew sad and lifted up her hand, from which flew the bird. Paul was surprised to see that it was a small white dove, which didn't come from these parts. It must have flown in from very far away. The Sámi woman went forward and when she passed him, the boy noticed clear regret in her eyes. He felt that she had really wanted to tell him something important.

The next days were very similar to each other. To Paul's mind they became a long single whole. The monotony of the landscape joined with the regularity of the journey. They could travel for two hours at a time, after which they had a stop and if they were hungry, a meal. They slept, as they had done up to this point, in tents. Only the Sámi woman refused to sleep with Lady and Little Lula and instead she prepared a bed for herself on the cart under the open sky.

The only thing that changed over these days was the attitude of Grouch. Formerly Ralph Wronski would never miss a single opportunity to be acerbic. But now he was silent. Even when during one stop Paul tripped over a stone sticking out of the ground and fell almost on his face, Grouch did not take the opportunity to taunt him. The boy wondered if Grouch's calm resulted from exhaustion or whether it was a sign of some deeper change. At present, however, there was no way to answer this riddle.

On the sixth day they made camp in open land, since they could not find shelter anywhere. Paul noticed that Traveller carefully studied his maps and in the evening he looked at the stars analysing their positions with compass in hand. Knight had the impression that the man was unhappy about something. When after a long time he had failed to come to bed, the boy left the tent so as to ask him if anything had happened.

'Yes, I'm a little worried about the direction we are travelling. I'm beginning to wonder if this girl is indeed helping us. She sees Tiger, so she knows the Crooked World, but really I don't know what her intentions are. In the end Enemy also has a good understanding of this world,' explained the captain.

'But why are you suspicious? Where are we?'

'We're travelling too far west to get to Alta. Furthermore, I get the impression that every day we're straying ever more from our northbound route.'

'And can't we show her with gestures that we're heading in the wrong direction? Show her on the map where according to you we are and where we would like to go? She doesn't look as if she's got a compass so maybe she's just taking us towards Alta by way of feel.'

Traveller gave him an irritated look. 'You're talking rubbish. Firstly, I've already shown her maps, she only shakes her head. Secondly, nomadic people never travel 'by way of feel'. Most often they are able to tell their position perfectly with only the location of the sun or stars. I don't think that the girl in this respect is any different from the rest of her people.'

'I'm sure you're right. But I don't think that she's bad in any way. Maybe this route is easier?'

'The maps don't show any kind of obstruction along the direct route. It seems to me that you've fallen for the woman,' Traveller gave him a malicious stare through half closed eyes, 'you're so keen on defending her.'

Knight shrugged and looked aside.

'I just don't want to make rash accusations against her... And for what reason have I got to straight away be in love with her?' he snorted, after which he added, 'you've got to admit she's a bit strange.'

'Yes, strange. That's what's beginning to worry me. If she doesn't turn around, in the end we're going to have to decline her help and continue on foot,' said the captain as if he had not noticed Paul's irritation. 'Well, it's nothing, let's go to bed. Although I must admit that I'm more and more thinking about setting up a night watch. Sleeping as unwarily as we've been doing is becoming dangerous. From my calculations we might soon be entering the mountain range that stretches along the coast. I don't think we'd be able to go any further by cart. If we stray too far south of Alta, we'll have to spend a lot of time crossing the mountains or turn back and go along them.'

With these words Traveller headed off to the tent. Paul followed entering straight after him and without a word lay down on his bed. For a long time he couldn't fall asleep. Before his eyes he saw the memory of what he had seen on the third day of their journey during their stop: the cold fire that engulfed everything but had only wrapped around the girl like a cloak.

A surprise was waiting for them the next morning. Neither the girl nor the cart was there. Traveller swore violently. Tiger went around the area trying to pick up the scent of the reindeer.

'This is impossible!' exclaimed Lady. 'After all she didn't say that she was going to leave us.'

'Indeed. Perhaps because she didn't speak at all,' said Grouch.

Lady looked at him angrily. 'Maybe she's somewhere nearby. Maybe she wanted to have a drive around and will come back?'

Traveller looked at her with irritation but when he spoke his voice was mild, 'Daisy, we are in open country. We can see everything all the way to the mountains in a range of many miles. Where could she hide here if she only wanted to drive around? She must have left us long ago in the night.'

Tears appeared in Daisy's eyes. 'I don't understand at all. She was such a good, helpful girl. Why would she leave us in such a manner? What are we going to do now?'

Traveller took her tentatively by the arm. 'Nothing's happened. We'll go on further on foot as we did earlier. We have maps and a compass and somehow we'll find our way. To have been able to travel by cart was an unexpected bit of help anyway so we should rather be glad that we could make use of it.'

Paul remembered his conversation with Traveller the previous day. He was not so convinced that he did indeed view the situation so optimistically. But Paul said nothing. Lady, however, let the captain's words cheer her.

After breakfast, which took place in silence, they started packing up, while Traveller spent a long time sitting over his maps considering the position that had been marked out in pencil. Paul took a look at it over his shoulder and froze. They were exactly to the west of the place where they had started their cart ride at an even greater distance from Alta than then. He felt himself take in a sharp breath of air.

Traveller suddenly turned around and looked at him. 'Don't say anything,' he hissed.

'But why didn't you say anything earlier? We've been going the wrong way since the very beginning. Yesterday I understood that we'd only strayed a little from our route!'

'I don't know. I simply don't know what happened. I didn't check the road so carefully at the beginning. I could see that we were going more to the west, but I must have gone blank. It's only two days ago that I noticed something was wrong. But don't tell anyone. There's no reason why they should worry about this.'

Paul thought that Traveller must have only been talking about Lady, because he did not expect him to care so much about Grouch and very few matters in her life worried Little Lula.

'In the end their going to realise anyway. We're now going to spend more time walking. How long are you able to hide this from them? Probably a couple of days.'

'Maybe, but now there's no point in starting a panic.' It was difficult not to agree on this point.

Soon they set off. Paul had to admit that at least the going was easier through such an open, almost empty space that now spread out in front of them. At a distance they passed by a great lake, the water of which shone like an emerald. When they stopped for a moment Paul looked at its green surface and remembered the ship voyage, which was such a distant memory that it seemed to have taken place a long time ago. He shut his eyes for a moment to recall that ever-present sky blue, that sun which roasted the body, that peace that he had in his heart then practising and preparing to do battle with Dragon. But what exactly were they now heading towards? Where was Enemy? What were they meant to look for in Alta? The key? But how? A sea of doubts again flooded the boy's heart. He remembered the Book that had last time given him so much strength, 'It's time that you made your way to Alta. You must go overland.'

They were meant to go overland, but why? He'd never thought about this. Maybe the goal wasn't Alta itself, but something along the way? Only that there could be many routes that led different ways… But there is only one main route, something in his head answered Knight. Only one way leads directly from the Baltic. The route from the South. But they had already strayed from it. He had to talk to Traveller about this. He moved forward in order to catch up with captain, who was striding away at the front.

Mr Wronski listened to him carefully. He only nodded his head thoughtfully. Knight waited patiently for his opinion but before the man ordered a stop and took him aside to talk to him, quite some time had passed.

'So you're suggesting that Enemy in the form of the Sámi woman diverted us from the main route, along which we were meant to find something?' Traveller summed up with a question.

'I… I don't know. I mean maybe it's so. I just thought that for some reason the Author of the Book wanted us to get to Alta overland. He didn't specify exactly which way he meant but it seems to me that the route from the south is the most obvious one that he could have meant.'

Knight flounced around with his explanations. Although everything did indeed seem to point to the Sámi woman not having helped them at all, he wasn't yet ready to openly accept it. The memory of her beautiful singing and the gentleness with which she had stroked Tiger and the dove meant that he was still unable to believe that she had had evil intentions.

Traveller looked thoughtfully into the distance.

'Do you think that we should go back to that route?' he asked. 'I had planned to go exactly north-east and join up with our previous trail three quarters of the way along it.' Under normal circumstances Paul would have been insanely proud that the captain, who thus far had rather been limited to giving orders, had asked for his opinion before a decision was taken. But now he felt too uneasy about the situation to pay any attention to it.

'I don't know. It's still difficult for me to believe in the bad will of this girl. If you had heard her sing… And that dove in her hand…'

'What?' asked Traveller surprised.

'On the third day during one of our stops… I followed her. She stood among the trees holding a small dove in her hand and again she hummed something beautiful.'

The captain stared wide-eyed at him. He had probably never reacted with such surprise at any other of the wonders of the Crooked World.

'And is there anything else?' he asked as if feeling that Knight hadn't given everything away to him yet.

'Well, aaah, it's hard for me to talk about this… Because I apparently saw this… but it probably didn't take place… I mean…'

'Speak clearly, I can see you're keeping something important back.'

Paul felt as if he had been pinned to a wall. He did not understand why what he had seen should have such huge importance. He also felt that this was his most wonderful secret, which he did not want to share with anyone. Something that had been given only to him. Traveller's stern look, however, did not give him any choice. When he spoke he felt as if some part of his very self was being ripped out.

'I suddenly saw everything in flames. Everything around me. It seemed to me that I too was burning inside, as if in the very heart. Only the girl stood unmoved in the flames. But then suddenly I realised that this fire didn't burn… it was cold. And then everything ended.' He wondered if he should add something. 'And then she tried to tell me something, but I didn't know what it meant.'

'What did she say?' asked Mr Wronski with a voice that croaked with anticipation.

'I don't remember any more. But… she repeated the same word three times: 'Ipmil'.'

Traveller stood dumbstruck with boggle eyes. Neither the wonders on the island of Shemesh nor Eyma nor even the secret of the Book had made such an impression on him. After some time Paul began to wonder if the captain, who was standing still, wasn't by chance about to turn into a pillar of salt. Just in case he looked behind himself to check that it was not something behind him that had had this effect on him, but he couldn't see anything. So he took him lightly by the arms and shook him.

'Is everything all right? Has something happened?'

Mr Wronski looked at him a little more soberly and came round a little.

'You really don't understand anything. I cannot make head or tail of why Friend made someone like you Knight.' Traveller turned away as if he were deeply disappointed in Paul. But Paul did not understand what was going on. How was he supposed to know what 'Ipmil' meant or what it was with that strange fire? Why had all of this made such an impression on the captain. He caught him by the arm.

'Captain,' he said gently, 'maybe you could simply explain to me what this is about? I don't know the Sámi language. I don't know what she said and I've never come across such fire before.'

For a while they were both silent. Traveller sighed.

'I don't know what I should tell you. Just tell me, do you think that it was Dragon's fire?'

The question surprised Paul. 'No, it didn't even come into my head. Really I don't know. When it had finished I simply thought it was a figment of my imagination.'

'Well, OK, but could it have been Dragon's fire?'

'No, it wasn't for sure. In the Book when the beast breathed fire at me, I felt the most terrible heat. That fire didn't burn.'

'Oh stop analysing it like that. It's important what you felt. You said that the flames touched your heart. What did you feel?'

Knight still did not know what Traveller was on about. What a strange question: what did he feel! But he was slowly beginning to realise that a moment ago he had thought of that event as his most intimate secret… Yes, it was something unusual, something wonderful, something that he wanted never to forget.

'I think I felt... simply happy. There was something wonderful about this. When I think about it I'm calm.'

Traveller looked upon him with distant eyes. To Paul it seemed that he was almost sad that he hadn't been given the opportunity to feel that fire.

"Ipmil'. I don't know the language,' he said slowly, 'but I do know what 'Ipmil' means, as it's part of a Sámi greeting.' Paul looked at him questioningly. "Ipmil' means creator.'

**Chapter twenty two**

# A MEETING
# IN THE AIR

Traveller's words resonated for a long time in the silence that seemed so complete that it sounded. Every drop of blood in Knight's body flowed through his veins with a great whoosh, the earth beneath his feet roared with its secret existence and the air sang the melody of life. Somewhere in the immeasurable distance the wheezing of charging reindeer bounced with a booming echo among the mountains on the peaks of which ice cracked. And somewhere beneath all of this a thunderous laugh could be heard, which filled the whole of creation with joy... Just as if it were the building material of everything that existed. For a moment it even seemed to Knight that the pale moon, visible in the pale blue sky would explode with the force of this laughter and in the immeasurable distance stars invisible to him were filled with light like fireworks.

The whole universe thundered with the joy of creation.

And just like fire, in just one moment it went out. So that loud silence vanished from Knight's head. A quietness arose, more ordinary and much less real than the earlier silent tumult.

Traveller was still looking at him sadly. In this look, Paul could read the story of the many years the man had used up in search of just what he himself had experienced in one totally undeserved moment: seeing the very depths of what exists. The depths that reach down below everything that is visible. The depths that touch the Maker of all creation: the very Author of the work. Knight knew that he would never with words be able to express to Traveller the immeasurable beauty of these depths, he would never be able to repeat the thunderous laughter, with which Voice brought to life the world of the Book.

Why was it he who had experienced this? They stood opposite each other for a long time: a boy only just verging on manhood, to whom, due to Friend's joyful caprice, had been revealed the beauty of this world, and a mature man, who in his own wisdom still stubbornly searched with all his strength for this same beauty.

Knight wanted to tell him to reach out with his hand and grasp it. Was it really so simple? He also wanted to tell him to stop leading and let himself be guided by he who knew better, by he who knew everything to the last page of the Book, to hand over responsibility for the expedition to the very one that will lead us straight to our goal. But that silence that fell between them, which was so full of unsaid words, was interrupted by Grouch.

'Have you so fallen in love that you need the support of such a kid? What is it, little brother? You look – you world conqueror – as if you've become rather melancholy,' and with these words on his lips, he laughed.

Traveller's face became concentrated with rage. He spun round to face his brother and spat on the ground after which he walked off without a word.

Paul watched what happened with sadness. He looked at Grouch, who in his miserable meanness was really so full of pain and jealousy. He remembered what Friend had once said. He had been good friends with Ralph until he had longed to be someone other than who he was. But could he really have been happy as a simple carpenter? And was Granny happy as a cook, he asked himself. He knew the answer. The memory of her gentle smile and the shine in her grey eyes were sufficient answer. Maybe it wasn't everyone's lot to become a knight. But really could anyone envy him the fact that since his battle with Dragon he had had to bear that terrible deformed picture of his own self inside? The monstrous face again wanted to come to the surface of his mind and he pushed it down deep inside into those same depths from where Voice's thunderous laughter came. He knew that when the time came to face the beast he would have to, above all, do battle with this nightmare reflection. What would he do then? And what had he done when at the top of the lighthouse, shut in the room of mirrors, each of which had shown an ever more ghoulish face? He'd dropped his torch and called on Friend.

This time he couldn't dally longer. Lady called them another time for a meal. The atmosphere was clearly tense. They'd already begun eating when

Tiger appeared, who could not get over the disappearance of the Sámi woman and sniffed all around in the hope of picking up her trail. He ran up to them cheerfully with a piece of dried meat in his muzzle.

'Look what I've found,' he panted after he spat his prize out on the ground.

'What, meat? We've got more than enough of that, brother,' said Grouch.

Tiger looked at him with contempt. 'I can see that observant you are not. This piece of meat comes from the parcel that the Sámi woman took with her. She must have lost it, which means she's travelling along the same route in front of us.' The last words he exclaimed with joy.

But no one reacted with enthusiasm. Paul looked with some interest at Traveller to see if this information had somehow affected his opinion of the girl; however the man sat with a face like stone.

'Well, aren't you happy?' asked Tiger surprised.

'What have we to be happy about?' replied the captain. 'We're not going to be able to catch her up anyway. Besides we don't know what her intentions towards us are.' On saying this Traveller looked aside, clearly trying to avoid Knight's gaze. Then, after finishing their meal he was so busy with packing up the provisions that Paul did not have the opportunity to talk to him privately. The boy very much wanted to find out what their plans were. After all, not long ago they had considered returning to the original route, due to the words of the Book. Paul, however, suspected that his story about the Sámi woman standing in fire had convinced Traveller to keep on travelling straight on and Tiger's find had only strengthened this decision. Paul was now sure that the girl was not on the side of Enemy: How else could she have experienced this fire? Clearly, Traveller understood this too and saw this as a sign that they were on the right trail. But the riddle of why she had left them remained. Knight very much wanted to hear the captain's opinion about this. His judgements on situations were often fairly accurate. Well, maybe with the exception of the last one.

They set off. For a whole day their route led them straight through what seemed a huge empty area towards a great mass of mountains on the horizon. After a certain amount of time Paul noticed that they were approaching a huge yet shallow valley, which looked like a massive scarlet pool. For a moment he thought that this had to be some trick of the eyes, but the cries of the others convinced him that the sight was real. The closer they approached the red flood, the more they were struck by the intensity of its colour. It seemed that such a thing could not be found anywhere else, at least not to such an extent. When they entered into the crimson sheet they discovered that the whole valley was covered by low plants whose leaves had this unusual colour.

'Arctic willow!' exclaimed Traveller in wonder. 'I've heard about this plant. It apparently looks completely normal until autumn when its leaves turn red and it creates huge stretches similar to lakes of blood.' The view was truly incredible. They slowly walked into this remarkable valley as if they were afraid to disturb the beauty of the landscape. Only Little Lula shouted with delight and ran straight ahead diving into the waves of red. Tiger followed after. After a while they began to play, to jump and to roll around on the ground with the delight that only befitted little children and animals. Knight very much wanted to join them but he felt some resistance within himself. To his surprise, it was Traveller who was first to run after them. He caught Little Lula in the air and began to spin her around to the squeals of her delight. Lady with a shout of joy joined in the fun leaving Paul behind with Grouch. It was strange but he did not want to leave him alone, stewing, as usual, in his own bitterness. When he looked at the man's face, however, instead of his usual grimace, he saw a thin smile. Ralph, it seemed, was not looking at all in front of him but rather somewhere in the depths of his own memory. Now Knight no longer waited for anything; he just left his companion to his own thoughts and chased after the others.

It was difficult to say how long they frolicked in this red fluff. In the end Grouch came up to them and played with Little Lula, while the others danced to the singing of Daisy. How great their joy was! What a beautiful world it was, which they had come to travel through! When they were all tired out, they sat on the ground to rest and eat.

For the rest of the day they waded through the red, slowly approaching the mountains. Their route was heading ever more upwards. They were in good spirits, even though Tiger didn't find any new signs of the reindeer cart. The next day they set off at dawn, which at this time of year broke before eight o'clock in the morning. Traveller expected they should reach the mountains around midday.

The scrub was becoming ever thinner. Although it still had that beautiful crimson hue, in places bare rock peeped out from beneath it. They had already been walking for about two hours and the clouds had begun to thicken as if they were gathering up for rain. All of a sudden, Knight slipped on some rocks and hit his head on the ground. Traveller gave him his hand and when the boy stood up, Lady exclaimed in horror, 'Oh no! You've hurt yourself really badly.'

'What do you mean?' said Paul in surprise. Though the fall wasn't particularly pleasant, he did not feel like he was injured in any way.

'You've got blood all over your face,' captain explained to him. 'You must have hurt yourself.'

'That's strange. It doesn't hurt so badly.'

Daisy took out a handkerchief, soaked it in water and began to wipe Paul's face.

It took a moment until the captain stated with a dry voice, 'Indeed you're not hurt at all.'

'Well, that explains everything,' said Grouch enigmatically.

'What does it explain?' asked Lady.

'Strange. Everywhere there's the smell of blood,' Tiger interjected unexpectedly.

'That's because there's no longer red Arctic willow. There's blood everywhere. A sea of blood,' continued Grouch.

Before he'd even finished, they all understood what he was thinking. For quite some time, they hadn't wanted at all to look down. Now they had no choice. They looked under their feet. On the rocks there was blood and the moss that covered the rocks was also saturated by it. What was worse, it seemed to them that the gore welled into a thick stream. They were filled with the terror of soon being flooded and drowned.

'Run! Upwards! Fast!' Traveller barked quickly.

They ran. Grouch grabbed Little Lula under the arms. Traveller pulled Lady. It seemed with every step the broad river of blood rose. A shadow covered the sun. Knight half closed his eyes and for a while ran blindly. Daisy's scream confirmed his worst fears. What the captain had feared for a long time had happened: Enemy was attacking them in the tundra, where they were completely out in the open without the possibility of taking shelter. Did that mean that they were going to have to fight Dragon in such unfavourable conditions?

No one now doubted that directly above them in the sky flew an enormous beast. It was only a question of time before it began its descent to attack them.

Unfortunately the mountains were not an inch closer and it was ever harder for them to run forward across the slippery blood-covered rocks.

The shadow grew larger. Dragon swooped down on them. Knight stood his ground and pulled out his sword from the layers of his clothing. For a short moment he saw the figure of Elf, whom he had long ago forgotten about. And as he was mentally preparing for battle with the monster, he felt someone grab his right forearm pulling his weapon aside.

'You idiot! Do you want to measure up against Dragon?'

'And what am I meant to do, he's attacking us,' he replied angrily.

'There's a time to fight and a time to protect yourself. Now we've got to run,' replied Traveller with surprising calm, while Dragon was momentarily slowing its flight.

'And where do you want to run? There's nothing here. We have no choice but to fight.'

'How little you understand! You push forwards as if you were blind and that mad Friend still insists on making you a Knight.' Traveller's last words were said with an almost pleasant sarcasm. 'I've called Arie.'

Before the meaning of the captain's last words fully sank in to Paul, who was stubbornly stuck in his own thoughts, they looked down under their feet and saw the river of blood turn almost in front of their eyes into a carpet of flowers. At this same moment a deafening cry resounded in the air. He who was to save them had come. With a flap of huge white wings a gigantic eagle appeared before them. To Knight he seemed much bigger than he had before. Dragon circled angrily above them as they climbed onto Arie's back. There was room for everyone, including Tiger. They flew high up in the air. For a moment they were at the same height as the beast, which was almost frozen motionless, and they could see it up close. The monstrous muzzle of Dragon was twisted into a horrifying grimace. His yellow eyes were empty and dead and from his mouth no fire came forth, only a feeble wisp of smoke. Still full of fear, Knight looked into the abyss of his mirrored wings. There in the depths, instead of a deformed reflection of their world, he saw fire. In one moment when Arie turned in the direction of the monster and looked upon him for an instant, it seemed that Dragon was burning up in this conflagration. He now looked truly terrible, like a disgusting fly of unbelievably huge proportions burning from within. There was none of that threat in him that

Knight remembered from their first confrontation. Arie quickly turned his glance away, as if there was nothing about this sight that could interest him, and with a loud flap of his stretched out wings, he flew off to the mountains.

Chapter twenty three
# IN THE MOUNTAINS

Nobody looked behind themselves to see if Dragon was following them.

Did it make any difference?

'That's not the end of it,' Elf whispered suddenly, who had caught onto Paul's coat with his little golden fingers.

Arie picked up the pace and soon they were hurtling through the sky at a breakneck speed. The swish of the air in the ears was deafening. The mountains grew in size in front of their eyes and soon they clearly saw great stretches of snow on the peaks. Ever higher and higher flew their powerful saviour all the way up to the icy heights. Paul could feel the bite of the ever cooler air, and he was very cold. Lead-coloured clouds gathered in the sky, which had not been there in the morning. Before they realised it had grown darker. And so they found themselves flying high in the mountains. After a certain time Arie began to descend and plunged between the steep slopes. Paul almost in disbelief noticed that a light snow had begun to fall. Had everything turned against them? A blizzard was gathering. The frost stung their faces and their lips froze in pain in the piercing wind. On the peak that they had just passed, Paul suddenly noticed little lights. He looked surprised that there could be people so high up and he froze in fear. Elf had been right. Even though Dragon had not decided to fight with Arie, he had not wanted to let them go so easily and was now following them with his shining yellow eyes from the very summit of the mountain.

How long had they flown? His benumbed limbs told him that it had been very long indeed. The darkness that was falling around them could mean that the sun had already gone down. When would they be able to stop at last? The number of questions increased, together with the growing tiredness and the initial relief at the appearance of Arie was replaced in their hearts by bitterness due to the ever harsher frost. Shortly, however, the eagle completely unexpectedly landed in a hollow in the rocks which provided them with a little cover from the wind. They slowly climbed down from his back.

'That was one of the worst nightmares of my life! What are you going to serve us up next?' exclaimed Grouch. In a single second Arie turned around and caught the man in his beak by the coat on his back and left him hanging above a precipice. The unfortunate man let out a terrible squeal and everybody else stepped back in fear as not much was required for them to voice Mr Wronski's opinion and share his fate.

'No, no,' whined Grouch with a weak voice, 'I... I didn't want to!'

Instead of putting the poor man back down on the ground, Arie only shook him more until he repeated his still desperate cries.

'No, I beg you! I didn't want to! I... thank you for the rescue! You saved us! Oh, great and wonderful Lion. You are our saviour. Thank you a hundredfold.'

And only now did the eagle delicately place Grouch on the rock on which they were sheltering. The unfortunate man was still breathing hard in fear but he threw himself on the ground and prostrated himself before Arie all the while mumbling, 'Thank you, oh, great lord of air and fire. You have saved us from the terrible Dragon and we will be thankful to you for that forever.'

The poor man looked as if he had lost his mind. Knight felt really sorry for him. Meanwhile the eagle sat back on his lion paws and, with head held aloft, looked down at him from on high.

'You should have stayed in Gdansk and worked honestly as a carpenter instead of sneaking onto a ship and setting off on an expedition for which you had no calling,' he added cuttingly, 'but since you're here, you'd do well at least to thank everyone for patiently bearing your constant spitefulness.'

With these words Arie at last turned away from Grouch and began to look into the impenetrable distance before him. Mr Wronski stood up and still tottering, began thanking everyone effusively for their patience. No one dared stop him in the presence of Arie, but nonetheless, Traveller, after a while, took out from his bag an extra sweater and began to dress his older brother like a little child. He stroked his head while he was doing it, quietly saying, 'It's OK. Everything's OK. We understand. We forgive you. Really we're glad that you're with us, because it's always more cheerful with you. You should drink something. It was indeed a difficult journey.'

Grouch sat down meekly and Little Lula cuddled up to him in silence. Lady took out their already meagre supplies and they began to eat. Arie sat with his back to them as if he wasn't paying them any attention.

When they had finished eating they began to wonder if they would be able to sleep at all in this place. Traveller was against it as he regarded it as dangerous to sleep in such a frost when they were not dressed warmly enough. On hearing these words the eagle turned around, but this time he had a gentle expression.

'Maybe you do indeed need a moment's rest. There's a difficult journey ahead of us. Get some sleep,' and after saying this Arie lightly moved his dove-like wings, under which spread a wonderful light, lighting up the entire rocky ledge they were sitting on. It was warm, almost soothing and Knight felt himself involuntarily falling into a deep sleep and dream again of walking in a large meadow full of red poppies.

When they awoke, the light around them went out. The darkness of the night was impenetrable. Arie stood fully alert looking into the distance. When they had collected themselves together, he turned around and said, 'We are in the heart of darkness. Some dreadful evil lurks in these mountains, but you are not allowed to think of that. Here in the ice and danger there is a little house. You must make your way to it. There you will find people who will help you.'

'You're leaving us?' Lady blurted out.

'Not yet, but I'm not going with you all the way. But I'm going to leave you something that will help you reach your destination. It's not time to talk about this. Get on.' With these words Arie sat down in order to make it easier for them to clambered onto his back. Tiger cautiously climbed up the eagle's body. Since the time he had first flown on him, he had been totally silent, as if the proximity of such a powerful predator had taken away his power of speech. When they had all sat down, Arie slowly spread his wings and ascended into the snowy darkness. Again they felt the piercing cold of the howling wind. Flakes of ice immediately froze their cheeks. They had been flying for some time when suddenly Knight realised that somewhere deep amidst the howling wind could be heard something that sounded like a hiss… He turned around and then he saw Dragon flying a little to the side above them.

The Beast looked at them with eyes full of silent rage. For a moment Paul and the monster looked at each other. Then in the gaze of the reptile appeared a contemptuous sneer. Knight knew that Dragon would not attack Arie, but in spite of this he was not going to drop his guard.

Next everything happened as if in slow motion. Dragon pointed his huge head towards an overhanging rock under which they were flying and spat out a jet of fire. The whole mountain shook and bits of rock began to fall on them. They heard a noise similar to thunder and saw a gigantic boulder teetering above them and slowly fall.

Knight's blood chilled in his veins at the horror. Dragon was not brave enough to attack Arie, but he certainly intended to impede his flight. And then, as if it were nothing, the eagle spread his resplendent wings even wider and from in between his feathers fire – of course – shot out.

A powerful illuminating cold fire that engulfed the falling boulder and blasted it into a fine dust. The ash fell on them like a soothing dew.

It had begun.

It was a terrible battle of fire. Dragon dared not attack them straight on, but he did everything in his power so that the rocks would injure them. He melted an ice-sheet with fire spreading from his maw and it flowed down on them just like hot lava. He smashed the mountains with his tail like a flail[6] creating rockfalls. With his claws, he ripped up huge boulders, which he threw in front of them. The huge rocks were like sandcastles or like piles of stones collected by a child, which could be knocked over with ease. All of this was accompanied by a terrifying roar, which went right down into the bone marrow, as if the cold alone had not been enough. Fire, ice, rocks, the terrible crash of stones and the howling of Dragon. Nothing apart from them seemed to exist. Knight had never imagined that he would come to experience something like this.

But this was all nothing. Like frost retreating from the warmth of someone's breath, like the gentle warmth of a hearth that slowly thaws chilled fingers, like the whisper of one's beloved in the darkness of the night, all of it: the

6   A type of melee weapon comprising a spiked ball on a chain connected to a handle

horror, fire, falling rocks, boulders and howls, melted away under the delicate touch of Arie's light. Everything it touched turned into a life-giving warm dew. Not once did the eagle falter. He flew steadily like a star following its orbit. The longer Arie remained unperturbed, the greater seemed to be the anger that overcame Dragon. As if he realised that there was nothing that could be done to shake his eternal adversary. As if he knew that here in this dangerous land where he had always ruled a power had entered against whom his own strength was simply the preposterous yapping of a little dog.

For Knight this entire flight had been like a ride on a roller coaster at a theme park. He felt the hideous terror of the situation and he had goose bumps each time that another boulder almost hit them. But at the same time the power emanating from Arie was simply intoxicating and when the power of his fire turned huge rocks to dust, Paul felt such joy that he wanted to laugh aloud. He knew that even in the chaos of destruction that surrounded them, he was safe on the back of the eagle.

Suddenly Dragon disappeared and there was silence. They flew on between the snowy peaks barely visible in the darkness.

'Ha!' shouted Grouch behind Knight's back. 'We've made it. He's gone. Oh, great and powerful Arie, nobody can match you!'

The voices of the others repeated this sentiment. The eagle took the cheers in silence as if his victory had been too obvious for him to accept the praise. Or maybe it was because he was too busy staring into the almost impenetrable gloom? Knight could feel under his skin that this wasn't the end, that before them lay many miles of travelling through the mountains, among which, as Arie had said, evil lurked.

They flew on for maybe another half an hour. They had time to calm down after the fiery battle. Then the eagle unexpectedly landed on the soft powdery snow. It must have been very late at night, sometime around two in the morning. Being exhausted they hoped that it was time for a stop. Little Lula had already been sleeping for a long time and was being held by Lady.

'What are you thinking? It's no time to rest!' Arie scolded them. 'You have to go on alone.'

'Alone?' Traveller was dumbstruck. 'In this darkness? We're in the mountains. We don't have enough light to go anywhere safely.'

Arie's eyes flashed threateningly.

'Oh, ye of little faith! After what you've seen, you still think that I will leave you to your fate?' With these words the eagle flapped his vast wings, from under which appeared a large ball of light that illuminated the darkness of the night around them. 'Within it you are safe. It will illuminate your path for as long as you wish. No one else can see it so you will remain unseen. I don't want you to freeze so in its glow you will be warm.'

Knight thought that despite his austere appearance and proud behaviour, Arie was very carefully looking after them. They stood a moment in silence. The eagle looked at Little Lula, who now slept sweetly in the arms of Lady. And suddenly he did something that Paul would never have expected of him. He turned his head to the side and with a sharp yank he pulled out one white feather from his wing. It was very long and, as it turned out, as soft as down, while at the same time being very strong since with ease the two ends could be tied together to form a cradle shape. It was big enough for Grouch to place Little Lula in without the slightest difficulty and he slung it over his shoulder. The head of the girl, who was now being carried in this rather unusual sling, rested on Mr Wronski's chest.

'Thank you,' said Grouch and his eyes shone with true gratitude.

Strangely these two words seemed worth far more than his earlier obsequious bowing to Arie, which had been done in a somewhat coerced manner. Even though the girl already weighed quite a lot and must have been quite a burden for Grouch, this seemed not to be of any concern to the man. He looked almost happy that he had been granted the privilege of carrying her in the feather.

'Show me the map,' Arie demanded of Traveller. 'I'll show you the place to which you've got to head.'

The captain obediently took out the drawings. The eagle showed them where they were with his giant lion's paw. It turned out that they had flown south west from the place where they had come across Dragon, which meant they had been heading in a different direction to the one they had been earlier. Their journey's end lay still a little bit further to the south.

After a while they were alone. Arie had ascended into the sky and disappeared behind the cover of darkness. Although they very much wanted to see him still, they were unable to enlarge the aura so much that it would illuminate the gloom into which he had disappeared. They set off slowly. It turned out that they had to traverse a ridge between two quite distant peaks. It was hard going and despite the brightness they made their way forward very slowly.

After walking for two hours they were very tired. No longer was anyone but Traveller hiding that they had had enough.

'Maybe we could make a stop if only for a moment? We haven't eaten for some time...' suggested Lady.

'I agree. We should collect our strength before moving on. We don't know how much longer we will be walking for. If we've got to reach that peak, we've got a trek of many hours ahead of us,' added Grouch.

Traveller kept quiet. He walked on, not paying attention to the words of his companions.

'Oh!' cried Lady after a while.

'Traveller, I don't think that Arie was demanding that we not rest even for a moment. We should rest,' blurted out Paul.

The captain stopped and suddenly spun round to face them. 'I know, I know you're tired. I am too. But, Knight, he did say something exactly like that. When we wanted to rest, he said there was no time for that, and that we had to go on. I believe that his light will protect us and ensure that we reach our goal safely.' Traveller wanted to atone for his previous lack of faith.

'But look,' Paul wasn't giving up, 'Lady can hardly go on any more, Grouch is carrying Little Lula, and we're all exhausted.'

Mr Wronski looked at Daisy and tenderness appeared in his eyes. But he immediately turned around back in the direction they were heading.

'I can give you some support if it helps,' he said to Lady behind him.

'No, thank you, I can cope,' she said proudly.

Traveller led on in front without a word. The others followed him in silence. The atmosphere was evidently tense. They carried on like this for about a quarter of an hour, when they suddenly saw a little light. They clearly picked up the pace. After a while it could be seen, in the spreading glow of the light, that before them stood a little house. Was this the place that Arie had sent them to? Their hearts began to beat faster. They were walking now as fast as they were able. Questions came to Knight's mind of where such a hut, being so high up and in such difficult conditions, had come from and why there was a light at such a late hour. But he was not able to answer them himself. After another ten minutes they at last reached the door.

They knocked. No one answered. They looked at each other scared. After all there was a light in the house... Then the door opened. An old man, with a slight hunch stood in the doorway. He was dressed in thick fur and had a broad face, typical of the Sámi. He looked at them and with a hand gesture invited them in.

Inside the hut was very cosily furnished in wood. A number of folk decorations also added warmth. In front of the lit fireplace stood three chairs of an uninteresting dun colour. Two of them were occupied. Someone sitting in one of the chairs said something in a voice croaky with old age. The person spoke in an unknown language. To Knight it seemed to sound like the language of the Sámi. The old man replied, probably saying something about the arrival of the guests. Two women stood up slowly from their seats. One of them was old with long grey hair, tied in a ponytail. She had rather European facial features. And the other one... Knight froze.

It was the Sámi woman.

And so she had arrived here before them. She must have driven her reindeer to their last breath. The fact that they had gone out of their way firstly heading too far north had certainly helped her. Deep down the question return to Knight of why she had left them in the first place. She smiled shyly. They stood as if stunned and she walked up to Lady, who was exhausted, tenderly caught her by the arm and led her to a chair. The old man was already helping Grouch take the sleeping Little Lula and place her on the simple bed  that was next to the opposite wall. The old woman prepared hot tea for them in the little kitchen after which she took some food from an opening in the ground closed off with a hatch and set about preparing a meal in silence. Next the girl brought them a number of furs in which they dressed after having taken off their wet clothes. Paul looked at her questioningly as if he expected her to explain her sudden disappearance, but her gentle smile made him realise that she was clearly being directed by the wishes of Friend.

When they sat down in the chairs and on an old battered couch, which stood against the wall next to a huge set of shelves full of books, they felt almost as if they were in heaven. It was so warm and cosy here and the hot tea and delicious food... No one minded the silence between them and their hosts. Tiger sat down next to the Sámi woman who delicately stroked him, just like the time Paul had seen her in the tundra. Falling into the warm reindeer skins, Knight felt himself falling asleep.

As he was thinking about having a short nap, the old woman called over to him, 'I hope you've all already had some rest.'

These words were so unexpectedly understandable to Paul that it was only after a while that he realised they had been spoken in English, which he was learning at school. The others were clearly equally surprised.

'Do you speak English?' asked Traveller fluently. The woman smiled with a light in her eye.

'I can see you're all surprised. Yes I do. That must be good for you.'

'Of course it is. It's simply that we didn't expect it. Do... do they understand us too?' Traveller pointed to the old man and the girl.

'No, they're native Sámi. They've never had the need to learn English. I come from the south and it was only after I was married that I came to live here.'

'Here?' asked Knight uncertainly.

'Yes, here. Are you surprised that one can live in such a house in such conditions?' the old woman asked him directly.

Paul felt embarrassed at having asked such a question, even though he really had wanted to know the answer. The woman did not, however, seem at all offended by his doubts.

'It's sometimes worth giving up all the comforts of the civilised world, the company of other people and even one's own safety, if in exchange one receives a treasure of greater value than everything else taken together.'

Knight raised his eyebrows, not daring to ask any more questions.

'Here among the mountain ice sheets next to my husband is a much richer world than anything down there in the lowlands,' she said with a smile. 'I know, it's difficult to comprehend. But I hope that you will soon find out about this for yourself. But now it's time that you got some rest. Beds have been prepared for you here in that room. Tiger can lie down on this blanket by the fireplace.'

On saying this she showed them a door leading to an adjacent room. Indeed there were four sheeted mattresses. It was the only other room in the house apart from the main room with the entrance.

'And where are you going to sleep?' asked Traveller.

'Don't worry. We can snooze in our chairs. We're not so exhausted by travel as you.' Only our daughter also has to rest after the difficulties of a long journey, but she can sleep on the couch.' And with these words she closed the door behind her leaving them alone.

They went to their beds without a word. The thought occurred to Paul that Traveller had been right: it had not been worth stopping to rest so soon before reaching their destination. Eventually he fell into a deep sleep.

The next day they ate a delicious breakfast, prepared by the young Sámi woman. It was made up of freshly baked bread and goat's milk. As it turned out, at these heights there were mountain goats that, although not usually farm animals, had been tamed by the old man and provided the married couple with milk. Other than that there was only honey. Despite the simplicity of this meal, after two weeks of eating dried biscuits, dried reindeer meat and whatever berries they had found along the way, everyone was pleased with the change and with the meal's freshness. After breakfast their hosts encouraged them to walk around the vicinity so they all dressed up warmly.

Now they had the opportunity to look at the mountains up close. They were vast and massive and they made a truly extraordinary impression. They rose out of the very valleys, which made them seem huge, although, as Paul knew from his geography lessons, these mountains were no higher than other mountains such as the Alps. From the height at which they found themselves they could see countless lakes below, which changed colours with the light of the sun and created an unusually mysterious impression. The house where they were staying was high enough for there to be snow on the ground at this time of year – that is in the second half of October. Above ice sheets could be seen flowing down in wide lakes from the peaks. The air was cold and sharp to breathe into the lungs. Knight felt that he was so light here that he could fly although he knew that this was only the effect of the low air pressure. He thought that there was something in this place that would give a man the strength to escape from the world. However, he knew that in the words of the old woman some secret still lay hidden which they had yet to discover.

Traveller sighed catching Paul's attention. His companion had a very dreamy expression on his face, which Paul had never seen before in all the time he had known him. Normally he never showed his feelings in this way. Clearly he had noticed Paul's inquisitiveness, since he turned to him.

'I haven't been in the mountains for a long time. As a boy I used to occasionally go hiking with my father. And with Ralph,' he added after a minute. 'Ever since I started sailing, I stopped going with them.'

Paul's expression must have shown his interest for Traveller continued, but this time there was sadness in his voice, 'Afterwards, my father had an accident in the mountains. That was a really difficult experience for Ralph, because they had to wait a long time for the rescue helicopter. From that time on my brother stopped hiking in the mountains and my father, to the end of his life, had difficulty walking. Since I was always sailing around the world, it was mainly Ralph who looked after him.'

Traveller froze as if revealing that what he was just about to say would cost him dearly: 'Really, I'm not surprised that he bears a grudge against me.'

Knight looked a little way down the slope where Grouch stood with Lady, who was holding Little Lula by the hand.

'I'm the kind of brother who yesterday wouldn't let him lead us through the mountains even though he knows far more about climbing than me,' added Traveller as if disappointed in himself after which he turned around and walked quickly off towards the house.

Watching his companion walk off, Knight wondered for a while if the captain did not regret having made such an admission.

Paul felt overcome by sadness. Why was everything not simpler? Why was Traveller not absolutely good and Grouch totally bad like it had seemed to him at first? Again he looked down the slope at the older Wronski brother. Slowly he began to go down to join the others just as Ralph was beginning to tell the others how he and his father had climbed Mont Blanc.

When they returned home, the couple and their daughter were busy with their embroidery. Only then did they find out that this was their main form of work. The old woman encouraged them to join in but, apart from Lady and Little Lula, nobody was interested. Tiger sat down by the fire to warm himself while the men sat on the couch wishing to look at their maps. Then Knight heard Daisy ask the old woman what was waiting for them there and whether Friend had left them something to do.

'I think that you'll find out soon enough. For the moment I would advise you to be patient. Friend asked me to play host to you until you are able to move on. I have to tell you though that you will probably have to stay here longer. Winter is coming and with it the polar night. This isn't the time to be making your way down the mountains. It would be better for you to stay with us and wait for information from Friend. You have shelter here.'

Again Paul was tempted to ask how this house could last through a mountain winter and from where they would have enough food to last a few months, but he held his tongue. Although he should have been glad that they had managed to reach all the way to that place without mishap, he felt sad to think that it would be terribly boring to wait so long. The others clearly thought the same as he heard Traveller mutter under his breath, 'Oh no.'

Only Little Lula, who had been watching in fascination the embroidery slowly take form, was joyful after Lady had translated the old woman's words to her and she exclaimed, 'That's fantastic! And can you ask if this lady can teach me embroidery during this time?'

'Of course' replied the woman with a smile when the question was relayed to her.

**Chapter twenty four**

# THE DARK NIGHT

And so passed the days. While the women prepared the meals, the men helped the old man look after the supplies collected in the shed at the back of the house. Next to it there was a store room for wood that required cutting into smaller pieces as well as sorting. Knight wondered how it had been carried up to such a height but decided not to ask. After work in the morning, it was time for lunch and when in the evenings the whole family sat down to their embroidery, the Wronski brothers and Knight politely kept out of the way and busied themselves with looking through the small library that the couple had collected together. They quickly grew bored, however, because the majority of the books were written in Northern Sámi language that was used by the Sámi people of these parts.

Most of the time was passed in silence as the elderly couple seemed to communicate almost without words and often they only looked at each other for long periods. The young Sámi woman did not say anything at all, just as she had kept quiet during their journey across the tundra. They themselves were not eager to break the silence with their conversation and most often remained silent. After two weeks, Knight realised that he had even grown used to this and overall felt somewhat calmer and the chaotic thoughts that had formerly often overwhelmed him, now seemed to disappear.

The worst thing was the boredom, which befell them in the afternoons during embroidery. Lady happily joined in the communal work and Little Lula was given her own little piece of material on which she could practice by herself. Traveller, Grouch and Knight suffered at this time unbearably. After a certain amount of time, Knight decided that he could not take it any longer, after which he took a small piece of material and began to learn from Little Lula. In the end he thought it was better than mindlessly sitting on the couch. At first the Wronski brothers treated him with disdain, almost as if he had betrayed their common cause, but after a month of staying in the house, they gave in and joined in with the work. Then it turned out that Grouch knew how to embroider. He turned out to be quite good at it, which the old woman acknowledged by asking him to help her with a dress which up to that time she had been working on alone.

In the evenings the old couple sat by the fireplace, took hold of one another's hands and quietly sang. These moments were for Knight blessedly peaceful and joyful. He would meditate on the mysterious and somehow melodious words of the ancient folk songs. Even though he understood nothing, he would wait all day until he could hear that wonderful singing again. Now he knew that the sound that he had once heard from the lips of the Sámi woman was a distant echo of a moving ballad sung by her parents. The girl would sit together with them, listening to the words that revealed their secrets to her.

Paul looked at these two singing people holding each other with wrinkled hands calloused by work and he thought about the mysterious reasons that had made the old lady leave the civilised world and live here in seclusion. Was this the reason? Was this what love was like? Were these short glances, with which the couple communicated almost everything to each other, enough to give up... well what? What was there down below that was more interesting than here? Knight realised with surprise that he had difficulty remembering the world that he had left far behind him. School, home, homework, games with friends, continually absent parents, music, cinema... And the next day would be the same again, only in a different configuration. Was it not better to spend time here beside a person who every day united whole-heartedly with the other? Who every day in silence offered the other person all their work and effort? Was this what love was?

Every day the warm milk, sweet honey and fresh-smelling bread gave the same affirmative answer. Every day the food had the best taste, working together gave the greatest pleasure, and singing raised their hearts in indescribable joy.

But the penetrating looks that the old woman gave Paul every evening before they slept spoke of a secret that lay still deeper. And every evening still the same unarticulated question returned to Paul: How was it possible? What secret did this little house lost high in inaccessible mountains still hold?

December came. The days were already so short that they hardly lasted three hours. Then the fact that the old couple had forbidden them to leave the house after dark also began to rankle. It turned out that the darkness in these mountains was not only natural and that with the dusk an hour of real darkness began in which everything that Dragon represented took control. This was why they had had to make their way to the house only in the light that Arie had given them. However, now they no longer had such protection and could not go out after dark. They began to think with sadness of the coming polar night, during which time they were to be imprisoned in such a small space. Now it was clear why it was possible to go directly from the hut to the wood and provision stores, without the necessity of going outside.

One day after dark, they sat embroidering when Paul felt that he could take no more. He was overcome with an ever more powerful sense of boredom and sleepiness. He stood up and made his way to the kitchen in order to make himself some tea. When he returned to the others with a hot mug he sat down comfortably on the couch in order to take a short break from the tedious work and look at the fire.

'Hey lazybones!' Grouch's voice tore him from his reflections. 'Maybe you could have thought about others. Go back to the kitchen and make us some tea.'

Knight felt as if the hot drink that was flowing down his throat, was causing something to boil somewhere inside his stomach.

'Get up yourself and make your own tea! You don't have to rely on others.'

'Others can do as they will, but I'm here working hard on this dress while you're having yourself a break from playing at embroidering. Move your butt and make us something to drink.'

Paul suddenly became angry. He turned around in his seat to look at the man.

'Move your butt yourself,' he said through gritted teeth, 'I won't allow you to make a lackey of me.'

'Oh there you have it, what a proud lord has become of our Knight,' Grouch added acerbically.

Paul could see Traveller raise his hand to interrupt their quarrel, but he was already too angry to ignore such behaviour from Grouch. He stood up from his seat.

'You're the lazy one who's making a great lord out of himself. And what are you? A carpenter? And as can be seen an embroiderer of girly dresses!'

Grouch screwed up his eyes in anger. The old man stood up and made his way to the other room where his daughter had gone earlier. They did not need to understand their language in order to grasp what was happening and not want to take part in a row.

'You're insulting me? You? And who are you? You tell me? You're a kid, a stuck up kid at that, who imagines himself to be someone important. Paul could not take any more of this. He was so angry with Grouch that he had to go out quickly to stop himself hitting him. Unfortunately the two small rooms in which sat the dispersed inhabitants of the house, didn't allow for any privacy. But where could one go when outside there was the polar night, which the old woman had warned them about? Suddenly a solution came to mind. At a quick pace he headed for the internal entrance to the wood shed. He entered the cold room slamming the door behind him.

He stood in the doorway in almost complete darkness. Only the faint light of the moon shone through a small window. He felt the cold. When coming in here only for a moment during the day, he had not paid attention to how cold it was. From underneath the opposite door, the cold of the Arctic entered in.

Nothing. Silence and darkness. He could only hear his heartbeat and see his breath.

Suddenly something stirred. The blood rushed to his ears. He looked at the door handle leading outside. Was it possible? Had it really moved?

Having walked quickly forward, he thought that he was like a condemned man, who instead of looking for how to escape, only rushed towards his own doom. He grabbed the handle and without waiting a moment to check if indeed someone or something was moving it from the outside, he yanked it hard and opened the door. The icy darkness penetrated inside. Knight felt the cold enter his lungs. Without heed of anything, he took two steps forward and in only a sweater he stood in the darkness of an Arctic winter, alone among the mountains that surrounded him, illuminated only by the ethereal light of the moon. His lungs slowly became accustomed to the biting cold but his heart would not slow down even for a moment. He remembered how Arie had warned them about the darkness of these mountains which was no normal gloom. But besides the cold was it really so terrible here?

He could feel his toes freeze and he looked down at his woollen slippers. In the light of the moon he saw how something similar to frost grew over them at lightning speed, climbing up along his leg. He was under the impression that a similar but invisible frost of paralysing fear was grabbing his heart. He knew the Crooked World well enough to realise that this was not a natural phenomenon.

Tortured he raised his head. The man that stood before him was surprisingly lightly dressed, in a dark flowing cape. Despite the numbness which was slowly overtaking his mind, the boy was intrigued by his uncertainty as to whether the figure standing before him with the exceptionally delicate and beautiful features was indeed a man. The overcoat in no way betrayed the figure.

'Hello, Knight.' The melodious voice also did not allow for the identity of the visitor to be ascertained.

Paul tried to make some kind of sound but his icy lungs would not obey his will. So mute, he was going to have to listen to this figure. Somewhere through his frozen mind the thought penetrated that it did not matter if he was dealing with a man or a woman. There could be no doubt that, whatever figure he had chosen at that moment, it was Enemy.

The thin crimson lips twisted into a smile.

'You recognise me.'

Knight shivered. A sudden feeling of nausea overcame his frozen body. He could feel the remains of his hot supper warming his frozen throat.

'Leave me,' he spluttered.

'Leave you? But no, my dear!' Enemy exclaimed with feigned care. 'You are so frozen that you wouldn't even have the strength to walk back to the wood shed and you'd die out here from cold. Anyway the door has already slammed shut behind you.'

The twisted logic of this argument seemed unassailable to him. The company of Enemy, no matter how dangerous, was now his only chance of survival.

'Come here. Grab onto me and I will lead you to the door of the house.' The dark figure extended a white hand towards him. Knight looked at the unnaturally long fingers. His only chance of rescue. The boy's heart pounded now like crazy and the blood pulsated in his head making thought impossible. He felt as if deep down in his very being he could hear some voice of warning

237

but that dreadful noise in his head was drowning out the words. Voice. Distant memories. Scraps of thought which tried to penetrate through his frozen consciousness. He held out his hand. Shivering from the cold he touched the tips of Enemy's fingers. Something dreadful went through his body, piercing his brain. Cold, cold, which hurt. It all changed into a cry of suffering. He was only a block of ice burning from within from a stab of pain, which could not be described with words.

Suddenly something burnt him terribly on the arm. He screamed with pain to feel a moment later the burning fire spread through his entire body as warmth that brought to life his extremities numbed with cold. He saw someone from behind him slowly pull out a long shining blade. Enemy's icy fingers went back when the old man pulled the boy back hard by the arm. Knight was not able to understand the words of his host. Enemy's face twisted horrendously. The beast spat at the old man. His spittle melted a hole in the snow, but the man, still holding the shining sword aloft, did not move a muscle. Paul saw how the terrifying creature again opened its mouth and from its throat came the sound of a piercing hiss. He could not bear it any longer. He covered his ears and closed his eyes. He felt himself slowly sliding on the cold snow.

Warmth slowly spread through his body. Even at the ends of his fingers, he could feel the baking heat. He slowly opened his eyes. He was lying by the fire wrapped in a number of blankets. On his bed, looking at the fire sat the old woman, holding a steaming mug. She turned to look at him having felt that he had awoken. Without a word she handed him the hot drink. Knight drank and drank and felt an amazing warmth spread through his body. And together with it came the tears. He was shaken by terrible sobbing. He was embarrassed to cry like that but his hostess seemed to pay no attention to it. She looked again into the fire.

He did not know how long he had been crying like that for. It seemed like forever. When he finally stopped, he could feel that his eyes hurt but he also had the impression that the block of ice that up to this moment had been inside his breast, was melting.

'I'm sorry,' he blurted out, 'I failed you.'

'Oh, don't be foolish. Nobody here was expecting anything of you so how could you fail us?'

Paul did not know how to take these words. He thought, however, that it would have been easier for him if the old woman had scolded him.

'Now all that matters is what you do with what has happened.'

To Knight this seemed even more cryptic.

'You may break down over having failed us, you may begin to fear, or you can learn something from it.'

It could be so, he thought. He half closed his eyes for a moment. Suddenly from the darkness of his mind emerged a dreadful misshapen figure. He opened his eyes wide, to banish this ugly image of himself. He gritted his teeth. He had the impression that some part of this terrible image had become true that night. As if the touch of Enemy's icy fingers had distorted his soul. He felt again the sobbing swell up in his breast. No. He was not going to cry this time. He was not going to feel sorry for himself. He had allowed Enemy to touch him and this could not be changed. But anyway the old woman had said that he could learn something from this. He could change this horrible experience into something that would improve him. No, not alone. He needed Friend. Yes, for sure. Alone he would only fall into the abyss of despair and regret. But the warm touch of Friend could carve out a work of beauty in his soul that had been distorted by Enemy.

He heard quiet footsteps behind him. Up to this moment he must have been in the room alone with the old woman while the others had been sitting in the other room. But now Grouch was slowly approaching him. His face was full of regret. Their hostess stood up from the bed and went off towards the little kitchen, to make more tea. Ralph sat down on Paul's bed.

'My lad... I'm sorry,' he said sorrowfully. 'It's all my fault. I was talking rubbish, just like always. I really didn't want to make you so angry. I feel so foolish.'

Suddenly a warmth that even the hot tea had not brought to his insides made Paul smile.

'It doesn't matter. Don't worry. Success had gone to my head and I got angry. It's really not your fault. I apologise too for all those bad words.'

Grouch did not appear convinced but suddenly he raised his hand and squeezed Paul's arm, giving him a little shake. Knight thought that never before had he squeezed him so affectionately. Suddenly he lifted himself from the bed and hugged Grouch slapping him on the back.

'It's all right now. Let's forget about it,' said the boy. 'I'm glad that we're together on this expedition.'

Ralph smiled. At first hesitantly but after a while he started laughing aloud.

'Yes, you're right,' he added. 'I wasn't expecting this. I only wanted to make the journey unpleasant for everyone. But now I really am glad that we are together. I've always wanted to go on some adventure.'

Knight looked into his wistful eyes and remembered what Friend had said about him at the very beginning. He was glad that since that time Grouch had changed so much.

'Come on everyone,' the old woman suddenly called out. 'It's about time for some hot tea.'

**Chapter twenty five**

# THE LETTER

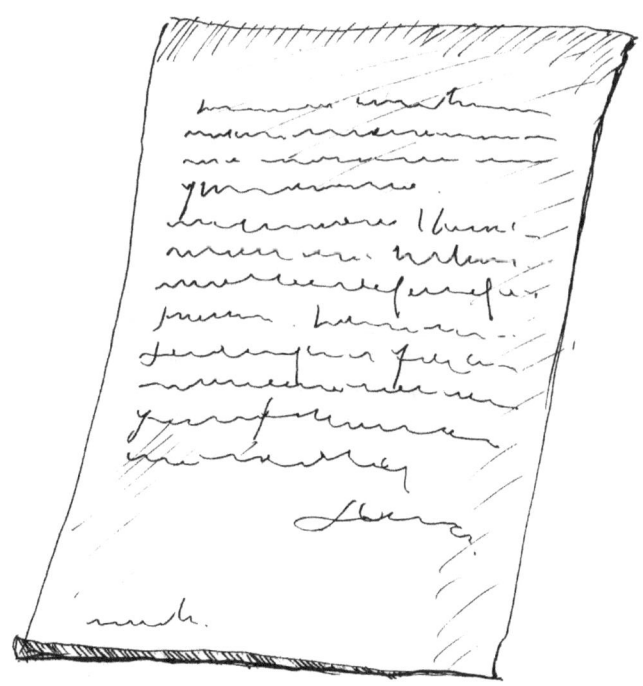

A few days later, a white dove landed on the windowsill. Paul instantly remembered the cold fire that the Sámi woman had been standing in with a similar bird in her hand. But how had it got so high up? Knight's surprise was further piqued when he saw that it had brought letters to the residents of the house. The boy quickly realised that this had to have something to do with the Crooked World. He certainly knew that carrier pigeons had been used to send information long ago, but certainly not any more… Moreover this was only the beginning of the surprises. When the old lady picked up the letters that were already lying on the windowsill and read out the names of the addressees, it turned out that as well as a letter to her and her daughter, there was also a letter to… Paul.

With raised eyebrows, Knight took the fat envelope from the hands of the woman, expecting news from Friend. His companions looked at him expectantly, clearly thinking the same as he himself. So what a surprise it was when he saw his name written in the hand he probably knew best in all the world. His heart began to beat faster. He did not want the others to see him opening this letter. He wanted – no, he had to be – alone when he read news from his Mum.

He ran into the room in which the old couple slept with their daughter, Lady and Little Lula, and slammed the door behind him. His hands shook feverishly. How was it possible? How had this letter travelled all the way here? He had not been home for so long; did Mum have any idea where he was? Mum. The word like an echo of something long forgotten and at the same time something so very dear, resounded now inside his head. The longing that he had long ago forgotten about, long before they had even set off on this adventure, could be heard in his heart with greater intensity. How could it be that they were so far from each other? Memories of her warm smile and the touch of her hands tussling his hair when he was still a child flooded back to him.

His still-shaking hands ripped open the envelope and took out a piece of paper folded in two. He opened it and began to read.

*My beloved son,*

*Oh! She used to say that so often to me when I was young!*

*I haven't seen you for so long. I miss you so very much. But I trust that you are safe in Friend's care.*

*So she knows him!*

*It's difficult for me to write this letter. There are so many things that I would like to tell you. I also feel now how much we have drifted away from each other over the last few years and how difficult it is for me to write to you now. My son what can I tell you after being separated for so many months? What could sum up what I've been going through during this time? My son, I love you. Son, forgive me. Forgive me for allowing us both to drift so far apart, for everyday cares and our daily support becoming more important than the games we played and the time we spent together. Forgive me for not always having been there when you needed me, that I didn't know how to love you in the way you deserved. But in my heart I always knew that my place, like every mother, was by her child. Forgive me that I did not know how to do it... What exactly?*

*To go beyond myself. Yes, that's it, to be there for you forgetting about myself. To go beyond oneself isn't that love? I always longed to be able to love you like that.*

*My son, I wanted to write about so many things to you in this letter and the only words that come to my mind are that I love you. I must have told you this too seldom when you were with me and the need to reassure you of this has welled up in me like a river.*

*Son, I know you have an important task and you have to be far away, but I miss you. I wish you'd come back. I would like it if Dad no longer travelled off on work. I would like to be at home more often. With you. I only regret that when you return you will no longer be the boy I last bade farewell to at Granny's house. Time flies and children so relentlessly grow up. Who are you now? What are your plans and longings? I know that you are Knight. I was not at all surprised by this. You've always been brave. You've always been very noble and cared for others. And I have always been proud of you.*

*I'm glad that you met Friend. I'm glad that you've set off after him on a journey, that you've found the courage to go where he leads you. You will only fully comprehend the sense of your journey when you complete it. Friend demands faith from people close to him and such faith is like a jump into the unknown. It is throwing yourself into the abyss after the person you love, knowing — only in theory — that love gives you wings. And you have jumped after Friend and set off on this mad journey. And now your wings are growing for you to fly off to where the real sun shines.*

*Fly son, fly away where Friend leads you. Fly to where your heart longs.*

*All my love*

*Mum*

Tears were streaming down his cheeks. His eyes had becomes so blurred that it had been difficult for him to read the last words. So many words, so many unsaid thoughts for all those years! He knew that he was going to have to read this letter again a number of times so that he would comprehend the full sense of all her words.

How long had he waited for such words! He had been waiting even though he had not known for what. He had needed them so much. He missed Mum. Although he was slowly changing from a boy into a youth who was choosing his own path, he would always remain a son – a little son – for his Mum and would always love her. And she loved him! Something that was apparently so obvious, but somehow lost in the bustle of everyday life. And she was proud of him. And she was not at all surprised that Friend had called him Knight.

He swelled with pride. His mother loved him and was proud of him. Could there be anything more wonderful?

She had asked for his forgiveness, but what had he to forgive? She had not always been there for him, as she had written. She would frequently become irritated, rather than simply love him. Yes, she was very emotional and she did not always want to play with him. But basically he had always felt that she was trying to change. For him. Because she loved him.

He was so warm that he took off his sweater.

He felt truly happy. He did not know how long he had been shut in the room but he was happy for this moment on his own.

He was glad that Mum knew about his journey. She knew Friend. What a surprise and what a joy! His cheeks hurt from smiling. He looked down at the paper crushed in his hand. He read the last paragraph.

*Faith is throwing yourself into the abyss after the person you love.*

But whom did he love?
Obviously he loved Mum. He loved Dad. And Granny.
But was that what she meant?

*And you have jumped after Friend and set off on this mad journey.*

Friend. In that case did he love Friend? The question appeared deep down in his consciousness, although he had never before thought about this seriously. He had always imagined love rather as something that was romantic, like falling in love with a girl, or something as ordinary as attachment to one's parents. If however he loved Friend, then he didn't love him in either of these ways.

He closed his eyes for a moment and again saw the large meadow full of poppies. He heard again Friend's laughter, which told him to grab onto clumps of flowers. He would have liked to have been there for real and not just in these fleeting imaginings. He would have liked to laugh together with Friend and run across these fantastic meadows. Free. Full of joy. Yes, no one else made Knight feel so loved, no one else knew him so well. No one else gave him so much strength to go on. No one else knew how to involve him in the unknown in a mad chase after... After what? After the remote and strange Crooked World, which either came or went, which either engulfed him, as if it were, in its miracles, or left him alone again with grey reality and tiresome toil.

He still didn't know if this was love, but he felt that he had indeed thrown himself after Friend into this adventure as if into an abyss.

*And now your wings are growing for you to fly off to where the real sun shines.*

What strange words, and yet Knight knew that they were true. But what did the "real sun" mean?

Again he was gripped by the memory of the fire that penetrated deep down, but did not burn. But the sun... the sun was no ordinary fire. The sun was like the life of everything that exists. In the end without it... there was nothing. Knight thought that cosmological concepts would not help him to understand. This was a mystery that he had not yet had the chance to delve.

*Fly to where your heart longs.*

Yes, he was certain of it. He longed for that fire. He longed for that miraculous moment when he had seen the Sámi woman with the dove in her hand among the cold flames.

Then he heard her melodious singing.

That singing. Now he heard it every evening. The old couple always sang that tune. The tune that had – he was sure – brought the unusual fire.

Suddenly he realised that both the Sámi and his companions were sure to be waiting for him in the main room. Only now did he notice that outside the window it was totally dark, which meant that he must have been sitting here lost in thought for a very long time indeed. So he stood up and went out. Seeing the emotion that remained in his eyes, the others guessed that he must have been deeply affected by the letter he had received, so they asked no questions.

**Chapter twenty six**

# THE PROPHECY

Slowly the days of the polar night came. It was already the middle of December and they no longer left the house. The dangerous darkness smothered everything outside with its sinister mystery. Paul prepared himself mentally to sit out this time of being shut up indoors to survive being in this small hut even if it turned out to be necessary for the entire winter. To his surprise, however, on the first evening – the time of which could only be ascertained with a clock – the old lady said that during the polar night there would be no more singing. This ritual was to be replaced by reading aloud before going to bed. This was not good news as neither Paul nor his companions understood Northern Sámi and although listening to music they could appreciate the beauty of the tune, they were not expecting dry prose in this language to be interesting for them.

The old woman pulled down a large dusty book from the top of the bookshelf and began to read. And just as he had predicted, Paul could feel himself becoming terribly bored. It seemed that the woman had already been reading for an eternity when she finished and announced that it was time to go to bed.

That was how the first few evenings went. Out of the corner of his eye, Paul observed his other companions of whom only Little Lula sat by the old lady listening to the sound of the foreign tongue. Tiger, as soon as the reading began, slept peacefully and Lady, Grouch and Traveller were clearly trying to suppress a powerful need to yawn. Clearly this was not an auspicious beginning to the polar night evenings.

Once when his thoughts were wandering towards his home in Warsaw, Paul was startled to hear the word "Ipmil". He listened for a moment to the monotonous sounds but he heard nothing further that would grab his attention. But later in the evening when the Sámis as well as Lady and Little Lula had gone into their bedroom to rest and Traveller and Grouch had lain down to sleep in the large room, Knight in the dull light of a candle pulled the book down from the shelf. He placed it on the table and opened it. Out of the corner of his eye he saw the captain watching him. Grouch was already sound asleep.

Paul looked straight at Traveller to make sure that he was not being reproved by him. But in the end what was so wrong about pulling down this book from the shelf? Mr Wronski looked at him attentively, but said nothing.

Knight opened the book at a randomly chosen page. As was to have been expected, it was full of strange words. He turned over a few pages but found nothing to grab his attention. He was a little disappointed. Hearing the word "Ipmil" had made him hope that this was no ordinary book. Maybe it could have even been the Book. But there was nothing now that would prove it. He was just about to slam the covers closed, when he saw that Traveller had jumped from his bed and was standing next to him.

'What's happened?' asked Paul in a whisper.

'What's happened? And what do you think will happen when you open this book?' answered the captain with a question, quickly thumbing through the old yellowed pages.

'Well, I don't know. I was just curious.'

Silence fell. Traveller's fingers nervously flicked through the immense volume and his eyes quickly scanned the pages. He seemed to be looking for something.

'Actually...' the boy wasn't certain what he was trying to tell his companion, 'I heard the word "Ipmil" during the reading. Do you remember? It was you who told me what it means.'

'Yes, that's what I'm looking for. I heard it too.'

They stood awhile in silence. Traveller was still occupied with flicking through the pages. Suddenly he stopped.

'Here it is. Look,' he pointed with his finger the place, leaning over the text.

Indeed among the many completely incomprehensible words, the one they were looking for could be clearly made out. They both leaned in closer, as if they believed that reading this one word they would be able to understand the rest of the text.

Traveller leaned the candle over in the vain hope, that by illuminating the page they would be able to find something more. But nothing spectacular happened. After a moment with a sigh of resignation they both straightened out intending to close the book.

Knight breathed in with a gasp. He had not been expecting this.

Around them reigned a deep darkness. There was no table, nor were there beds or armchairs next to a glowing hearth. He could sense Traveller next to him breathing deeply, attempting to take control of his anxiety.

But Paul had the strange impression that despite the darkness, he recognised this place. He looked down at the Book. He could now clearly see that it stood on a pedestal and emanated a strange light. He had the impression that with every moment the glow was becoming brighter. Only now did he notice that around them there could be seen ever more clearly some distant illuminated figures.

Yes he was certain now. They were their reflections. They were in a mirrored room. Was it not the same one as in which he had once found the Book at the top of the lighthouse? Was it possible that they had returned to the same place that they had left a few months earlier? Were they in City?

'We're in the lighthouse,' he whispered to Traveller.

'I know,' replied his companion through pursed lips.

'The mirrored windows are closed. Is it possible that we are on the island where there was the ruined City? On Migdal?'

'It looks like it,' replied the captain drily. 'Come on, the exit was on the left over here. We only have a candle. We must be careful not to waste light.'

Knight looked again at the Book, but he still could not read anything in it. They walked off to the left. Paul automatically counted his steps. One. Two. Three. Four. Five. Six. Seven. Eight. Nine. Ten. The door. They opened it wide. The two branches of the spiral staircase led downwards. They took the one that was closest to them. Going down they went past a number of rooms that Paul remembered from his first visit to this place. Passing by them he only cast his eye upon them, but as far as he could see in the dim light, they were not so empty and covered in cobwebs as they had been then.

They reached the very bottom and stood in the door. Traveller took in a loud deep breath of air. In the light of the moon, the sprawling densely built-up City could be seen and in the distance the peaceful and impenetrably dark sea. Here and there lights shone out from within windows. Knight felt his sword, which the captain had thankfully ordered him to carry with him even in the house. Only now did he feel how hot it was under all these layers of clothing. He began to undress and his companion did the same. But they did not know what to do with their garments. They were not after all going to carry them about with themselves.

'Let's leave them in the lighthouse. Despite everything, it doesn't look like it's often visited,' proposed Traveller.

So they did so. When they felt lighter in normal shirts and just trousers, they decided to go down from the hill on which the lighthouse stood and walk through the city in the hope of finding something that would explain why they were here. Knight in the end had no doubt that there was some concrete reason why they had found themselves in the Book. Voice would certainly not have placed them here without reason.

They went down the dark slope. At first they walked along wide beaten-earth alleyways, along which there were loosely spaced woodland huts. A number of them looked rather poor, they were wooden with neglected yards. The further they walked on, the wealthier the homes looked. In the end they reached a place where the greenery ended and the densely built-up streets began with two-storey tenement buildings, interspersed with lower more opulent buildings decorated with carved columns. At night, the empty streets did not seem quite so oriental as they had when Paul had arrived in City through the hollow in the tree growing in the desert. Nevertheless it could be seen that everything was built out of light-coloured stone.

They walked aimlessly, turning sometimes here, sometimes there. Suddenly they arrived at a small square, which might have even been a kind of patio which was bordered on the side from which they entered by columns and on the other three sides by building walls.

Clearly without realising it they had found their way into the courtyard of one of the villas. In the middle of the little square there was a shimmering water feature around which grew lush oriental plants and flowers with strange scents. They hesitated wondering what to do now. They should return down the street. The sight of the water reflecting the moonlight was attracting them as they were thirsty. They had no scoop so they cupped their hands into the glowing liquid and drank from them greedily as if from little goblets.

'You're thirsty?' a quiet female voice asked them.

They jumped back as if they had been burnt and looked around. On their left, in the door stood an elderly woman with a jug in her hands. She had obviously come to draw some water too.

'Yes,' replied Traveller uncertainly. 'Yes, we were walking this way and we felt thirsty.'

The old woman went up to them slowly, looking at them carefully. It was only now that Paul realised that they were dressed in strange garb for the inhabitants of the city. Their modern shirts and simple trousers were very different to the clothes characteristic of the natives, at least as far as he could remember from his first visit here. The stranger was wearing a light dress over which she wore a richly decorated robe.

'Where are you from?' she asked with interest.

'Oh we're...' Traveller was clearly troubled. 'We're from beyond the island. We sailed here last night. We wanted to see City.'

'From beyond the island?' The lady looked at them through slightly screwed up eyes.

Only at that moment did Knight realise that Traveller did not know the history of City nor that the inhabitants here did not believe in the existence of anything beyond the island, so his reply must have certainly astonished the lady.

'Yes,' carried on the captain. 'Unfortunately we don't have any clothes with us that are suitable for a warmer climate. We're too far from the north...'

Paul gave him a sideways glance: after all the island was at the northern end of the Baltic, even though it really looked like a southern oriental country.

Suddenly Traveller fell silent. He clearly looked astonished by something. He looked at Knight as if he was expecting help. But Knight could only raise his eyebrows, since he did not know what it was his companion was thinking of.

'She can understand us. What language are we speaking?' Now it became clear also to Paul that he did not know what kind of sounds were coming from the mouth of his companion. He was not able to recognise the tongue, although he could understand it. He was well enough acquainted with the Book for this phenomenon not to surprise him much.

'I don't know, but the Book is ruled by its own laws.'

'Are you saying something?' asked the woman uncertainly. 'I just asked how it's possible that you are from beyond the island. After all nothing else exists beyond our City... At least that is what our leaders claim.'

Now it was Traveller who raised his eyebrows in surprise. Paul swore deep down for not having earlier told him, if only in brief, the history of this place, which he himself had come to know when he had been in the Book the previous time.

'Yes, we are from beyond the island,' said Paul taking the initiative in the conversation. 'We know that your leaders say that no other world exists and this is why the lighthouse was closed, but it's not true. We have come from afar, but nonetheless we have decided to stay here for the night... in order for us to avoid the danger of ... people opposed to us.'

The woman's eyes shone in the light of the moon. She was clearly excited by Paul's words.

'It's amazing. Simply amazing,' she exclaimed and lowered her voice. 'You see, my husband has also always claimed the same. I mean that there are other countries... and because of that he was thrown off the City council. It's wonderful that you've found your way to our house.'

With these words she left the copper jug which she had been holding all this time in her hands, she nodded at them to follow her and went towards the side door. They went inside. Inside it was very opulently furnished. On the walls there were colourful pictures, which they could see in the dim light of the torches fastened to the door-frames. There were also decorative tapestries hanging, the red colour of which sewn with golden thread made the inside warm and cosy despite its size. Everywhere there were marble urns, in which there grew impressive plants. There was not much furniture here, which in no way filled the huge empty space of the room. The elderly woman led them into the next room where she told them to wait asking them to sit down on something that resembled a chaise-longue. She herself went into a room, which they presumed to be a bedroom. They heard a male voice from there which must have belonged to the woman's husband. After a long time, the master of the house also appeared in the doorway and came over to meet them. He was called Boniface while the wife introduced herself as Helen.

Their host was an older man with a long grey beard. He had a dark complexion and lively eyes. He smiled at them amicably.

'My wife's told me that you've come from beyond the island and fear persecution from the authorities here.'

'Well, yes,' said Traveller, again taking over the lead in the conversation. 'Supposedly they claim that other countries don't exist so we would prefer not to put ourselves at risk.'

'Mmm,' it seemed the man was completely somewhere else in his thoughts. 'Yes, yes, Helen, please find some clothes for these men so that they can walk freely around City. I see that you speak our language so I don't think anyone will suspect anything.'

Their hostess soon returned to them with clothes, loose tunics. However they did not know what they were to do with the swords tied to their belts. They decided to ask the old man openly what they could do with them. They changed quickly in the room adjacent and returned to their hosts.

'Dear... Boniface,' Traveller clearly felt uncomfortable addressing their host by his first name. 'We have weapons that we don't want to leave behind, but we cannot hide them in these tunics. Could you help us?'

The man looked at their swords in curiosity. That's no problem, we have decorative belts from which swords can be hung. I see that your weapon is short. Maybe you would prefer our classical swords?'

'No thank you. We're used to these ones. This one is a special weapon which opens up with an internal spring.' And with these words Traveller demonstrated to Boniface the mechanism that opened up the sword.

Their host raised his eyebrows, clearly surprised at the invention that he had been shown.

I have to warn you that carrying swords, you will be considered to be part of the upper class of the citizenry, which might cause certain problems. Nonetheless if you are decided, please, here are you belts.' On saying this he pulled out two beautifully embroidered belts form an ornate chest of drawers, with grips for fastening weapons.

'Thank you very much. We would like to walk around the town tonight in order to assess the situation. Will it be safe?'

'Yes,' replied Boniface. 'That shouldn't be a problem. Maybe, however, you would like to sit down and eat something? I'd be very glad to find out what you're planning. Since you're armed I can assume that you're not here with purely peaceful intentions... Although I am against the City council and I'm happy to see people from other countries, I don't want to be responsible for any disturbances.'

'We do not want to start any fights,' protested Traveller.

'No, of course not. I assume that for the two of you it wouldn't be to your advantage. By the way do you have many companions on the ship you sailed here on?'

With the comment of their host, they understood they had already made their explanations too complicated.

'No, basically we're alone,' he said. During this time the lady brought them a tray of fruit and sweet cakes and she sat down together with them in the wooden armchairs. Boniface was silent, on hearing these words he only raised his eyebrows questioningly, while Traveller looked critically at Paul.

'Do you know something about the Book in the lighthouse?' blurted out the boy.

The married couple looked at the boy for a while in silence.

In the end Helen spoke, 'We've heard about the Book.' She began carefully after which she began to speak more openly. 'Some of the citizens that do not wish to believe the government, talk about the legends of the Book, which supposedly contains the entire history, the past and the future of our City and every other country. Supposedly, the lighthouse was closed because of it. In some homes you can find fragments that have supposedly been copied from it.'

'Supposedly? You don't believe in it?' asked Paul perturbed.

'We're not talking about what we believe,' interrupted Boniface. 'We are telling you what the situation is like.'

'But what we're talking about now is what you believe,' exclaimed Knight passionately. 'It's that which everything depends on! If you believe…'

He stopped and wondered what he was to tell them. 'What' was it really that depended on whether they believed in the Book.

'Well, what is it if we believe?' asked the master of the house.

'If you believe, then everything can still be changed. City might not be destroyed.'

At this moment Traveller stopped pretending that he agreed with Knight and began staring at him intensely.

'Destroyed? Boy, surely you don't know what you are talking about. This City is developing unusually quickly. Everything points to us soon reaching a level of development that our forefathers could have only dreamed of. Science and technology are developing at a pace unheard of. Soon we will even have ships that catch fish by themselves. Scientists are working on methods to transfer thoughts telepathically and excavations on our island allow us to examine our prehistory going back millions of years. Imagine, lately they have discovered that the monkeys from which we come from had wings and could fly. And that's not saying anything about law! We have already come to such a point in our respect for all beings that the last council, with regard to evolution, extended human rights to monkeys. Maybe I am no supporter of the present government but there is no way to deny that they are looking after the development of our City!'

With Boniface's every word, Knight stared wide-eyed. Goodness gracious! When he imagined flying monkeys with human rights he had to stop himself from snorting with laughter. How twisted was this picture of reality. But was his own world not like this? Maybe instead of tunics, everyone wore jeans and t-shirts. They had a complex sewerage system and instead of drinking from wells they used pipes, but in light of what Boniface had said was City not a caricature of the modern world from which Paul came? At least the monkeys here could fly on wings while their own had to humbly hang from trees.

In one moment it became clear to him why the Book was the light which should illuminate every country. Only the Book could allow one to look on all of history. Stuck in the here and now we could only marvel at machines for catching fish and laws for monkeys. But where were we heading? To eternal never-ending development?

No, the Book was the history of the battle with Dragon, and Dragon had not yet said the final word. His fiery breath turned everything to ashes including the remains of the unfortunate flying monkeys. And what would remain?

He already knew the answer. After all he'd already been here: among ruins covered by an overgrown forest, where only the Book would remain untouched on its pedestal.

But was what he had told Boniface true? Was it still possible to save City? After all, he had seen the ruins himself. Was rescue possible when even those inhabitants who still believed in other countries thought that City's development was unstoppable?

He must have spent a long time in thought as he heard the master of the house clear his throat and say, 'Young man, just as I said our City is developing now at an impressive pace and there is no reason to believe that it awaits destruction.'

'But I've seen it destroyed. I was in the Book. We came out of it to you.'

'That's nonsense. The Book is only a book. Maybe it is a certain historical record, but we cannot treat it as magical.'

And so how, after hearing these words, could Paul explain the truth to him? The man did not want to know it. Since he had already denied the power of the Book in his assumptions, how was he to listen to its Voice?

'Come with us then. We'll take you to the Book and we'll read a section. Maybe then you will believe.'

Boniface was silent looking at him. He was clearly debating whether he should agree to this proposal.

'The City council does not even believe that we exist. You believe that we exist so would it not be worth taking a risk and also believing in our words?' asked the boy.

'Yes, but would it change anything? Even if we believe your words and the Book foretells our destruction, how does it change anything if we believe or not?'

This question floored Knight. Indeed, where had the idea come from that City could be saved?

*Because I am a merciful Author.*

Knight well remembered the deep sound of Voice. He felt indescribable relief. So Voice was with him here and now in the Book, just like the last time.

*Of course, I am always here.*

And what about the City? Did that mean it could still be saved?

*Yes. I have just told you I am a merciful Author. As long as the inhabitants want to create their history with me, I will not forget about them.*

And what if they don't want to? And what about City? Did that mean it could still be saved?

*You already know the answer. You saw. If they defiantly use the pages of history and constantly try to grab my pen... Well, then I'll stop writing about them.*

But supposedly some citizens have copied passages from the Book. What will happen to them if you stop writing about City?

*Those who remain faithful will be given another land to live in.*

And how many faithful are needed for City to be saved?

*As many as are needed for City to return to me when the time of testing comes.*

Oh!

Knight screamed deep down. He felt that this was a criterion that would be impossible to fulfil.

Don't lose heart. Faith. Well, it reproduces like rabbits. You should know about this.

Like an echo, at the sound of these words, an image appeared in Knight's head of the many rabbits that were under Grouch's chair in Gdansk as well as in the caves of Shemesh. He had long ago forgotten about this. He had almost forgotten about Rabbit, whose Knight he used to be after all. He had never thought about it in this manner. He had simply thought that the figure of Rabbit, which was a part of himself, had been there to force him to take action, that it had been a kind of literary device of Author. Could the little animal have meant something more? Could it be that since that time in the house of the Wronskis, his diffident following of Friend had not grown into a strong faith – even bordering on certainty – that the will of Voice would lead him without fail through the pages of the Book?

Faith.

*"It is throwing yourself into the abyss after the person you love knowing only in theory that love gives you wings. And now your wings are growing for you to fly off to where the real sun shines."*

And so City could still be saved.

*Yes, you must find seventy people who will believe.*

Knight looked at his host, knowing that he had been silent for a long time.

'I don't know if it will change anything,' he said slowly, 'but I know that we must try. Are you coming with us to the lighthouse?'

'There's no need,' Helen interrupted suddenly. 'A friend of mine has a passage of the Book written down. We can go to her place.'

Her husband looked at her suspiciously, as if this was the first time that he had heard of it, but he did not make any further protests. The woman suggested that they set off while it was still night.

They walked in silence. Boniface was clearly not in a mood for further discussions on the fate of City and Traveller seemed rather irritated by Paul taking the initiative to speak.

Before they left the house Helen stole a glance at Knight and gave him a meaningful look. He felt deep relief seeing that he nonetheless had an ally. He supposed that the hostess knew at least a part of the Book and shared

Paul's opinion as to the future of City. The boy only wondered what he would do when they arrived. What could be written in the Book that would convince Boniface that it was worth undertaking the effort to save City? He simply had to trust that all would work out well.

Everywhere was dark illuminated only by the light of the moon, which sometimes penetrated into the depths of the heavily built up streets. The tall sandstone buildings with the little windows gave a little bit of the impression of a prison. Knight looked around alertly, being aware that it was here in this City that he had first seen Dragon. Was the monster here now too? Did it know that they were here?

After a ten-minute walk up a slope, somewhat to the north of the hill on which the lighthouse was, they stopped before the doors of one of the tenement blocks. Boniface ordered them to keep quiet. They went into the courtyard, where they found a beautiful garden. Here Helen asked them to wait and went inside herself in order to tell her friend of their arrival. She did not come back out for a long time, after which she came to them accompanied by a younger woman of plain appearance. In the weak light of the torches, her hair, which was tied into a tight bun, had a reddish colour and her eyes were bright and green. In her hands she held a large bundle of papers.

'Welcome, my name is Dominique. I'm glad you've come to me. Helen tells me that you come from the Book to save our City and that you want to show it to Boniface.'

'Yes,' replied Knight uncertainly. 'I am Knight. And this is Traveller.'

'Knight and Traveller? Is this possible?' Dominique seemed to be in great shock.

'Well… yes.'

'And so you really are from the Book,' she exclaimed excitedly.

Paul and Mr Wronski looked at her in silent astonishment, fearing to say something that would destroy the unexpectedly good impression that their names had made on Dominique.

'It's just that one of the fragments that my father copied down many years ago concerns the arrival of Knight and Traveller to City,' she explained to Helen and Boniface.

'Show me,' said the man sharply.

'Come inside,' she replied.

They went into a large room on the other side of the courtyard opposite the main gate. The room was decorated similarly to the house of Boniface and Helen, with numerous wall paintings. When the lady of the house had lit a torch, in its light Knight could see what the pictures portrayed. They were various scene paintings. At first it was difficult for Paul to make out what was on them, as they were so faded with age. Yet in almost all of them the same man was depicted. Knight did not need much time to understand that that brown-haired man with the warm smile and the blue eyes that shone even in the picture was Friend. The pictures appeared to be scenes from everyday life: Friend having lunch by the table, Friend in a boat, Friend in the garden among the flowers...

'Who is in the pictures?' blurted out Paul.

'That man? I don't know. Those are very old frescos. My parents once claimed that it was the founder of our City, but I don't know how they knew it. In the pictures he looks more of a dreamer than an enterprising founder of the former town.'

The mysteries seemed to multiply. When Traveller looked carefully at the pictures, Paul sat down with the others on the chaise longues that were in the middle of the room. Dominique unfurled the parchments on which the Book had been copied in thin handwriting. The woman was clearly looking for some fragment. Suddenly she shouted out in joy and handed over the pages to Boniface. Together with his wife he read the text. Knight regretted a little that he could not look at what was written because he himself was exceedingly curious as to how their arrival to City had been described in the Book and what according to the Book they had done.

Traveller, who had still not sat down, stood strategically placed behind Boniface and began to read over his shoulder.

The married couple spent a long time on the text. While reading, Helen gave Paul a warm smile. This raised his spirits. However as they read on the faces of the readers darkened – and especially the face of Mr Wronski.

In the end Boniface suddenly tore himself from the parchments. There was total silence.

'This is impossible,' and his voice shook, although it was difficult to say whether it was from excitement or anger. 'I know. What is written about your arrival is all true. At least up to now.' With these words he turned to Knight, 'But I cannot believe in what is written about City. It's untrue.'

His declaration sounded so decided and final that nothing further could have been done. Paul only opened his mouth looking for words.

'What do you mean, "untrue"?' argued Helen. 'Why should you not believe in it? Since everything about the appearance of the two messengers is true, why should the rest be a lie?'

'And why should I believe more in the Book than in reality?' Boniface was now almost angry. 'Reality is such that City is developing brilliantly, even despite the fact that its inhabitants do not believe in other countries. Why should Author destroy such a wonderful civilisation as ours? Why should he want to? This would be nonsense, even cruelty. I don't believe in such an Author!'

While listening to this tirade, Knight crossed his gaze with Traveller. His sad eyes said almost everything. He shook his head in an expression of resignation. Whatever was written there, it did not give much hope for salvation. But nonetheless Paul felt that he could not give up. He could not leave things the way they were. He was going to fight to the end.

'But you yourself said that the description of our arrival is true. Why should the rest be a lie?' he objected.

'And why should it be true? Why would Author want to destroy our City?' Boniface continued stubbornly.

'Because City has rejected him. He offered the Book to it so that it would be guided by it, but City locked it up at the top of a lighthouse,' he exclaimed almost angrily. 'Why write about it more?'

'But what are you talking about, young fellow? It is we who write our own history. Author might have written it once and left it in a lighthouse but now our fates are in our hands and everything points to the prophecy about City being destroyed not being fulfilled.'

Knight was left speechless. It was only at this moment that he understood the bottomless abyss of incomprehension that separated them. Boniface did not see fate as a story being told, the ending of which – although foretold in the Book – was still being formed. He did not understand that the Book was not just a dead description of history. That it was their lives, here and now, and beyond it there was nothing. Now Paul fully appreciated the sense of what Voice had once revealed to him about the freedom given to his characters.

But how could he explain it to him? How could the greatest secret of existence be explained to someone who did not want to accept it? No, he could not do it. To explain it, it was necessary to feel it, to experience it. After all, not long ago he would not have believed himself. He looked helplessly at Helen. She believed. He could feel it. Her anxious eyes had been following them during this exchange of opinions with the indescribable hope that Boniface would understand. But there was nothing to be understood. Now all that was necessary was only to believe.

'This is senseless. Such a discussion is leading us nowhere,' said Traveller. 'Are you coming to the lighthouse? There you can convince yourself as to the words of the Book.'

'I have them written here,' objected Boniface. 'Why should I bother going to the lighthouse? How am I supposed to know that the Book is still there? And if it is the City authorities are sure to be guarding the access to it.'

The situation looked hopeless. Knight did not quite know what Traveller was counting on, however he understood that there was some kind of chance. Boniface's resistance seemed unassailable.

'Darling, please do it for me,' said Helen. 'Even if you don't want to believe in it all, come with me.'

With all her bearing she seemed to beg him to listen to her. The man looked at his wife with a certain affection and sighed.

'Forgive me, my dear, I'm not able to believe in this fantasy. I can see reality, and it contradicts everything.' When he said these words, Helen's eyes filled with tears. 'But since it is so important to you, I will go.' The woman closed her eyes and squeezed her husband's hand. Knight felt relieved.

'Still the problem remains of how we are to make our way there without being seen.'

'That shouldn't be any difficulty,' interjected Paul. 'We came to you from there and no one stopped us.'

'I wouldn't be so sure,' said Traveller. 'The fact that we came from there unobserved doesn't mean that no one is guarding that place. But we are armed. Will you, ladies, be coming with us?'

'Of course I will,' said Dominique who had been quiet up till now and Helen only nodded her head.

'Good, in that case you will also need weapons. Do women in your City use swords?'

'No, that is not the custom,' replied the hostess. 'But I think that we can hide small daggers under the tunics. Judging by the prophecy, we have to be ready for everything. The end is nigh.'

On saying this she stood up and, from a chest of drawers standing in the corner, took out two sharp daggers with ornate handles. She and Helen put them in their belts and covered them in folds of material which they draped over. Traveller warned that it would not be sensible for them to use too bright a light on the road as it would could raise the unwanted interest of the night watch. So they took a number of small torches with them, of which they lit only one. Thus prepared for the road they walked out into the darkness of the night.

Something had clearly changed. Immediately Knight was struck by the pervasive sense of danger. He heard fearful cries – although if he were to say from where he would have probably said from within his own self. He was under the impression that with every step the street under his feet squeaked like a rusty door. He looked up in the sky, although he feared what he might see in it. With a bright moon as a background, flying shapes could be seen that looked like giant bats.

Then with full clarity, the memory of the battle in the cave came back to him when the horrible birdlike creatures had attacked Arie.

He felt that little time remained. Would they be able to save City by the morning?

**Chapter twenty seven**

# ON THE WAY TO
# THE LIGHTHOUSE

Everything seemed to turn against them. As soon as they had turned into the first street that led up to the hill, some man came out of a side gate.

'Oh, Boniface! Is that really you?' he asked jovially. 'Who are you walking with so late at night?'

'Aah, these are... my guests,' he replied uncertainly.

'Guests?' the stranger burst out laughing. 'And what are you doing with them in the middle of the night so far from home?'

'Well...' Boniface was clearly uneasy. 'They stayed late into the evening at Dominique's and we were worried that they wouldn't be able to return to us after dark, so we went out to bring them back,' interjected Helen soberly. 'Forgive us but it is very late so we would like to get back home quickly.'

'It's late, late. It's two in the morning already. I'm just wondering why you are heading in the opposite direction?' replied the stranger with venom. The woman froze. No one had an answer for this somewhat obvious observation.

'Forgive us, sir,' said Traveller coldly, 'but who are you to demand an explanation from us as to what we are doing? Why are you out of your house in the middle of the night?'

The man only looked angrily at Mr Wronski. He straightened up proudly and passed them by walking down the street.

'Be careful who you mess with Boniface,' he said over his shoulder. It could be clearly seen that for Boniface, who was entirely unconvinced as to this venture, this was all too much.

The man turned to Helen: 'You see, darling? This is idiotic to risk our good name and safety for some fantastical stories.'

'You weren't afraid to risk them when you stated in a City council meeting that other countries exist beyond City,' she replied to him angrily. 'And now what? You're afraid?'

The man clearly did not want to reply to such a question so his wife continued, 'Since it is so dangerous to walk down the street at night in one's own City, do you still believe that we are living in such a wonderful civilisation? If our country was so wonderful we would be free and we would be able to do what we want! But that's not the way it is! Dump your illusion that we are living in a wonderful world and look at yourself. You've been thrown out of the council for your views and you shake with fear that someone might snitch to the authorities about your night-time walks. Is that freedom?'

Boniface walked on in silence. Even though his wife's words had probably not convinced him, he had to bear himself with honour and prove to her that he was not afraid. Or perhaps they had? Maybe some grain of doubt had been sown in his heart?

They walked on in silence. Knight said nothing but everywhere he saw quickly moving shadows. But whenever he turned round to see what had thrown them, he saw nothing. He felt that this was not a good omen.

All of a sudden, they heard cries. Before them above the houses they could see a bright glow. They picked up their pace. When they could see behind the next corner, in the distance at the end of the street they could make out flames which were destroying a low building blocked from view by the larger tenement buildings. Around it there was already a small crowd of onlookers.

'And what now?' asked Dominique. 'Are we going to go on, or are we going to go around to get to the lighthouse?'

'What am I hearing?' said a stentorian voice behind them. 'Who wants to go to the lighthouse?'

As if in slow motion they turned around and saw a gigantic man behind them with a smile, although not a sincere one, on his face.

'We do,' replied Traveller aggressively. 'Do you have a problem with that?'

Boniface was shaken by Mr Wronski's demeanour.

'But, but. Your honour… I'm sorry that my friend has offended you…'

Only now did Knight recognise the man standing behind the giant. It was the speaker he had heard long ago in the Book preaching to the inhabitants that other lands did not exist and then he had jumped out from the hollow at him as well as at Daisy and Tiger with a weapon in hand. A shiver went down his spine. Was it possible that their leader also recognised him?

He did not have to wait long for an answer. The man looked at him with a shine in his eye and said, 'Don't we know each other...'

There was nothing to wait for. Knight in a lightning movement pulled out his sword from his belt and opened the spring. The blade opened out completely and before anyone had the time to protest, Paul slashed at the speaker blindly. He managed to lean back slightly and the blade barely cut his tunic and only grazed his chest. Despite this he stumbled and let out a continual scream. Boniface shouted horrifically.

'Run,' said Traveller quickly.

They threw themselves into headlong retreat. Now they could only escape in the direction of the burning house. They ran as fast as they could. Suddenly they saw the fire take hold of the high tenement block standing a little closer to them. The onlookers began to disperse in fear.

'Is there some side street here?' asked Traveller while running.

'Yes, there,' said Dominique pointing with her hand.

Indeed a narrow street soon appeared that ran at a sharp angle to the side. It meant that they would unfortunately be heading away from the lighthouse. They had no choice. They turned into it.

Helen and Boniface were clearly beginning to lag behind. Such a run for such elderly people was exceptionally tiring. It meant that either they would separate or they would slow down. But they did not intend to leave the old couple by themselves. Traveller stopped to wait for them and then with a drawn sword he stayed at the end of the party. All of a sudden, they saw a group of six men with swords some hundred yards behind. And so the chase had begun.

Dominique, Boniface and Helen were now running at the front, while Knight and Traveller were at the back. Paul was struck by the realisation that this was senseless. They had no chance against their pursuers, especially when they couldn't run very quickly. So what in that case should they do? Would Voice help them? Suddenly he saw that one of the tenement buildings had a large half-open iron gate. Without thinking much they all entered together and slammed it behind them. They did not have the key and the men chasing them had certainly seen where they were hiding.

Almost involuntarily, Knight placed his hand into the folds of his tunic that were draped over his belt. There in the pockets of his trousers his fingers closed in on a wire key that he had made a long time ago at the Little Sun. He placed it smoothly into the lock. It was a perfect fit. He turned his hand. At the moment when they heard the click of the lock, someone yanked at the handle from the other side of the gate. They breathed a sigh of relief. But what now. They were locked in someone's home, into which there might easily be another entrance. There might also live someone there who was totally opposed…

'Who are you?' asked a quiet voice behind them.

They had hardly heard this question in the racket the men were making yanking at the gate. They turned round slowly. Opposite to them in the middle of a small courtyard, stood a small boy of about eight or nine years old.

'We're travellers from another country,' blurted out Traveller. 'We're running away from the City authorities who want to hide the fact that we exist.'

Whatever kind of impression it was that Mr Wronski wanted to make by saying everything directly, he had clearly failed in his attempt. The boy looked at them unmoved.

'We're looking for shelter,' the captain added calmly.

'In that case, please come in,' said the boy bowing his head. Despite being the age of a child, he made a particularly dignified impression on them.

When he led them forwards through the wide entrance door, it seemed to them that he was leading them into his very own palace. After they had entered a small living room, Knight felt that they couldn't just act like guests. After all that band of City ruffians was still probably bashing at the gate. They had to do something.

'I know you,' the boy said unexpectedly. Paul froze. How could he know where they were from?

'The Book told me of your arrival,' he explained. What a relief! So there was no need for further explanations. They had found their way directly to the home of an ally. But who was the boy?

'My name is Jacob,' he said as if he had guessed Knight's question. My parents were taken by the City authorities recently because they warned against forgetting the Book. I've been left all alone. Can I join you?

The question very much surprised them. Traveller clearly frowned. They already had enough trouble with having to keep pace with Helen and Boniface without taking on the burden of a little boy on their shoulders.

Only then did Knight understand his mistake. He had forgotten what Voice had said. After all it was not about fighting with the City authorities or doing anything spectacular. They had to find at least seventy who believed and only then would they have a chance of saving City.

After all who was this boy if not a believer? A believer in the Book and its Author.

So before Traveller had the chance to diplomatically refuse, Paul blurted out, 'Of course. We need everyone who believes in the Book. We must convince as many citizens as possible of its existence and only then will we have a chance of saving City.'

'What rubbish,' wheezed Boniface, still out of breath. 'I've had enough of this. You were only supposed to lead me to the Book and now it turns out that I am to take part in the saving of City. I've been dragged into some hopeless chase and fight.'

'But what is hopeless? The battle for City or the chase itself?' Traveller angrily asked him. 'It seems to me that now you have already stopped believing in the possibility of saving City. At last you see with your own eyes how it is heading for destruction.'

'I don't see anything of the sort!' Boniface answered him in a rage. 'I only see that you have dragged me into a conflict with the authorities.'

'Now there is no way out, my dear. You must take the risk and run away with us. Our leader has seen you in our group so there isn't anything else for you to do anyway,' added Helen.

'Our group?' Boniface had almost reached the limits of his anger.

'Now you're already with them and not with me? Now you say "us" when talking about yourself and them?'

'I'm talking about us when I mean those who believe in the Book, my dear husband. Either you believe and you are one of us, or you give up fighting for the truth.'

'What bombastic words. And what does it mean for me?'

'Everything,' added Jacob, 'or nothing.'

Those gathered around stared questioningly at the boy. What did he know?

'Don't you know what the Book says?'

*For I will lead these seventy who believe to the summit where the real sun shines. There I will save them. And I will build for them a New City where Dragon will be no more.*

The solemn words of the Book echoed in the silence that had fallen. Suddenly Boniface replied coldly, 'Dragon? And so you believe in a Dragon?'

Nobody said anything. Everyone tried to understand the sense of the Book's prophecy.

Ignoring the older man's comment, Jacob explained, 'Just as you intended, we must get to the lighthouse. City awaits destruction, but there we'll be safe.'

'So the "real sun" means the lighthouse?' asked Knight. Really he felt almost disappointed. When he had read those words for the first time in his Mum's letter, he had thought about that all-encompassing cold unreal fire. But the lighthouse? The Book did indeed shine with its own internal light but this was not the same. Something of what he was going through must have been visible on his face as Jacob clearly turned to him.

'Are you disappointed?'

'Well, I… somewhat imagined "real sun" differently.'

'I think the shine of the Book is only a foreshadowing of the "real sun". Despite what happens, we have to gather everyone who believes in the Book and lead them to the lighthouse.'

It was astounding how this boy spoke with a voice of authority. His proposal now seemed entirely sensible, so they did not have any choice but to agree to it. As could have been expected, Boniface objected.

'Have you gone mad? You want to gather together a whole throng of people and lead them to the lighthouse! How do you intend to oppose the City authorities? And anyway, why am I supposed to care about your safety? Since you believe in a Dragon, my sensible arguments won't convince you anyway.'

With the man taking such a position, there was nothing more to say. If Boniface was not going to accept the idea that the truth about City may be other than that which resulted from his cursory observations, then they would not be able to convince him by themselves. The only chance was to drag him by force or by trickery up to the lighthouse.

'But how can we find those who believe?' asked Dominique.

'There is one more home where the inhabitants have the Book written out,' said Jacob. 'We must go to them.'

'It's not enough,' interjected Knight. 'There's only a few of us. We still need sixty or so people. We have to go out into the streets and gather up the people from them.'

'That's a big risk,' said Helen commenting on his idea, while Boniface only snorted.

'We have to take it,' said Traveller unexpectedly. 'Is there another way out of here?'

'Yes there is a passageway into the neighbouring house, which is empty, so we will be able to get out from there unobserved.'

'Good. Does everyone have a weapon?'

With these words, the boy ran into an adjacent room, and returned after a while with a small dagger, which he stuck in his belt in a similar manner to everybody else.

'Excellent. Boniface, Do you want to risk it and come with us or do you prefer to wait until the City authorities throw you in prison for complicity in attacking the leader?' asked Mr Wronski caustically. The man did not answer but screwed his face up in anger. They took that as a good sign and left being led by Jacob. Boniface followed after them. When they found themselves in the courtyard, they went through a narrow door leading to a side building. They expected to see a deserted dusty room, but what they saw was much worse. Jacob, who had entered first, screamed and jumped back, falling into Traveller, who was coming up behind him. He only had time to push him to the side and reach for his sword before a giant spider – perhaps two metres across – attacked. The captain swiped with his sword and stabbed the monster in the belly. It staggered back and retreated a few metres. Then it stood looking at them with numerous eyes. They heard it breathe angrily. Behind it they saw a large empty entrance hall covered in webs from which hung a multitude of smaller and larger spiders. Boniface gave a stifled cry. The others pulled out their swords. The people and spiders stood opposite each other as if weighing up whether it was worth attacking.

'Let's go back,' whispered Helen.

'And then what?' grunted Traveller. 'You think it's better to run away from this beast than to attack? I prefer to fight.'

After saying this, Traveller took two steps forward with his sword held high. The injured spider let out a terrible hiss and leant back a bit on its legs. Mr Wronski moved forward another two steps until he stood almost at sword's length from the hideous creature. Knight followed on after him.

Then the spider suddenly threw itself forwards, opening its disgusting mouth. Traveller jumped to the left at the same time slashing at the eyes of the beast with his sword. The creature howled picking itself up a little on its front legs. At the same time Paul crouched down and when the spider was above him he raised his sword straight up deep into the innards of the monster. The limbs shook convulsively.

'Push it away,' suddenly shouted Traveller. He did not have to say it again. Paul pushed the hilt of the sword with all his strength a little to the right. The beast was so dreadfully heavy that he completely crumpled under its weight. Falling to the side it hit him with its legs. They were heavy and armoured; it seemed to Knight that he had received a few heavy blows from a cudgel. He screamed out in pain and moved back dropping his sword which was stuck in the belly of the spider.

He would not have paid the pain much heed had it not been for the sinister growl that came from everywhere. The now dead monster may have been the biggest but it was not the only one of the spiders that were in the room.

'There are too many of them, they'll bite us all,' yelled Jacob.

'We have to cut the spider web and quickly run to the exit,' commanded Traveller.

Paul stood still stunned by the pain. He felt that he was unable to pull out his sword from the belly of the spider. Helen pushed the boy a little forward as she passed but he had no strength or will to go on. Suddenly from behind Paul's back out flew a little light and grabbed the hilt of his sword. This somewhat helped Paul recover his senses since he had been convinced that Elf had not come with them into the Book. He also had not expected that such a small figure could lift such a heavy sword. Amazed, he watched as Elf with one yank pulled out the sword from the belly of the spider, lifted it in his delicate hands and gave it to him.

This was enough to bring Paul fully back. He moved forward, cutting with the sword almost blindly only taking care not to injure his companions.

The spiders attacked them from every side. There were countless numbers of them. It was certainly a miracle that they were able to knock them all down from their webs or cut them up with their blades. Elf flew as quick as lightning here and there, cutting up the monsters' armour as if it were butter with his shimmering wings.

The way out onto the street was on their left in the middle of the long room where they were. It was almost entirely covered in spider webs woven like a shroud. Traveller, together with Dominique and Helen, who had shorter more agile daggers, cut at it while the others defended their backs from the spider attacks. Suddenly Jacob quietly cried out and bent over in two, but Boniface caught him under the arm and held him up. It was a miracle that they reached the door. It opened surprisingly easily and everybody, as if pushed out from inside by some unnatural force, fell out onto the street.

And there... Screaming and stampeding, people running off in every direction...

'What's happening?' Dominique shouted out to some women running by.

'Fire! It's spreading everywhere terribly quickly. Run!' shouted a young woman from behind them.

'To the lighthouse, to the lighthouse,' Knight began to shout. He understood that now was the chance to gather up the people: As they were running away from danger in panic, they might want to take shelter in the one truly safe place. He forgot about the pain that had recently overpowered him. He ran forward shouting, 'Run up the hill! To the lighthouse! The flames won't reach us there! To the lighthouse!'

He shouted so loud that he felt his throat rasp. His companions immediately grasped his idea and running after the crowd that was fleeing downwards they began shouting together with Paul.

'Upwards! To the lighthouse! The fire will not reach there.'

Their shouting started to get through to the terrified people. Some stopped and looked around to find a way up.

Suddenly Knight noticed that on the roofs of the nearest houses perched some monstrous birdlike creatures eyeing them out in the crowd. But he did not intend to give up. He was going to continue calling out. Since Voice had sent him here to help these people believe in the Book and in this way save City, so he was not going to leave them now at the mercy of Enemy, who had taken on different figures. City droned with many screams and cries. Over the clamour of people, the sound of everything being destroyed by flames could be heard. The heat of the fires could be felt on the face.

Their calls were clearly beginning to cause confusion among the people. Some rushed down to the coast as if they had not heard them at all towards the black depths of the sea. Others stopped. Only the tiniest fraction of the inhabitants turned back.

Traveller suddenly called out, 'We must split up. Knight, you, Dominique and Boniface, run up towards the lighthouse and call out to people. Jacob, Helen and I will run off to those friends of the boy that believe in the Book and along the way we'll call out to everyone to run upwards. In this way we'll send more people towards the lighthouse and we'll meet up there.'

This suggestion, although sensible, contained within it one terrible danger. Separating under these circumstances? That would mean weakening their combined strength in regard to Enemy. But on the other hand… it increased the likelihood of saving the greatest number of people.

'OK, you're right,' Knight felt that he was saying this despite himself.

The others listened without a word. Boniface was so numbed by shock that there was no problem separating him from his wife.

Knight turned left up the next street heading upwards and, together with Dominique and Boniface, made his way quickly towards the hill. The birdlike creatures were now circling low above the streets.

He could not, however, run as quickly as he would have liked, since Dominique had begun to stop the people running down the hill and personally entreated them to change direction. Although at first he was reluctant to accept this, he understood that they had a greater chance of convincing others to run upwards through City.

With his left hand he caught some old man and pulled him towards himself.

'Run upwards. The flames will not reach us there; we'll be safe in the lighthouse.'

'Safe?' asked the old man.

His voice was cold and sneering. Only now did Knight take a conscious look at him. He was short and hunched with a heavily wrinkled face.

'Yes! That's where the Book is. You must believe that City can only be saved through the Book.' Paul himself did not know why he had dared to try persuading the man so openly.

The old man smiled showing his few teeth. He looked so repulsive that Paul let go of his arm and took a step back. He felt a disturbing shiver. The man had a long dishevelled beard and dark eyes. In fact they were black to such a degree that it was impossible to tell apart the pupils from the irises.

Knight felt a wave of nausea come over him. Only now did he recognise who it was that stood before him. It was the very same old man who had blocked his exit from the cellar in the Little Sun at the very beginning of his journey. It was Enemy.

'I think we know each other,' said the man sinisterly. Paul hesitated. He could have lifted up his sword, which he still held in his right hand, and simply cut the old man in two or he could have left him and ran on. An unbearable moment of hesitation. And if Enemy, despite his unimpressive appearance, was to chase him? Or set the bird-like creatures on him?

Before he had been able to make a decision, he heard a scream from Boniface, who had up until that moment been standing and heedlessly waiting for him. He turned around.

His companion had been attacked by an armed man who wore an emblem on his chest showing that he was from the City authorities.

So these traitors are not going to let it go, thought Knight angrily and with sword raised and no longer paying attention to Enemy, he attacked their opponent. Surprised, the man tried to defend himself, but Paul could feel an almost superhuman strength within him. Jumping, he raised his leg high, which kicked aside the barely raised sword of the guard and with the flat side of his sword he struck the man a stunning blow on the head. Defeated, he fell unconscious to the ground. As Knight stood over him panting in rage he felt someone touch him from behind with the point of a blade underneath the ribs.

'I told you I would remember you,' sneered the old man from behind his back. 'And now I can delight in your death.'

All around them a crowd of people ran down into City, but no one paid any attention to Paul. No one cared about the settling of some score, which was taking place here. People only cared to save themselves. Boniface stood still bewildered. Out of the corner of his eye, Knight saw Dominique sneak up on Enemy from behind and with a single dexterous stab, she stuck her dagger into his back. Paul jumped out of the way of the blade that still twitched at his back. He turned around and saw the old man with a horrific grimace on his face stagger on his legs. From his throat came an inhuman gasp. He began to slowly fall to the ground.

To Knight's extreme horror, he did not collapse on the ground, as could have been expected. The lower he fell, the more uncertain the shape of his figure became, as if he were dissolving into a thick black mist. When his head had almost reached the level of the street, it suddenly turned completely black so that for a moment all that could be seen was the mouth still twisted into a grimace, after which it turned into a hideous monster that was not reminiscent of any creature. It had no form; it was like a shapeless black mass from which peered two eye sockets that seeped blood and in the place where there had previously been a mouth yawned an infinite emptiness. It seemed to Knight that he saw in it a terrible chasm, as if the throat was unending.

He shuddered. He felt that he could not let himself look at this bottomless pit of evil, which breathed out at him with its killer breath. He looked at Dominique. They exchanged fearful looks and picking up Boniface together, they ran upwards, still shouting at the people passing by to turn back.

Someone tried to stop them.

'Have you gone mad? You've got to run down to the sea. You can take cover in the waves by the shore, where the fire cannot reach.' With these words he ran off further down while they still tried to catch those passing by and show them the way back up. But there were ever fewer who would listen to them. Clearly the belief that safety could be found in the water had spread through the frenzied crowd.

Suddenly, they saw the bird-like creatures dive down and catch people at random from the crowd and throw them screaming to the high heavens into the air, while other beasts caught them in the air and tore them apart in front of the dumbstruck crowd. Still more terrible cry resounded. Prolonged screams resonated in their ears. The bird-like creatures were having themselves a fiesta of dread.

It seemed to Knight that he was so frightened his own blood was congealing in his veins. He stopped breathing and his legs were as heavy as iron. He thought he was not able to move. Like a faint ray of hope, the delicate light of crystal wings flashed above him. The soothing presence of his loyal companion flooded Knight with warmth. He felt that he could run and Elf would protect him from the attacks of the monsters.

They hurried on. Suddenly the street came to an end. Some narrow stairs led upwards. They began to push their way through the people running down. When they ran up to the top it turned out that they had reached a kind of city viewing platform from which a view of part of the island spread out beneath them. Above, the thin lighthouse dominated over a forest sparsely dotted with buildings. Only now did Paul notice that from in between the closed, mirrored shutters, a faint light shone, as if no barrier could suppress the light of the Book. It squeezed its way outside through the narrowest of gaps. Yes, the truth could not be totally hidden; at most it could be obscured. This site gave Knight hope.

Suddenly, the screams that could be heard all around, turned into a wall-destroying yell. Paul turned around and looked down to where it seemed to him this dreadful clamour was coming from. There in the distance could be seen the coast as well as the sea that stretched up to the horizon. Only there was no longer an endless calm surface. It was a wild untamed element, which in its anger rose up and with the power of the foamy waves fell on the unfaithful City engulfing the citizens who had not been expecting anything.

The site that rolled out from the platform was a picture of indescribable destruction. The fire and water almost combined their powers, engulfing the people who were scrambling around in panic. Numerous walls and buildings fell with a boom, throwing up clouds of sharp gravel into the air. Knight knew that this was a picture of destruction. So had Voice decided to destroy the city without waiting to see if they would succeed in gathering up those seventy who believed? But why? No, this was not yet the end. Voice could not lie. He was waiting for them to reach the lighthouse. After all, not all City had been destroyed by the elements yet.

Suddenly something caught Paul by the throat. A picture of Traveller and his companions came to his mind. No, he did not want to think about this. Voice, after all, would not allow something terrible to happen to them. He could not lose faith wondering about this. He turned to Dominique and Boniface who stood dumbstruck looking at the destruction of their land. He shook them.

'Come on. We have to look for people who want to run towards the lighthouse. Now they won't be able to run down towards the sea so we have a better chance.'

Dominique looked at him with silent dread in her eyes. She only nodded her head although it could be seen that this had been a great effort for her. Boniface still stood motionless like a pillar of salt, looking at City, which had been his entire life.

Only now did Paul notice that there remained few people left around. The majority had already run down from the upper to the lower parts of City. The few, just like his companions, looked on in silence at the ferocious battle of the elements, which seemed to be competing about which of them could engulf and destroy the most.

Knight caught people by the hand and called out, 'Go upwards to the lighthouse. There we can still find shelter. Don't you see the light coming from there? That's the Book. Remember it! Don't you know how it once protected your City with its light? It can still save us. Run upwards!'

Saying nothing, Dominique caught people and pushed them up the lighthouse hill like puppets with no will of their own. Some, due to their efforts, began moving upwards as if they were stunned.

But at the same time voices spoke up: 'Don't listen to them. There is no salvation for us any more. We will be devoured by those birds or by other beasts that are circling above us. It's better to die in the fire than to be torn to pieces.'

Suddenly someone climbed up on the platform's wall and jumped down into the abyss of flame that reached up towards him. Knight now wanted to run up to the wall to see where he had fallen but he was terrified when he noticed that other people were heading in the same direction to throw themselves down in a similar manner to their own doom.

'No, no!' he cried. 'What are you doing? Do you think such a death is better? Why are you throwing away the only hope of being saved?' His voice was drowned in the screams of the dying. The bird-like creatures were still attacking, diving down with a terrifying screech.

Someone caught his forearm.

'What are you saying? Will the Book really save us?' It was a young man who in his left arm held a small terrified child. The little boy hugged the arm of his dad but, what was really heart-rendering was that in the eyes of the father regret could be seen as well as the fact that he was fearfully lost.

'Yes, believe me, please. Those who make it to the Book and believe that they can find salvation in it will survive. Please believe me,' Paul felt that he was almost begging this man he did not know.

Then he noticed that behind him there was a young woman, almost certainly his wife. Her tearful eyes were fixed on the bundle which she held in the folds of her tunic by her breast. The quiet mewling of the frightened baby moved Knight's heart. By her legs, stood a boy of about five years of age who grasped his mother's dress with his tiny little fingers.

In its pain and despair, that young family was so beautiful that it took Knight's breath away. The innocence of the terrified children and the despair of the helpless parents drowned in something that emanated from them. Paul could feel an almost palpable love binding them together. While all the other inhabitants ran downwards into the City in chaos without paying any heed to the fate of their loved ones and caring only to save themselves, this family had stayed together, prepared to share the same fate, whatever it might be.

Tears flowed down Knight's face involuntarily. He could not allow them to die. Even if he could only save them, he would do everything so that they would not die. It was unimportant if he gathered up seventy to save City, as Voice had demanded. No. He would fight with Author of the Book himself to save these people who emanated a love that united them.

'Come. We must get to the lighthouse.'

He pulled the man and moved upwards. After him came the woman with the children and bringing up the rear there was Dominique and Boniface. Around them there was continual shouting:

'Don't believe them! Up in the lighthouse there are even worse monsters than here!'

'Doom awaits you there!'

'Dragon is in the lighthouse!'

The mention of Dragon went through the Knight's body like a dreadful growl. But that most fearful of beasts had not yet appeared. What could this mean? Was the worst battle still before them? Now so little distance remained between them and the lighthouse.

People joined them, a middle-aged man, an elderly woman, a few terrified and disorientated children...

Knight feared to count how many there were. He did not want to base his hope on dead numbers. He preferred to believe that Voice would save them without regard for how many there were. He was surprised to note that with the omnipresent dread, the destruction and the feasting bird-like creatures everywhere, above their small group appeared a glow the colour of a rainbow. He looked up and saw how not high above them ephemeral creatures with variously coloured crystal wings rose up in the air. He had seen them before, long ago, in the cave where they had fought with Eyma. Now they were protecting them from attack by Enemy and they were guarding the way. So Author was still supporting them.

Knight felt how much he longed for Voice to speak again in his heart. He longed to hear cheering words, some... any assurance that all would be well. An endless silence was all that replied to his longing. Paul experienced the empty space inside, where previously Voice had spoken. Why was he now quiet? Why did he not support him in this terrible moment?

Suddenly he slipped and fell. The young father of the family held him up a little, enough that he could recover his footing on the ground. He looked at his feet. He was standing on some kind of paper, which slipped on the damp rocks. It was some torn out piece of a page. He did not have too much time to look at it and he wanted to leave it and move on, when his attention was caught by a tiny drawing in the very corner of the piece of paper. He picked up the sheet and slowing down he looked at the picture.

It was a portrait of a man. He had black hair and lively blue eyes. Knight did not have to wonder who it represented. Although he still felt the emptiness within and Voice was silent, he knew that Friend was reminding him of his presence. So they were not alone. Paul did not try to understand why Friend had not come openly with help. He knew that the meanderings of such considerations would lead him to doubt and to inevitable despair. He had to believe. Even though the murderous fire was all that lit up the darkness of night, he had to believe that where they were heading shone the true sun.

He crumpled the paper in his hand and place it in his tunic by his chest as if it were his greatest treasure. He had the impression that warmth was spreading from his heart throughout his entire body. He ran off after the others, who had managed to overtake him a little. Suddenly he heard an ominous growl. He looked back.

Had he known what he would see before he turned around? He probably had. His whole body, already tense like an instrument string, had been waiting for this moment. He knew that what he most feared had to appear.

But it was not now. When he looked down the slope towards the sea, he saw a terrifying monster multiplied in its enormity come out of the sea. Although he had seen it before from the bottom as it had filled the entire cave with its huge size, he had no doubt that it was Eyma that had appeared from out of the depths. Numerous limbs sprang from others like budding shoots. The beast was so huge that emerging from the ocean it created the impression that it would consume the entire island. Its slimy tentacles came out of the water and began to climb up the streets of City crushing those few who had so far survived. To Knight it seemed that Eyma had wound its limbs around the whole island as if it had grasped a delicious doughnut that shone with icing ready to be devoured in one bite.

He knew they had little time. They could not watch the monster which they had no chance of fighting anyway. He turned again to the others who were dumbstruck looking back at the beast.

'Faster, faster! We have to get to the lighthouse before Eyma reaches us!' he shouted.

His companions again moved up the hill like mindless sheep. They were so paralysed with fear that they allowed him to lead them without resistance. Now they moved up the dirt road between the sparsely spaced buildings. Knight saw that in the window of one of the houses there were a number of people looking at the destruction of City. They were clearly frightened to leave and run away anywhere.

'Dominique, lead everyone to the lighthouse. I'll try to persuade someone to join us.' With these words he ran up to the house and without knocking he burst through the door. Two men standing by the window, most probably a father and his adult son, as well as an elderly woman looked at him in terror.

'Come on! Run for it! The monster that came out of the sea will reach you. You must come shelter with us in the lighthouse. The Book is there, which will save us.'

He had been counting on them immediately getting up and running after him, but they stood unmoved, staring at him without comprehension. He went up to them and caught the old man by the hand.

'Let's move! We've got to escape!'

'Have you gone mad?' he asked hoarsely and pulled his hand from Paul's grasp. 'Have you seen anything of what's going on outside? There's no chance we're leaving here.' Saying this, he took a few steps back from Knight.

His son and the older woman, who could have been his mother, were still looking at Paul without moving.

'You will die here. Do you think that as the whole of City has burnt down you will be saved in your little house?'

'And it's supposedly better for us in the lighthouse?'

'The Book is there!' Paul heard himself shouting out in anger.

'And what about it?'

This question cut through Knight like a sharp sword. He really did not know what it was about. He only knew that Voice was leading him there, that salvation might be there, but what kind? Why?

'If we're going to die, then at least it is with all our possessions.' On saying this, the man made a gesture encompassing everything around him. Paul looked around involuntarily. It was a very ordinary home, neither poor nor particularly wealthy. When he gazed on all the different equipment in the home he saw that it was all infused by a black mist, similar to the one that the evil old man had turned into. There was something awful in these fumes. And it was not some danger that they had innately. In some monstrous manner Paul knew that the mist was not characterless, that there was some evil hiding within it with its own purpose.

He took a few steps back. Once again he glanced half-consciously at the inhabitants of this home. And so they wanted to die with their possessions. No, he was not going to save them now. They had made their choice. He turned around and ran out. He immediately realised he had lost a lot of time. His group of companions were already far ahead of him. The fire had consumed the viewing platform on which they had stood not long ago. The bottom of the island had already drowned in the dark turbulent waters, from which Eyma still stretched out his macabre limbs to crush buildings and grab citizens. The moon looking down on him dripped with blood and the sky was full of flying beasts. The air shook with the shouts and screams and the darkness that engulfed everything was so thick that even the fire had difficulty illuminating it.

Knight again started running upwards. And every now and then he stopped seeing people hiding here and there. He caught them and showed them the way to the lighthouse, but most of them did not even want to listen to him. They preferred to dwell in their limitless despair, absorbed in the contemplation of their own demise, deaf to the truth, which could free them from the shackles of darkness.

How limitless must be the darkness that would make a person abandon his own salvation! How terrible must be the gloom that hates the happiness that would lift a man up above meagre reality into the sphere of absolute freedom!

Knight had the impression that many of those he was trying to convince to take shelter in the lighthouse had already lost their lives. Their empty look masked a bottomless abyss hidden inside. Why? The question was continually pressing on Paul's lips. He so very much wanted to understand how a person could choose their own demise. And why Voice was allowing it. Why would Arie not come and save all the inhabitants from destruction?

Arie comes to those who call him.

At last. He had been waiting so long for Voice to speak. But why not? Why could he not also save those who did not call him? After all, he could save them.

Are you sure?

Of course! I am certain that you can do anything. You could also send Arie to those who do not want to believe.

So look.

Knight stopped running. In the distance the group of his companions were running upwards. Here and there a few people were hiding among the houses. Someone stood before him in the middle of the road looking at the destruction that was happening behind his back.

Suddenly a miraculous, warm clarity took hold of the gloom. Knight heard the flapping of powerful wings and looking up he saw a powerful bird flying above him. After a while that wonderful glowing being descended and landed softly by the man standing in the road. With his glowing white wings and his almost soft figure, the eagle stood out sharply from all his surroundings full of monstrous bird-like creatures, black mist and sticky darkness. The man stood dumbfounded staring at Arie.

'Come, climb on my back. I can save you. I will take you and we will fly far off to another island,' he said gently.

The man stood looking at the beautiful eagle, which so contrasted with the entire nightmare that surrounded them. Suddenly a terrible scream came from his throat and he stumbled back with his arms out in front in a defensive gesture.

'No,' he shouted. 'Help! Some monster wants to eat me! Someone help me! I would prefer to die in the fire!'

With these words, the man started to run, he passed by Arie, who stood calmly still, and ran down towards the murderous fire. Knight turned around and looked speechless as the man fell with a scream into the flames.

Paul was overwhelmed by the bitter danger. And so it was like that. So one could abandon salvation, which was not only a hazy promise of protection from the flames in a high lighthouse. One could abandon salvation, which appears suddenly out of the darkness in all its bright glory. So does everything depend on this? Does everything only depend on whether I want it? On whether I believe? Knight closed his eyes in desperation.

*Yes. It is enough to want it. And then I as Author assign a role to every character in my tale. I can lead him to a happy ending if only he allows me to write it and he doesn't spin his own version of the story. Those are the rules. Everyone who denies his role will have to leave the pages of this story. Now the time has come to at last purge the plot. There are many characters living in it who do not want to hear me. And it is now time to bring it to an end.*

Only will it be a happy ending? Knight as if in slow motion looked at the nightmare all around.

*Oh, yes. I am – I must admit – a sentimental Author. I like happy endings. It's already been a long time since I thought up how I would like this story to end and now the time has come to write the final pages.*

And what will happen next? What will happen when you finish writing the final pages? Will anything continue to exist?

*Oh, yes. You see, I didn't tell you earlier... My story is only a beginning. Really it's hardly even a prologue to the Great Story. Although in principle there will no longer be the Book or the tale... Then you will already be more than characters. The Great Story is now life itself and you, my characters, will come from the Book into life with me.*

As deep inside Knight listened to these words, fire took hold of the houses a little behind him. Only now did the all-consuming heat reach him. Would it consume him too? As if in a dream, he opened his eyes. Before him stood Arie as if waiting for something. Paul knew what he had to do. He climbed up on the back of the bird. The powerful eagle unfurled its fluffy wings and climbed into the air. Knight suddenly felt how the brightness that surrounded the bird and which so astounded him, penetrated into him. Now he had the impression that he himself shone, that the thick sticky darkness dissipated before him, just as it did before Arie.

The bird rushed up towards the lighthouse. It flew low above the earth to the few surviving people. Most looked at it from afar with fear and ran away as it approached. Only two children hidden behind some bush, looked at him with clear joy and climbed on his back. Some well-dressed woman jumped towards them with outstretched hands. Arie also took her. Suddenly they saw a poorly dressed man who was running upwards by himself. Arie caught him in flight in his beak and with one sweeping movement threw him on his back.

Suddenly he turned from above the road to fly over the forest. A shout came to them from within the vegetation. Someone was calling for help. The eagle flew in between the trees where they were not quite so dense. Knight jumped from his back and began to call out. He saw someone struggling towards him through the undergrowth. Paul pulled out his sword and with sweeping strokes began to cut everything that separated him from this unfortunate fellow. He succeeded. He pulled the lost boy towards the majestic figure of Arie and they climbed on the back of the eagle. The bird again took to the air to fly towards the lighthouse. The fire was almost everywhere.

Suddenly from above the trees Paul saw a rider dressed in long white robes which billowed behind him in the wind, just as did his long white hair. He rode on a white horse whose mane and tale seemed to be aflame. The rider held a sword in his hand and he raced his steed upwards between the trees towards the lighthouse. But Arie flew on and soon the mysterious figure had disappeared from view.

From high up, Knight could see a group of people climbing up from the other side of the hill. They were surrounded by the bird-like creatures and the flames were almost licking at their heels. From afar Knight could make out the lonely figure of Traveller, who among the general turmoil cut at the disgusting bulk of the attacking beasts with his sword. Around him the others only bowed their heads in despair waiting for the blows from the crooked beaks.

Only now did Knight appreciate the unbroken resolve of his companion and guide. Traveller did not know the meaning of the words "give up". He fought on relentlessly, even though the battle already appeared a foregone conclusion. The strength and speed with which he used the blade of his sword to cut at everything that endangered his group of companions was breathtaking.

Arie sped in their direction at breakneck speed. The increasing mass of bird-like creatures dispersed before him, just as it once had done in the cave. And just like then, Knight felt that he was tensing his muscles ready to attack. Suddenly it was as if he jumped in the air with a terrible cry. Paul realised that the fluffy feathers beneath him were disappearing. For a moment he had the impression that he was just about to fall, having nothing to hold onto, but at that moment Arie placed his powerful paws on the ground and with a mighty roar, shaking his golden head, he attacked the bird-like creatures tearing them apart with his lion's muzzle.

It was the first time Knight had seen him in the figure of a lion. He was impressively large and his coat glistened like the purest gold. His main was wholly woven with a light that dispersed the surrounding darkness. Indeed everything seemed to now be buried in this mane like in a soft puffy eiderdown. The gloom was lifted only by it being shaken and the fire retreated from the power of his lion roar.

'Quickly upwards!'

The voice, which itself was as powerful as thunder, hastened them to run up to the lighthouse. There was no longer any time for any kind of explanation. Knight, arm in arm with Traveller, as well as the group of people they had gathered up made their way to the thin building on the summit. Arie protected them from behind pushing away a wave of darkness that was closing in on them.

How little now separated them from the place of salvation! As if in exultation, they ran this final distance safe under the care of Arie. They saw Dominique running into the lighthouse still dragging Boniface, as well as the people who they had collected along the way. Knight had no idea how many of them all together there were. There were certainly forty or fifty but whether the number was high enough to reach the required seventy of that he was not certain. For a moment a shudder went through him. And what would happen if it was not?

They burst into the lighthouse. Its doors turned out to be surprisingly wide.

## Chapter twenty eight
# IN THE LIGHTHOUSE

The brightness that dazzled them was not from this world. Little motes of air like gold dust filled the infinite space of the sky and under their feet shone oceans of ice. Everywhere there were the most various of creatures, which filled the skies in the limitless distances of the stars. They sparkled with many colours which were so vivid that just looking at them would awaken unutterable joy in the heart. The ice was full of people and animals standing with dignified raised heads, like figures carved out of marble. But nonetheless the life that teemed in them was reflected in the echo of the heavens. The melody of the universe, which sang a song in an unknown tongue, made every particle of their bodies vibrate.

In the middle of the limitless sea stood the horse with the burning mane, and on it sat Rider. His blue eyes glowed from an immeasurable distance and his face shone, as if it had been cast in metal. In his hand he held a long sword of maybe three metres. The hooves of his prancing horse, as if carved out of stone, broke the ice, which cracked all the way to the furthest horizon only to seal again after a moment.

Behind him on a gigantic throne that reached up to the heavens sat Author himself. It seemed to Knight that somewhere in the depths of his memory he recognised that majestic face with the grey eyes. But there was no possible way to describe his figure. He held the Book open on his lap. The quill in his hand was so gigantic that if he had held out his hand, he could have knocked down most of the stars in the heavens with it. Now it lay motionless on the page, ready at any moment to write another page. Author however looked with unmoving eyes at something behind Knight. Paul turned around. Behind them in a flawlessly sky blue space stood powerful Dragon. Its wings were spread wide, although now it was not moving. Around him everywhere there were the vile bird-like creatures with the white eyes frozen in the air like a swarm of insects preparing to attack. Around its legs there was a horde of ghoulish creatures and among them the old man from the cellar of the Little Sun, the leader of the City council and many other faces... And although their heads were not deformed, monstrous twisted bodies grew out of them, all of which were so indescribably varied and at the same time so nightmarish that they no longer looked anything like human limbs. In deformed hands they held long spears, pitchforks and twisted swords...

In this bright space, which changed with a mass of colours reflected in the millions of coloured elf wings, the sight of Enemy's army was truly vile. All kinds of monsters breathing hatred, twisted by their own base desire sharply contrasted with the undisturbed peace of the beings hanging in the sky, with the statuesque lack of movement of the people and animals with the frozen figure of Rider and with the unmoved power of Author.

'The time has come.'

Knight recognised Voice, who here in this space sounded like the bang of all creation. Everything showed that it was time to conquer the rule of Dragon.

The beast gave a drawn out howl, but it voice was drowned out by the all-powerful roar of Arie. Knight could not see the eagle anywhere and he had the impression that the roar had come from all around, from the air, from all the creatures that were gathered here, from his companion and even from himself.

He pulled out his sword in front of him. At the same time Traveller did the same as well as the surviving inhabitants of City. But they were not alone. Countless ranks of marble figures stood with them ready for battle. Only Rider remained unmoved on his horse.

Two armies – one black, stinking, breathing smoke, dripping with poisonous blood, as well as the other reflecting the light of countless colours, clear and bright – moved against each other.

The flash of a raised sword.
Metallic noise.
Stroke.

War cries.
Blood.

Blood like tar, black and smoking with an intoxicating stench.
Bottomless throats, from which poured forth streams of hatred.
White, dead eyes, burning with the desire of destruction.
Fire from the maw of Dragon, which melted into the gold particles in the air changing into an invigorating breeze.

Spears.
The crash of weapons.
The roar of the beast.
Monstrous screams.
Blood.

Silver blood flowing onto the sea of ice changing it into a meadow full of flowers.
Cries of pain turning into the most wondrous singing.
Wounds, from which flowed invigorating fountains.
Pain, which turned into the ecstasy of joy.

Quenched with battle, Knight glanced behind himself at Author, who in his undisturbed peace was writing the final pages of the Book. Suddenly, his quill stopped and he raised his eyes. His gaze fell on still-motionless Rider, who as if feeling this gaze upon him, raised his sword even higher and spurred on his horse. Its burning mane flamed like lava and the granite hooves crashed into the ice. They moved. Everybody – elves, people, animals – ran to the sides to make way for the majestic figure on his steed.

The beat of the hooves entered into their blood and caused the very stars to shake.

Dragon roared and leapt forward towards what seemed the small figure of Rider.

Sword held high.

Muzzle down.

The blade which like the nib of Author's quill went to one place.

Fire.

Neighing.

The cry of darkness.

The flash of blue eyes.

Hateful yellow eyes.

The brightening white within the fiery mane.

The endless gloom of poisonous wings.

The steed's thin stone legs.

The twisted murderous claws.

The billowing rushing robes.

The outspread wings dripping with poison.

Time that turned into an eternity.

Dragon was killed.

Together with him came the end of the darkness and the universe once again took on its melody of happiness.

Full stop.

He closed the Book.

They both stood arm in arm. With shallow breathing and semi-closed eyes through which the dull light of a candle barely registered in Paul's stunned mind. He knew that his companion was standing paralysed just as he was. A sudden snore jolted them from their stupor. Grouch turned over in his bed. Only now, still breathing deeply, could they look around the small chamber. And in it: a couch, two armchairs, one bed, a barely glowing fireplace… and the Book lying on the table closed. The damaged cover was evidence of its long story. How much had it gone through? How many fates were written within it? How many tales?

And so what had happened to City? What had happened to Boniface, Helen and Dominique? What about Jacob?

Only did this now matter? Author must have taken care of them. He, Knight, had taken his own path. He had reached the very end in order to be able to take up arms again. To fight for his City.

And Traveller, he too had learnt about his own possibilities. He had taken his own path to the lighthouse. He had taken on the fight. He had experienced the power of fire that did not burn. He had dived into Arie's mane.

And so they had fought the first battle for themselves. The fighting would continue until the day when they would also have to battle for the world and everything in it.

Knight closed his eyes and again he saw that final moment. The power of the sword pen which was buried in the heart of Dragon. He did not have to fear.

'Now it's time to sleep,' Traveller said calmly. 'There's still a lot ahead of us.'

Mr Wronski took the Book from the table and placed it high on the shelf in its place. Without a word he lay down in the armchair. For a moment he looked into the fire after which he shut his eyes. Had he fallen asleep?

Knight spent a long time lying with his eyes closed looking at images from his memory or rather from deep down in his soul, in which he still saw the sun afresh shining in the sky in the light of which Dragon and his army melted away like figures made of ice. The real sun.

**Chapter twenty nine**

# EXPLANATIONS

Morning came. Although it was hard to call it morning since the polar night still covered everything completely in darkness. But in Knight's heart it was full of light. The Traveller's quiet smile also told the story of a beautiful land bathed in sunlight. Suddenly the thought crossed Paul's mind that he missed this place, but at the same time it was not now the longing that had seemed to tear his heart in two on the island of Shemesh. Then he had been overcome by despair, which had come from the knowledge that he could not stay there. But now inside he was filled with the hope that although his time, his time of City had not come yet, he would be given the opportunity to return to that world.

'Today is the 24th of December,' said their hostess.

Oh, today is Christmas Eve, thought Knight. How full of meaning that feast day now was. He was not surprised at all when in the evening Friend came knocking on the door of the hut. They ate a celebratory (for their circumstances) supper after which, for the first time since the beginning of the polar night, they went outside. It turned out that there was a beautiful aurora, which lit up the mountains with a red and green glow. They sat in its light on a bench that had been brought out by their hosts.

They were silent. What was there to say in the face of such wonderful promise? The changing colours reminded Knight of the elves' crystal wings fighting with Dragon. His Elf had disappeared somewhere as if he had joined the joyful choir of light in the heavens. Friend smiled mysteriously as if he knew what was hidden in the magic of this colourful concert. His blue eyes shone joyfully.

It was difficult to say how long they lasted sitting out in the frost. But they were not cold at all. They returned to the hut to lie down. This time Friend did not disappear without a word, but he said goodbye to them.

'But can't you stay with us?' asked a disappointed Tiger.

'I am always with you when you need me. Besides we'll see each other again soon.'

'But will you at least explain to us what more we are to do?' asked Lady, unaware of the story of the battle for City.

'What do you mean? You have to find the key for Granny and then you have to sail back home on the Whaler.'

'But must we wait here for the end of the polar night? When are we going to be able to move on from here?' Daisy questioned him further. Knight was himself surprised how little he cared to know the answers to the questions. Of course he wanted to return home but now he knew that Friend would lead them and they need not fear that they would lose their way. And were they still to wait a long time in this hut? Somehow he was not worried about this. In the end it was nice to spend time with this family listening to the mysterious words of the Book in the evenings. He was surprised to realise that he had found his inner peace, which was now allowing him to wait patiently for the next stage of the journey.

'You'll see later. When the time comes to move on, you will know,' replied Friend mysteriously after which he was gone.

The next few days passed by lazily. Knight and Traveller told the story of what they had experienced in the Book to the others, who listened with cries of disbelief and fear. But the happy ending brightened their faces.

'And what happened to City?' asked Lady.

Paul realised that, in some way that he could not comprehend, the fate of Daisy was connected to the story of City. Her curiosity therefore had a deeper cause. But neither he nor Traveller were able to give her a satisfactory answer, so they sat awhile in silence.

'What happened?' asked Lady appearing disturbed. 'So then it was destroyed?'

'I think...' began Knight uncertainly, 'I think yes and no.'

Lady frowned. For sure this was not what she had wanted to hear.

'I mean ... This particular City together with everything that was evil within it was destroyed... But...' He still hesitated as to how to say the truth he felt. 'But everything that was good within it was saved... and... was transformed.'

'Transformed? What does that mean?' his explanation was clearly insuffi-
cient for Daisy.

'Aah, you see, it's rather difficult...'

'I believe that in City's location there is a New City, which will be much
more brilliant and better than the previous one,' calmly interrupted Traveller.
'And so the razing of City occurred and at the same time it made it possible for
something incomparably more perfect to arise.'

Lady thought for a while as if trying to comprehend the sense of what had
happened and assess how good a resolution it was.

'OK, well, let us say that that is what happened. But explain to me in that
case how this relates to what we saw on the island when we were there. There
was no New City there, only ruins.'

For this pertinent observation they had no good answer.

It had to be admitted that Knight had already been worrying over this
question earlier. Why had they seen City destroyed but at the same time saved
in the lighthouse? Maybe the space of the lighthouse hid within it the secret
of this New or in other words transformed City? How was it that they knew
that City had been transformed? After all, they had not seen it. But somehow
they had this certainty in their hearts. They had led the believers from City to
the lighthouse, they had seen the final battle with Dragon but they had had to
return here to this little house in the normal world... What world? Was this
"normal" world so intertwined with the Crooked World that it was impossible
to see the boundaries between them? When Traveller long ago had described
the history of the island, he had said that the few people who were saved from
its destruction were able to escape by sea to other countries. Supposedly they
had also kept maps... But they had seen the total destruction of Migdal!

The secret of the Book suffuses through all of history. In each one of its
times is contained the truth about the ultimate goal, about the great Epilogue.
Every moment contains an eternity within it and leads into the gate of the
Crooked World. You only have to want to see it. The battle with Dragon for
City and its destruction is a picture of the last battle with Dragon for the entire world. And although City was destroyed, it was saved in the memory of
Author, who wrote about its transformation at the very end of the story. Time
and space, this world and its eternal image, the heart of every single person
and all of humanity are intertwined together so that at last in the Epilogue

everything can find its resolution. Every person, every City, all of humanity are fighting a battle for their survival. Every one of these stories will in the end find its finale.

Only now did understanding come that Paul's heart had long ago sensed. Knight knew he was fighting an internal battle for himself, he had fought a battle for City, now a battle for the world awaited him. How was he to win it?

Find the key for Granny.

That's right. In City his task had been to lead as many inhabitants as possible to the lighthouse. Now he was to do exactly the same thing, only in a slightly different manner. He was to help as many people as possible go through the gates of the Crooked World. He had to start with Granny. But where was he to start looking? He'd made his way so far and still he did not know where to find the key.

You must go to Alta, there you will know where to search further.

'Hey, Knight, are you with us?' Tiger pushed him lightly with his nose.

'Oh, yes, yes, I was lost in thought. I think that... City was destroyed and we saw its ruins. And what happened in the Book was the final renewal of City already at the very end of the Book, in the Epilogue. Maybe it sounds strange but this was... the future.'

'But in that case what happened to those inhabitants that you led to the lighthouse? Were they saved or did they die?'

'I don't know but I think that Author took care of them.'

Once again the memory came to mind of Boniface and Helen, Dominique and Jacob, the young family and so many, many others. Also of those who did not want to run to the lighthouse... What happened to them? He wanted to know, but at the same time he felt that this was nothing to do with him. This was a matter between them and Author and only He could pass judgement on it. He was also convinced that Voice would not allow anyone to die who would want to be saved. In regard to which he had seen for himself how few wanted this... Painful memories of the father and son with the elderly grandmother whom he had tried to save returned to his mind. What, however, had there been to do? It was better to stop fretting about such considerations, he thought, when suddenly Little Lula jumped on his lap.

'Oh, stop all this talking now. It's time to play,' she joyfully exclaimed clapping her hands. 'Let's play pat-a-cake.'

Knight did not have any younger brothers or sisters and he could not re-member such children's games, so he did not know how to play. Strangely enough it was Grouch who explained the rules to him. He had to slap Little Lula's hands before she managed to pull them back. When he managed to catch them, they changed sides. They spent some time happily playing the game. Knight could hear Lady asking Traveller about more details of what had happened in City. Then she told him something about herself, but Paul was no longer listening closely since Little Lula had begun to teach him other various rhyming songs, thus drowning out the conversation between the captain and Daisy.

**Chapter thirty**

# THE OLD WOMAN

Time once again became marked out by their everyday routines around the house. Meals, embroidery, reading. Even though the evening read had previously been a source of dread, it had now become a source of real joy for Knight.

He greedily listened to the words that were incomprehensible to him. What secret did they hide? He would close his eyes and allow the melody of the Sámi language to sweep over his mind. Even though he could not understand the text, he at least had the hope that, with his whole self, he could absorb its meaning. In the darkness under closed eyelids he would revel in the foreign words sensing that if he could only understand them, he would comprehend everything: the sense and the purpose of all of history. He knew that this was unrealistic but honest contemplation changed him from within. He felt as if he were bursting with joy. He spent his days fully trusting in what was to come. He started caring less and less about the time and place of coming events and instead he began to think ever more of Friend and his blue eyes.

Now he had come to understand the secret of this little house in the mountains. He knew why the old lady had given up her entire life in order to live here at the side of her husband. However strange to him it seemed, he understood that in the darkness of the mountains they were the guardians of the Book. He was envious of them that its sense lay open to them. Oh, why was he not able to find the Book in some language that he better understood? But, on the other hand, whenever he wanted, Voice would reveal the Book's meaning to him. Did that mean that not everything could be accessible to him?

He spent a long time wondering if he should talk to the old lady. After all, she knew that they didn't understand anything of the readings. But nonetheless she did not try to explain the meaning to them. Maybe she realised that listening to the words alone could change someone's heart regardless of whether they understood the sense of the sentences. Besides, he would probably have to admit that he and Traveller had taken down the Book and together had entered into its story.

In the end he decided that there was not much to lose. One evening after the reading he turned to the woman and asked if they could talk for a moment. Because there was a most beautiful aurora, the old woman suggested that they dress up warmly and go outside.

'I've been waiting a long time for you to finally pluck up the courage and talk to me.'

Paul was very much surprised by this statement.

'I... hesitated. I wanted to ask you about the Book. It's just that I don't know exactly about what. I think I wanted simply to find out if you could explain to me what it says.'

'But you were in the Book. You should know it.'

And so she did know.

'Yes, but the story of City's destruction is probably only part of the Book. And I would like to know what else can be read in it.'

The old lady fell silent. Knight was worried that he had asked too bold a question. It was funny. He was not afraid to fight with monsters but he was afraid of this quiet little woman. She, however, smiled after a little while.

'The question should rather be what do you want to read in it?' Paul raised his eyebrows. He was not totally certain as to what she was talking about.

'The Book has everything in it,' she said seeing his confusion. 'What in that case do you want to know? I am not able to tell you all its secrets. Besides, I've spent most of my life getting to know only a tiny number of them. Even if I wanted to, I would not be able to explain its entire meaning to you. But if you have any questions, I can, as far as possible, try to answer them.'

Knight fell silent in thought. What exactly was it that he wanted to ask? He was simply so full of the desire to find about the Book and he did not have any particular expectation as to what he could learn from it. Suddenly he was struck by something the old woman had said.

'But you were expecting me to want to talk to you, so you must have something to tell me.'

The woman hesitated as if she had been caught doing something red handed.

'Yes... well, I can see that you're quite sharp. So yes there is something that I ought to tell you. But... I thought you would ask about it yourself.'

She looked at him as if expecting the question that she wanted him to ask. But Knight's mind was totally empty. It seemed to him that all the questions that had recently come from his heart had in one way or another found their answers. Oh, he was so curious about the secrets the Book contained but he had no idea about what concrete question he was to ask.

Suddenly from the dark depths of his mind something slowly began to emerge. A question that had been bothering him for some time, even though he had not even been aware of it.

'Why?'

The woman sat still silent and he wondered what exactly the word "why" meant. Why what? As if somewhat more clearly from the depths of his consciousness arose something whose cause he wanted to know.

'Why me?'

That was it, why me. Why among all the people in the world was it him. Why had he met Friend? Why had it been granted to him to come all the way here? Why had he seen the last battle for City? Why for one short moment had he been given the opportunity to see the golden light of the Real Sun?

Old Woman read these questions from his face as if from an open book, even though he had said none of them aloud.

She was silent. Did she expect he himself to find the answer? She did not look surprised by his question. Obviously this was what she had expected. So why was she still looking at him? Was it about something else? Some burden was crushing down on his chest. What was it?

'Why me?' Paul's voice now turned into a cry that came from the very bottom of his existence. 'I want to know! I led a peaceful life in my flat with my Mum and I wasn't expecting anything from my life. And so why? Why did I get pulled out of all that? I followed feeble clues like a blind man. And where have they led me?'

'You talk as if you're offended,' Old Woman noted calmly.

'No, no! Never in my life has there been anything better... I am a different person. But... why me? Why not somebody else?'

'And since it could have been someone else, then why not you?'

This question floored Knight. After all this was no answer at all. Though it was the truth, he nonetheless wanted more.

'You're right,' the woman knew his thinking almost as well as Friend. 'An answer with a negation is no answer at all to a question about the reasons for being chosen. Only you see the problem is this that being chosen is just what it is. It is being chosen.'

His head was already spinning.

'The essence of being chosen is being chosen?' he asked in disbelief.

And so he was not going to get an answer to his question, he thought with regret. The old woman looked at him for a moment in silence. She must have known that whatever she said was not going to please him entirely.

'Yes, being chosen is being chosen by somebody. Somebody chooses. You do not have any insight as to why this person and not some other was chosen. Being chosen is a blessing but it is a blessing that remains a secret. Author of the Book chooses his characters. Not for their specific abilities or great achievements, since after all... he created them. He's the one that gives them their abilities. He is the one who makes their achievements possible. Characters belong to Author.'

'But he also gives them freedom,' said Knight, recalling the words of Voice himself from somewhere in his memory.

'Yes he gives freedom. They can choose other paths than the one he has written for them, but then... Well, they won't be chosen. They will disappear from the history in which they did not want to take part.'

Yes, he had already heard this, or rather he had read it.

'But what kind of freedom is that? Since I must fulfil Author's plans anyway and if I don't, then destruction awaits me?'

The old woman smiled as if he had asked a naïve question. Why were there still so many doubts, even though he had already experienced the incredible power of the Author?

'Oh, because he's still writing. The story has not yet reached the end. It can still be changed. Your choices, your decisions, they have meaning. They shape the story. There's only one thing you cannot do. You cannot deny the story.

You cannot cast out its Author. Is that not a huge space for freedom? Besides you might not completely fulfil Voice's plans. That does not mean that you won't see the real sun but... but the more you fulfil his plans the more you will be yourself. That means who Author wanted you to be.'

Knight considered this. Yes, it all made sense but somehow he still did not feel satisfied.

'I know what it is about all of this that troubles you,' she said unexpectedly. 'You're troubled by how unfair it is that you were chosen and not somebody else. You're irritated by a possible lack of fairness in regard to others that results from you being chosen. You know that you don't have to worry about yourself. You rebel against others not being able to experience the same thing.'

Yes, that was exactly it. She was right. He was happy to have been chosen as Knight, but he continually had the impression that he had been granted an honour that he had not deserved while others were much more worthy.

'This is what the entire secret is about,' the old woman continued. 'Because it's not just us characters that have freedom. It is Author that is its source and he has a true freedom that we cannot comprehend. His freedom is also revealed by the fact that he chooses whomever he wants. You can say it's unfair but then wouldn't fairness be something beyond Author? Something that limits him? No, it cannot be like that. Author is completely free. It might sound shocking but he is also free in regard to what is fair.'

'Does that mean he can be unfair?'

'That's a badly formulated question. Author is. We cannot talk about him in future tense. He is fair or he is not fair. If you had asked the question 'is he fair, or is he unfair?' I would have replied that he is fair.'

'What in that case does it mean to say that his freedom is beyond fairness?'

'It means that he is not limited by the rules of fairness. He is free and can choose whomever he wants in whatever way he wants. He can choose characters for completely mundane tasks. He can also choose them for truly great works. In this regard he is completely free.'

'But doesn't he become unjust in this way?' Knight asked on.

Everything that the old woman had said seemed logical but at the same time difficult to comprehend.

'But does fairness really depend on everybody receiving the same thing?' she answered with a question.

'Well... no. Well, I mean probably not.'

'Fairness is when you receive what you need.'

'And not when you receive what you deserve?'

'No, that's called a system of justice. In love it is important to fulfil the needs of the beloved person and not reward good deeds or punish wrongdoing. Author loves all of his characters and chooses them for the roles for which he created them.'

'But some he casts aside and so he does punish.'

'No, those are characters that have cast aside Author and they disappear from the pages of his story. They themselves choose their own annihilation.'

'But...' Knight thought awhile. 'But there in the Book, City was destroyed.'

'Did Author destroy it?' asked the old woman.

'Well... Enemy... Well, it was Enemy who tried to destroy it.'

'And what did Author do? Did he try to save the inhabitants?'

'Well... yes, I think so.'

'You think so?'

'It still seems to me that he could have done more to save them...'

'Are you sure?'

Knight started to think. In front of his eyes he could see all the people whom he had tried to convince to run away to the lighthouse. In the end it was they themselves who had not wanted to. They had chosen their own destruction. But maybe it had been he, Knight, whose persuasion had been to weak. But then, they had even refused salvation when Arie had appeared...

'No, I don't know. I would like to believe that he couldn't have.'

'Exactly. All that we can do is to believe,' the woman added thoughtfully.

'But couldn't he have fought Enemy alone rather than try to talk people into running to the lighthouse? That way he would have saved City and he would have given the inhabitants another chance to believe in him.'

'And don't you think that he had already given them many chances? He gave them the Book to light up their land, but they rejected it.'

These words still sounded in his memory.

'He still tried to speak to them on more than one occasion. They did not listen. If he had waited longer, the few that he was able to save would also have fallen away.'

They fell silent.

'Everything apart from this is a secret.'

Knight spent a long time thinking about these words, staring at the aurora that was shining against the dark sky. How much he struggled with it all. How much he wanted to understand why he had been chosen as Knight.

'Because that's the way Friend wanted it. There is no other answer.'

She had again replied to his thoughts. He turned around and looked at her straight. How come she knew what he was thinking? Up until now only Friend and Author had been able to reach into the depths of his soul. Who in that case was she?

'How do you know? How do you know what I am thinking about? Who are you? I don't even know your name even though we've been living here for such a long time.'

'My name's Sophia,' she replied calmly as if this one name explained everything.

'How do you know so much about me?'

Her eyes lit up with a thousand colours of the aurora. She gave a mischievous smile.

'You see, I too was chosen by Friend. Not chosen, like you, to fight, but chosen to study Author's secrets of wisdom in quiet and alone. That's all. If I am able to guess the train of your thoughts, it is because in the silence of the mountains one can even hear the movement of a soul.'

This required some thinking about.

'And your husband? And daughter? Who are they? When we came here in the cart, I saw your daughter holding a dove in her hand. Suddenly everything was aflame, but nothing was burnt. Then she tried to tell me something. I remember the word "Ipmil". Traveller said that it meant Creator.'

'Oh, yes,' exclaimed Sophia with a smile. 'You see, Theresa is very much devoted to Author whom we call Creator, since with the power of his imagination he created the entire world. She spends her time revelling in His presence. This causes Him joy so He blesses her with evidence of his presence. The fire which even surrounded you then is one of His signs, one of the rays of the sun that lights up his country.

'And your husband?'

Sophia looked at him carefully and her eyes glistened reflecting the red of the aurora.

'You're asking a lot of questions. You won't get answers to all of them.' She was silent for a long time. Knight felt foolish for having started to ask such intimate questions.

'One thing I will tell you,' she said unexpectedly. 'In the days of his youth he too was a warrior. Just like you.'

She smiled at him, not showing him the sharpness she had done a moment ago. He wanted to ask about a lot of things, such as why in that case he was now living in these inaccessible mountains but he felt that he should not ask further. Besides it was probably better that he did not know everything. Great secrets have more charms than simple solutions.

## Chapter thirty one
# THE RED HOUSE

In the middle of January, the sign that they had been waiting for finally came. Theresa handed them a small branch with a few small leaves. It had been brought to them by the dove that Paul had once seen. According to Sophia it meant that they were to set off again on their journey. In answer to Traveller's question about what they should do when the aurora ends and darkness falls, the old woman stated that they shouldn't worry about that. If Friend expected them to set off, he would certainly take care that their journey was safe.

Indeed when they were ready to set off, the sky lit up with an exceptionally bright range of colours and the mountains were illuminated by the glow reflected off the snow. It was a good sign.

They said goodbye to the married couple and their daughter. Even though they had spent so much time in such a small house, that little family still remained a mystery to them. The young Sámi woman's eyes shone like fluid crystals. Knight was surprised that she had become so attached to them. He very much wanted to know why she had left them in the tundra to make the rest of the journey to the mountains on foot. But he realised that the girl did not understand him and he did not want to question her mother. He hugged Sophia tightly. Since their conversation he had felt a blessed peace rule in his heart. Now he was surprised that he had struggled and wearied himself with a problem that seemed to him completely incomprehensible. Friend had chosen him as a Knight. And now when he had at last completely accepted it, he felt the joy of freedom.

They set off.

They spent a long time wading through deep snow. Little Lula, as usual, was the least tired riding on Tiger's back. Lady during the hardest moments lent on Traveller and Paul and Grouch brought up the rear.

They walked exceptionally fast. Traveller kept studying the sky carefully. Luckily it turned out that the end of the mountain chain separating them from the sea was already close so that when they would start going down the darkness would cease to be such a threat to them. Besides now after a four-hour hike the slope they were going down was no longer so steep and rocky and as a result the going became easier.

At one moment when it seemed that the aurora was weakening they heard a strange whispering sound nearby. They stopped. For a moment everyone looked around, but nothing could be seen.

They took another few paces forward when suddenly the aurora vanished. They were cast into darkness. Knight heard Lady's breath quicken and Little Lula's high voice ask, 'Well, what now?'

Exactly. What now? There was the sound of a bag being opened, the scrape of matches on the box and a flickering light in the hands of Traveller, which he used to light the torch.

At least they could now see a little of the road before them. Would it be enough for them to make their way down? And what about the powers of darkness that hid in the mountains? Maybe they were not here in these slightly lower parts? But they had heard that whispering sound. So they weren't alone.

Suddenly on the edge of the light cast by the torch the silhouette of a four-legged figure could be made out. A huge beast lurked in the darkness. But they could not see what it was. Tiger crouched. Traveller quickly pulled out his sword and Knight and the others also reached for their weapons.

'Leave your swords. They will not help you,' they heard a deep voice say. 'Walk downwards.'

Strangely, they obeyed. Traveller slowly put away his blade. They walked down almost paralysed with fear. In the voice there was something demanding that brooked no disagreement. So they went on listening carefully for the soft almost soundless footsteps of their guardian. What was he leading them to?

The darkness became slowly lighter. They walked in this way for around another two hours, until they began to feel their strength was failing them.

Lady was walking ever more slowly and the others matched their pace to hers. Tiger was breathing deeply, trying out of the corner of his eye to follow the creature that was hiding in the darkness and was awakening in him such a fear. Suddenly Traveller, who was holding Daisy, stopped.

'We are very tired. We would like to stop for a moment and eat,' he said into space.

A low rumble answered him. It was difficult to take this for agreement so Lady tugged on Traveller as a sign that she could go on further. Mr Wronski moved on although at the same time he began to pull out the sandwiches that Sophia had prepared them for the journey from his bag. Guardian – for that was what Knight had called him in his thoughts – did not object so they shared out their food while walking and ate. After having eaten Grouch picked up Little Lula who clearly needed to sleep. The child rested her head on his shoulder and immediately fell asleep. The unburdened Tiger now moved with a little more vigour. He was continually trying to sniff out the presence of Guardian. Suddenly he looked Knight in the eye. It was difficult to say how Knight understood this but the anxiety in the eyes of his animal companion was so clear that everything became clear. Guardian had no scent. Tiger could not smell him and hence he was very worried.

What could it mean?

Most probably only one thing: whatever it was that was following or leading them was not of this Earth. Really they could have guessed this earlier, but now it became particularly clear. There remained doubt as to whether Guardian was Enemy of not.

They continued walking downwards for another half an hour when suddenly they realised that the hills behind them were slightly lit up, as if they were surrounded by a bit of an aura. Paying no heed to Guardian, Traveller stopped and turned towards the slope they had just come down from.

'Indeed,' he said, 'it's around the middle of January when the polar night ends in this region.'

'Are we safe?' asked Lady in a slightly rhetorical manner while not paying heed to Guardian.

The halo above the mountains became ever clearer. Knight, however, had the impression that out of the corner of his eye he could see a light that did not come from behind the mountains at all. Such a light flickered in his memory.

He understood that Guardian could not be Enemy. He turned around. On a great stone that stood a little to the side of the path they were to go down lay the giant figure of Arie. He now looked almost completely like a normal lion with the only difference being that from his shiny sides a giant pair of dove-like wings still stuck out. Paul wondered for a moment about the reasons for his transformation, but soon he realised that it was not so much that Arie had changed, but rather in his heart, in Knight's heart, there had been a radical metamorphosis that had allowed him to see more. Guardian's mane now emanated light flooding everything around. He himself looked on them patiently allowing them to take pleasure in the fragile rays of the sun. Knight was sure that the lion was smiling even though the expression of his regal face remained inscrutable.

Suddenly Little Lula awoke and raising her head above Grouch's shoulder, who was at that time looking up, she saw the majestic figure. She shouted out in joy and escaping from her carer, she ran straight towards Arie. Now the others also turned around and saw the shining predator. The little girl jumped onto the high boulder and threw herself into Guardian's mane. There was the sound of a low purr, which echoed all around, even in their hearts.

'I was afraid that we would no longer see you,' said Little Lula. 'You are so beautiful.'

The smile which – as Knight now understood – shone in Arie's green eyes, lit up everything around. Guardian rubbed his mane joyfully against the girl and then – oh! – her entire figure turned into pure gold. Knight, who was brought up on fairy tales in which the turning of a hero into a gold statue did not normally mean a happy ending, held his breath for a moment out of fear but then he saw how a golden Little Lula was still stroking Arie's hair and he became calm.

'It's time that you rested,' he said in a low growl. 'Today is a very short day, so our stop may not be long. Rest while you can.'

They laid their roll mats on the ground and lay down. Because they had eaten earlier along the way, they no longer felt hungry. Tiger approached Arie and lay on the ground next to the boulder. Very soon after the light above the mountains began to weaken. Traveller stood up demanding that Lady lie down until all had gathered. With his nose, Guardian nudged Lula, who was resting on him.

'Take out your watch,' he said.

From under her coat, the girl took out the watch, which Knight had long ago forgotten about. She held it by the chain and, waving it like a pendulum, showed it to Arie. For a moment they looked at the face. The bright aura around the mountains appeared to stop moving. Just a moment ago it had been disappearing fast. Time. Knight looked carefully at the little round watch. Whilst still on board the ship the thought had occurred to him that this mysterious object might somehow affect time. Now he was almost certain of it, which did not bring him any closer to solving the mystery as to how it did it. Arie told them to rest a little longer before setting off again.

After another hour the aura above the mountains clearly began to weaken again. They gathered themselves together and set off. Now being accompanied by Guardian, they had no fears as to reaching Alta.

They spent the next few days travelling. The nights were clearly becoming ever shorter and the travelling was becoming ever easier. In the distance they could see the shining blue of the sea, which penetrated into the valleys. The mountains between the fjords looked like bony fingers in shallow waters as if an elderly person had dipped his hand in the space of fluid time.

The low red houses made Alta a very picturesque place. In the shining crystalline snow they looked like droplets of blood on the white cloth of the ground. When they reached the first of the buildings, they were truly exhausted by the long journey. Guardian encouraged them to keep on walking. They had to reach the slope of a rocky mountain that was on the far north of the headland. Knight sighed at the thought of the further miles that still awaited them but he walked on slowly. But soon he was taken by an even greater sadness when he realised that Arie had simply disappeared. They were alone. Although there was relatively little ground left for them to cover, the loss of Guardian was painful.

They walked parallel to the coast. When they walked by the port, Traveller spent a long time looking for the Whaler, but without success. Paul could see a wave of anxiety on captain's face but he was too exhausted to fret about the missing ship right now. Besides, well, nothing could have happened without the knowledge of Author, so he did not think that they had any real reason to worry.

They walked on slowly so reaching the slope of the mountain took them a few hours. High up on the slope from the side of the sea a small red house could be seen buried in the snow. From what Arie had said, that was where they had to go. Grouch suggested a short stop before they began the climb. It was a sensible idea so they stopped to rest and eat something. The slope was not particularly steep but wading through thick snow made the going difficult. Knight looked with interest at the intense red of their destination. Arie had said that someone was waiting for them there to help them find the key for Granny. Finally, Knight thought deep down. He had been through so much since the beginning of this journey that he could not wait to at last find out where the key was, the key for which he had after all decided to undertake this journey.

The black door contrasted with the colour of the house. They knocked. Nothing happened. Lady banged loudly. Suddenly the door opened. In the doorway stood Friend with a broad smile on his face.

'Welcome,' he said joyfully. 'You're here at last. Come on. It's time you had a decent rest.'

With a gesture of his hand he invited them in. There was a warming fire burning in the fireplace. They sat down tired and without a word they took a warm meal from Friend's hands. The fish that they had was probably the best thing that Paul had eaten in all his life. With each following bite an incredible warmth began to spread through his body. The taste of roast meat was so exquisite, that nobody wanted to finish eating. Friend smiled to see them in such good appetite. He also gave them mugs with a hot drink. Knight had no idea what it was. He only felt the sweet liquid, the sweetest he had ever tasted in his life, flood into his mouth and slowly pour down the back of his throat. Oh, what bliss!

When everyone had finished drinking and eating, they spent a long time sitting and looking at the fire. Nobody felt the need to say anything. The feeling of being sated and at peace was so strong that any kind of words became unnecessary. In the end Friend engaged them in conversation.

'You're not curious as to why you're here?' he asked with a light in his eye.

The question seemed strange to Knight, almost absurd. Was this not where they had been sent? Was this not the goal of their journey? Somewhere at the back of his hushed mind returned the memory of a key for Granny, about the missing ship and many other matters but nothing seemed of any importance. The others were also silent.

'I see that being here in my small house is enough for you,' said Friend commenting on their silence with a smile.

'And so you live here?' Knight asked even though as soon as the question had left his lips he realised how foolish it sounded.

'Here... and not here. I can live anywhere and at the same time there is no place where I could really lay my head,' Friend answered him lost in thought. 'Anyway, yes, this is one of the places where I like to spend time. I can see that you lot like being here too. I think that you now need a little sleep.'

He led them into a room where there were four large beds, a child's bed and a large bedding mat on the floor, perfect for Tiger. For Knight it was a little strange that this place was just right for them but he did not spend much time dwelling on this. As soon as his head hit the pillow, he fell fast asleep.

**Chapter thirty two**

# THE RETURN

He was back on Shemesh, the rainbow island. Only this time it was full of people. And not only people. Fish jumped high in the air. On the rocks there lounged wild cats and the skies swarmed with various brightly coloured birds. The last time he had been here he had suffered so much. His heart had almost been torn out by this beautiful world but at the same time he had felt that he could not live here. Now he was filled with joy. He wanted to dance and sing. He had the feeling that every living thing, just like him, wanted to sing one unending song of happiness.

He saw buds opening in a single moment into the most beautiful flowers after which they would explode with a riot of colour which would light up the shimmering air with a million colourful sparks.

He saw birds which danced with loops in the air and spread around them a rain of golden dust.

He saw fish, which jumped out of the water singing the most beautiful arias, after which they would fall back into the lake and their song would still be playing in his heart.

Everything took part in the great hymn of happiness and joy.

He walked slowly looking at the falling cascades in the flows of which hid the time and space of everything that had ever happened. In the waterfalls there were written all events that had already taken place as well as what had yet to come. Suddenly, he saw flash by tall stone columns among which walked people dressed in linen togas. Somewhere else in a highly ornate parlour a woman with very red cheeks and a tall wig on her head was laughing.

Paul thought for a moment that he would like to look at everything to find out about the history of the whole world as well as his own. At one moment in the glow of the flowing water, he even managed to catch a glimpse of a man that was disturbingly similar to himself. He wanted to walk up closer and see if this was not his future self, but suddenly something caught his attention. He stood still. He looked in the lake already sensing what he was about to see. His grandmother was lying on a bed. She looked very pale. He looked upon what was happening before his eyes with surprising coolness, even though he knew that she was dying. But instead of the pain that he was expecting to see, he had the impression that Granny's whole figure was surrounded by an aura of happiness and joy. Her tired face appeared to him to be a picture of ecstasy. Was she suffering? Now he understood that this question made no sense. In the mirror of the lake, which day and night reflected the light of the Real Sun, her pain was transformed and seemed to him like a grain of sand in an ocean of happiness. Here the beach ends washing away the sand of suffering; it is time to step into the bottomless depths of eternal joy.

But still worry entered into Knight's heart. What about the key? After all, he had not found it… He stretched out his hand and reached out to take the hand of his beloved grandmother through the sky blue surface. He did not have the key for her but maybe he could pull her through into this beautiful world of eternal life? When he grasped her bony fingers with his hand, he felt a sudden sob fill his breast. He lay his head on the bed still holding that most precious hand. Someone was stroking his head.

'My dear, my dear. Come with me. It's all over now. She's no longer suffering. She is happy now for sure.'

Kneeling, he lifted his head and lay it on the lap of his mother sitting on the bed. Tears flowed down her cheeks, but she was calm. Paul let go of his grandmother's hand and at that moment he noticed that her hand was grasping some small object. Tears flooded up from his breast when he saw a tiny wire bent into the shape of a lock-pick for a door. He should have guessed. She had sacrificed her entire life to working in the Little Sun and that was where it had been meant for him to find her the key to the Crooked World.

That same evening he heard Mum inviting Mr Wronski to come over and pray for a moment by the body. In the depths of his pain Paul was curious to meet Traveller. But maybe this was all a dream? But the key… Again, just like on the first day of the adventure, it was evidence that this had not been a trick of his over-active imagination.

Later, when the doorbell rang and Mum went to open the door, Paul – still lost in his own thoughts – heard Mr Wronski introduce Ms Stacey Gherkin. He snorted with laughter. That happened quickly, he thought. He heard the voice of another man. In a moment, Traveller, together with Daisy and Grouch stood in the doorway. They greeted each other. It was not the time to share stories of their journey so they stood in silence for prayer until the hearse came to collect the body of the deceased. It was a very sad moment, but Paul with every part of his being tried to keep the thought in mind that when had come back from the Crooked World, Granny had gone there and now she was enjoying the beauty of that wonderful island.

The guests wanted to say goodbye and leave quickly so as not to disturb the peace of a house in mourning. But Paul was very much surprised when Mum asked them to stay.

'Please sit down. I would like to hear the story of your journey. I haven't found out much from Paul,' she said finishing with a slight smile.

'I too am rather interested in finding out how Paul got back,' and saying this Traveller looked at Knight. 'I think that he would best be able to tell you the story of our entire journey. I can only add that after he disappeared the first day in the house in Alta, we waited for a few days for our ship to arrive, after which it took a four-week cruise for us to reach the port of Gdynia. We arrived back without mishap ten days ago.'

This concise description set Paul's head spinning. A few days, four weeks, ten days? How was this possible? After all, he had been on Shemesh just for a short while!

'And how did you wind up here?' asked Grouch.

'I… I don't know. After we fell asleep, I suddenly found myself on the island of Shemesh and then after a moment… here. I don't know how. It was all so quick so I can't quite understand how come you lot had the time to go on such a long voyage.'

'Aah,' sighed Lady understandingly, 'on the island time flows completely differently.'

'Well… clearly it does. Mum, do you know how I got here?'

'No, I don't. I was sitting alone with Granny. I was worried that you would not get back in time. I left the room for a moment, I came back and you were kneeling by her bed. I don't know how it happened.'

Well, I suppose I'll ask Friend about it some time, thought Paul resignedly. He now knew that he was not going to find out about it. There were still a few matters that needed explaining.

'And what about Tiger and Little Lula?'

'Little Lula is in the Little Sun,' replied Lady.

It was as if something had hit Paul in the stomach. After all this how could they just leave the child in the institution?

'But don't worry,' added Lady quickly. 'In a few days' time we're going to hold a modest marriage ceremony, which of course you are invited to...' on saying this she turned to Mum. 'And after that we will be able to begin the adoption procedure. Currently we're visiting Little Lula every day and we've been able to take her out twice for a whole day. Unfortunately this can't be hurried anymore.'

Paul was overcome by a feeling of relief. Thank goodness, but there was one more thing...

'And Tiger? Did he return to his cat form? Is he somewhere here?'

Three pairs of eyes looked at him in silence. It seemed as if nobody wanted to answer the question.

'Well, spit it out. What are you staring at me like that for?'

They swapped glances. Paul felt himself getting anxious.

'Well...' began Lady, 'I don't know how to tell you this... Tiger is dead.'

Paul felt as if he had been struck on the head. How could this be possible?

'Dear Knight,' said Daisy leaning towards him, 'we should have guessed it earlier. When we were on the island... he died. And he was transformed into Tiger. As long as we were in the Crooked World, he could accompany us, but he could not come here with us. He returned to the island.'

He looked at her in shock. Again he wanted to ask how it was possible but he knew that it was senseless. He felt that he should be glad. He remembered how much Tiger had wanted to stay on the island. And he had stayed there. Knight had also felt an unassuaged longing there for a happiness whose magnitude he could only guess at. But did he have the right to feel sorry for Tiger and demand that he return to them from the land of happiness? No, in his heart he knew that he did not. But still the regret remained and, if this were in any way possible, it had further deepened his sadness at the passing of Granny. Mum put her hand on his shoulder. 'I know it's difficult. To be glad for the happiness of those who have departed and to be sad that they are no longer with us, isn't it? But let your feelings go. There's no point in pretending it doesn't hurt.'

'If you'd like some kind of pet, we've got plenty of rabbits to give away,' said Traveller with a glint in his eye.

They spent the next few days preparing for the funeral. In the meantime, Paul set about unpacking his bag, which Traveller had brought him. He slowly took out his things, breathing in their smells. During the sea voyage they had become infused with the acrid smell of salt and damp. Most people would have taken it as the smell of mould but for Paul this stench brought with it a range of wonderful colourful memories. He reached down to the bottom of the bag and felt something that had the characteristic shape of a book. Suddenly he remembered the novel he had bought himself long ago in the bookshop, the one which had a title and a cover that had so intrigued him. He pulled out "The Quest for the Key" asking himself, just as he had done on the ship, whether it was possible...

Suddenly someone knocked on the door. After a quick 'come in', in walked Traveller.

'Hey, Knight, I wanted to ask you over to our place. Come round. We'll spend some time together and talk about our adventures. Little Lula will be there too.'

'Thanks...' Paul hesitated.

He looked down at the book in his hand. Again he had been interrupted just as he had been about to open it. Of course he wanted to go and visit his companions, but first he had to satisfy his curiosity.

Suddenly, he realised that someone was gently taking the book from him.

'Leave that. Besides, you know what's written there.'

In Traveller's eyes, there shone a slight smile.

'And how do you know? I bought it before I came here but I've only read a few pages...'

'But you know Friend. You know that he loves to jest and that is one of his favourite jokes.'

'But what kind of joke is this supposed to be?' said Paul becoming irritated. He did not know what Traveller was talking about.

'Everything, the whole story – hmm how can I explain it to you...' his companion hesitated. 'Not everyone is ready to experience such an adventure as you have just done. Enter into a world completely different to what is normal and everyday. Sometimes a book, a story, may help such a person... It may help him believe that there are worlds other than the one contained by his own four walls. But even if he does not believe it, at least he may discover in the story some part of himself, maybe he will dare to dream and in this way become more himself. Friend simply likes such stories.'

All of this sounded very strange to Paul.

'But I didn't even start to read this book; I did not get to anything unusual. How was this meant to help me enter the Crooked World?'

'No, no, not you!' Traveller almost snorted. 'It's about others. You did not need so much encouragement to enter the Crooked World. The fact that you were the one who bought the book is Friend's joke. Above all, it's about others. Maybe your story will mean that someone will want to meet Friend and will dive into our wonderful world.'

'What, you mean that my whole story, everything that I went through... that anyone can read about it, and that all they have to do is buy the story in a bookshop?' Paul was shaken.

Traveller burst out laughing.

'Oh, of course. And what did you think? You're not the centre of the universe; this entire journey wasn't just about you. Anyway, don't worry about it. Nobody but us will know that you are you, and bookshops are full of such stories anyway so there's no reason to feel exceptional. Come on, let's go. Dinner's waiting.'

'But wait up...' something was bothering Paul. 'I know that even though Author knows the ending, we still have an influence on it, but in this case... since the book had already been written before I started out on the journey... that means I couldn't have been killed. If I'd read the book earlier, I wouldn't have had to fear being killed by Dragon.'

'That's not completely true...' Traveller hesitated 'It's difficult but, as you might have noticed on our journey, the question of time in the Crooked World is quite enigmatic. Hmm, maybe you'd be better off asking Friend about that but right now come on, let's go.'

From that time on Paul spent every day at the Wronski house, which was undergoing a minor refurbishment. After the wedding, Daisy was going to live with them so certain changes were required. Grouch was also preparing a room for Little Lula. It turned out that Ralph was a talented sculptor and in his hands wood would take on the most fantastic forms. He made all the furniture himself and decorated it unusually intricately with carvings of animals. Among all the different creatures the most commonly occurring one was the mysterious figure of an eagle with lion paws and dove wings.

The most beautiful piece was, however, a bed for the little girl, which looked as if it lay between the feet of a giant lion. The day before the funeral Paul's Dad arrived in Gdansk. He said that his business abroad had finished and now he was going to spend more time with his family. He and Mum began to wonder if they shouldn't move into Granny's house as then Dad would be able to better organise work in his shipping company. This was a wonderful prospect for Knight. It was true that he was sad about not being able to go to school with Peter but the fact that the Wronski household was in the near vicinity made up for the loss of this relationship.

The funeral ceremony took place the next day. Paul was surprised by how many people came to say goodbye to his beloved grandmother. There was also a group of children together with a number of their carers from the Little Sun and among them was Little Lula. When condolences were being offered to Paul's parents at the cemetery, he stood a little bit off to the side. Most of all, he wanted to be alone. He looked at the long line that was forming leading up to the grave. Most of the people he did not know at all. He looked on without interest at some woman with a shock of red hair, behind whom stood a man in a long overcoat and a black hat pulled down low over the face.

When he went up to Mum and took her hand in his own, he saw her face light up in a smile. But Knight did not want to look at this, so he moved off even further to the side. The sadness went through him right down to the depths of his being and he felt that he was unable to look upon the happiness of others. He walked on slowly between the headstones.

After a moment the stranger came up to him as if he was determined to offer him his condolences. Paul reluctantly stretched out his hand. He looked down at the ground wanting to make the stranger feel that his presence was unwelcome.

The firm grip of his hand, however, made him raise his gaze. In the shade of the hat he could not make out the eyes of the stranger but he could have recognised that infectious smile anywhere.

'And so you're here?'

'Yes. Do you think that I could have ever left you?' Friend joyfully asked.

'No... Actually I didn't think that. It's just that I'm sad.'

'I know,' said Friend growing serious. 'It's always difficult.'

'What? Death?'

'No. Life.'

Paul looked critically at his companion, who had just taken off his hat.

'Come. Let's go a little further off and we'll talk.'

They walked off in silence. At the end of the row they sat down on a little bench that was mounted on some ornate memorial.

'What do you mean?' Paul doggedly asked. 'Why is life so difficult?'

Friend looked at him in silence. Knight felt foolish. He knew that this entire journey, which he had taken part in, and everything that he had seen on the island of Shemesh, should have been sufficient as an answer. But the memories seemed to pale as he was overwhelmed by the experience of the death of a beloved.

'Well, exactly. Why is it that it is life and not death that is difficult?' spoke up Friend in the end. 'Someone whom I once befriended said something like this that the suffering of this world are not worth the magnitude of future happiness. You can believe it or not but it is true.'

Paul was silent. He remembered the indescribable joy that he had felt on the island. He believed that Granny was there now. So what was he sad about?

'I know, I know that you're right. But I'm still sad.'

'I understand. It's always difficult,' he repeated himself like an echo.

In fact Knight was grateful that the man had not tried to convince him that Granny was happy and that he should not be feeling this way, or something like that. He understood his sadness and that was what counted.

'Tell me one more thing.' Curiosity momentarily pulled Paul out of his grieving. 'What was all this about? All of this great journey that went all the way to Alta in order to find a key that had been in my pocket from the very first day... I've been thinking about this a lot.'

'It was purposeless,' replied Friend and his eyes lit up with joyful sparks.

'What do you mean, 'purposeless'?' replied Paul angrily.

'Do you remember when we met under the oak?' he asked off the point.

Paul was surprised. Under the oak? What could he be talking about? Under the oak... Oak. In the desert. Yes. There was something like that. Three men had been sitting there and one of them had been similar to Friend...

'That was you?'

'Of course. Anyway my dad told you something then.' Knight stared goggle-eyed. He should have known.

'You can take any way you want. If you allow me to lead you, then you are sure to arrive where your destiny lies. When you found the key, or rather the lock-pick... you could have returned to your grandmother to find out if it was the right key. But you weren't ready for that. You needed a longer road in order to understand at least a little of the secret of the Crooked World. So I led you a different route. I could have chosen a completely different one... but I did not do so.'

Paul looked at him with eyes wide open.

'And so all of this was for me to understand?'

'Both yes and no. Don't think that everything revolves around you.' Friend gave a kind smile and Paul was reminded of what Traveller had recently told him. 'Others also needed this road. But yes, it was only about understanding.'

'Only what is it that I've actually understood?' Paul paused as he thought of all his adventures, the history of City, the letter from Mum, and the conversation he had had with Sophia. 'No that's a stupid question.'

'You need a little time so that everything will grow a little more in you,' continued Friend. 'It's necessary if you want to take part in the next adventure I am preparing.'

'Really?' asked Paul animatedly.

'Of course. There's no time to rest in this world. There are always many things to do.'

'And what about this adventure?'

'I can't tell you yet. You'll find out soon. Now come on. Let's go back to the others.'

'But wait!' For Paul it was still necessary to have something explained.

'That book I bought in the bookshop... It had my whole story written up in it. I could have read it and known what was going to happen. Traveller tried to explain to me that it isn't like that but I'm still not sure.'

Friend looked at him with a light in his eye.

'And did you read it?' On Friend's mouth there was a mischievous smile. 'So how do you know what is in it and what could have happened?'

It was the end of March. Paul was a year older and had to finish the last class of lower secondary school. It turned out that Mum had managed to get a dispensation from lessons in the remaining school year in return for home tutoring. Due to which he would be able to complete his final year subjects on a commission basis and take the lower secondary graduation examinations in June. Paul did not ask about the details. He was sure that Friend had had something to do with it. If all went well, he would be starting upper secondary school in Gdansk in September.

He was studying hard, while his parents were organising the move. After his exams in June they finally packed everything up and moved into Granny's house. The boy was sad to say goodbye to Peter. As soon as they saw each other, they immediately hugged one another. Suddenly what had so painfully divided them seemed unimportant in the face of their feelings of friendship.

Having experienced his own weakness, Knight was aware that others also make mistakes. Besides his friend had apologised for what he had said at the end of the previous school year. Paul had also been sorry that he had made fun of his mate. Only now did he remember Friend's words about how one day he would understand that Peter had not wanted to hurt him. Paul was sure that this time the holidays would not be boring. Every day he went to the Wronski household, where Little Lula was shortly going to start living. There he learnt from Grouch how to carve figures in wood. When two months later he was at last able to form the shape of Tiger out of a large wooden block, he was truly happy. He had a strange feeling the cat looked at him with living eyes. Moreover the Wronskis gave him a whole herd of rabbits, for which he and Grouch built a wooden hutch in the garden.

Once Paul decided to go for a walk by himself to the port. While he was looking with interest at all the tall ships, he suddenly noticed Grouch standing with Friend, looking at the distant sea. Shortly they walked off far from Paul. The boy very much wanted to ask Ralph what he had been talking about with Friend but when they met up, Grouch's expression of joy was enough for Paul to understand that it was none of his business and that Friend could visit who-ever he liked and whenever he liked.

Little Lula was a frequent guest in the home of her future parents. She often sat cuddled up to Daisy resting her head on her shoulder and listening to the most varied fairy tales made up on the spot by Lady, in which the heroes lived through various crazy adventures. Paul liked to look at them and imagine that it would be so forever, that now the once-sad woman with the still unwithered violet in her hair would hold the abandoned child who was able to lighten the world with her smile. And just as she had done throughout their journey, Little Lula brought everyone a lot of joy with her happy games. She particu-larly liked to sit in her new room and play with her small mysterious watch, which she still carried with her. Knight was always promising himself to ask Traveller where it had come from, but he would always forget. Something told him that this mysterious object would yet be put to use. When Paul sat in his new room, he would sometimes have the impression that he could see a sud-den flash of gold moving somewhere around just under the ceiling. When he tried to look for it with his eyes, he never succeeded. But he was certain that Elf would not have left him even here. Although he rarely ever thought of him, his unceasing companion, particularly in the hardest moments, was a source of true joy for him.

# EPILOGUE

Paul looked out of the window. In the bright light of the spring sun, he saw the city. His new city.

City. This word, like an echo, conjured up memories hidden deep in his heart. The crackle of fire, the screams of the dying, the hiss of monstrous beasts...

As if in response to the memories that came to mind, a dark cloud covered the sun. This gloomy form conjured up in his soul the sight of another shape in the sky.

City. How grey and ordinary. Somewhere in the mysterious space where he heard Voice and from where in moments of fear, the blackest despair would make itself known within him, he heard the words of Boniface: 'City is developing now at an impressive pace and there is no reason to believe that it awaits destruction.'

City. Boniface and his flying monkeys. Technology and development. The unquelled anger of the ocean and the heat of unextinguished fire. All of these memories hit him like a wave breaking on a rocky shore.

Was it possible?

He glanced at the people hurrying down the streets going about their everyday business.

Was it possible?

He felt that something was stabbing into his ribs.

He reached under his shirt.

In surprise he took out a crumpled piece of paper. Where had it come from?

He flattened out the crumpled sheet.

With a certainty that went through his entire body, he folded up the paper. He knew what he would see on it.

A man who smiled to him as if alive drawn by a skilled hand.

Suddenly it seemed to him that he could hear footsteps in front of the house.

There was no knock, but in spite of this he went to the door.

No one was there.

And yet he had been certain that he had heard something.

He did not know from where they had come from or whose steps those had been.

Their echo, like a promise, resounded in his heart bringing that almost undisturbed certainty.

Friend would come.

Author will place a full stop.

If you've enjoyed this book, please consider leaving a review on Amazon or Goodreads (or ideally, both).

Many thanks!

THANKS

At the end comes the time to thank all those people without whom this book would not have come about, or at least not in the form that you have just read.

Above all, I wish to thank my husband Krzysztof, who was the first to say that I should write a book. He continually encouraged me to do so and then accompanied me during the writing and the publication.

I would also like to thank my parents who were its first critics.

Thank you to my uncle Henryk Eliasz as well as to Karol Madaj for their opinions.

Thank you to Ania Adrich as well as to Sylwia Murawińskia for their help in working on the text and its editing.

I would particularly like to thank my friends Katarzyna Meissner and Maria Maruszczyk for all their help and advice which would be difficult here to even describe. Thank you to everybody who helped me with the crowdfunding and particularly to Dorota Wiśniewska, Magdalena Grzybowska and Marek Turski.

But above all thank you to my children. For being here and for making me who I am.

# CONTENTS

www.ingramcontent.com/pod-product-compliance
Lightning Source LLC
Chambersburg PA
CBHW050733230626
47052CB00002BA/9